The Pet Hawk of the House of Abbas

The Silk Road Trilogy
Volume 1

THE PET HAWK OF THE HOUSE OF ABBAS

DMITRY CHEN

TRANSLATED BY LIV BLISS

EDWARD & DEE

ISBN 978-1-940585-00-0

Edward & Dee
RIS Publications
PO Box 567
Montpelier, VT 05601-0567
www.russianlife.com
orders@russianlife.com
phone 802-234-1956

Cover photograph (claw): Michel Loiselle (dreamstime.com).
Cover design: Vanessa Maynard

749 C.E.

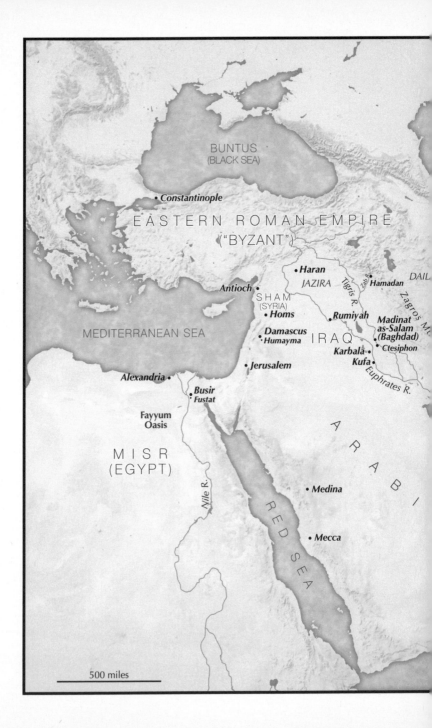

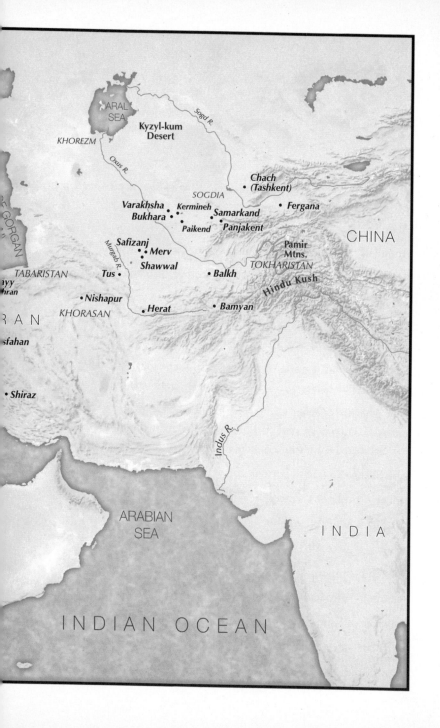

DRAMATIS PERSONAE

Characters marked with an asterisk (*) are historical personages

Abdullah* – paternal uncle of Abu Jafar (Mansur)

Abdullah* – military commander, a son of Caliph Marwan

Abu al-Abbas* – Abu Jafar's younger brother, also known as as-Saffah (He Who Spills)

Abu Ayun* – military commander loyal to Abu Muslim

Abu Ayyub al-Muryani* – Abu Jafar's chief secretary

Abu Jafar* – birth name of Mansur (the Victorious), treasurer of the House of Abbas; also known as Abu-d-danik (the Pinchpenny)

Abu Muslim* – rebel against the Umayyad Caliphate in Khorasan. Also known as Abd al-Rahman, al-Marzawi, al-Khorasani and Sahib al-Dawat (the Founder)

Abu Salama* – aide to Barmak and agent of the rebellion

Adijer – owner of a winery in Merv

Anahita – Adijer's daughter

Arwa* – wife of Abu Jafar

Ashkend – impoverished landowner; see Khalima

Ashofteh – physician in Merv

Aspanak – Nanidat Maniakh's brother

as-Saffah* – see Abu al-Abbas

Barmak* – former ruler of the Kingdom of Balkh (an individual about whom little is reliably known)

Daud* – Abu Jafar's paternal uncle

Hashim* – head of Abu Muslim's secret service

Hussein* – grandson of the Prophet Muhammad by Fatima and Ali

Ibrahim* – Abu Jafar's older brother

Isa ibn Musa* – friend of Abu Muslim, relative of Abu Jafar

Khalid* – heir to the throne of Balkh

Khalima – friend of Nanidat Maniakh's youth, now married to Ashkend

Mansur* – see Abu Jafar

Marwan (II)* – Umayyad Caliph, known as al-Hemar (the Donkey)

Muhammad* – Abu Jafar's son

Muhammad* – "of Humayma," father of Abu Jafar, Ibrahim and Abu
    al-Abbas

Nanidat Maniakh – head of the silk trading house of Maniakh

Nasr ibn Sayyar* – Arab general, last Umayyad governor of Khorasan

Salam al-Abdrash* – Abu Jafar's aide

Sulayman* – Abu Jafar's paternal uncle

Yukuk – Nanidat Maniakh's advisor

Zargisu – childhood friend of Nanidat Maniakh

Ziyad ibn Saleh* – Abu Muslim's secretary

SELECTIVE FAMILY TREES

THE HOUSE OF ALI

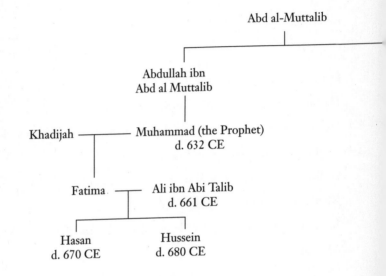

Abd al-Muttalib

Abdullah ibn
Abd al Muttalib

Khadijah ———— Muhammad (the Prophet)
d. 632 CE

Fatima ——— Ali ibn Abi Talib
d. 661 CE

Hasan
d. 670 CE

Hussein
d. 680 CE

THE HOUSE OF ABBAS

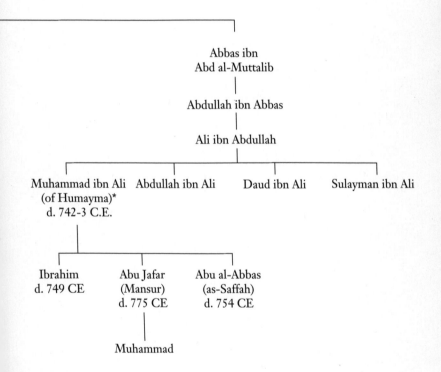

Abbas ibn
Abd al-Muttalib

Abdullah ibn Abbas

Ali ibn Abdullah

Muhammad ibn Ali   Abdullah ibn Ali   Daud ibn Ali   Sulayman ibn Ali
(of Humayma)*
d. 742-3 C.E.

Ibrahim   Abu Jafar   Abu al-Abbas
d. 749 CE   (Mansur)   (as-Saffah)
           d. 775 CE   d. 754 CE

Muhammad

Note: The relative age of the three brothers of Muhammad of Humayma shown here has not been determined, but they may be assumed to have been younger than he.

Book I

The Book of the Murderers

I saw the glittering Samarkand, its meadows, torrents, gardens,
I saw the wondrous blessings the city strewed around,
But my heart rolled up its carpet, to quit the court of hopefulness.
What else to do with pockets empty, not a dirham to be found?

1

WHAT DO YOU HERE?

It all began with that rascal of a boy, just an ordinary little scamp from the streets of Samarkand and the first resident of that city I came upon as I rode into the cold, black shadow of two gate-towers that soared up into the pale blue sky.

"The Hawk!" the imp with the sun-bleached hair howled to his undergrown accomplices. "The Hawk is here!"

I recall looking around – *A hawk? Where*? – and, seeing nothing feathered in the vicinity, continued on into the peacefully gaping maw of the gigantic, iron-clad gates. Meanwhile, though, the boy had run on ahead, deep inside the citadel, and was wailing there at the top of his lungs: "The Hawk has returned! The sun of hope has warmed us this spring! He is here, and the times of turmoil will soon be ended!"

At which point he poked a finger in my direction for no reason I could see, then shook a threatening fist at the top of the wall, toward the dull metallic gleam of the city sentries' helmets, and vanished into an alley.

"The city must surely have found itself new legends and new heroes," I told my weary companions. "We're no heroes, though. All we want is rest."

Had I only known what awaited me at my home in place of rest! But that all happened later. For now, I was just going leisurely along, my heart brimming with a sweet sorrow.

"Ruined art thou, my Samarkand; thy beauties are destroyed," said the poet. Thirty-seven years of war, squadron after squadron galloping down these very streets in clouds of dust. Temples looted, gods consumed by fire, countless caravans of booty departing westward to Merv, accompanied by columns of slaves. And again wars without end, first others against us, then brother against brother and stranger against stranger, and piles of fresh corpses heaped on hills both near and far...

But, though mauled, despoiled, deprived of hope, my city looked astonishingly alive amid the pale pink spume of trees in blossom. It rang with merry voices and smelled of morning-baked bread.

And, miracle of miracles, here, on small wooden balconies built into the sturdy towers at the outlet from the citadel, sat the everlasting elders of Samarkand, their faces tilted toward the mild spring sun. I could have reached out as I rode by and placed a respectful hand, for only an instant, on their knees, to assure myself that they were not a dream. Because those old men seemed not to have stirred from their platforms since the day I had left the city two long years before.

From under their caps, reaching down from temple to chest, thin braids hung – the very same braids they had worn when Gurek was young. Young, full of hope, and preparing the city's defenses to withstand the army of Qutayba ibn Muslim. But Gurek and Qutayba were long gone, while those old-fashioned braids were still in place, except that, once fair, they were now hoary.

"But Harith ibn Surayj!..." one began in a voice of reproach, pointing a finger topped with a long, crooked nail toward the sky.

"But Harith ibn Surayj indeed..." another with a gray braid interrupted, jabbing his finger forward like a sword.

Yet Harith ibn Surayj, insane son of the Arabiya – for so we had named our overlords – though born here in this land of mine, was dead, dead, and dead these several years. And his rebellion against the Caliph had been crushed, and already new gangs of rebels, new mounted bands, were galloping hither and thither along the roads of Sogdia and Khorasan, pursued by the troops of Emir Nasr ibn Sayyar. But the old men beneath the towers still remembered the glorious battles they had fought, God knows on whose side, and in truth, who today can tell which was the brother's side and which the stranger's?

The citadel now behind me, next came the knotty, wizened trunks of ancient trees to the back of a square crisscrossed by lone riders on donkeys or ahorse, and beyond the trees, blind walls the color of sand and flat roofs. More trees then, lifting their naked, black, fractured branches to the pink and gold rays of morning. And then more buildings, markets, streets and people.

The city, round as a loaf of bread, had been tipped just a little by God's good hands toward the south, to face the sun. Its vast circle was capped by towers barely discernible on the far horizon.

We bore right, down narrow streets, between walls where leafless grape vines twined. And here was the canal, cutting deeply into the earth's flesh, and crossing it, bridges of every size. And behind them, to the west, a smoothly rounded hill sprinkled with the city's best houses, their walls painted delicate pastel shades. Thin trickles of grayish-pink smoke drifting upward. And swallows, hundreds of swallows, flickering streaks of movement in the azure heights.

And then at last, the house of the family Maniakh. Or, more precisely, not a house but a whole neighborhood, since no one in all the city knows with certainty where our family holdings, which had expanded without let or hindrance through three centuries, really end.

"Druta, bratar. Greetings, brother."

My worthy sibling, Aspanak by name, was looking quite well, as was his way. Rotund he was, well-fleshed, flourishing and outwardly almost good-natured. Now, though, he was looking on the world with reddened eyes, and his face was pale, as if he had kept to his room all winter long. He blinked in the light and made no great show of joy to mark my arrival. It was as if we had parted only yesterday, as if I had not spent two entire years in the elegant capital of the Celestial Empire, never venturing away.

"The boy is mine," my brother confessed on the instant when I laughingly hinted to him that unknown strangers had greeted me quite differently, almost rapturously, down in the city. "He received a whole dirham for those raptures of his. And he's made good money these past months too, for telling his tales of the Hawk in the marketplaces. Yes, yes, about you. Don't bristle like that, Nanidat – you don't live here. The people need heroes, need hope. So for the time being you are the Hawk, and then... then we shall see. And shall talk," my brother added casually, his watery eyes cutting sideways to watch the servants reverently leading my horse away. "But if you want a brief, a very brief, account of the matter in chief, everything is most strange here. The revolt in Merv has been so successful that... Well, the Caliphate may as well not exist. Here at least. We're now without a master."

"So that's how it is?" I asked in bright surprise.

"That's how it is," Aspanak sighed. "All has hung by a thread for weeks. At last there comes to pass that which our house has sought these many years and that, strange to say, is more fearsome than aught else. Because... because we know the world that is departing but we still don't know what's to come. Yet there's more to tell. While we were rejoicing to have finally hidden ourselves away from the Caliph's sight with mutinous Merv as our screen, here... oh yes, here in Samarkand, as in Merv itself, murderers are suddenly at large. And I need not tell you what it is they do. They commit murder."

"Really? Murderers, but not in your employ?" I was the picture of sympathy.

"No, and there's the rub," my brother responded. "No one knows who employs them. They work in pairs, with very sharp, very slender daggers, and make their kill – never mind who, so long as it's a person of some note – a judge, an aide to the Caliph's governor... So, then, they're at the beck of Abu Muslim, rebel of Merv? But next we know, the commander of one of Abu Muslim's squadrons is butchered in Merv... All and any, indiscriminately. And then, when the two murderers have done their deed, they don't run away. Instead, they calmly let the bodyguard slaughter them on the spot. And a month or two later, another pair finds different prey... But we'll talk more in time, of course."

"You do understand that when we talk you must not expect much sense out of me," I reminded him gingerly.

Aspanak was vexed. "Yes, yes, I've forgotten nothing. But you still should know... Very well then, today there will be guests to mark your arrival, and you'll be hard put to wash and change in time. Listen to everyone. Nod knowingly. You're the Hawk, after all."

I spread my hands and rolled my eyes up to the sky, mimicking my brother.

"Good enough. Since you need me to be the Hawk, today I'm the Hawk. So be it. But then a day at the bath-house. A hunt. Again to the bath-house. Bring me all the new musicians. And for you I've brought an interesting Lanlin wine. And another from Taiyuan."

"Oh, if it's wine you want, you'll be amazed at what fills our goblets this day," he said.

At last he was smiling.

STARTING UP FROM A DAYTIME slumber that had descended on me in the blink of an eye, I dressed carefully in a new robe cut in the Samarkand style but of blue Luoyang silk with silver threads, a Kashmir kerchief to caress my neck, roomy Iranian trousers, and a light cap with a whimsical twist at the crown, and finally dabbed behind my ears a few drops of precious fragrance from the Imperial south, from gentle Guangzhou.

The coming evening promised to be sweet, because there were in this world those – my friends of yesteryear and companions of my youth – to whom I very much wanted to show my face, wind-worn as it was from weeks on the road. To show it and to modestly accept their sincere delight in the man I had become – to their utter astonishment, let it be said.

Then the hoof beats of the city's best horses were heard, and soles scuffed softly over the smooth paving of my courtyard, lit now by the crimson rays of sunset. The glimmer of golden sashes sported by our local dehkans, several duly festooned with swords. And then came the offspring of ancient merchant families, who may have been swordless but had long outmatched the wealth of the dehkans with their lands and castles and exorbitant taxes to pay on all those riches.

Clever, kindly faces. My friends.

Standing on the lowest stair, I bent in the slightest bow, my eyes avidly seeking face after familiar face.

"Maniakh of the House of Maniakh, what do you here, back in your own home after an absence of two years?" I heard the first guest say.

"What do you here?" The phrase had come into fashion some twenty years ago, when I was just a lad. And at first it was, of course, not intended as a greeting to a host welcoming his guests. But the wits had had good sport with it over those twenty years. Now we had "What do you here, when there's naught here to do?" and "Do you here what I think you do?" and "Whatever you do here, let us do it together." And in reply had come a countless multitude of even wittier responses, begotten by Sogdia's most sophisticated minds. Our minds.

As for "Maniakh of the House of Maniakh," it signified but one thing, being used to address the oldest living member of a clan and the head and master of the household, even if that oldest living member was still well on the kind side of forty. And even if the way of life he had chosen was eccentric at best, if he had quit the home where he was master to take modest rooms in an upper gallery above the aristocratic Eastern Market of Chang'an, the immense capital of the world's largest empire, which the caravans took two or even three months to reach.

"Maniakh of the House of Maniakh, can you have tired of relieving the Emperor of his stocks of silk?"

"I have. I'm beginning a new enterprise. Since every respectable person in Samarkand will in good time take up residence in Chang'an... No, but it's hard to believe. No sooner have you read in a letter from home that such-and-such a one has found success in Samarkand, be it in music, dance or the art of the kitchen, than you'll see his smiling face on Mingdao, the grandest street in all of Chang'an. And with a plump purse at his belt. There's a slip of a girl by the name of Mevancha who had scarcely learned how to dance – though excellent legs she has, and tireless too – and she's already in Chang'an and already a shining star. And when there's a place in the world where we're so dearly loved, where we're a valuable commodity, there's a living to be made from that. So prepare yourself for the road. I'll make a living from you too."

"Maniakh, have you ever seen Yang Guifei, whose portraits are beginning to appear even here in Samarkand, although made by such as have never set foot in the Celestial Empire?"

"I may have some fame among the local merchantry, but not enough to place me alongside the Emperor's beloved. Although I did see her once, if you can call it seeing, my good friend. She was as far from me as... as that plane tree. I actually saw only her back, draped in red and sky-blue silk. She's as light as thistledown. She flew up into the saddle, her foot hardly touching the low bench they brought her. Quite young she is and not at all as stout as you hear tell. At that distance, I could not make out her face, but I saw the sparkle of bejeweled pins above elaborate coils of hair, and I saw the horse's croup and also two ladies, one with a long-handled fan and the other with a fly swatter."

"Maniakh, what do you here, when the wizards of your new land have sold you the secret of eternal youth? Look, Sabit, he alone of us all has not changed. Like a boy, yes? And this is one who has traveled the Road no less than eight times, over hungry deserts of stone, through the snows of mountain passes, across treacherous rivers in flood. Yet you still have the eyes of a child. Great trader, share that secret."

"Oh, the secret of eternal youth is very simple, my dear." To my disgrace, I could not recall her name. "They take the seed of a near-grown colt, for which purpose a young filly is presented to him, hind end first... No, don't douse me with wine. It's surely too good for that. And, while I think of it, let me have some now... So, then, that colt..."

"Maniakh of the House of Maniakh, what do you here, if, as we have heard, you are without peer in procuring the best silks? You are wreathed in glory, Nanidat, you wretch. But, you know, your father once called on mine to complain that his boy-child was growing up amiss and would end badly, as a poet or a musician... So it was, Nanidat, so it was! And not too very long ago."

I was all beaming smiles and without time enough to spare a kindly word and glance for every friend who followed friend. But my soul was overflowing with melancholy. *What has become of you, the best of Samarkand's best?* I thought, *Why has the light fled from so many eyes? Why is the skin of that woman, for whom two nephews of a mighty ikhshid of Sogdia once pined as one, so faded and so crudely powdered – and in this, the prime of our lives?* And from a far corner of courtyard, the gloomy gaze of a former friend, downcast to have me see that his silken robe had known better days. As if it mattered to me which of my friends had risen in the world and which had fallen on hard times. Or what malady afflicted that heir of an ancient family already renowned here eleven hundred years ago, when the city gates were opened to the conquering Iskandar the Two-Horned Lord and his threadbare host. Why did he, a man of my years, look almost old?

Dimmed, dingy, droll and dear, some deprived of your youth, others of your wealth, and all of your hope. The conquerors will perhaps depart one day, but not vanquished at your hands. Your war is already lost. Ruined art thou, my Samarkand.

Do not fall into that old trap, Nanidat, the voice within whispered on. *You simply need to find nothing good here. How else will you explain to yourself why you abandoned the city of your birth?*

"Maniakh of the House of Maniakh, is it true that you not only speak the language of the Empire of Tang but have also learned to write those strange signs, not one of which is like any other?"

"I have even invented six new signs that are like nothing at all. And every one indecent."

"It remains, then, only to learn the hideous language of the Arabiya and you will have no equal in all the world. It's simple, my dear Maniakh. Their language is naught but 'la-la-la-la' interspersed with a horrid hissing. Trash it is, and I've told my son he mustn't learn it but he..."

The patriot faltered then, remembering too late that certain words were not to be spoken in that house – or, more precisely, in my presence. But two others hurried to his aid, falling over each other to distract me.

"No, no, be easy. They of the swarthy faces are vanquished. Don't you know that? Consider them gone. This Caliph will be the last. You can forget their language if you will."

"What does that mean – gone? What about those who were born here in Sogdia and live in this land of ours? Where are they to go? Shall we kill them, every one? And the one in five of our own who is already at home in their empty temples, what's to be done with them?"

I was beginning to compose my next witty reply when...

"Maniakh of the House of Maniakh, why do you stand there like a graven image, while I die for you still, as I ever did? Won't you look at me?"

And I turned around and dissolved into the grayest eyes in all of Samarkand.

She always made play with her words, the bold Khalima of the House of Vgashfarn. She had delighted in sending the blood rushing to my face with such talk when we were young, because we both knew that there was a spark of truth in it. But here the gray-eyed beauty was not alone. At her side was a dehkan, one I did not know, with a truly Sogdian face – the hooked nose, the stiff, short beard, the prominent green eyes. She brought him to me and said, with a bashful dip of the head: "How long were your travels, oh Maniakh, fine and fair! I was widowed while you were gone, and have married again. Let me introduce you. This is Ashkend, son of he who commanded the squadron from Neshef in the battle at the Iron Gates. Two castles to add my own, vast but neglected landholdings that we shall put to rights. And he's a good man. Be his friend, Nanidat. You're so alike."

And that, it seems, is when it all came to pass.

But no. First, I brought the goblet of wine to my lips at last and was about to take a sip, for no reason other than to make a pause in the conversation.

The wine, though, would not permit such informality. Behind the warm aroma of over-ripe blackberries lurked something dourly unfamiliar – a touch of old skin? Or, on the contrary, of young, living skin? Drawing another greedy breath through flared nostrils, I sensed a hint, just a hint, of leaves fallen from frost-bitten trees. What a treasure! A wine of warriors and sages.

I raised my eyes and caught sight of my brother watching me with great satisfaction.

"And I was wanting to flaunt my wine of Taiyuan before you," I called to him over the heads of my guests. "What is this? Where from? From Merv?"

"From Merv of course," he replied, his mouth stretching from ear to ear and making slits of his eyes. "But not just Merv. And it is not only that it has lain in a sealed pitcher for eleven years. There's a whole story behind that wine. And such a story!"

I surveyed the room. One dehkan was swirling a goblet under his nose, deep in thought. Another was licking his lips abstractedly and gazing at the ceiling. What peerless thing had my brother brought from his stores this glorious day?

At long last I took a sip for myself and almost laughed aloud at the wine's merry, tender tang that instantly gave way to a trace of sweetness.

By then we were all moving from the courtyard into the hall.

In times past, a hundred years ago, this whole process had been no more than the custom of meeting guests on the threshold with a goblet of especially good wine. The guest took his first sip at the door, then proceeded in dignified style into the hall, with its long ceiling beams and colorful wall paintings below – fabulous beasts with elongated, sinuous bodies, warriors in chain mail, and women with huge blue eyes – there to settle into his rightful place by the wall. Then the food would appear, followed by musicians and dancing girls.

But apparently, many decades earlier, some lady had said to the assembled company something on the order of "Oh, but do let's savor our wine out here. See how beautifully the sun sets over the hills." Or maybe the guests began caring very much to examine not only all the new outfits but also the arrivals on horseback and the mounts they rode into the courtyard. Besides, how often do we converse at our leisure, except when on a hunt or otherwise frolicking in the out-of-doors? And as a result, the goblet of welcome had transformed into a large part of the evening, the favorite part, a time when everyone was free to speak with everyone else, to form circles large and small, and then, gradually and still chattering, to move into the hall and, finally, to sit, motionless as the stone giants in the cliffs above Bamyan.

And so it was. We straggled in a gaudy, perfumed throng into the hall, goblets in hand, and Ashkend, Khalima's new husband, who had me by the arm, was asking me what had become of the great, broad-beamed, starry-eyed poet with the booming voice whose sour spiced soup the Emperor had once stirred with his own chopsticks, so that by drinking it the man would sober up at last and again be fit to compose more of his impromptu verses. There had been no news of him from the Celestial Empire for three long years.

"Oh, my esteemed friend, nothing has become of him," I replied with a shake of the head. "It's just that the patience of even the most enlightened emperor sometimes runs thin. The poet is no longer called to court. Because that genius, sad to relate, drinks every day. And very serious wine he drinks too – double-distilled, transparent as water and searing in the throat."

Ashkend was all surprise. "That wine isn't for drinking, though. Only healers use it, but for wholly other purposes."

At that time, I distinctly remember, we were standing face to face in a hall full of people, and my brother was preparing to seat the guests but was in no hurry to do so.

"Tell the renowned poet that," I shrugged. "But once you have begun downing that dreadful potion in good earnest, you can't stop. You drink it day after day and..."

A great number of things happened then, and with a fantastic synchronicity.

Two servants, evidently domestics of our household wearing identical cotton jackets, trousers and short headbands, were moving about the hall with clumsy, shuffling steps. Following an Imperial custom that I had introduced at some point, they were bringing trays of hot towels for the guests.

What ails their feet, the both of them? I recall thinking.

In those days I was not yet able to carry on an entertaining conversation while at the same time noting everything that was happening around me. Two young men were shuffling along as if in a trance, and how was that of note?

One was shambling about behind Aspanak's back. The second crossed close to me, past my left shoulder and out of my field of view. And at that very moment, from the wall where other servants were standing, three or four slight but very agile figures darted toward the center of the hall, the run ending with an odd forward lurch.

There was a slight jolt in my back then, on the left shoulder blade, and a dull thump at my feet, behind and to the left. Someone had crashed to the floor. Then the clang of a chased metal tray.

No, two trays, one nearer and one farther away. This was a puzzle indeed. Behind my brother's back, two of the little men were mounted on a bringer of towels like riders in the saddle, which had made him drop his tray. And all this almost before my brother could begin to turn.

I cast a sideways glance at the goblet of Mervian wine in my hand, delighted to see that although jolted, I had not spilled a drop, and so continued: "... and that secret is known to the entire Celestial Empire. But it values its great poet not one whit the less."

My words resounded in a fearsome silence. I met Ashkend's eyes, and the look in them was one of horror and pity.

And from the other side of the hall... slowly, so slowly... my brother reached out a hand to me.

With my right hand I raised the goblet to my lips and took another sip. I remember the pleasure of tasting again the ravishingly tart freshness that gave way to a hint of sweetness at the back of the tongue. And I shrugged my left shoulder, not understanding what was wrong.

The shoulder – or, more accurately, the shoulder blade – responded with a jab of pain.

I turned a little, saw the floor tiles behind me spattered with tiny drops of blood, and the other bringer of towels, his legs twitching under the weight of a man who, judging from the movements of the arm hooked around the neck, was trying to twist off his head.

And again, that piercing pain.

"Nanidat..." My brother was speaking almost soundlessly, but I heard him well because the hall was still very quiet.

Ashkend was for some reason trying to pry the goblet of Mervian wine from my hand. By now almost everyone was staring at me in silence.

A thought flickered through my mind. *Am I wounded or am I murdered?*

Someone caught me as I fell.

2

ZARGISU

"Never did I think that such would be our meeting. This is… This is too much." My brother, sitting at my bedside, shook his head.

Unnerved earlier but now for the most part easily over my fear, I was luxuriating in my soft bed and benevolently watching the white, purple-trimmed ends of his headband swinging to and fro across his chest. My left shoulder was tightly bound. Our family physician had labored over it and told me it was certainly not the worst wound that had ever been seen. The skin was torn, yes, and the injury went deeper yet, but that was the extent of it.

"And just imagine," Aspanak continued in a flat voice, still rocking his head and fleshy cheeks from side to side, "if he had struck not in falling, while reaching out to you, but with a sure hand. Then the blade would not have glanced along the bone but… That's the left shoulder blade, you know. It would quite simply have been the end of you. My whole family is aghast and sends you every possible kind of greeting. Very well, but now look at this."

A strange object lay on my brother's plump, white palm. It resembled a block of wood shorter than a hand's length or a toy left unfinished by some craftsman.

"This is the way it's done – very easy and quick, if you know how."

My brother pushed a metal strip back with his thumb, seemed to split the little billet of wood effortlessly in two with his fingers and began to turn the whole thing inside out.

Between the two halves, I now learned, a long, slender blade had lain concealed. Aspanak's fingers guided the two halves each through a semicircle, bringing them together to form a handle, and that strip of metal – commonplace copper it was – deftly locked it all in place. In design, it faintly recalled, if it recalled anything at all, a fan from the Celestial Empire.

"Previously I had only heard of this weapon, but now they are being found by the sentinels in city after city," Aspanak said quietly. "Nothing out of the ordinary but a great convenience that may be carried wherever one wills. To the eye, it's a simple little billet of wood. It takes some time to open, indeed, but in our case the knives were at the ready and lying on the trays, under the towels. So simple... Those two had been working here for several months. Our house, needless to say, is better guarded than the palace of Nasr ibn Sayyar himself: I am not so easily accosted, not I! Especially of late, when the talk from Fergana to Damascus itself is of those murderers and naught else. And, note you, I was surely the one they first wanted. But it took no time at all to grasp that you are the head of our house and that once you were here, two blows must be struck in place of one, while I was thinking you safe and sound here. And so the tale is told. We can take comfort in the fact that none before us has lived through such an attack. But as for the rest of it, all went on as it always does. You didn't see that. They had already led you away. What I mean is that both the murderers are dead. No one has yet been able to take even one of them alive. Although they make little effort to flee. They're usually cut down on the spot by sentinels, since the murders are committed in a crowded place, somewhere in the center of the city, and the murderers gladly bare their own necks. But our guards, you understand, are no sentinels."

"They were wraiths," I said, with a hint of pleasure. "And so you did what you set out to do."

"But did it badly," my brother acknowledged. "Yes, we have a squad of wraiths – between you and me, only eight of them as yet. And really, no one pays them any particular mind. Small and in fine trim they are, and masters of their craft. But, as you see, those masters are still too slow on their feet. They've learned to safeguard me but evidently they have yet to commit to memory that none here is above you. In their minds they know it, yes. But in the hands and feet, not in the minds, of wraiths is where the memory must reside. It's a good thing that even one of them gathered his wits and made the leap. But – again between you and me – no wraith in this world could have guessed what would come next. They were protecting us, while my regular guards had the murderers in hand. And then the pair of them, both at the same time, squirmed away from the guards and sprang – not on us, though, but on each other, like... well, like two men in love... and no wraith could have understood in good time what was happening. Just imagine: each had another knife, an ordinary kitchen knife. They stabbed each other neatly in the neck, spoke one word in chorus, smiled and turned up their toes."

And Aspanak – slowly, as always – spread his hands. That strange knife was still clasped in one of them.

"One word?" I repeated.

He shrugged. "I'd say it began with a 'pa.' Or a 'fa.' A long word, though. Four syllables between, I'd say. And a sound drawn out at the end, like an 'e-e-eh' or more of an 'a-a-ah.' No matter, though. In short, that's how they work. Who? They hail from Khorasan, by the look of them. Or from Balkh. Why? That no one will tell. For money? But why would a suicide want money?"

"All I understand at this point is that I won't be able to visit the bath-house for another week," I told him reproachfully.

He waved the hand holding the knife. "Two weeks. Although the physician will remove the bandage the day after tomorrow, and then we'll know better. But with a wound like that you'll still be able to walk, ride, hunt... A trifle, a trifle. But what comes next, that's the question.

So now let me tell you something. You need to know what is happening with your trading house, when all's said and done."

"Which was going along quite well four months ago, judging from your letters," I reminded him.

"Letters... They're about matters of the moment. But looking ahead... Two years," he said, surprisingly succinct. "That is how long we can hold on if the rebellion in Merv grows into a full-scale war and the trade routes are closed for as long as it lasts. I made the calculations three times. For others, mind you, it will be even worse. And it would have been worse for us too, had you not been as bold as you are. No one here has such merchandise as you procure, and only you and I know its worth. Well, and the rest you can imagine for yourself. We have the merchandise, but if they close the roads to Kufa, Damascus, Alexandria... And demand will fall off too. I don't have to tell you that silk is a peacetime commodity. A bolt of silk has been known to command a hundred dirhams in a world at peace. But when war comes, silk will at best be stockpiled as a substitute for money... All that remains to us are the lands of Roum, which some call Byzant. They will still buy everything, but you'll have to carry the silk north, around the Sea of Gorgan. And if the war spreads southward to Balkh, Kashmir will be closed to us and everything south of it too..."

"If we take and sell all we possess in Chang'an alone, you and I will have enough to live long and tranquil lives. And then there's our private caravanserai in your Byzant," I reminded him, for all that I was not a little shaken by what I had heard. It was like reaching a summit only to find the mountain falling quietly away beneath your feet.

My brother signaled his assent with a wave of his hand and continued. "Well, we've worked long and hard to roil the waters and now, when all was going well, now..."

I was intrigued. "What's this?" I asked. "Who worked hard and for what? Is this yet another of your boys telling tales in the bazaar? What fables are these that put the trading house of Maniakh behind every plot in the whole wide world, from the lands of Roum to Chang'an?"

Aspanak's eyes narrowed, his round cheeks bulging up to cover them from below. He was smiling.

"Not every one, as you can see for yourself, Murderers with knives in wooden cases – that's no plot of ours. That's a plot *against* us. By and large, though, the devastation that broke our father's life is a thing of the past. Our house stands firm again, and in more than the silk trade. With plots or without, we wield all the influence we ever did. And one of the seedlings left behind by our grandfather has set fruit. And such fruit! The story is long, but it began in the interesting little village of Humayma, by Damascus. A group of travelers once came to that village, converging on the home of a gardener there... Humayma is generally renowned for its gardens, and it lies, what's more, at the crossways of three important roads, a good place for trade... That gardener's name was Muhammad, which is a very common name. But not every Muhammad is a direct descendent of the uncle of another, a wholly other Muhammad, peace be upon him. That uncle was Abbas, and he could well have inherited the cloak, the staff and the ring of that other Muhammad, the one and only Muhammad. But, as we all know, he did not become caliph and to this day, other kinsmen of the Prophet, men of the House of Umayyah, possess that legacy in its entirety... This, now, is something that almost no one knows: exactly who it was that came to visit the gardener. Their names were Maisar, Abu Iqrim and Hayyan, an apothecary. But that apothecary was also a wandering trader in fragrances, and he had been sent by our grandfather. It's a long story, as I said, and I myself do not know how our grandfather here, in Samarkand, could have directed a search for such as would throw the Caliph's empire into chaos and thus weaken its power over Sogdia. I know only that perfume traders passed through all the Caliph's lands, sent there by our grandfather. And this I know because our grandfather once boasted that they had made up the cost of it and more, because the Arabiya will readily soak themselves in all those fragrant liquids by the bowlful, and the price is naught to them... And so, the apothecary Hayyan made a grand job of it. He turned that gardener of Humayma into a superlative conspirator."

"Meaning that he came along and asked, 'Would you care to rebel?' "

"Well, one can only imagine what our travelers said to the gardener of Humayma. Maybe it was in this wise: 'Good Muhammad of the House of Abbas, would that you might raise your head from your worm-riddled earth and see what transpires in the world of the faithful. The Prophet, peace be upon him, is in his grave nigh on ninety years. His heirs have subjugated Sham and Misr, and their Damascus and Alexandria with them, and as a result, naught remains of the proud empire once ruled by Constantine. The swart-faced horsemen have worsted the Berber peoples and the inhabitants of the realm beyond which lie only the fearsome waves of the sunset sea, that being the land of al-Andalus. The Shahanshah is vanquished, the great empire of Iran is scattered as the dust. And now even those loathsome manikins from Samarkand... Not that they have quite capitulated – for some reason they fight on – but they're in a poor way. So, then, our gardener friend? All is conquered, but where is there peace in the land of the faithful? A horror, this is, not peace. A chaos, my good fellow. Brother slaying brother, armies in hot pursuit of one another, and the lords of the faithful are not righteous caliphs at all but instead not one as will mend another. So bethink you now, old man Muhammad, you in whose veins runs the blood of the Prophet, will you go on this way, growing your figs and quince and apples?' 'If that is how matters stand, then I am with you,' he of the House of Abbas would say to them then."

My mood, not surprisingly, had brightened. My dear brother was once again in fine fettle, now that he had left off belaboring himself for the near-successful attempt on my person.

"In point of fact, they bent his ear a whole week," Aspanak acknowledged. "But there is more to the tale. So tell me, have you managed to calculate when our wise grandfather sent his man to the village of Humayma?"

I was silent.

"Twenty-nine years ago," he said, his face unreadable. "Remember what year that was. All who had come away with their lives were paupers, in rags and tatters, but proud. Samarkand was destroyed,

Paikend, city of merchants, was destroyed, Bukhara barely drew breath, Balkh was all but obliterated, but the beast Qutayba ibn Muslim had been killed. And who contrived his strange death we know, you and I. That was no boy with our money in his pocket telling tales in the bazaar about our trading house, Nanidat. It was a brilliant operation... Let whoever was present at the time preen himself over it, for the victory is all but secured. After the beast Qutayba, all the other emirs have been but puling babes. And now we don our glittering chain mail, the best in all the world, and throng together, now one last push and we shall sweep that vermin away forever back beyond the river, to Merv, and there we'll have at them again. And to think, Nanidat, that our grandfather, who in those days was mustering regiments for Gurek, who had dispatched secret couriers to the Khagan in the Great Steppe and to the Radiant Emperor of the Celestial Empire, to think that he, for safety's sake, did not trust in his own successes and, also for safety's sake, sent his apothecaries to Humayma and his cloth traders to other kinsmen of the Prophet, those of the House of Ali, and all the rest of it. As surety, for what if Samarkand were to be shattered again? As indeed it was. But one of the seeds sown by our grandfather proved golden. It was little money, Nanidat, only a handful of dirhams. But there it is: sometimes one dirham brings more benefit than a whole sackful of dinars."

"So," I said, half-rising from my bed. "Are you telling me that all that has transpired in Khorasan over the past three years has been our doing?"

"Not all," my brother said. "We have money, but not enough to pay for every soldier, to guarantee every detail. But in the main, yes. The gardener Muhammad proved himself a great man. He deputized twelve naibs who began to test the lay of the land, determining where in the Caliph's domains supporters might most speedily be gathered. Many of those naibs were executed, have no doubt of that. But, interestingly, no one has yet found the way to Humayma. You and I know the name of that village, as do a few others, but the Caliph, no. And year has followed year, and so it was that in Khorasan, to the far eastward site of vanquished Iran, all was going most excellently for the gardener. Because Khorasan had not forgotten its own vanquishing. Khorasan was waiting for someone to give the word. That Khorasan lies full on our western frontier, that it stands athwart the way from Damascus to Samarkand, that it slices the Caliphate in two – you understand, Nanidat, that none of this was dismissed as mere chance. And our grandfather sat here where you and I speak now, in these same rooms, whiling away the days with his favorite plaything – the plot – year after year. And no one knew of this. Well, Nanidat, the gardener Muhammad died undiscovered, and another became head of the House of Abbas in his place, a person whose name I shall not speak aloud. He sent yet another envoy to Khorasan, by the name of Bakr. The burden of the conversation was more than likely how to collect from the conspirators of Khorasan one fifth of their income. At first no one thought that they might rise in open revolt. Bakr's right hand was a slave boy born near Kufa or maybe in Khorasan itself. In the beginning, he rode hither and yon, from Humayma to Merv and back again. But that slave proved at last to be a veritable leopard. Three years ago, he sent out an order. In the first days of summer, it said, we shall raise black banners and begin an open war. All were to don black garments and gather under arms in the village of Safizanj by Merv. And now we have what we have."

"Once a slave, now a leopard? My dear brother, you're speaking of the mysterious Abu Muslim. Then he's your man, and Khorasan is now ours? But if that is so, all that remains is to remove the Caliph's governor, Nasr ibn Sayyar..."

But my brother only sat, his shoulders creeping up toward his ears and a mournful smile on his face.

"I have been in no haste. I did not want to repeat our father's mistakes," he said at length. "It had seemed so many times that with the merest jolt, the enemy would disappear. This time, I thought, let someone else do the work for us and do it all. Meanwhile, we and Nasr had become the best of friends – for two years he has spurned no offer of friendship. And the Caliph's governor was, to be sure, in no position to spurn the friendship of one who had opened a school for copyists of the Holy Book..."

"Now I understand all the talk about your dutiful visits to their temples."

Aspanak looked at me sadly.

"No one can hear us in this place, Nanidat. So you may believe that what I shall say to you now is said in all sincerity. It was of course necessary to be on friendly terms with Nasr, but... There is one God, and I'm not sure how important to Him is the temple from which a man beseeches Him. Who said that?"

"I did, naturally. When your camels are amid bare rocks a week's journey from any temple of fire, you go to a temple of Teacher Fo. Or you simply place your hands on your knees, palms upward, under the vault of heaven. Yes, I said that. But Teacher Fo didn't vanquish our land, didn't put our books and our temples to the torch, didn't..."

"Yes, yes. But then again, the Book of the Prophet didn't vanquish our land of itself either, and it put nothing here to the torch. It's a formidable book, Nanidat. 'Allah is the light of the heavens and the earth. The parable of His light is as if there were a niche and within it a lamp: the lamp enclosed in glass; the glass as it were a brilliant star.' If you could only understand how that sounds in the language of the Arabiya... It shouldn't ever be translated. It's music, Nanidat. Music from there."

And he jabbed a finger skyward.

"You've learned their language?" I made no effort to hide my envious respect.

"While you learned the language of the Han and can even read it... But none of that is important now. Because matters have been moving overly fast. Nasr ibn Sayyar has been killed, Nanidat. Somewhere in Iran. Just now. No one here knows it yet. The Caliph has no more governors in these parts. My... informers say he was crushed by the sorrow of the latest drubbing dealt him by that fine fellow Abu Muslim, because the governor was not in the bloom of youth and unaccustomed to defeat. And who wouldn't be crestfallen after writing to the Caliph imploring him for aid – and in verse, no less – and receiving nothing in return, and then seeing your army vanishing away under the blows of some upstart? Other informers, though, have reported his death to me in somewhat different terms."

And, in a manner that spoke volumes, my brother dandled the dagger in its wooden case on his palm.

Again I was intrigued. "To particulars, then. The first who could have arranged the murder is the rebel Abu Muslim."

My brother was quick with a response. "And Abu Muslim ordered his two closest confederates murdered too? He could have had them destroyed without turning a hair, because he has less care for his own than for strangers. But were you and I almost cut down on orders from Abu Muslim as well? No, those men with daggers... This is not the Caliph's doing nor the rebels' either. This is some third party who is simply destroying everyone of any significance. And one who knows very well who is of significance and who is not."

"Someone working against the Caliph and against the rebels at one and the same time... Has Caliph Marwan at last wearied one of his own? But then it would have been simple enough to remove only Marwan, with no needless complexities... Yes, but then again, the berid, the Caliph's messenger service in Khorasan, Abu Muslim has, of course, scattered to the winds..."

"All of it, and he did not scatter it but with no great ado massacred both the simple postal workers and those who were not so simple," my brother assured me. "You're far distant from our affairs but see, Nanidat, how quickly you put the most pertinent questions. Which confirms yet again that, for all your innate idleness, once you begin anything, you end by doing it better than any."

I was silent, acknowledging that I had spoken too rashly. Soon, though, I had a new question for my brother.

"But if I am innately idle, then how, by your good graces, have I become the... the Hawk? Will you at last explain what bird this is and why I had no sooner become it than someone tried to run me through?"

At that, my brother's face took on a very familiar expression, one I had seen time and again in childhood, when I had bested him with my bow or at tug-o'-war, and he was still refusing to concede his most evident defeat. For which he would have forgiven anyone but me.

"Well, then, answer I must," he said at last. "The Hawk. He is a magical being, part warrior, part sage. Obviously of the House of Maniakh, since that very bird is on our father's standard. And of course it is you, for who else could it be? Not I, indeed, for I am seen here every day. No storybook hero, I! But you're here for six weeks at most, then take yourself back from whence you came, and the last time you disappeared for two long years... The general idea is that the Hawk will save Samarkand, and the people sorely needs such fables at a time like this. They feel that decisive days are near upon us. But it is, you know, a trifle and has naught to do with any serious matter. And all would have been well, had that pretty pair not fallen on you too, and with such astonishing speed. Must I tell you again how I feel after that? But wait. Say nothing. Because the Hawk was only the first thing. And there is a second, of utmost importance. And that second is: No, Nanidat. No, I do not propose to drag you into this family affair. It's enough that our silk trade is what it is because of you. I won't try to coax you to go looking for whoever sent those murderers, and I won't promise you the best bodyguards in Sogdia and Khorasan, the best helpmeets and advisers. Because I know better than anyone why, since those days long past, you have taken in hand neither sword nor... Say nothing, please don't... And no one will ever dare judge you or ask you... No, never."

We were both silent. Because it was plain so see that Aspanak, for all that he was telling me "no," had something more to say to me but, since could not bring himself to speak, was prolonging the awkwardness. I watched and waited in silence.

"It's Zargisu," he said at last, his voice too loud. "It's Zargisu, and what's afoot now where she is, in... in Merv, is strange, inexplicable"

The "strange" and the "inexplicable" fell on very deaf ears. What next escaped my lips came somewhere between a cry and a hiss:

"Zargisu? You said Zargisu? In Merv, at the very heart of the rebellion? What possessed you to embroil Zargisu in the family... affairs?"

My brother then made an inimitable gesture to admit – and sincerely so – his error, raising his hands toward the ceiling and turning his eyes in the same direction.

"I embroiled Zargisu? Ask rather if I could have stopped her! Imagine for yourself: we have been waiting year after year, wondering when it would begin. And now Abu Muslim is raising his black banners in Merv, his army grows by the month, and victory after victory is declared aloud for him on our public squares by the drivers of passing caravans. Abu Muslim cannot be stopped! All of Iran rises to his aid! All eyes glow with hope! And so on and so forth. And then pops up before me our timid little, irreproachable little Zargisu and tells me that if I do not find for her an assignment in this war, she will sell all she owns and set off alone. 'And you'll perish within the week,' I try to explain to her. But she understood that very well and she was only... ahhh... threatening me with her imminent demise. And you know, Nanidat" – here my brother caught his breath – "she was magnificent! I, like you, have known Zargisu almost all my life. But it was only then that I saw what ancient blood can be. She was not asking. She was not even holding it over me. She... was informing me that she would sell all she owned, buy arms and journey to the land of her forbears, with my help or without it. There, where all her brethren, the princes of Iran, flock together under the banners of the Leopard of Merv."

My brother fell silent then and began drumming his fingers rhythmically on his knee. Now, now he would tell me all. But I already knew what he would say, and I grieved ahead of time.

So his next words were all the greater surprise to me.

"Well, naturally, given such a choice, I decided that she should best be in the good company of our people in Merv. They would protect her, caution her, teach her. And... You thought, Nanidat, that you knew the girl. I thought the same. But we were both wrong. She was sheer perfection – wholly fearless, fantastically resourceful, astonishingly patient... All her dispatches were pure gold – golden as the Imperial dinar of Byzant."

I said nothing, hearing well that "was," that "were." I watched and waited. And he drummed his fingers on his knee.

"And then Zargisu was... gone," he said, and that was not at all the word I had expected to hear. He caught his breath at last and hurried on.

"Next, after only three or four months, all of Khorasan began to crawl with very, very unpleasant rumors of a demon woman – and, as you already understand, Gisu, or something very like, is her name... Hear what they say about her, Nanidat. Even a seasoned warrior is afraid to encounter her sword, because she will cut him down as if he were a novice – unexpectedly, boldly and... unerringly"

"Our mother never tried to initiate Zargisu into the caste of women warriors?" I broke in.

"No, no, of course not... So, I continue: she tortures her captured enemies, long and hideously. And how will you enjoy the tales of how she wanders the field of a newly joined battle – accompanied, note you, with a small squadron that is devoted to her to the point of utter adoration – and finds a wounded warrior. Imagine a woman skewering the vanquished enemy to the earth with a dagger or a broken spear, running him through like a moth on a pin! And what she does to him then... She binds a certain part of him with a cord, as I hear tell. How he must wish for it to fall, but no, it stands. I have never heard the like and do not care to think on it, but this is what they say. And then this woman hoists up her chain mail and other garments, mounts the poor thing like a horse, and rides him until she has had her fill. And then she finishes him with a dagger blow. Picture the scene. I can even hear the rhythmic ring of metal, clanging, clanging... How is this to be understood, Nanidat? And the point in chief is – what do those nameless murderers have to do with all this? On the one hand, nothing, because they seemingly preceded it, but... And what are we to do, especially since that woman's appearance on the fields of death coincides right oddly with the devastation of my – of our –

entire system in Khorasan? Of which she knew so much. I cannot even imagine who else there is for me to write to. We had a hospital on the outskirts of Merv. We created it, we maintain it, and it has been a great convenience. People wander hither and yon, then come to seek a physician's care... And we also had a very interesting piece of property in Merv's eastern purlieus, not far from the river crossing and the road to Bukhara. A pleasing wine was it not? Well, that winery, rich and renowned, was our second base of operations. And now, I no longer know if it's ours or not. I know almost nothing, save that Khorasan is at this time the very place where we need to know everything that can be known. And that we have prepared ourselves over long years for this. And that, all at once, here we are. And then those murderers appear and deal us one blow apiece."

He sighed and was silent.

The House of Maniakh had lost its network of people at that most critical moment and in that most critical place? I was beginning to understand my brother: at such a pass he must stop at naught. Including bringing me home from the Empire, for few enough even knew Zargisu by sight.

I was prepared for him to say: "For this one commission I will give you the best bodyguard in all the world. Only find her, Nanidat, and deal with her as you see fit. You alone are capable of this, and I simply cannot leave the city in these crucial times."

And I already knew what my answer would be.

It would be "no." Once again, "no."

My brother was observing me in silence.

I began to form my lips to pronounce that "no."

"Enough," Aspanak said unexpectedly. "That will do for today. You now know the matter in chief. Lie here a while. I require nothing, ask nothing of you. The details may wait until later. Enough, enough."

It was all I could do to remove my robes and feel my shoulder, numb and throbbing slightly under the bandage. Then, with a groan, I lowered myself back onto my soft bed.

The thousands of spectral murmurs in the Samarkand night –
distant hoof beats on the road, a woman's laugh scarce heard, the hum
of a string plucked by chance – seemed dreamlike. But the very waking
truth was the golden gleam of Zargisu's hair as she slipped away along
a garden path and turned, as it were, for an instant on hearing me
whisper, "What have we done to you?"

And then from our courtyard, from the very foot of my chamber
wall, came the sounds. A dull blow. A doleful moan. And the ring of
metal.

3

THE FOURTH PARADISE

The following morning was one of the best in my life.

It began, though, in some trepidation. Amid the chaos and cries that rocked what should have been the most serene and secure place in the world – my own home – my brother, guarded by four of his wraiths, burst in at a dead run, his face contorted, as the battle raged on below, at the foot of my chamber wall. He wrenched me from my bed and, running still and breathing hard, hauled me away below the ground.

I KNOW OF NO OTHER city that rises aloft with such elegance, now smoothly, now steeply, up into hills between two large canals and a multitude of smaller. Chang'an, the capital of the Celestial Empire, is lovely for being an absolutely flat chessboard of green precincts that runs from below the south face of the Imperial palace on its low rise. Constantine's proud city, the capital of the lands of Roum, is a single vast hill thickly sown with houses and colonnades that breaks off on the seaward side, beyond which gleams a scattering of other lights across the narrow straits. But the green hills of Samarkand, with houses that soar up the walls of narrow ravines above the canals – no, other such hills the world knows not.

And this is not least because each of those hills is riddled beneath. With underground pipes that carry water. With underground stores and chambers. With underground baths from which the moist aroma of steam-infused herbs and switches carries up to the passersby – and on cold days can be also seen, in ephemeral plumes that rise from domes set in the ground. And with underground passages, like the one along which my brother was now leading me, still at a dead run with his hand on my elbow, to bring me out at last at a good distance from the outer walls of our home that was in truth an extensive neighborhood. There he brought me out and all but flung me into the saddle of a horse that stood ready for the road. Whenever he could catch his breath as we ran, he had gasped out fragments of sentences that I remember as:

"The sentry may be there in good time... But we ourselves shall destroy them all... Never in three hundred years has anyone dared deal so impudently... with the house of the family Maniakh... We shall come to the bottom of this. And for you, westward with all speed. To Bukhara and thence to Merv. Sit out the trouble there. Because if it's you they want... I don't know what's happening and care to take no risks... Time, I need time. Go to Merv. And there go either to Adijer's vineyard, which lies on a hill just short of the river – everyone knows it – or to the physician Ashofteh, in the new infirmary behind the artisans' quarter south of the fortress. You will find your feet. No one knows you there. Naught matters more. Now haste, make haste! The saddlebag holds all you need. We'll send for you later. To Merv, to Merv. The answers to all questions are there! . ."

And before I was fully awake, I was trotting through the wide open – at night, no less! – Bukhara Gates and along the desolate dawn road that led westward.

But when I did wake, when I gave an indignant shake of the head, when I knew that I was travelling with no attendants, I knew not where and I knew not why...

Then I fell into the best of moods.

In the first place, no one pursued me. My brother had carried one thing off well, at least: I had fled unnoticed.

In the second place, I had no doubt that my brother would not willingly throw himself into any fray. His swordsmanship was no better than mine, and he too was no way discomfited by that. So I need have no cares on his account.

In the third place, I knew that he may well have been right – that if those curious folk with the knives wanted very much to kill me, whatever the reason, there was no more obvious thing to do than to steal away. Which did not, of course, mean that I could not have sat the trouble out in my own home, especially since it came complete with underground vaults. But I had not made the journey home to cower beneath the earth. I wanted rest. And how better to rest than westward bound on a deserted road?

Particularly since – and this was in the fourth place – I did not propose to seek "the answers to all questions" in Merv, or anywhere else, for that matter. I was nurturing more interesting ideas than that for the near future. Or, better yet, many ideas. But I would be the one to choose among them, rather than permitting my own younger brother to command my every step.

I slapped the saddlebag, which, by a longstanding family tradition, in addition to all else that was needful for an unexpected journey would always hold a good amount of money.

This pouch too was certainly not empty.

Excellent. And now let's think what we shall do next.

It would, for example, have been my pleasure to spend a long and idle week on the rolling hills of the Great Steppe, which at that very time were covered in swathes of yellow and orange tulips. The Steppe was a safe and splendid place for he whose father was of an ancient and much respected Turkic race. It soothed the soul and warmed the heart.

At which point I squared my shoulders – and felt the bandage.

No, this was no time to spend feckless days among the tulips. The day after tomorrow, my brother had said, the bandage must be changed.

And besides, why journey to the Steppe when I was already in paradise?

The man charged with selling our house's silk in the Western lands, with furnishing it to Byzant by way of the market town of Lamos, had told me once that the Arabiya believe there to be four earthly paradises.

The first was where two rivers, the Tigris and the Euphrates, converged, where the black soil known as sawad bore all the fruits and grains the soul could desire. And where to this day stand the ruins of prostrate Ctesiphon, capital of the unhappy, annihilated Kingdom of Iran. I had never been there, to the former Western territories of Iran whose name is Iraq, but the great round city of Ctesiphon with its huge-domed palaces was known and remembered by all.

The second paradise was the valley of Bavvan, which was also in Iran and of which, to my disgrace, I knew naught.

The third paradise was, of course, Damascus and its environs, so lush and green.

And the fourth paradise was the endless, flowering garden that lay between Samarkand and Bukhara – the Sogd river valley.

Which is exactly where I was.

I reined in my horse. To the left I could still see bluish peaks, their inaccessible heights strewn with silvery threads of snow. The mountains of Tokharistan. And to the right, in the tender spring grass on which my horse trod, the blood-spatter of tiny scarlet poppies. Beyond, flowing in dense surges over the rolling hills, the lacey spume of trees in flower. And amid that foam, clambering up the slope, flat roofs and the smooth curves of low walls twined about with grape vines.

Because this paradise was populated, and even well populated. The villages here nestled into each other as two lovers do.

It was morning. The first little donkeys were already passing through the gates, and from behind the walls came the aroma of the world's best bread. Someone was dragging a bundle of twigs down the street, and a woman, her brows lightly knit and her head thrown back, was examining the white clusters of flowers that drooped over her wall. In three months, she would be testing, every bit as intently, the firm, velvety nuggets of her unripe apricots.

But the Arabiya, certain as they were of having captured all four paradises, did not know that there were also willows whose gray-green domes hung over hundreds of rivers, streams and canals in gentle Luoyang, and dizzyingly fragrant fields of flowering lotus and peonies in the Imperial park of Shanlin Yuan by Chang'an, and yet many, many other gardens that could be called paradise.

But my paradise was here. And I was in no hurry to depart from it, neither to Merv nor to any other city.

For in this place too, a wealth of pleasures awaited me.

I could buy a large woolen shawl in the nearest market, wrap myself in it and pass the night on some hummock, breathing in the scent of flowers. There is no scent like it, neither in Shanlin Yuan nor anywhere else in the world.

Then, after changing my bandage, I could spend the following night or two in the most costly caravanserai, summoning the best musicians of those parts to play for me as I dined. For that, one need not even be the richest man in Samarkand.

I could visit a jeweler in the next hamlet to select a sky-blue lapis lazuli set in silver or even a blood-red ruby from Balkh, mined amid the bare rocks of the Pamirs. And then when I wearied of it, I would give it to the first girl I met, who would, naturally, be such as may help dally away some pleasant afternoons in a warm room, on clean rugs and linens. With light, wide-set eyes, a small, sharp chin and a nose somewhat long and slightly curved, the sweet faces of my homeland's women being already so unfamiliar a sight to me.

And since I had been wounded by those hard-hearted murderers, that girl... should be assistant to a physician and adept in delivering the unfortunate from a variety of sufferings. If they, helpless and immobile as they were, requested that of her.

I pictured her quite clearly, straddling my outstretched legs, her naked back turned toward me and rising and falling as I watched, the muscles of her hips tense, and between them two tender half-spheres, contracting and releasing and making inroads in my heart. Or maybe not contracting, but only scarce shuddering and quivering? That I would have to learn when the time came.

And the next day, I might invent something else to give me pleasure, might journey wherever I would and hastening nowhere.

And no one would seek to meddle with me, not least because no one in the great, wide world, not even my brother, would know quite where I was.

Sometimes it was simply tiresome to journey with an honor guard and time after time to all but read on the lips of those we passed, "That is one of the Maniakhs, oldest of his clan, and not too ill-favored, either."

But today I was at last alone, and free.

And in addition, I well knew that I had earned this. Because among my friends – those with whom only yesterday I had been sharing goblets of that astonishing Mervian wine – many were talented and wealthy. But my life, mine and not theirs, had been such that it remained only to bow the head humbly before the grace of Ahura Mazda or of Tengri, God of the boundlessly blue sky – name Him as you will.

Or, by contrast, to raise one's head proudly skyward.

To be born wealthiest of all, to be the elder son of an ancient family of such renown, and one of whom the most varied tales are told in hushed tones – such was your gift, o kind and dreadful beings of the radiant blue heights. But one must also know how to make good use of that gift. Let any man try entering his life encumbered by the burden imposed by a far-famed ancestral name known to all who live in Samarkand. And, that burden notwithstanding, also be the first among the best and the best among the first – one who had struck bargains that would long be recounted to children studying the art of commerce.

Traveling the Road once, struggling for three long months through snowbound mountain passes and across dry riverbeds, amid biting winds and wells of bitter water, and beset by the voices of demons in the night – that is great fame and a great labor. But to travel it eight times... such a thing few scions of even the best trading houses would ever resolve to do. It was amusing to think that had I wished to become a caravan-bashi, I could have done so within the year, for all that few titles are so highly respected in our world. The caravan-bashi holds in his hands dozens of lives, including his own.

My back was strong, my eyes were sharp and clear and excellently well-attuned to a woman's sidelong glance. And even my teeth, with very few exceptions, were in their place. I was able to feed myself and provide sustenance to several hundred more. And few had seen, as I had seen, half the world and read such a quantity of scrolls and books in his own languages, those being the languages of the Turkic peoples and the Sogdians, and in the languages of others, of the peoples of Iran and the Celestial Empire. Few, too, had heard the voices of so many of the world's best poets or strings strummed by its greatest musicians.

Your life is splendid, Maniakh of the House of Maniakh. The victory is yours.

And today, this paradise, this world, belongs to you, and no murderers roaming in pairs can prevent you from relishing that world.

For safety's sake, though, I surveyed the road, which was clearly seen to the very horizon, but there were no pairs of murderers with baleful faces within eyeshot. A group of artisans rode along, carrying something that rattled and rang – copper platters? – and evidently making for the nearest market. Then two broad-beamed old patriarchs on mules, and what if they were two? And another pair, this time dots on the far horizon behind me, where the sun was scrambling aloft and flooding the sky with gold, making it hard even to know what they were riding. If donkeys, I need think of them no more. And even if horses, I could, mounted as I was on a steed from the stalls of the House of Maniakh, throw them off my trail with no great difficulty. And in the end, I could not be shrinking from all who traveled in pairs along Sogdia's liveliest highway.

The first caravanserai awaited me near Kermineh, which is where I first knew that although I could usually stay in the saddle as long as I wished, I would do better to spend that night sleeping as long as I cared to. Sleeping until the night melted away and even until the following day's sun began clambering leisurely across the sky. For when all was said and done, the last night had been but a poor thing and had ended untimely, so why not make up here what I had lost? Especially since the cup of blood that had been shed was also worth something, it having been mine own... And, while I thought of it, I might still be able to make my way, before nightfall came again, to Bukhara, where a truly presentable physician could be found.

The stalls of that first caravanserai on my way, as I noticed the following morning, held several horses belonging to travelers but they were not stabled in pairs as horses are wont to be, and so, fending off the ignominious thoughts, I journeyed on. And as I did, I tried not to remember how, before lying down to sleep, I had tested the thick plank door that closed every room of every caravanserai – but against the petty thieves that come by night, of course, not against drowsy murderers. And besides, my brother had said that those oddities preferred to strike their blows publicly, in a crowd. So I should be most wary not in my room at night but, for example... I shook my head and stifled the unworthy thought.

But there came another in its stead: *Who needs to murder in public view, and for what reason? Why, murderers who, strange as it may be to believe, simply want to die, because some people do wish for strange things. But they who send them, why do they not order the victim's throat slit quietly in a dark alley?*

Assume, then, that someone wants these murders to be common knowledge. But then, in turn: Why? Well, for example, to put fear into someone. Or to put fear into all at once. Or...

At that point I had to remind myself that I already had two professions, my current vocation and the one held in reserve. Silk trader now, that is, and, as I had earlier determined, caravan-bashi for later. But here for some reason I was also entering into an affair that even my brother did not concern himself with but was, rather, left to those expressly employed to keep the special accounts in his... that is to say, in mine... well, then, in *our* trading house. So let them rack their brains over such matters.

And this was what happened next. Having travelled not even half a parasang, I decided to return to the caravanserai, to purchase for my journey the very fine-grained, layered bread that they had served at breakfast and had taken my fancy. I could wrap in it anything I bought on the road and so dine without even dismounting.

Because I had by then decided that, on second thought, I was indeed hurrying, and westward at that. I no longer cared to spend the night on a flower-strewn hill. Our trading house owned a small private caravanserai – a trading yard, to speak true – in Bukhara. And I seemed to have decided against seeking a village physician, since I would be taken to someone worthy and well-approved in Bukhara the very next morning.

But at that moment, I recalled what my wheezing brother, winded from much running, had said about Merv as he dragged me toward the outlet from the underground passage – that "no one knows you there."

Did that mean that I had best not show my face at our caravanserai in Bukhara because they did know me there, because my name would be told to all, and that would not bode well for me?

But there were, in any event, dozens of caravanserais in Bukhara's southern purlieus, in any of which I could be recommended to one of a multitude of good physicians.

While thinking on all this, I failed to notice how I had galloped all the way back, except that on the way something had... A trifle, naught but the strange look in the eyes of one of two travelers coming toward me on two very mediocre nags. A look... well, as it were a fleeting panic in those eyes as I swept by.

But on the other hand, who would not panic if at any instant he was about to be flung from the road by a man going at a dead gallop who...

Who had but a short time ago been pressing on in the other direction. But to know that, they would at least have had to notice that the man had first been riding westward. And if they had noticed that, then...

"Just now there were two horsemen on the road," I said to the baker who was bringing me his fine-grained, fresh-baked flatbreads. And I began to describe the horsemen in some detail.

The baker, not surprisingly, knew nothing, for he had never left his ovens. But he retailed my questions at the top of his voice across the enormously spacious courtyard. An inordinate amount of talk at cross-purposes ensued, after which the entire courtyard knew that a westbound traveler was in fear of someone. *Every man should indeed tend to his own business*, thought I, *for what's my brother's is my brother's and what's mine...*

Even so, I did determine that those two had arrived here, at this caravanserai, immediately after me on the previous evening. They awoke early, while I still lay abed, but tarried by the public water cistern, prattling with everyone about nothing. It was as if they were biding their time. And they did not set off until after I had gone. Those tidings, needless to say, brought me no joy whatsoever.

And then I did something that I would under no circumstances permit myself today. I sped back toward Bukhara, again at a full gallop, in hopes of storming past those two, whoever they may be, and continuing at near the same pace, to reach my goal by evening.

The idea was sound: no dagger there is that can kill a galloping man. My mistake, though, was that, having not met the two anywhere on the road and having decided that they had simply turned off toward some village – homeward, that is – I allowed a calm to descend on me.

Today, of course, I would certainly suppose that those two, once over the first wave of panic, would have drawn the tolerably accurate conclusion that I had left something in the room and so would soon come their way again. And they would serenely wait for me, lying on the crest of a hill well out of sight from the road. And, if time passed and I did not come into view, only then would they bestir themselves.

But in those days I knew naught of such things. So, calmly now, I reached the purlieus of Bukhara at end of day. Where, as on the day before, I was much put out that I could not bathe in regular fashion but instead had to torment myself, bandaged shoulder and all, with basins of water and damp rags lathered with soap. But when that was done, I lay myself down to sleep untroubled, in an excellent caravanserai where no one could know me, although still feeling unwontedly weak as I took to my couch.

The events of the following morning, though, were unpleasant indeed.

Probably the wisest thing I did that morning when I quit the caravanserai's square and spacious courtyard was to take with me my purse – a long, narrow, leather pouch that could, if desired, be wound about the waist. I know not if I would be alive today were it not for that... not even that prudence, but that happenstance. As I recall, I had almost left the purse in my room, since the safeguarding of my money was usually left to one of my attendants, but remembered in time that I would need it to pay the physician. For dinner I did not propose to pay, since I would return in good time to eat at this caravanserai or someone would stand me a meal at our own.

My musings on whether it behooved me well to burst so unceremoniously and in broad daylight into my own caravanserai brought me to the simple and very good idea of first observing it from a respectable distance until I spied a face familiar to me from Samarkand, while still preferably at some remove from the yard itself. Then I would hail that man, and the rest would go of itself.

After again cursing my brother Aspanak roundly for the predicament his stupidity had put me in, I seated myself in the spring sunshine where a knot of caravan drivers and other merchants had gathered to drink whatever pleased them best so early in the day – Sogdian beer or the sherbet of the Arabiya or simply water – and began my watch over our caravanserai gates.

It was not in my plans to feast my eyes on the charms of Bukhara that morning. It is not at all a bad city, as cities be, although stone slabs do not pave its streets as they do in Samarkand and although the best location in all the Bukhara oasis is not Bukhara itself, no indeed, but Varakhsha, seat of the bukhar-khudats, which sprawls nearby and to the north-west, in the desert of red sand aptly named Kyzyl-kum. Bukhara's governors had made their home a thing of beauty, with stucco carved into medallions rife with vines, flowers and wild beasts, which had become the stuff of poetry.

Bukhara itself, though, had always been a comfortable and somehow languid city. And so unlike any other that, although it had long been part of Sogdia and the bukhar-khudats had supposedly submitted to the ikhshids of Samarkand, no one fully believed that to be so.

Our caravanserai was situated, naturally enough, close to the road, amid a multitude of public caravanserais and warehouses. From here the citadel could not be seen, and it was also a good distance to the artisans' quarter, chaotic, noisy and yet to see the green of spring, where a ruck of the Arabiya lived.

The conquerors of my land.

But they were here too, in this very spot, settled comfortably on the prayer rugs that brought Bukhara its fame. And much engaged in their favorite pastime, which was to loll there and babble blissfully on, every minute clutching each other by the sleeve.

Did they know that their Caliph's deputy – our Caliph's deputy, I would have said had I been speaking aloud – was murdered, murdered after a long and hapless war with the latest in a long line of rebels, that mutinous Merv now stood between them and the Caliph's palace in Damascus, that ahead lay either another war, as if this paradise had not seen enough wars these thirty-seven years, or something other? The unknown. A new state? A new Sogdia, but with its capital in Merv? Or a confusion of city states – Samarkand, Bukhara, Chach, Fergana – all awaiting a new overlord? And who would he be? Again a khagan of the Great Steppe or perhaps a yet-unknown potentate of a resurgent Iran?

Be all as it may, these people with faces seemingly carved from dark wood had good reason to be perturbed at that time. But I observed no perturbation. What I did observe was that they were indolently conversing not only among themselves but also with their Sogdian neighbors – with those who had for long years waged war against them. What were they speaking of? Not about the harvest, to be sure, since the Arabiya had yet to learn how to till the soil here. War was another scarcely desirable topic. But trade, quite possibly. Although, like as not, they were hardly announcing how ready they would be, at the first opportunity, to wrest our trade routes from us.

They will never leave, I thought, as I had oft thought before. Because more than half of them had been born here, on my native soil, and many of Sogdian mothers. They had never so much as seen the yellow sands of the country from which their warrior fathers had come. And here they would remain forever and a day, because we could not kill every last one of them.

And I will never again see the Sogdia my father and grandfather knew.

Maybe the very name of Sogdia would disappear, when all my fellow countrymen would come to prefer instead the spine-chilling consonance of a word from the language of the Arabiya, Mawarannahr – "that which lies beyond the river." And dahsht, the Sogdian word for desert, would be forgotten too, and the fact that in my land, silk is called by the sumptuous, toothsome name of prenak.

But then I was drawn away from my mournful thoughts and even laid aside my goblet of very tolerable light wine of a greenish hue.

Because the caravanserai of the trading house of the Maniakhs in Bukhara – my caravanserai – was looking other than it should.

I could not speak surer than that, having had no training and no experience in the affairs that occupied my brother.

But something was amiss, and I now had the agonizing task of recalling what precisely I had seen on the other side of that broad street in the time it would take to have the purveyor of wines admit me to the place where men and women never go together, and even to stand there alongside a companionable, swart-skinned, black-bearded conqueror.

What exactly was amiss, then? Well, for example, a man had ridden out through the gates – I had near forgot his face but without the slightest doubt he was one of ours – on a mule. And had made toward the center of town. And what of that? He was holding some bundles and rolls, which meant that he was on one of our usual errands. So what had drawn my attention?

Another, this one on horseback, who had for some reason been keeping watch in the street, by the gates, had plodded off behind, making no effort to hide. Our man even turned around to assure himself that his escort was there. And having done so, silently went his way.

For how long had escorts been lingering for our traders not in the yard itself but outside the gates? There was nothing so terrible here, note you, except that in the normal way they would have left together.

I was tying to remember the look of he who had followed behind. A Bukharan, to be sure, but likely one of those who felt at home in the conquerors' empty temples. Who maybe had already changed his real name of Mahich or Vius and become an Abdul or a Rashid. Which was no rarity. This was, to all outward view, the most ordinary Bukharan.

But if he was an escort while also a bodyguard, why had he not even exchanged nods with our man, even though they had plainly seen and recognized each other?

This puzzle I could not crack. And then I remembered another nicety. Over all this time, six or seven men had walked or ridden into our yard. And their faces... were faces like any other, although several did not have entirely the look of those who might normally frequent a trading yard.

Such people had no place there. I could say naught more distinct than that. And I even cursed myself for having frittered away half a day without having seen or understood a thing, and all instead of doing something more... astute.

And by astute, I seemingly meant either questioning the vintner regarding the affairs of his neighbors across the way or simply striding over there, entering into what was, after all, my own...

But then I began slowly trying to tuck myself deeper into the shadows, although the cool spring day was even cooler there. Because two horsemen were sauntering down the street, and I knew them both. Or almost knew. Because they had the posture in the saddle, the turn of the head and the general bearing of the two of whom I, craven coward that I was, had been in such fear through the two previous days on the road from Samarkand.

They turned smartly toward our yard and without hesitation passed through the gates.

An ague seized me, while I kept to my dark corner below the wall, wondering: *Shall I flee? But what will that gain me? At best, the pair will be cheated of their chance to look around and recognize me when they leave again.*

Then came the cries from behind the gates, the one full of fury, the other of pain.

"Yalla, yarab!" – "Oh ho, you Arab!" – all the dusky-faced conquerors, until then deep in their peaceable conversation, said at once, as they turned to look toward the gates.

Some on that busy street began to approach the gates closer, craning their necks.

I surmised that I would fare better in a crowd and soon thereafter, amidst an agitated multitude, was pushing my way into my own caravanserai. At which time it came to me clearly that I did indeed understand nothing.

Because a stable hand – whose face was, when I thought of it, foggily familiar to me from Samarkand – was struggling to hold two horses, one of which was shaking its head from side to side while the other tried to rear. And hard by those horses' hooves two bodies lay, the spots of blood and the unnaturally twisted arms and legs, to say naught of their immobility, attesting to the unlikelihood of their ever rising again.

The dust was still settling.

My pursuers, then, would stalk me no farther than this yard.

But that was no reason to rejoice. Instead, I backed – slowly, not wishing to stand out from the crowd – toward the gates and once outside, made my way, trying not to break into a run, to a place thronged with people. So as to hide among them and vanish.

A trader's healthy instinct tells him that if he begins to discuss terms and discovers that he understands exactly naught of what is transpiring, then he must bid a courteous farewell and apply himself elsewhere.

But here, another instinct was hinting, no farewells were in order. Because what had transpired here was not simply incomprehensible and very unsavory, but an unsavory affair that had some connection with me.

And so it was indeed time to flee.

Not like a panic-stricken fool, though, but quite otherwise.

4

THE SILVER STIRRUPS

The man who departed that very evening along the road that led southwest to Merv was not at all he who had arrived in Bukhara the day before.

That man was I, who had known enough, after fleeing my own trading yard, to retreat to the narrow streets and there find a quiet place to sit, swallow some soup, which was tasteless on my tongue, and think long and hard. And to reach some rather unpleasant yet unavoidable conclusions.

Chief among which was that the danger was real. And that it would be futile for anyone to try to puzzle out in haste what had transpired here. Especially one who had, to boot, made himself almost a foreigner in his own land.

And, that being so, there must be no courting even the slightest risk.

Cowardice is no shame. Stupidity is. There is naught to fear except... danger. And not to acknowledge danger is the supreme stupidity.

I did not fear the ghouls of the desert, those long-limbed and abominable monsters with the legs of goats that lure travelers into untamed places and devour them there. I myself, by Lop Nur, had once been shown a long ridge of gray rocks behind which three caravan drivers had been lost to sight a year previously and had never returned. I began to look hard, and in the sickening shimmer that trembled over that ridge, I had glimpsed for an instant a mottled head... But I was not afraid. Both because men from the princedoms of Ind had told me ghouls are only illusions of the day that are born of starshine and melt gradually away in the brighter light, and also because I was not alone and the entire caravan stood ready to throw a bridle on any who might become spellbound and suddenly take to scaling that accursed slope. And so the ghouls, to speak seriously, were no danger.

But here I was altogether alone and had no notion who was hiding behind what ridge, who was a friend and who a foe, and why I even had any foes at all. Nothing could be more dangerous that this, for in Lop Nur I had at least known where the ghouls were lurking.

So it was high time to turn coward. And, more, to be the best and the most cowardly coward in all of Sogdia.

Let us, then, begin with a simple idea, I thought. *My two pursuers were killed as soon as they entered our trading yard. And no one had best betake himself to a place where people – my pursuers though they be – are killed.*

Whether others would search for me, whether they would walk or ride, in pairs or alone, I did not know. But I could surmise that they would begin by watching for a solitary denizen of Samarkand on the right side of forty and dressed as I had been when I rode away. On a horse of fair quality, ash-gray in color. Toward the west.

What of that could I change? I took to giving most of my attention to my money pouch. To that time, I had done as any well-bred man should and had not slavered over every near-weightless dirham with its uneven edge and four-line inscription, but had plunged a hand into my purse, drawn out a coin, and handed it to its rightful recipient. And had refused the little silver daniks I was owed in return.

But now I remembered that dirhams were money too. And for a long time, as I sat over my soup, I tried to determine by feel how many I had.

When the count was done, I proved to have few enough. More than I needed to journey back to Samarkand, but what would be my lot there, other than the prospect of being a prisoner in my own home and knowing no peace even then? True it was, though, that from my home, the road led east. To the frontiers of the Celestial Empire. Back to Chang'an.

But I also had money, enough and to spare, for the road that led in the opposite direction, to Merv.

I was in Bukhara, in rough measure half-way between Samarkand and Merv. Around me stretched what had once been an unremarkable country by the name of Sogdia, but thirty-seven years ago had become the eastern outskirts of the Caliphate. And now, as my brother had said, no one knew who ruled here. Westward of Bukhara lay Merv, capital of Khorasan, the easternmost portion of Iran, which had been conquered a century back by that same Caliphate. But if Khorasan was now in rebel hands, then Sogdia was, as my brother had also contended, a no man's land. And, strange as this may sound, for a solitary traveler that did not bode well, for anyone could fall upon him and, say, make off with his horse. So Merv was not the worst place to be, since there was at least some authority there.

And westward from Merv began Iran, which was, as I heard tell, still subject to the Caliph. But that was one place where I did not propose to go.

Yes, but what would I gain on reaching the almost unknown Merv, which I had but ridden by once on my way to Constantine's fair city? Well, two locations where, as my brother had said, I *may* still be able to show myself.

So much was true, but what if those locations resembled our trading yard in Bukhara? . . And then I remembered that my brother had said nothing about Bukhara. An oversight, that, or no?

And in Merv I would also be within the domains of one whom for almost three decades my family had been fattening and quietly leading to power. And if the Leopard of Merv could not protect me, then who could?

Especially since, once in Merv, I would be able to send a letter to my brother asking for money and seeking protection for my journey back to the Celestial Empire, if I did decide to return there.

But I did not want to write such things to my brother. Instead, an altogether different idea came to me. *Dear brother*, I would write, *you are skilled in so many things where I am not. So why, then, even after sending the unfortunate Zargisu to Merv – on her insistence, you'd have me believe – are you still at such a loss that you actually resolved to consult me on the matter? Grant me, then, that you* were *desirous of asking me to take a hand in this.*

What was it that I could do but no one else could? An interesting question.

So I should set off eastward without delay, although aware that in Zargisu's little home on the Western Canal, not far from ours, I would nevermore be greeted by a slender, tall-grown girl with wind-whipped hair the color of just-burnished copper?

But a world in which Zargisu's little home was forever empty would be a lackluster world indeed, however many gardens it might contain.

At the end of all, it would suffice me to know where she was and how she fared. To meet her, to speak a while, to understand what of the strange and hideous talk of her was true and what was not. And then, let her touch my hand in farewell, and the world would once again spread an endless road of beauty at my feet.

Putting away my thoughts and casting an anxious glance at the sun, I again placed a hand on the pouch holding my dirhams and was again unpleasantly surprised by how very few they were. Glad I was then to have bought no rubies.

And now – what person would my murderers be seeking? A man of a certain age... and that was hard to change... dressed thus and so, and mounted on a light gray horse.

Instead of a dirham, I handed my host in payment for my soup the agreed quantity – a modest quantity – of daniks and inquired of him the way to the cloth and the leather markets.

At the cloth market, after some listless haggling, I was able to discard my knee-length Sogdian robe, quilted and trimmed with a rather rare, dense silk, and my loose trousers called sardwil, and replace them with far less costly garb. I was now dressed in plainer trousers, a kuftan of Iranian cotton, and a gray aba, the large cape that almost all the Arabiya had worn ever since arriving in this land of mine, it being simply indispensible on long journeys for the protection it gave the rider against the combined assault of dust, sun and cold.

My Sogdian cap, made of felt but trimmed with silken cord, was replaced by a keffiyeh, also gray, and a black iqal to secure it.

With a sharp intake of breath, I realized that I no longer resembled a man from an ancient Samarkand merchant clan, although in this case that was cause only for joy.

Having entered the shop dressed as I had been, there was no hope of securing a reduction in price, especially since my robe and sardwil were already well worn. So I ended by making a simple exchange under the trader's superciliously sympathetic eye.

But then later, at the leather market, I no longer looked overly rich. And I repaid the prior indignity in full, albeit visiting my revenge on another trader altogether.

He was selling donkeys.

My idea was plain enough: if I was still sought, the seeker would already have galloped his way through each of the city's dozens of caravanserais and found the one where my horse was stabled. And then his questions would begin. My outward appearance and clothing were simple to describe, considering that, in general, few travel alone. So that, come what may, going back for my horse would put me at risk and I had, after all, just pledged to myself that I would be the greatest coward in all Sogdia, if not in all the world.

For a new horse, at least a good one that would throw any pursuers off my trail, I had not the coin. And what was the sense in throwing them off, if night would follow, when there must be rest, if not for cowards then at least for their horses?

And so I decided that, rather than trying to leave my pursuers behind, I must do the contrary and let them run ahead on their horses. And then I would make other plans.

The donkey I needed was standing a good ten paces away when I took up with the owner over an entirely different beast. Prior to that, I had strolled unhurriedly down several other rows of the leather market, with its saddles, harnesses, and live merchandise, to gauge the present going rate for donkeys in Bukhara.

A battle over a consignment of silk that is almost too large to cram into an entire caravan's packs can take exactly the same amount of effort and skill as buying a donkey. So I was not one whit concerned that the sun was already sinking in the west, because this signified that the buyer's time had come. And besides, while it is certainly not always possible to sleep in the saddle of a horse, donkeys seem to be made expressly for that purpose. And I had firmly decided to travel during the time least expected by my presumed pursuers – all night long, if need be.

"I have no requirement to transport rocks. I require it to carry only me. But to carry me long, well, and with no commotion," I told the donkey vendor, trying hard to look stubborn, wary and outright witless.

"Then that one, the black one... Fifteen is all I ask... Do you know how to choose a donkey? Almost like a horse, but..." The Bukharan with a felt cap clapped tight on his head and a flower behind one ear was beginning by trying to win my trust.

I did know how to choose a donkey. If it gives you a womanly smile, batting long lashes, do not trust it, for it could well prove guileful and capricious. And if you see one that looks as strong as a bull, do not rejoice because you do not yet know how far, all its strength notwithstanding, it will be willing to travel without rest. In general, if a horse is in character better than any man and a camel will at bottom always be a malignant brute, donkeys are complicated creatures. I cannot say that I know them as I know horses, but the principal secret I have, and it is that they are chosen by character, which can only be determined by intuition, and that's the sum of it.

"Not for fifteen, no, but for five I would have bought it... Do you take me for a Maniakh?" I muttered.

What I did to him next would have been enough to incense anyone. Without warning, having taken my price up to ten, I began to shake my head, and against all the rules, retreated, saying, "No, five it shall be." And for a long, a very long, time, sticking out my lower lip, I eyed yet another donkey. Then at last, when the merchant was well and truly maddened, I waved a hand and took myself off, but on the way stopped by the beast I really wanted and extended a hand to it.

"But this one, now..."

"Eight, if you must," the proprietor said with a gust of breath. By then, he wanted one thing only, which was to see the back of me, and that without further delay.

And it was, as I already knew, an excellent price for a donkey young but still canny enough and with legs accustomed to keeping a brisk pace. And almost white, as was typical of the donkeys thereabouts.

Silently I found eight dirhams, not even putting myself to the trouble of counting them out, handed them to the merchant, and took the bridle.

The donkey gave me a sly look.

And we set off, he and I, toward the setting sun, leaving the city. He who had once been a proud horseman in Sogdian garb was now jouncing along on a donkey, his face swathed in a keffiyeh.

But it must not be thought that in all this I had forgotten the one other problem that all along had been, not greatly but persistently, troubling me.

My reckoning was that none had ever yet died of a deep slit in the back. The physician had bound it up. My brother had mentioned that even with such a wound, one could walk, ride and hunt. Which was, in rough measure, what I was doing. Then what was I feeling? My shoulder blade seemed to itch and was throbbing a little, but something of the sort, I surmised, is supposed to happen when a wound knits up. As for poison, no one had said a word about poisoned knives, and besides, what poison would it be that was not felt at once but lay in wait for three or four days? So if any risk was to be taken with my health, there could be no risk less foolhardy.

The donkey and I cut across a dense torrent of camels bringing goods to the city for all that night was now falling.

Oh, the sorrow, I thought. *Bukhara's far-famed New Year bazaar is in full swing. Twenty days of frantic trade, the last of them on the first day of the coming year.*

And five days thereafter came the New Year of the Magi, and between those two events, an intemperate drinking of wine, passersby soused with water, and music and poetry resounding from the best houses.

Novruz. New Year's Day. Voices chant to the sun the eternal "May your red radiance come to me; may my yellow weariness go to you." Vessels on a platform – seven, to mark the number of the immortals. In one, food; in another, seeds; in yet another, coins... Two candles, one for the light and one for the darkness. A mirror to reflect evil away. Fish to signify life, colored eggs as a symbol of fruitfulness. And, at the platform's left front corner, the Great Book.

But where shall I greet the holiday this year? I wondered. *On the other side of the desert, in a city where I know no one and no one knows me? Where I will probably sleep through all the merry-making, because my head is so unwontedly heavy?*

Then came a time when I shuddered, woke up for good and all, and glanced around.

The sky to the east was already pale gold. The paradise around me had ended long ago, and the road leading southwest was like a dark and endless snake winding its way amid bare, dark-red hills. I had spent the whole night astride a donkey that had proven a wholly quick-witted and agreeable beast. But now even he needed to rest.

Yet I had, it seemed, not woken for that reason. Then what had roused me?

That was it: hoof beats behind me, coming from the north-east. Man is, all the same, an unusual creature. Under threat, his sight and hearing are not what they were before but far, far sharper.

Ahead and a touch to the left, a mountain, the same mountain still, rocked from side to side on bowed legs. I was, of course, not journeying alone, but had attached myself, as it were, to a group of travelers. No one cares to have an uninvited companion on the road, but it was night and they were all in and out of sleep. And besides, a lone man on a donkey is no visible cause for alarm. The camels' feet rustled softly across the ground, their rhythm never changing. And my donkey's little hooves clipped and clopped along.

And behind me, entirely other hooves – a horse's hooves.

I slumped into the shape of a pothook and wrapped myself more snugly in my aba.

The hoof beats were fewer now, and farther between. And then two shadows came to lie on the rocky path just to my left – long, lank, indistinct, and rounded above. For a time, they kept their place, then both began to extend fleshless tongues to touch me and my donkey. To touch and pull back, touch again and again pull back.

Then I distinctly heard two horses breathing close by me, and their shadows lay over the camel's shaggy hindquarters.

And after a long, a very long, moment, the two horses overtook the caravan to the left and the clatter of their hooves went on ahead.

I did not care to turn my head by even a hair's breadth, because the most fearsome of all would be to meet that pair eye to eye.

But you were killed! I wanted to cry out to them.

Yet still I did turn my head the slightest bit. They were, of course, not at all the ones who had followed me from Samarkand and had perished in my Bukhara trading yard. Two completely nondescript men, these, wearing grayish abas like mine but with their faces quite uncovered. The horses were Turkic mounts, from the steppes – nothing to look at, that is, yet hardy enough.

And a while later, the sound of hooves came again from behind.

This was a man alone, on a better mount. A true Iranian. On his head he wore a Khorasani kalansuwa, which left his face open for the world to see, and an uncommon face it was too – slightly sunken at the bridge of the nose and with a stubborn thrust to the chin. In body he was tall, very tall, and thin. I would even say that he was quite simply a fine man, although not for his countenance but for his heedless, confident grace in the saddle. It was the grace of a warrior no longer young but strong and experienced.

His gray eyes sliding over me with a studied indifference, he rode to the head of the caravan I was trailing, whence his pleasant, rather husky voice carried back to me.

Then the hooves sounded faster, also passing on ahead.

"Hey, you there!" It was a man's voice, from up in front. And, without a doubt, it was me he was addressing. "Hey, you on the donkey! How long since you attached yourself to us? There's been all sorts traveling this road since early morning, asking questions..."

I knew exactly what he meant and, like one going to his doom, I turned left, up into the smooth, sandy hills. The donkey shook its head in gratitude.

All he and I had to our names were a handful of dirhams, useless in this wasteland, a large flask of water, a few thorn-bushes, and the remnants of a loaf of bread. And something of the cool of morning, which in these parts could easily – even now, so close to the New Year – turn to a fierce heat.

The donkey avenged himself on the thorns while I tried to sleep and not sleep at once, and below, the road dinned with the thunder of horses' hooves and the ring of metal. It was a large mounted squadron riding by, throwing up dust and stones – not a single spear there was but rather a multitude of scimitars in scabbards, chain mail in bags strapped to saddles, the dark, bearded faces of the conquerors, the Arabiya, and mixed among them, blond, Sogdian heads... Who was galloping so, and where, and why? Was it Lord Tarkhun resurrected, once more to lose his grasp on the all but defeated Qutayba and again be deposed by my grandfather and see Gurek installed on the throne in his stead? Was an army of Sogdian rebels, sixty thousand strong, descending yet again on Merv, as in the days of Harith ibn Surayj, only to lose the war there yet again? Or had others arisen who desired to repeat our victorious war, waged eighteen years before, that had plunged the lavish lands of Sogdia into an unthinkable famine? Or was Abu Muslim already here? Or were these people just galloping into nowhere, simply because an entire generation had now grown up that could make naught but war?

And what sense was there in placing on those festive platforms the paired candles, the mirrors, the chalices, the fish and the colored eggs, if long ago God had abandoned the people of this land and they Him? Five hundred lashes were prescribed for he who defiled the earth with a dead body – only birds and dogs could pick the bones of the departed – but we had littered our paradise's earth with thousands of corpses, had drenched it in rivers of blood. And what did we want now – and in that "we" I included myself, who had also once ridden out on such a horse, with a sword at my belt, to do resplendent, victorious battle, and...

Then a merciful mist clouded my eyes.

I was brought from oblivion by a gray ground squirrel propelling a pebble toward me with its minute paw. It stood a while, looking at me askance and making motions of displeasure with its tiny snout, then instantly dissolved away at the edge of a round hole in the sandy hill.

The hoof beats of two horses drawing near from the west now demonstrated to me the weakness in my brilliant plan. I had fared most excellently when the two horsemen had overtaken a man in counterfeit attire on a leisurely donkey. But then, after galloping quite far ahead, they had probably come to know that something was amiss and were now retracing their steps. Then, after resting awhile, they would resume their search, riding again from Bukhara to Merv. That stage of the journey took three or four days, although longer on a donkey, offering plentiful opportunities to scrutinize all who shared the road.

So I was not at all surprised to see, after a seemly interval, the tall warrior speeding down the same road and also the opposite direction.

Now all that remained to me was to sit on my hill with a flask soon to be drained, a donkey and a ground squirrel, or...

A WOMAN'S HEART IS MADE to melt before a man beset by calamity.

I was a long time choosing my caravan, and began my descent to the road only when I was certain that the place of honor on the lead camel was occupied by a woman of middle years and estimable corpulence, covered against dust and sun by striped Bukhara fabrics that swathed at once her head, haunches, and the rest of her.

"That you may," she replied, after peering into my face. "But we can go one better. Get yourself into a camel pack and sleep there a while. Your donkey will follow on a tether."

A gift, a very gift! No horsemen would ever be moved to suppose that the ordinary white donkey hitched to a camel had only that morning been carrying the hunchbacked man they sought. I was rocked back to sleep against the camel's swaying side. And awoke surrounded by the long shadows of evening, looking into a crimson sun that lay on the horizon.

"AND NOW WE SHALL TALK, young man," said my savior in female form, squirming contentedly into her cushions and patting with a chubby palm the dusty rug she sat on, to have me sit by her. "And of course you have no food... Nay, put away your dirham. We have supplies aplenty. Should we rather discard what we do not eat? And so, alone on the road, with sickness, by the by, in your face and no food... So, so, so. What has befallen you?"

When lying, my brother says, best lie truthfully. And so, with a sigh, I offered up the following to that full-fleshed, dignified face.

"I am of a wealthy and well-respected merchant family of Samarkand. Because of a woman who had to make away from the city and travel to Merv, I have also had to make away. All the more so since, due to this business, someone has hired murderers, and one attempt has already been made on my life. I'm wounded in the shoulder. Now I must go to Merv, where all the problems will – or so I hope – be resolved." *Was that well done, my dear Aspanak?* Yet, if you look close, it was almost all the unadulterated truth.

"So," the caravan mistress said, handing me another cup of water. She was satisfied. "Drink, drink. You do look ill, and you tremble. Well, then, that is an interesting story. You're a good liar. And now I shall have my say. You are certainly of a good family... Such is your face, for those with eyes to see. You've lived your share of years, but still have the look of a boy. Now about that wealthy family... Why would it not buy your way out of all that unpleasantness? No, the chances are that you are no merchant but higher – a dehkan to the life. But your father was too good a warrior, for which reason your lands and castles have been confiscated by those ibns and those abus, and now you... let me look at you again... now you are a dapirpat, a scribe."

Indeed, I thought. *Here's another trade, aside from merchant and caravan-bashi, that I could take up here and now. To sit over a papyrus with kalam or brush in hand, copying the decrees of ikhshids and emirs, and documents on the levying of the kharaj and the jizyah. . . Tedious, yes, but that I could also have done. How much one learns about oneself on such merry travels!*

"And now, as to the woman – tell me more about her, won't you? Whatever you will. Her face. Or some other trifle."

Her face? How long is it since last I saw her? Two years and more? All I remember now is her back and her waist, bent slightly as she turned, a gait achieved with a great economy of motion, and her hair – oh, such hair! Her mother did not err in naming the girl Zargisu, the golden-tressed.

So then, with another sigh, I gave the matron a tale about something else altogether.

About how we lay on a rug, Aspanak, that loathsome lad, and I, both with hands clasped together and chins just grazing them. And directly before our eyes stood two identical and marvelous objects. They were large... my God in heaven, simply enormous – bigger than both our heads!.. heavy, compact constructions, like little dwellings made of pure silver. Their flat, polished bases rested sturdily on Zargisu's rug, and the two side walls of each curved smoothly upward to meet at a silver loop in the form of thick, knotted vine strands.

And in the milky gleam of those walls was a whole world, a half-forgotten world of vanished beauty. Interlaced in cambered coils were singular beasts with arched necks, arrows arrested in flight behind them, and letters in human form, and above them all, a khosrow, a shahanshah, his lance angled downward.

These were the silver stirrups of a prince of vanquished Iran.

They had been in the battle of Qadisiyah, Zargisu said. One hundred and thirty years before, when the swarthy-faced conquerors had sped through the black dust rising above that accursed field, to break the line of heavy cavalry, of warriors armored to the eyes, then had rammed the array of war elephants, and even that invincible formation they had broken. And the princes in their impregnable armor fell, their iron feet sliding strengthless from silver stirrups. And so too did General Rustam fall, leaving only a verse behind.

"O, Iran! Whither have gone the many kings that once adorned thee?.."

Naught had remained of the greatest of all empires. There was only a slender girl with a face specked with freckles and eyes the color of dark honey, a stiff-backed little column sitting before us on a rug.

"Now you're not lying, you beautiful boy," the stocky woman said softly. "Of the rest I know not, but that much is true. You do love her."

Love? I wanted to retort. *What love is this? I never, after I was no longer a lad, so much as laid a finger on her. We simply grew up together, the daughter of a mother escaped from an empire undone and the sons of an ancient Samarkand clan. That, and no more.*

But I was silent, gazing into the woman's dreaming eyes, which shone in the campfire's light.

And then out of the darkness, a sharp, quick hailing. And at the very edge of my mind, I heard in the silence of night the distant, and unmistakably slowing, hoof beats.

Of two horses.

The matron pushed me, with unexpected force, out of the transparent circle of rippling light and into the dark.

"To the camels." She spoke quickly. "I have six bodyguards with goodly staves. Get yourself into the camel pack, and stay there. You'll find a slit in the pack side for whatever need you may have."

From inside a woolen sack that smelled of dust and raisins, I heard voices. Long, persistent conversations. And then quiet.

At last a woman's whisper through the wool: "It's a bad job," she said. "They begged. They were very insistent. Of course I didn't take them into the caravan. They had a good view of my guard and their staves. They've built a fire on a nearby hill. And they can see us very well. So stay there and sleep, dapirpat."

Through the upper slit in the sack, one after another, three cushions fell onto my head.

I woke again when the sack, and I along with it, was being hoisted, with much cursing, onto a spitefully wheezing Bactrian. Then the sack rocked, and the rocking went on without end.

Toward noon I heard again her hushed voice. "They're traveling alongside, in the open. Which means they know you're here. And there was a tall one too, hardly seen before he was gone. Does he want you as well?"

"I don't know," I replied, in all honesty.

The sun rose ever higher.

Through the side slit I tried to breathe and through that same slit, with horror in my heart, I did the thing of which my rescuer had spoken, imagining the two horsemen... but never mind them, imagining everyone in the caravan seeing the yellow stream seeping into the earth. The water in my flask grew downright hot, then was gone, and through that slit someone shoved a fresh flask. My head burned with fever and – I could no longer hide it from my own self – the pain that griped my shoulder was different now. This was, clearly, a bad job indeed.

I do not remember how long I rocked in that horrible sack. At last, hard by my ear, I heard a voice, but male this time.

"Hey, dapirpat, where are you going, exactly?"

"To a vineyard. A famous one. Very costly wine, almost black in color. On this side of the river, not quite to Merv," I reeled off, for I had nothing left to hide.

"Then you must in truth be a boy from a good family, to be acquainted with such as they," the voice growled amiably. "With such as have no conscience. To take so much for a single flask, even when the wine is young... If it's wine you need as good as that but at one-tenth the price, only ask me. Very well, your donkey is being brought to you. Those friends of yours have fallen back a little, although they're still here. And there it is, your vineyard, afar on the hill. Merv too is now in sight. Listen to me. Push your legs through the slit, bend your body, then thrust out your head, spring onto your donkey, and off to the right, up the hill, at a trot. Your beast, belike, has tired of walking on with naught to carry. Now: ready, push, go!"

Drenched in blinding, gilded sunlight, the world rang with birdsong. On a rocky hill to my right, an even roofline could be seen, and my donkey, teeth bared in spite and ears laid back after I had plumped down on him, was carrying me upward amid rows of grapevines.

To the west, beyond a motionless ribbon of river, the ashen shadow that jutted above the horizon was the outline of unreasonably, unimaginably huge, round towers with a wall between. They could well have been built by a giant long dead.

To the east, behind me, I could still easily see the tiny caravan of three camels, a bulky female figure perched unmoving atop one of them, and four mules with their riders.

And some distance away, two diminutive horsemen, black against the road.

Then, trailing them, yet another – a mote of dust, a streak on the horizon, likely visible to me alone.

5

THE DEAD GENERAL'S WINE

The man who met me at the very gates had the look of a peasant, which is to say that his legs were dusty to the knees and his garments were no shining model of elegance either. There were, moreover, several others in the courtyard as dusty and sweaty as he, and together, in no way like master and men, they were loading camels with huge clay jars tied in pairs. But only one of them, his face overgrown to the eyes with stubble of an indeterminate shade, had turned a gaze at once both sad and right malicious on me, and had at length uttered a portentous phrase, with a meaningful pause in its midst.

"You seem to ail... today."

"I am wounded. And I have been pursued these last six days" was my honest and very quiet answer. "Seven, if you count the day I spent in Samarkand."

The man with malice in his eyes became very serious, went to the gates, and surveyed the road a while. Then he turned to me.

"Well, if you allow that I've had no guests from Samarkand for almost a month past, all could be worse. At least you found your way here. And now I'll give you joy: no one is scaling our hill from the road. Let us reckon that they're gone for now. So you may dismount from your long-eared beauty and... What is your name, my sorely rumpled guest?"

"Maniakh," I said, undaunted. "Nanidat Maniakh."

"You make bold to say so," he said, the creases around his mouth growing deeper. "But in this house there is one most pleasing way to determine if we are indeed speaking of my good client. Here is the first question for you," he continued amiably, linking arms with me to lead me into the cool of his home. "Where are we now? What place is this?"

"This is the place where our family buys a remarkable wine," I replied.

"So it is! Although I would have been more particular and called it the wine of the House of Adijer. My wine, that is. And you, of course, have drunk it, if your name is indeed Maniakh," he went on, inclining toward me confidingly.

"I was drinking it when I received my wound," I replied, feeling myself about to dissolve most shamefully into tears, for my journey was now truly over. "It was a formidable wine."

"Yes. Now where's Anahita? She remembers better than I what exactly we sell to the House of Maniakh. But I'd say they buy only two wines. One's relatively simple, although not entirely ordinary... a very good selection, that, but the other... Few in Samarkand can boast of having tasted it. I have only thirty pitchers left, and the following harvest was not quite the same... Anahita! Where is that wretched girl? Well, and as for your wound – I see that it troubles you, for you're holding your arm somewhat awry – that's easy enough. Best we don't touch it here, but as soon as the heat subsides, you will be with the best physician on this side of the world. It's over the river, not far at all. And now let's get you to a place that's comparatively cool. Down below, that is... Ah, here at last is the child who one day will take up my business, and we shall see if it goes along as famously then. I won't behold any of that, of course, but you may well."

All the while, stepping out on long legs and with constant winces, smiles and an occasional twitch of the head, he was leading me down a flight of stairs, to a half-sunken chamber that was cool indeed, and there he tried to bring some order to the long wooden shelves ranged along the wall, interrupting himself to give a questioning sort of look to the girl who descending to join us. She, though, directed eyes, dark and melancholy as her father's, toward me, but the melancholy in them very quickly gave way to pity. *What must I look like?* I asked myself, and again I wanted to weep. There was a slight spinning and a buzzing in my head, and my skin felt like a stranger's.

But the tears receded, because every instant spent in the cool of this place was happiness to me.

The room had... an odor. It smelled tart, lavish, festal, cozy... but no, there's no describing the aroma of a large, apparently very large, courtyard and home where wine is made. It was a smell to quaff from large goblets. There was naught to compare with it but the damp air, perfumed with switches and herbs, of a steam bath in the instant before the Khatun, true mistress of the Karluks and renowned in Samarkand for spending a week in our underground bath-houses, never once emerging into the light of day, makes her entrance, casting off the last of her garments.

Adijer's half-sunken chamber also contained a singularly low wooden table and alongside it chairs no less low, which gave me to understand I was already in Khorasan, for all that I had yet to cross the river.

"Anahita, this is a guest from the House of Maniakh," he said, with a slight, nervous rub of the hands. "So, then, bring us..." And he whispered into her ear, while she nodded so eagerly that her dark braids bounced. "There now, and while she's bringing it all, let me remind you that we also work with golden grapes here but are famed for the black. Because... How many varieties of the grape are there in these parts?"

I raised a marveling brow. That I did not and could not know.

"Three and a half thousand on the long-suffering land of Iran alone," he continued on the instant. "And what wealth there is also in the lands where Byzas once ruled... And from the vicinity of Jerusalem, the wine of Ashqelon you of course know... But here, to no one's great surprise, we celebrate the Shiraz wine. Yet the variety that grows on my hills stands alone. Nowhere else will you find it. It is our pride. It came here long ago, from afar. There was a war" – Adijer gave a fleeting grimace – "seven hundred years back, I seem to think. And into the lands of the Shahanshah there wandered, who knows why, the army of a man... most likely his name is now remembered only here. They called him Crassus, Marcus Crassus. He was, of course, killed" – and at that my host brushed away something that was of no consequence to him – "for the tale is told that the Shahanshah took great pleasure in the works of Euripides, who is near the same as Aristotle but far easier" – this with a wry smile – "and who wrote these lines:

We have fetched from the mountains
The prey we have fresh killed –
The hunt brought great success.

"And imagine, they carry in the head of that very same Marcus Crassus. That was not here, note you, but in Haran, far to the west."

He broke off then, and passed to and fro between me and the table, which had been cleared of its clutter.

Sighing, I looked at the chaos surrounding us. Everywhere clay jars lay and stood, their size ranging from modest to such as could accommodate not one man but two. And dippers, and rags, large and small, and goblets and cups also littered the room. I very much wanted something to drink.

"And here, in Merv, which was then called Margiana, his warriors settled. There was plentiful land in those days," he went on. "It was an interesting time. They weren't even given into slavery. My ancestors, by the by."

The dark-eyed girl had in the meantime returned twice and left again, gradually covering the table with pitchers, an uncommonly large number of goblets, and also water and fresh-baked bread. The bread for some reason left me unmoved, but the water I began to drink at once, and thirstily.

"You do right. You need to cleanse your mouth in preparation for what is in store," Adijer remarked, in the way of one accustomed to teaching.

Then a tender, virginal hand, so cold it made me flinch, was laid on my forehead, and a worried voice said, "Father, I think the wound is giving him a high fever..."

Adijer hesitated, then heaved an uneasy sigh and said: "A pity, that. Well then, my esteemed guest, you shall not drink much wine at present. Just draw its aroma into your nostrils, test it with your tongue, take a small swallow, and no more. It will even cheer you. And then, as I said, off to the physician... So, Anahita, when next you go outside, tell them to saddle a mule, the one that's mild in temper, and we'll take two fellows more hale than he to serve as our bodyguard. So, then, the warriors of Crassus had brought in their marching packs vine slips from home, from the hills of the empire that men called Roum. Of a variety that is a true treasure. Although it's hard to manage – ah, so hard! – and will have truck with only the meanest, driest soil on a west-facing slope. Sheer torment, it is. But it has made us what we are today. To few it is given to drink such wine when it is young. And here it is, our new vintage."

The first thing to strike my senses was the powerful aroma rising from the first goblet, even from a distance away.

"If you know Damascus cherries..." – I nodded – "not candied, that is, but very fresh, then that's what you're tasting." Adijer's voice was coming to me through a mist, for the fever was hard upon me again. "And the flavor is not for the weak. It binds the tongue, because this is a very thick-skinned variety. Our nights can be cold here, and that's how the grape protects itself. What else do you sense?"

"It glistens like oil. And it is very thick, like syrup," I replied through the mist.

"Yes, yes, well said." The voice was encouraging. "And that is indeed all that may be said about this wine. But look what happens to it if you cellar it for two years in a sealed pitcher, and also if, as was devised by this intolerable chit of a girl" – he inclined his head toward his daughter – "you squeeze the grapes very gently, not really squeezing them even, but letting them crush each other with their own weight."

And there was a tender sweetness now at the back of the tongue, and new aromas too. Especially one that had nothing light about it but, rather, brought to mind a horse's sweaty hide, along with something more.

I heard my own voice. "Do you know what this smells of to me? A woman in the heat, the fire, of passion or the hot skin of an animal. For whatever reason, though, it pleases me."

Adijer nodded, content, while his mildly discomfited daughter retreated to her pitchers.

"Just so," he said. "At first I was afraid that clients would be daunted by that interesting undertone. But that proves to be what draws them. Which goes to show once again that you and I are animals, all the same. But the pitch of it must be tamed, must be combined with the aroma of very ripe fruit, and then it can be laid down for nine, ten, even eleven years. And now a question for you, Maniakh my good sir. You have before you three goblets of wine. Which costs more by the pitcher-full than a young camel? Which is that wine of generals and kings? Which of the three did you, as you tell me, drink some days ago in Samarkand?"

This test could hold no fears for me. The few sips of wine that had returned me to life for a time had been swiftly followed by some morsels of flatbread and a cup or two of water, and now all was quite right again between me and the world.

I leaned over each goblet in turn, inhaling their scent and recalling as I did the one day I had spent this year in the house of my birth. One goblet I promptly set aside, for its wine was like a lovely woman, smelling of night-blooming flowers and sweetness... but it was not at all what I had been drinking when that knife blade hooked into me.

The choice between the two that remained, though, was no simple matter, for each was worthy of a king. But they would be, in a manner of speaking, two very different kings – the one strong, open-handed and kind, although a simple man by nature, while the other... Ah yes, an overripe blackberry supplanting the cherry and last year's foliage merging with the inimitable odor of a heated animal.

But the assistance I needed came at last from the glancing lightness that this third wine laid on the tongue, and also the strange hint of sweetness at the finish. I did more than smile – I laughed.

"You see before you the long-awaited guest from the House of Maniakh," Adijer, who had been watching my face all this time, told his daughter with a sorrowful grimace. "He has passed the test. And now it is my turn, for I too have a test to pass, and you had best not hear our conversation. Go up into the courtyard, girl... And drink more of this wine, you envoy from the House of Maniakh, now the pitcher has been broached. You have earned it. None other in the world could make such a thing – only our land, our labor, and a little good fortune. We shall have more serious converse of wine, you and I, when your wound is healed and the fever falls. The mule is likely ready. And for now all that need be known is..."

And here he shook his head in vexation, clearly not wishing to own to me that my brother's affairs had gone crosswise here. But I knew that well enough without his help.

"Well, as you know, my role in this long tale was very simple. I passed on letters, and sometimes people unknown to me attached themselves to caravans of mine, going either from here or from Samarkand. When all comes to all, I only make wine, and so... And so I simply did not know what to make of it when one day..."

The expression on his face changed then, as he gave an ear to what was happening above.

And I too heard the clatter of many hooves, the clang of metal, the neighing of horses. It was as though the entire courtyard had suddenly filled with armed horsemen.

"What is this, and so soon?" he asked, bewildered now and with another nervous rub of the hands. "I'll go and explain all to them... And in the meantime, you..."

He wrenched my bemused self from my seat and forced me to crawl, feet first, into an enormous, wide-mouthed clay jar that lay on its side.

It had long held no wine, which clung on only by a hint of sourness in the earthy smell within. I scrabbled to find a foothold, while my host had already covered the vessel's mouth with a large, dusty piece of sackcloth, thus depriving me of both light and air.

Long, long moments followed, until, spilling down the stairs into the chill of the empty cellar, came a rabble of soldiers in iron mail or quilted leather, the smell of their bodies for an instant blotting out even the indelible aroma of wine.

They were carrying – not dragging but carrying – Anahita down with them.

Behind them came Adijer himself, and two of his daughter's maidservants, and then others, every one at a loss as to what to do. There was no doubt of what would come next, although I refused to believe to the very last that this was neither jest nor dream.

I was assailed by the sharp, sour smell of a soldier standing full in front of my wine jar, but what happiness that he was standing with his back to me, for had he turned around, he would have seen, a mere three paces away, my eyes behind the burlap. I had pushed the cloth aside to make a spy hole, with no thought somehow that this slight movement might cause the entire thing to slip down from the jar and reveal me to the general view. I was, in truth, not thinking of anything at all, save that this was no longer a pair of murderers. This was something far more fearsome – a throng of armed men, panting heavily and for some reason in very ill humor.

Suddenly the room grew quiet. A thin-legged and very strange little manikin, who, like most of the rest, had his back to me, was speaking in the language of the Arabiya, which I did not understand. The only clear thing was that he was commander of this squad.

"A-a-a-h," one of the women responded, in the feeble voice of one already lost. And Adijer, his face altogether gray, first took a step forward, then stopped short, uttering no sound. The pause was becoming intolerable, when suddenly, closing his eyes, he threw himself on the leader with a shrill cry.

Never shall I forget the moist crunch of a sword piercing a breastbone. I have seen my share of deaths but had never before witnessed a man put to the sword while I watched. Adijer hunched over, as if seeking to rest his cheek on the blade that protruded from his breast, and only when the soldier, his armor ringing, plucked back the sword did he fall.

What followed was an oddly inanimate scene: no one stirred, not least because the soldiers hardly moved unless ordered to.

The short-statured man gave an impatient wave of the hand, and the maidservants began to remove Anahita's short scarf and her jacket, revealing her small, supple breasts. The three turns of fabric that had covered her from the waist slid down, so that she was made to step out of them. And I was startled by the thickness of the black hair on her womanhood, by her short and rather thick legs, now faltering under her as the flesh of her inner thighs trembled fitfully. The maidservants led her to the low table in the center of the room and, whispering, helped her down onto it. And I looked on from the wine jar's mouth, fearing even to breathe. Anahita lifted her head to survey those standing around her then, with the slightest movement of her thighs, tried to rise. In so doing, she spread her knees, and that small movement brought a sudden commotion that grew into a horror surpassing aught my fevered brain could ever have devised.

My eyes averted from the tumult before me, the heart pounding so loudly in my chest I wondered that none other heard it, there I lay, a sorry caitiff afraid even to stir, for the jar rested but unsteadily on its side. I would have accepted an arrow to the head to end the torment but not a sword in the breast, because the feel of that sword was all too clear to me while the body of the great vintner still weltered in his blood by the door to the stairs. No one so much as glanced at him now.

So weak, so sick and broken was I by the end of it all that I almost failed to note when, in answer to a brusque command, the unfamiliar soldiers of an unknown army began preparing to leave the room in file, their amusements done. They were taking nothing with them from the house.

Then their leader turned his profile to me, and I almost cried out.

For before me I saw the face of a demon, with disfigured, nubbled skin, and brows and lashes burned all away.

But with two steps, he disappeared from my sight. And the rest followed him.

The last soldier hung back and took up from the table a pitcher that by some wonder no one had upended, had not even brushed. I recognized that dust-begrimed pitcher as the one containing the precious wine of generals and kings.

He snatched it up to his lips and just as quickly pulled it back with a twisted grimace. And flung it into a far corner.

The wine had not pleased him.

After a time of silence and naught but silence, I began to extricate myself from the jar. The maidservants looked up, their faces haunted by the abomination they had witnessed here. And after but two staggering steps, I pitched forward on my face and remember no more.

I came to myself on a rug in the corner, with a dampened cloth on my forehead. The unhappy Anahita was gone from the cellar.

My head was hot and crowded with sluggish thoughts. The fever was upon me with fresh force, and in my shoulder, a new and different feeling now not only itched and burned but rankled me too. And I knew that if I did not apply without delay to a physician, any physician, any at all...

But now a servant was loading me into the saddle of a mule, after which there was a broad boat that carried both us and the animals over water, in the evening twilight. I watched the enormous towers passing off to the right as we moved toward the southernmost part of the city.

I feared more and more falling from the saddle into the dust. And I also feared that when the physician finally saw my shoulder and felt my pulse, he would say, with supreme indifference: "It is too late. From whence you carted him, there you must cart him back again..."

In sum, there was no place more nightmarish to me than that to which I was being brought.

That I had been delivered to a truly fearsome place I knew to a certainty when I heard a wild, overstrung wail resounding from beneath low-hanging tent eaves across which the orange shadows of lamps swayed. At any other time, I would have turned and bolted without a backward glance. But my head roared and racketed, my lips and eyes were those of a stranger, and something was stirring in the wound on my shoulder blade and gnawing at me from within. And, most importantly, I was afraid to fall. For I knew well enough that were I to sink with a sweet sigh to that hard and lightly fissured ground, I would fall asleep on the instant and maybe never wake again.

Rapidly casting a professional eye over my arm and shoulder, which I now feared to move, a girl with a stern face led me past rows of people lying on the ground, past other girls such as she who were busy with sticky, blood-soaked cloths, and into the largest tent.

There stood the semblance of a high cot, almost the same as the one I had so recently quit, except that on this cot a long, bloody clot of meat lay, convulsing and uttering hideous howls.

A disheveled man with bloodshot eyes pounced on me. "What, another one? Who are you?"

"Maniakh. Nanidat Maniakh," I obediently responded.

And met with the most unexpected of all possible reactions.

"Maniakh? And I am Shapur, votary of Mazda, and Shahanshah, who rules Iran and lands apart, and am descended from a race of gods. You're no Maniakh, you're a whelp! A ragamuffin and a mountebank! Had you truly been of the House of Maniakh, you would not have had the audacity to show yourself in this place! For three weeks I have received not a dirham from that much-respected house, so now come and explain that to those who are brought here, forty and fifty of them each day! There's nothing for them here, neither food nor herbs. So, say there is no darnel to be had, but even poppy juice we cannot buy, and try to bear such pain without it! But why am I talking to you? You're but a lad and naught else. Well, then, hold this down."

And to my utter astonishment I found myself leaning with all my weight against the bloody stump, which was not even groaning now.

The red-eyed man was working his ghastly will on it, slicing pieces from it, dampening some places with cloth after cloth, and unceremoniously stitching it up with what must have been a tailor's needle and thread. And all the while he was muttering to himself.

"Hmm, that's a spear. That's what a spear can do, yes... in and twist, and now I must decide what to do about it. The bone's gone, we can assume. So shall we amputate it all away? Hmmm... And whenever will that stripling quiet down and leave off pummeling people? Best he should kill them all at once... Yes, the great Doctor Bukhtishu himself would faint dead away to see what we do here. Finished. Bandage. And then... he survives, he doesn't survive. Such is the game we play."

Soaked from head to foot in another's blood and furthermore well beslimed, I began to sink down to the slippery floor.

The doctor noticed me again. "And what exactly did you want here, stripling? Where? Ah, the shoulder... Ah, a dagger... How very dainty you are. With wounds such as this people take to their beds for a week and then return to the saddle... Hmm. So, so. You did wrong to neglect this paltry wound... a nick is all it is. But have you ever seen worms crawling out of it, white worms with black heads? No, no, don't you dare do that here. There's filth enough without you to help. A deep breath through the nose... and bear up. Hmmm. If the fever isn't down by the day after tomorrow, you may thank the House of Maniakh that there are no medicines and that you will die of such a trifling thing. Else I would have had you on your feet in a trice. Here all we do is cut it away, clean out the debris, carry it off, and throw it out. And sew it up. Done. Bandage... Now, I'll give you a clean jacket – in the corner, take one – and instead of trousers, wrap yourself in this... You'll be like one of the Arabiya. It's simpler. Girl, off with him to a far corner. He'll sleep now. Tomorrow we'll change the bandage. He's a Maniakh, I'll have you know..."

I staggered away, prodded along by a girl not of few words but of no words at all, and fell onto a vacant cot that smelled of sheep.

My shoulder, arm, and entire flank burned with a fierce fire, but the pain no longer frightened me somehow, for now it was a four-square, merry, warming pain. I wanted to sleep and cared not at all if there were two nameless men on my trail, or even three, or if I had left them all behind. My journey was in any event at an end, and I simply could not take another step.

In a listless, dream-like state, I watched a tall, well-knit fellow settle himself at length, by feel, on an empty cot alongside mine. The poor wretch's face, his eyes included, was almost entirely hidden behind a bandage. He lay down, heaved a deep, deep sigh, and, to all appearances, promptly fell asleep

As did I, so that what followed was only a dream. For two shadows were resting on me – long, so long, extending from the tent's entrance all the way to my cot. I felt no terror, for I knew that all I had to do was sink yet deeper into sleep and dream something other. Maybe even Zargisu's voice, saying to me when next we met: "I know all about you. You have traveled the Great Road eight times already. You are the envy of every trading house. The merchandise you purchase knows no equal. You are celebrated. And I am glad."

Yet the other dream, the very nightmare, would not go away. The two were close now. One stopped a small distance away and even turned his back to watch lest someone should enter the tent. The other stooped slightly over me, and his hand began to slide out from his bosom. And since it was all only a dream, the kind of dream in which you can stir neither hand nor foot, I was not at all surprised to see a wooden handle spreading fan-like and the slightly bowed barb of a slender knife appearing from it.

But when will this dream be over? This is not me and this it is not happening to me, I wanted to shout to the murderer bending in obeisance before me. *My place in this world is either beneath the stars of the Road, amid bare rocks and dry river beds, or among motley torrents of silk set a-flowing by a mildly vexed silk vendor. There he stands, in thick-soled sandals, the folds of his sleeves hanging to the waist, in a brown cap bristling with pins, and his beard so sparse it has but three hairs in it. And the Sogdian, his brow lightly furrowed, examining with many a cavil his bolts of cloth – that is I, as ever was. I cannot be here, in a city of rebels, where people are murdered and women ravished, where I understand nothing and know no one. I cannot be lying asprawl in this place, wounded by who knows whom and for who knows what reason, with a throbbing shoulder, looking up at a dagger poised to fall on me from the tent canopy above.*

And then a shadow, tall and spectral, began to rise. It was the shadow of the wounded man with the bandaged head who had lain on the other side of me. He made what seemed to be one long, unbroken movement, while at the same time tearing away the dressing with his left hand, to reveal a face familiar to me, with a somewhat flattened, sunken nose and a protruding chin. As he reached out his right hand across my body toward the murderer, I saw in it the fleeting glint of a long, very long, and elegantly curved blade. And in that endless movement, his left shoulder seemed to be turning away from me, farther and farther yet, unbalancing him so that he almost fell, while he drew the sword in his right hand toward him, as if hauling on a rope.

And it seemed to me in my dream that the murderer hanging over me with his dagger was vomiting over my chest, for he gave a strange cough and something warm gushed from his mouth.

But the tall swordsman had already stepped over both our bodies and was moving toward the other murderer, who then did something very strange. He did not try to defend himself – it was clear that he had not so much as a fighting chance against the sword and that even to take flight, leaping over those who lay there, would be senseless too – but instead he clumsily stuck himself below a rib with just such another long, slender knife and began to fall. And as he fell, he uttered a word, scarce heard, that ended in a drawn-out "a-a-ah."

I touched with a finger the thick liquid that had soaked the jacket so recently given to me, sighed, and sank into the soundest sleep.

6

PAIRIDAEZA

I seemed to sleep a day away, or perhaps a little less, awoke brimful of happiness, and met the fixed stare of light-gray eyes.

The tall warrior was sitting by me, in no great haste to be anywhere else. Furthermore, he now bore no resemblance to any warrior. What had he done with his long sword? Calmly, closely, I examined his face, with its jutting chin and folds of skin so sharp they could have been traced by an artist's hand.

Not rising, I inclined my head – or, more simply, pressed my chin to my chest – and said, "Thank you."

The warrior nodded.

At last I broke the lingering silence. "The danger is past?"

He compressed his lips and pondered a while, then nodded again. I considered that and asked what I now know to have been the most fitting question at such a pass.

"Why?"

And again I heard the voice I had not heard since the caravan – low, assured and somewhat husky. And I thought that the voices of those born to sing need not always be high and pure. If this man, for one, had suddenly burst into song, many would have come to hear.

"Because those people were very ill-trained. Their attention was diverted, which cost them dear. And further... they usually do all ahead of time. They hire themselves out and work there until they rouse no more suspicion. They prepare. Which means that while you remain here, within these tents, any fresh murderers will need to find themselves a place in the hospital, either as assistants to the physician or as patients. Which is not easy, for the great healer Ashofteh is no man's dupe. And then they will strike unexpectedly and in full sight of all. So we still have a few days."

"*We* have?" I asked after a time.

"I know how you named yourself to the healer," he said reluctantly, and was again silent. Then he added, "My name is Yukuk."

The pauses in our conversation were becoming ever more strained.

"But that isn't even a real name," I replied at last. "It's a byname. It means 'owl.' And it's Turkic and you, esteemed warrior, have the look of a Khorasani."

"That byname sufficed all these years past, when I worked for your trading house," he said with more than a modicum of irony. "But I see it's unknown to you. And that means... that means a great deal."

"People sometimes call me the Hawk, so we both come from birds," I said, for no known reason – although, shameful as it is to confess, seemingly to make an impression on him.

"You must keep to your bed," the warrior by the name of Yukuk said at length. "But meanwhile, you yourself know what to do."

To speak the honest truth, I had not the least idea of that, and the meaning of his words cast no light in my poor head until much later, after several days had passed. Yet it was a simple and obvious thought: I would have to ascertain what manner of man was hiding behind the byname of Yukuk, for all that he had saved my life.

That was what my hoarse-voiced companion had meant me to hear.

The following pause was becoming altogether unpleasant, and I still did not know what to do with those protracted lulls. And so I surrendered to that most simple of ploys and finally broke the silence myself.

"Very well, then. I have a few days. But then I need to discover how... how to find a certain woman. Strange things are told of her. She is said to force herself on warriors on the battlefield, although that to me seems impossible. And then she kills them."

"Oh, that woman," Yukuk said, giving me a look in which there was much to read – surprise there was, and even, I wanted to think, respect.

It was now for me to maintain a dogged silence while he thought on what I'd said.

"It would seem to me that you'd be better served making sense of who wants to murder you and why," he finally added. "But if you're assuming some connection..."

And he fell silent again. But I had been caught by that trick for the last time. I sighed and closed my eyes.

There was the rub. Indeed, I did now know to a certainty that there was a connection. Because I had heard quite well the word that the second murderer – the self-murderer, in truth – had uttered before he died.

It was the word of which my brother had spoken, beginning with something of a "pa," some four syllables between, and a long sound at the end, like an "e-e-eh" or an "a-a-ah."

Pairidaeza.

"GISU, GISU," SAYS MY BROTHER – not yet ten years old and still to run to fat, but already as mean-spirited as can be. "What does it sound like in the language of Iran, that far-famed word that means 'garden,' just an ordinary garden? Paradizo? Paradiz?"

"Pa-i-ri-da-e-za," the little red-haired girl responds, stumbling for the fragment of an instant over the "r" and pronouncing it deep in her throat.

What followed was unpleasant indeed. And, wrinkling up his eyes in delight, my brother was, naturally enough, the one to begin it.

"Gisu," he declared, "it's too lovely a language for you alone to know."

"But it's my language," she retorted after a moment's thought.

"Now it will be mine too."

"And I want to learn to say the 'r' like that as well," I chimed in.

"But you're so lazy you can't even remember simple words in the language of the Han. So says your father, yes, oh yes," Gisu taunted me. "I still have hopes of Aspanak, but you..."

I was well and truly angered now. "Then if exactly a year from now I can speak your language, sing its songs, and write a little, then I... I will be permitted to bite you on the rump."

"Until the blood flows," my ruthless brother added for reasons of his own.

And, after another moment's thought, Zargisu nodded her flaming head. First to Aspanak, then to me.

A year later she was compelled to lie prone on a rug, with a very solemn face, panting slightly as she fumbled with her garments.

"Now you may," she said in a stern voice.

And I, callow idiot that I was and in fearsome embarrassment now, did bite into the lean right buttock that I could scarce see there among the folds of cloth. My teeth were sharp then, I know not why, and almost immediately there was the salty taste of blood. But I even took a terrible pride in my victory. I had earned my prize, since I could converse placidly with Iranian traders in the marketplace, and even my dealings with the language of the Han were going along far more merrily too.

Then my father sent for me.

He was ill at ease, winding around a finger the braid that hung by his ear. Mother was not there. This was to be a conversation between men, and that troubled me.

"As firm as the iron of the Great Steppe, she was. She declared that she had lost a wager," he said in a low voice. "And I cannot punish you because, insofar as I know that girl and her mother yet more so, once they have given their word, there's naught else for it. She would simply have made you perform that foolishness. So then, punish you I cannot. But talk to you, that I can do. Do you know, lad, that some things can never be made right?"

And that brought promptly to mind the many things that had transpired in Samarkand over only the last few months, and I understood at once that, yes, some things can never be made right.

"The marks of your teeth will last her whole life long. You didn't know that... And it can be seen that those are indeed teeth marks. Imagine, now: in six years, or seven, it will be time for her to marry."

I felt myself turning pale but did not know why. *Zargisu? She will marry? Only six years from now?* That was, of course, long enough, more than half my life, but... It was a striking thought.

"This is a special family, but it will be long before you understand that," my father said thoughtfully, running the soft, sharp toe of his boot across floor tiles as green as winter-frosted water. "I've helped her mother all my life. Do you know why? Because she is the only woman whom I may deem beyond reproach. In everything. And the girl is growing up to be the same. Remember, then – after this, you will be responsible for her as long as you live. Now you think you've made an easy escape. But one day you'll understand what it means."

Lying on a stinking litter amid the recuperating and dying inhabitants of the rebellious city of Merv, I thought that not until this day had I truly understood his words.

Pairidaeza. Again I heard the word in my head, spoken not in a girl's voice now but in a woman's. And it sounded not at all as it had on the day we made our shameful, foolish bet, but as I heard it at a later, a far later, time.

After Zargisu, on learning that I was soon to be married, nodded to me with an inscrutable smile and said, "I am glad." And after the battle at the Iron Gates was behind me, and all that followed had befallen me, when there befell... well, everything that did befall. Add to this a few more years, when I had returned from my second journey to the far-famed city of Chang'an, and the talk of all Samarkand was "Look now – the man has, it seems, made something of himself. His misfortunate father would not shame to own him now, and a pity it is that there befell him that of which we know, you and I."

Zargisu met me then at the threshold of her little home. I had been told that she had enlarged the house, a gift to her from our family, with her own funds, which she now had in abundance. Because Zargisu had become a rug maker, employing a good twenty girls to weave those rugs in her courtyard. She had made the first knots as I watched many years before, and by this time the orders for the products of her workshop – rugs of a dark blood-red with white designs, the pride of Iran the beautiful – would keep her women busy for a year and a half ahead.

She led me across the forward courtyard, which was that veritable workshop, and through a file of rooms to a rearward court. And there I stood, dumbstruck.

Before me, between whitewashed walls, there ran into the distance long, perfectly straight walks of cypresses, young, not yet full-grown, and carefully trimmed, that divided the space into even squares. And although I knew that the garden was not all that large, it was so made as to seem endless.

There were, too, walks of white sand. And also channels straight as a lance, along which pure water, cold and sweet even to the eye, ran, with glassy ripples puckering its surface for the briefest of moments.

Each of the squares between their cypress borders was a riot of color. Here were rose bushes, the plum-hued petals sprinkled with still drops of water. Here was a smooth field of flame-bright petunias, and to the right, uniform lines of yellow narcissi.

"Around that corner are jasmine bushes, but they aren't flowering now. Come again in spring," she said with a strange excitement in her voice. "Then there will be white laleh... What would that be in..? Oh yes, tulips, of course. The walls will be wreathed in vines by autumn. And I forgot the little irises, greenish blue, the color of deep water. They will please you. Because wherever you may have been, there must be one place on earth where you can come and rest, knowing that they are glad of you there. No matter what has befallen you, no matter what the course of your life has been. So tell me now, be done with your silence. Is it well with you here? It is well?"

She almost cried the words aloud and stood motionless on the path, inclining slightly toward me and spreading her hands to the side, palms upward.

"May I just sit a while in that arbor?" I asked, to make the strange moment pass.

And then came the scene from my dreams – but no scene it was, just Zargisu taking a few steps down the path, toward an arbor awash in a sea of carnations, and making a turn toward me as the wind whipped her hair, which gleamed with a golden fire.

In the arbor, she, a teacher to the life, raised a long finger that seemed to be freckled too and turned it in my general direction. And together, letter by letter, we said the word "Pa-i-ri-da-e-za," then roared with laughter, not in chorus but as one.

I OPENED MY EYES AND again encountered Yukuk's unmoving gaze.

"I come here constantly," the tall warrior said with a nod, seeing that I no longer slept. "When there is need, I shall be easy to find."

And out of the corner of my eye I saw, in a corner of the tent, why it was that he came here. A little, short-legged girl, the one who had made such a clamor on a previous morning at the sight of two corpses and pools of blood amid the rows of patients, was worming herself under his cape. And then she all but vanished, squeezing herself into the space between Yukuk's arms, at which point the tent flap opened and a second of the hospital aides appeared. Quickly taking the measure of matters, she said "Ha!" then lightly jostled the first aside with her hip – "Shift yourself," she seemed to say – to gain for herself a place under the cape of the tall warrior, who stood as still as any statue. All three laughed quietly, but I only sighed and once more closed my eyes.

It must be said that two corpses and the floor around my cot soaked in blood, to say nothing of the cot itself and the clothing but recently issued to me, had had a stupefying effect on the ministering girls and on Ashofteh, who – head of this institution though he was – had also come running to see. Strange to say, though, no one took me to task over it. Instead, they began to treat me charily, silently handing me another set of garments, which were black this time, the color of the Merv rebellion.

"Our hour has come. When in the village of Safizanj, by Merv, we light a large signal fire on the square, all are to gather, having donned black apparel, and are to raise black banners," the now-invincible Abu Muslim was reputed to have said almost exactly two years earlier. And the people came, from Herat, Nishapur, Balkh, and Merv itself, and in due time the crowd streaming toward that fire became a river, and at its head they drove a donkey with sticks, crying "Awake, Marwan!"

"They have named the Caliph 'al-Hemar,' the donkey, because he tirelessly tramples all roads and tramples them again with his army, beating down first one rebel and then the next," my convalescing neighbors explained to me, in long and listless conversations. "And so he has trampled his last. Now let him do what he can with the hero of Khorasan, whose host at present numbers over a hundred thousand."

A day later, my shoulder was carefully examined by the woman with an impassive face, who did something very painful to it, bound it up again, and waved me away. And I knew then that there was naught more to fear, save a slight stab of hunger. It was late at night, when the healer Ashofteh also slept unfed, because all day long he had been beset by an unending torrent of men with the most ghastly wounds. *But who is warring against whom, if Nasr ibn Sayyar is dead, and the forces of the Caliph himself dare not show their faces here?* I remember wondering.

And I was wanting to drag myself back to my cot and sleep again, sleep... when from close by came the sound that had been ever in my dreams since that terrible day when the wine-master lay dead beside me: the fitful stamping of many hooves in the courtyard.

A man was being carried toward me, held under the arms, while capes fluttered, hiding the lamps' trembling light. His feet trailed along the ground, one arm cradled the other, and, his head thrown back, he was uttering a thin, hoarse wail.

Here, in the principal tent, by the table where the wounded were incessantly cut and sewn up again, I stood alone. And so that heated throng of soldiers was making straight toward me, interrupting each other and waving their arms in my face.

Although barely able to keep my feet, I beckoned to the nearest of Ashofteh's helpmeets, after which it remained only to make a start somehow until the luckless healer would rub his eyes and come.

"Onto the table, face down, and remove the garments from his shoulder and arm," I said with assurance, and they began to lay the shrieking man down. He placed a trembling cheek against the ill-washed board, and I was confronted by one eye, utterly mad and yellow as a wild beast's, in which the flames of the lamps quivered.

"The best healer on this side of the world will soon be here," I said into the ear protruding from the dark curls with their oily glister, "and you must fear no more. What will be, will be. But you shall have to endure, because the pain will for a while be yet more terrible. If you but twitch, the healer's hand will tremble too, and then all will be even worse. But we will hold you."

He, though, only whined quietly, while drops of sweat streamed from his damp face onto the table, mixing there with his tears.

"Marwazi!" a grimy soldier breathed into his face as he clumsily tried to remove the sufferer's quilted leather coat. "Marwazi! Khorasani! Do you wish me to give up all my blood for you?"

And love blazed in his eyes.

So. Who else in these parts would be called so simply "You of Merv" and "You of Khorasan," and be offered all a man's blood, to boot? Interesting guests, these, in our modest home of pain and hope. But who has wounded the Leopard of Merv?

"The blood of one man cannot be given to another," I told the soldier testily, while the thought flickered through my head, *What if it could? And if so, how – poured into the veins from a jug?* "He needs now not blood but herbs to take away the pain. Or poppy. Or even just ice."

But Ashofteh, small, solemn and self-possessed, was already coming toward us, pushing aside the robust, iron-clad soldiers. He leaned over the wounded general, whom I was still holding, ready for the healer's command to bear down on the unfortunate creature with all my weight.

"White wine, double distilled, diluted with water, one part to four," the healer told the women brusquely. "All who need not be here – out, all of you out, for the pain will be such that..."

The soldiers obeyed instantly and took themselves off, shoving each other as they went – and the first among them was he who had just now been offering his blood.

"Light, light. Bring all the lamps here," the healer continued through lips now pale, for he had at last seen exactly who lay on his table. "Ah-hah, here's just a scratch with the tip. Of a sword. This swords can do, yes... But going on, to the elbow... Oy-oy. So hear me now, sovereign lord. Your arm will be whole and will even work. The bones are intact. But here, by the elbow, there's a cavity, with long gray threads passing through it. If they're knocked, the pain will be so hideous that... So you must bear up and not stir. Do you hear me, lad?" He was suddenly addressing me. "And how would it have been had I not kept beneath my cot the last – the very last! – pouch of a certain thick, brownish substance? How would it have been then, eh?"

I bowed my head in shame for the House of Maniakh. But Ashofteh had already sprinkled something from the little bottle that he had brought with him and was issuing more orders. They brought him clean cloths, the wine, needles and thread, knives – the whole ghastly arsenal that I too had so feared when I lay on that table.

"Ah-hah..." the great physician muttered to himself. "Here need just be closed... There. It's already working. The pain has become a small thing. It feared us... What, then, were you without a shield and trying to fend off the blow with your bare arm clad only in leather?"

The man on the table was breathing noisily into my ear. He gave off a suffocating aroma of roses.

His sufferings, though, were all but over.

And very soon, standing on his own feet and trying to shake off the comrades in arms who clung to him, the invincible Abu Muslim was speaking to the healer, his still-damp face smiling now with a childlike sincerity.

"I shall never forget you for this," he said. "And you also." That last was addressed to me.

And Ashofteh and I, both at once, laid hand on heart.

Another day passed, my fever fell, and my shoulder griped me now with a sure, subsiding pain. And then I knew that I wanted not just to drink, since water aplenty was brought to all here, but to eat something. Something other than the strange food that had come to me with baffling interludes between – the pale soup with cubes of a radish-like vegetable or with a sinew or two from some animal, the grayish bread... Although the desire to sleep was still greater.

On what seemed to be the fourth morning, I discovered of a sudden that I felt quite simply well, weak though my legs remained and for all that I was now uncommonly light and empty within.

And uncommonly ill-tempered. I was in great need of something.

I began by inspecting the place I found myself in, for I did not yet care to think of venturing beyond the gates. It was a courtyard, large, sparsely treed, and surrounded on all sides by long galleries that rested on columns of wood and stone. All told, a typical caravanserai, that had at one time apparently sheltered those unable to afford better. But since the city was already hot, most of the patients were placed, as I had been, in tents that ran in rows across the courtyard.

And behind the courtyard were the kitchens and... a large midden, consisting of clay jars and of sacks set one upon another. This entire enterprise rested on broad slabs of yellowish stone.

At the very edge of one slab I discovered a rather imposing pile of apricot stones that had fallen from somewhere. Evidently the cook had tossed dried apricots into a pot, used the flesh for whatever purpose, and thrown the stones out – and rightly so.

They lay a pace or two from the nearest sack, away from all else. And although I was not deluding myself as to the outsides, knowing that some person, or even some animal, could have been sucking on them, the sweet kernels – which I imagined to myself most clearly, those elongated, delicately brown seeds with their wrinkled skin and a pith, slightly bitter, that creaked against the teeth – had never yet been touched by anything in this world. Naught could ever be cleaner.

I looked about me with great care and saw no one.

Then I found close by a stone that would serve, and did not stop until the pile of apricot pits was naught but empty shells marked with dark, moist spots that shriveled rapidly in the sun.

I sat a while deep in thought, then said to myself: *Not only the richest man in Samarkand but any man, whoever he be, could likely fall no lower. It is time to think on what to do next.*

7

THE DAPIRPAT OF MERV

And I went in search of the healer.

Ashofteh was resting on his heels by the wall, his hands limply dangling. It was still morning, but his face looked utterly fatigued.

"So there, then," he greeted me. "And are we leaving already? A need for food already? A stroke of luck, that. Or in a day or two..." And he nodded toward the gates.

I sighed deeply under his telling gaze, which said to me: *Do not fret yourself, I shall take no money. How would you come by any money?*

Lying in my bloodied corner, I had already had occasion to count what jingled at the bottom of my purse. Four dirhams. I could give one to the healer to ease my shame at least a little. At the end of all, one dirham could buy a whole sheep, alive or slaughtered, complete with skin, wool and meat – although what would the healer want with the wool and the skin? – or a huge sack of dates or...

The three dirhams that remained would serve me for food, but I also needed lodgings. And such funds made a mockery of the journey back, had I even had the heart to return to the winery in search of my donkey. And even if the donkey and the house with its magical wine were still of this world.

And therefore I had gained an altogether clear idea as to what I could do with the remains of my money.

I must begin a new undertaking that would, if nothing else, help me regain my strength over the next week or two. And use the time to conceive something more astute, which would, at the very least, entail having someone carry a letter to Samarkand.

And I also knew what that undertaking would be.

What could I do? Well, it was all most simple. Only a few days ago I had been thinking on that very matter. First, I could trade in silk – *Better than any other in Samarkand*, I added in my mind – but that required considerable capital, a reputation, and all else that the House of Maniakh had spent years in winning. Not to mention how that House began its tale, with the first Maniakh, the great Maniakh, the man who had journeyed on a highly delicate mission, first to the Shahanshah of Iran and then to the Emperor in Constantine's city. As a result of which, the world knew one war the more, but while that war raged on, the elaborate guile of Maniakh was stealthily creating the now-celebrated trading route that ran north of the Sea of Gorgan, skirting the lands of the Shahanshah. And so the world was changed – and for the better.

Such work, it was plain to see, would not be mine in the near future. Indeed, I might not even have the good fortune to come upon apricot stones in a midden ever again.

I could have made an excellent caravan-bashi, plying the road from Samarkand to Chang'an and back. So much I had learned. But in my present fix, that would hardly serve either.

So, what else am I? "You're a boy from a good family. And now you're a dapirpat, a scribe."

Excellent. A dapirpat, then. The perfect work for a person scarce recovering from a wound. A quiet, sedentary task. All that remained was to settle with the healer.

"Esteemed Ashofteh," I said to him. "Let us begin from the very beginning. Your hospital is suddenly receiving no money from my trading house. That occurred" – I remembered Adijer, hapless genius of the winery, telling me how long it had been since he had seen anyone from Samarkand – "three or four weeks ago. Yes?"

"Then, good sir, you persist in asserting that your name is Maniakh," the weary healer replied. He was still addressing me in coolly distant terms. "Very well. Two corpses by your cot and no trace of they who settled with them. That is almost proof. Much is being said of your House, know you, and lo and behold... So, let us assume that you are in very truth a Maniakh, some poor kinsman of the great silk merchants. And yes, we have ceased receiving money from your family. Three or four weeks ago it was indeed. Do you wish to commiserate with me? But I shall find money here, yes I shall. It will be given to me. I'll go and ask. If I can tear myself away from that table you know all too well."

And then the infirmary will no longer belong to our family, I told myself.

"The family will send you money," I assured him. "But first I need to be again what I once was. As you've seen for yourself, I have had every manner of... unpleasantness here. So I offer you all that I have, which is myself. In the evenings I can hold your wounded patients by the shoulders or the legs, as I've already done twice before. And, while I think of it, the first man who lay there when I was brought here, did he..?"

"He died, of course," Ashofteh said morosely. "Who could bear such a thing? But what were you saying?"

"I will work for you," I went on. "Half of every day I will attend to those who lie here. I will study."

He understood instantly. "And for that, as befits a pupil, you'll keep your cot and such meager food as we can scrape together for you. And meanwhile, you'll find your kinsmen or friends... Hmmm. You do not fear grime and blood, lad? Because there will be more than enough of that for you here."

"If the healer's path begins in grime and blood," I said, "so be it."

"The healer's path..." he said weightily. "No indeed – the grime and the blood are both the continuation of that path and its end. But the beginning is when you see a sick man and say to him, 'I want you to live.' He could die anyway, note you. But dozens of my patients lie dead who would have lived had someone simply spoken to them of an evening and then told me how their healing progressed. And there's one other thing of importance. To make the blood run aright, there must be a working of their arms, shoulders, legs, and sometimes, carefully, the place where the wounds are drawing together. A pressing on certain points on the body. I have no one to do that. But you could, if you can only learn some simple things."

"How did I come to such horror?" he suddenly asked both me and himself. "You have surely heard of the school of Bukhtishu in Gondishapur? It is not far from here, in Ahvaz... We would spend days on end there disputing what to put in a medicine that would send it faster to the site of the pain. Or, in other cases, to make it go there by degrees and all day long. We contrived various ways to mix medicines with sugar or rose water. All seemingly in the way of Dioscorides of Roum, but a great deal, a very great deal, of our own we added too. But here, what is there of Dioscorides? Here they carry people whose legs or arms, or such as remains of them, must be amputated. What healing can there be, when this is naught but a line of butchers' stalls in the market? Yes, well, I accept your offer, lad, but say no more to me of the House of Maniakh. You may never become a healer, you may never bring money, but your offer is honest if it is naught else."

With a sigh I returned to my cot.

And the next morning, a new life began.

At the very least I needed two small brushes to write the Sogdian script. And a pair of reed kalams to make a good appearance. Ink in a wax-sealed vial. A palette on which to pour a drop of ink and dip the brush. And, oh, if I could only find a stick of dry ink from the Celestial Empire, to dissolve a shaving or two in water on just such a palette, each time making the ink afresh. All of that, though, was to be had somewhere in Merv.

What do they write on here? I wondered next. Paper from the Celestial Empire there surely was, but only as a luxury. Then papyrus it would be, two sheets of every quality. And I also needed to buy a firm board to place on the rug between my knees and lay the papyrus

on. And a satchel to carry it all, so shaped that the ink would not spill...
Money, ah, money...

Oh, great God in heaven, I also needed the rug on which the client
could sit facing me and mistrustfully watch the movement of my brush.

It then came to me that I would have to carry, like a pack-donkey,
all these tools of my trade to wherever my future place of work would
be. And therefore I would need a rug with ties.

And all of this was taking place in the milling crowds of Merv,
which were already making my head spin, because they were crowds
in which the beards and locks of most of the men, peering out from
under a great variety of head coverings, shone – nay, gleamed – in
diverse shades of red, from saffron yellow to dark crimson. Iran had of
late gained the name of Land of Red Men in Sogdia, where that brash
manner of caring for the head's vegetation had yet to be learned.

Then the women, their braids hanging below their caps... But after
what had happened in the home of poor Adijer, I still did not care to
look at them, though I myself knew not why.

And when I at last emerged from the closest market, where I had
bought everything needful for my future employment, and found my
way to my goal, I threw back my head to stand and stare.

Who had built that horror so many centuries ago? All of Sogdia
and, like as not, all of Iran is studded with castles that rise like dark-
stained teeth amid mountains and valleys. There are no such structures
anywhere else in the world. Neither the long, low city walls of the
Celestial Empire nor the camps that the armies of the Emperor of
Byzant pitch in an instant and wheresoever they will are like those
castles in any way.

But the fortress of Merv was quite simply a huge mountain of
ungainly proportions, ascending from within an oasis on the river
bank. Its round, sand-colored towers were crimped into the folds of
the walls and, far above, their uneven black edges alternated with the
unendurable radiance of the sky, which was scored across by kites
whose wings formed tiny crosses. Those great slabs of rock were the
very stuff of fear.

The gates to the fortress, set between two heavy entry towers, were choked with a motley press of people going in and out of an enclosure surrounded by walls that crushed the earth and were notched with steps cut anglewise into the stone, since soldiers must be given a way up.

Here, in the inner enclosure, were houses, large and small, that huddled at the foot of the walls. Some of their denizens had tried, with no marked success, to bore holes into the walls themselves, since, at the end of all, those walls, and the towers too, were but an enormous mass of compressed earth and old rock that held naught within. But, when it came to making holes, the swallows had done a better job of it.

The northern side of the enclosure, flooded as it was by the merciless sun, was almost empty, while on the southern side, in the shade, the people swarmed like bugs at the foot of those monstrous edifices.

And there, in the cool beneath a plane tree, I found what I needed.

Three men sitting in a row. One older and black-bearded, to all seeming one of the Arabiya who had been born here, in Khorasan. And two younger, one with an unreasonably large nose. Also local but saffron-haired, they gave me a glance with a trace of arrogance in it, quickly placed hand on heart, and again leaned over their papyruses.

And there was papyrus aplenty, since all three, every one on his own rug, was busily working his brush or kalam, while clients waited patiently. And, to my joy, there were rather more clients, a whole four more clients, than there were dapirpats.

After a lengthy and courteous conversation with the black-beard – whose mixed blood had given him two names, the Iranian Ajir and Hussein ibn Ibrahim or something very like from among the names of our conquerors – I spread my rug on his left hand, closer to the gates and farther from my two ill-disposed rivals on his right. The row of dapirpats now began with me. I sighed with satisfaction and began to look around me, for there was much to see.

This was the eye of the Mervian rebellion. The portion of the enclosure that from a certain point flowed away like a river into the ravine between enormous towers was half-empty, separated from the other part by soldiers in full armor. Behind them were the roofs of little houses and the awnings of tents set amid gnarled and horrifyingly ancient trees.

There the new ruler was ensconced.

The Leopard of Merv and his closest confederates did not spend their nights here. But, as I very soon learned, from time to time and sometimes every day, one after another or in groups, they passed on excellent mounts between the entrance towers and proceeded into the well-guarded depths of the enclosure. Meanwhile, the crowd that had belike gathered to see only this wailed its rapture and wept, gulping down the orange dust kicked up by the horses' hooves.

And then people brought their petitions to the new overlords.

But those petitions first had to be written.

MY WORK BEGAN ON THE instant, as soon as my rug was spread. I tried not to scrutinize overmuch this man of Merv, with his heavy nose and ironic eyes, while he, in turn, tried not to give me overmuch of his attention. But at last he yielded.

"Newcomer, what languages do you write?"

"I? Pahlavi and Sogdian, esteemed sir," I replied, following that with a modest "I doubt the language of the Celestial Empire would interest you."

The big-nosed man sighed and said something about the need to write the language of the Arabiya.

"Yes, but we are in Iran," I responded yet more modestly. And, having thus won myself a new friend, I added, "It is not a matter of the languages I write but the languages in which this letter will be read."

That all the inhabitants of Merv, regardless of their origins, understood the language of Iran I had already learned from my neighbor Ajir. Also that we were under no compulsion to present our petitions in the language of the conquerors. For, when all was said and done, the Caliph had lost his power over these parts.

There followed a difficult conversation about money, in which, to my disappointment, I learned that a dapirpat's labor was measured not in dirhams but in daniks. My first client expressed himself respectfully dubious as to my abilities and even my hand, which was to me a simply outrageous assertion, and so it continued until I proposed that he pay me after his petition was accepted.

He was thunderstruck.

"And what's to prevent me then from passing you by and departing through the gates?"

"But, esteemed sir, do you not wish your affairs to prosper?" I inquired of him. "And for that will you not need the aid of those powers that know what justice is?"

And I raised a finger aloft.

The order was placed and accepted, and I began to record the lines of the appeal one by one – to Abd al-Rahman, to Sahib al-Dawat, to the illustrious al-Khorasani and al-Marwazi... in short, to Abu Muslim. And then my client pondered, while I gloated on his torments, before suggesting that he tell me in plain words what he needed, and I would compose the letter myself, simply, clearly, and beginning with what mattered most.

What he needed was to be released from the jizyah, the tax on non-believers, on the grounds that not only he himself but his father too revered the true Prophet, peace be upon him, and, that being so, they ought not to pay it. The dishonorable rulers of old had not wished to heed this poor wretch and...

All diligence now, I dipped my brush in the oily black liquid.

In three days, my reputation as a tolerable dapirpat was made, since some were merely drawn by my Sogdian appearance and good manners, others presumed only that I was no worse than the other three, and so forth.

And again and again I wrote those tearful entreaties to the bulwark of justice, to Abd al-Rahman, to Sahib al-Dawat, to al-Khorasani...

The rebellion had been much like a show put on in the Western Market of Chang'an. Though it arouses strong feelings galore, in good time it must, like any show, end. And its standard-bearer must then occupy himself with the very matters that had first brought the people thronging to him garbed in black

And those matters, I came to know soon enough, were exactly such as were then transpiring in my home, in Samarkand. The words "jizyah" and "kharaj" I could now write before they were spoken and with my eyes closed. The crowds were demanding of Abu Muslim fair taxation and the return of lands that had earlier been appropriated to members of the dusky Arabiya. And – the most raveled of all – the endless succession of caliphs in Damascus had utterly confounded the question of the link between reverence and revenue. Those who visited the empty temples and venerated the Prophet Muhammad should have had far less to pay. But no one in the Caliphate had expected the vanquished peoples of Khorasan and Sogdia to begin bowing before the new Prophet too, and in ever increasing numbers. And, which was no great wonder, to then demand relief from the tax. The caliphs had never quite decided what to do in cases such as this. And, worse, every one had had a different answer. So the newly converted were taxed here but not there, now but not then.

Such was the state of affairs that had fed all the glorious, terrible and hopeless wars waged in my Sogdia. To watch it happen again on enemy territory – or former enemy territory, was it? – afforded me no little pleasure.

Can a young and, as I have heard, unlettered man who has triumphed in every battle puzzle his way through all this chaos? I wondered as I carried to my home, which was the hospital, my thin rug, the satchel that held my dapirpat's instruments, and a handful of dried black grapes, another handful of ruddy dried apricot halves, a bunch of fresh herbs, and a flatbread, still hot, its dough flavored with onion fried in sheep's fat.

None of that was for me. I had already consumed on my own account a whole flatbread and a sizable serving of meat soup. All the rest would be a gift to two of my charges.

Because I had by then made the rounds of many cots and come upon no small number who hovered, as it were, between sickness and healing.

I had looked into their faces, had applied myself, under Ashofteh's impatient gaze, in pressing my fingers into certain points on their unwashed, evil-smelling bodies, had even begun at last to understand how much might be done with the bare hands. And while I was about it, I took their pulses, finding them either steady or otherwise.

Then too, I was seeking men from Sogdia and found them – first one, then another, then a third. All of them men who were struggling to recover from ghastly wounds received in who knows what battles and skirmishes. The first was very quickly discovered.

"What is your name, brother?" I said one day in my native Sogdian tongue to a youth whose face had taken on, probably forever now, the color of green Jerusalem olives.

"Nanivandak," he said, with no particular difficulty but also reluctantly. He would not look at me.

And I shuddered. We were near namesakes, our names both dedicating us to the same Nani, ancient goddess of our land.

My fingers began their journey along his leg, torn apart by the spear that two months back had pinned him to his saddle. I remembered Ashofteh's grieved whisper: "The leg is almost whole. He need not even be lame. But still he keeps to his bed. He ails constantly, first one way, then another. I fear he too will die, because the left side of his heart is no longer producing the breath of life."

"I am making the blood run faster through your leg," I told the boy. "Tomorrow I will come again and send it running more merrily through the neck, up and down."

Now the boy turned his head and looked into my face.

"I am called the Hawk," I said to him. "Have you heard of such a one?"

He looked at me in silence, and there was a slow change in his eyes. He did not believe me but he very much wanted to. And, wonder of wonders, he had indeed heard of the Hawk.

"And furthermore, it was my lips that said it, and I well remember it was they who spoke so – not I, but some other on my behalf. And further to that... I want you to live."

ON THE TENTH MORNING, I dove, as was my wont, into the plane tree's salutary shade, to discover there both my friend Ajir diligently plying his kalam and the two on his right also working untiringly with their own papyruses, and to learn that for me – for me and none other – two residents of the glorious and rebellious city of Merv were waiting. And that to the two dirhams that I, my daily expenditures notwithstanding, earned by my labor, a third would soon be added.

I rolled out my rug and reached into my satchel for ink.

Then there occurred an event – or, rather, a whole chain of events – with which, yet again, a whole new life began for me.

Here yet another string of camels, all gray clumps of dusty hair, was floating into the inner court of the Merv fortress, their soft hooves almost stepping on our rugs. And even before the first camel halted, a nimble, dark-skinned lad with eyes full of curiosity came sliding down its tousled flank. He had already run around the creature twice before an ungainly, gangling, swarthy-faced young man with thin, unkempt hair of a strange, pale-orange hue slid down its other side.

"Abu Jafar, treasurer of the House of Abbas or some such," Ajir, to the right of me, said disapprovingly. "Gracing us with his presence again. His byname is Abu-d-danik, the Pinchpenny."

The House of Abbas "or some such"? So here there had fallen full on my head one of the two people who... And then I began to remember something of what my brother had told me. This would be the very time to go to those people and say...what? "Peace be upon you, I am the richest of Samarkand's merchants and my grandfather gave your forebears, descendants of Abbas, the first good money they ever earned, for setting a revolt in train. And now it chances that poverty has driven me to work as a dapirpat here, in Merv, so what say you to giving me a little money, inasmuch as I greatly wish to eat savory food, sleep in a presentable place and, at last, set out on my journey home." Dubious, all of it, and not the most fortunate idea that ever was. Yet...

But at that instant, I had eyes only for another traveler with that caravan, this one dressed in uncommonly clean and respectable attire when compared with the Pinchpenny. He cautiously descended his camel's flank, to stand square opposite me and my writing set, essentially by my very feet. A young slave with a face pitted by the pox was assisting him.

This owner of light-blue eyes that radiated kindness and were wreathed in plentiful wrinkles and also of a soft, hoary beard was more than known to me. He was even very well known to me.

When he had come to Samarkand in times past at the head of a cavalcade, to visit our house among all else, many had come running to look at him.

Because he hailed from a great city at a crossing over the River Oxus, a city amid plains that ended in the inconceivably high wall formed by the steep, bare peaks of the Hindu Kush. And beyond that city was Bamyan, with its two enormous stone statues of Teacher Fo, as he was called in my beloved Empire. And beyond that, the enchanted realm of Gandhara, where the statues of that same prophet were smaller but executed with a magical beauty. Their faces seemed alive and they beamed with warm yet aloof smiles.

The heart of that entire region was the city of Balkh. And in the center of Balkh there soared aloft, like a mountain peak, a sharp-tipped stupa constructed over precious relics – two charred bones from the funeral pyre of Teacher Fo, who had once been Prince Gautama.

Around that stupa stood a spacious monastery, a city within a city, and the abbots of that place also ruled the land. They were called Paramukha, but, that title having long been handed down by inheritance in the same family, it became at last Barmak, which would henceforth be that family's name

This last of the Barmaks – he whose traveling cloak the pock-marked slave was now shaking out – was the one who forty-five years before had met with peaceful overtures the armies of Qutayba ibn Muslim, which then were but dreaming of the rout of Samarkand. And, obedient to its abbot's word, the monastery of Teacher Fo became, without the slightest torment and almost in the course of a day, a temple of the new Prophet. And Balkh became part of the Caliph's empire, also with no needless sacrifices.

That tale the men of Samarkand remember to this day, some with condemnation and others with envy, as they mourn their own temples, put to the torch by the beast Qutayba.

In sum, it was in no small wonderment that I sat with brush in hand below the wall, well aware that before me stood the erstwhile – or maybe not the erstwhile but the now and present? – King of Balkh, which was Bactria in the language of Roum, and overlord of the land whence come the world's best camels and excellent iron to take into battle.

It burst from me unbidden. "Barmak of the House of Barmak," I asked, "what do you here?"

When I said it, the winsome old man was resting his hands on his knees, in a pose bereft of all majesty, and trying to work the knots from his legs. He stood two paces from me.

Hearing himself thus addressed, he straightened, turned, looked at me for several moments through narrowed eyes, and said "Ha!" With a smile, he uttered the first letters of my name – "Mani..." – then stopped, chewed his lips and pondered a while if he should, at this time and in this place, speak a name such as mine aloud. And, finally, he decided on an evasive answer.

"Dear young friend of mine," he said, "how interesting and how rightful it is that you are here, for I had heard that you were quite elsewhere. Yet this is how matters come about. I am so glad."

And the overlord of the land of camels gave another radiant smile.

"As to your question," he continued after a brief pause, "I can indeed answer it and that right simply. I am tutor to that boy. A fine occupation, it is, no worse than... hmm... serving as a dapirpat in the fortress of Merv. And, between ourselves, it pleases me well. But there is much I wish to tell you, so... so let us meet again tomorrow, outside those gates, before set of sun, and I shall show you an astonishing eating house no more than three hundred paces from here. This is your first visit to Merv? Then, you see, my idea is most apposite..."

And, throwing his arm around the shoulders of the dark-skinned, nimble lad, the sovereign of Balkh set smoothly off, following behind the Pinchpenny, who was already striding, his arms awkwardly swinging, into the depths of the enclosure, toward the roofs that sheltered the ruler of Khorasan.

Yet who was that boy whose tutor was a king descended from an ancient and immeasurably esteemed clan? And why did that king stand at the side of a mere treasurer from the rebellious House of Abbas?

But another caravan was already entering the courtyard. Abu Muslim was evidently hosting guests to be reckoned with this day. Now there were coal-black Iranian warhorses, snorting as they bent their proud necks toward the dusty earth. The riders, and there were but three, wore jingling chain mail, and he who rode ahead was nothing short of magnificent. If the man who bore the byname Yukuk was comely to behold but could never be called beautiful, this one was beyond a shadow of a doubt beautiful and, unlike Yukuk, young besides – twenty five or even thirty, but no more. He had a strange nose that came out at a sharp angle then descended on the vertical like the blade of a battle axe. And the proud set of his head, his hair in its elegant waves, and his bold eyes made of him a singular and spectacular sight.

Yet all too comely to behold, I thought from my shadowy refuge as I coldly watched the fine fellow, all smiles, proceeding slowly amid the enraptured crowd. *Comeliness in such a degree works woe, for he will likely be either a blood-soaked murderer or as stupid as a ram – although, it may be presumed, in all but warfare.*

Meanwhile, the fine fellow had passed on, into the depths of the courtyard, where there was no crowd but only Abu Muslim's soldiers, leaning on their spears. After that, I was hard put to make anything out there. But the gates now admitted yet another warrior flanked by a chakir, a hireling soldier, on either side – no fine fellow, he, and older than the one who had gone before. Not Iranian but manifestly of the Arabiya, with a grizzled black beard. And as he went, he bowed, with hand on heart, to the crowd – right, left, and back again.

I watched the spectacle with abstracted gaze, thinking all the while of Barmak, of money and of the way home. And in the meantime, the men of Merv, enamored as they were of their warriors, the warriors of the invincible Abu Muslim, were bringing to them the wares they traded here – their berries, their scarves, everything but their rugs. There was no talk of money, of course. Rather, the traders were imploring these darlings of the people to take whatever they would and pay naught or only to touch a piece of merchandise, for good luck. Even the two dapirpats who had to this day sat impassively to the right of Ajir and me, thus closing our line, had succumbed to the general ecstasy and moved toward the warrior with the graying beard. One had contrived to lay his left hand on the belt of this hero of the common folk and the other, he of the big nose, had even taken his Iranian courser by the bridle.

A trifle only remained, which was to tug on the warrior's belt or perchance on the folds of clothing at his breast, so that he would be taken by surprise and would fall by his own weight onto the blade held upright in the hands of my former neighbor.

I had, to my own great surprise, already sprung up and taken a few paces forward with my hand held out before me in warning, but I proved tardy.

Although the thoughts that caused my tardiness were entirely fitting to the situation.

I was dressed much like the two murderers and had spent several days seated alongside them. I would have done well in explaining that I had naught to do with what had transpired here, but only until they asked me my name. And where I lived, why there and nowhere else, and what I was doing with a wound on my shoulder... None of which could be associated at all with the crime, but as topics of conversation there were surely better.

Which signified that my career as dapirpat was ended, that I had best not even gather up my brushes, kalams and papyrus, but instead continue in the way that I had, in fact, already begun, which meant not to stand, mouth agape, and watch the chakirs cut down the murderers, who would whisper their "pairidaeza" as they died, but to hide myself as swiftly as I may in the very heart of the crowd, which was now all abuzz with excitement, and make toward the gates. And so away.

Barmak of the House of Barmak has made a most timely appearance in Merv, I thought. *Because in this place none but he can help me decide if I should pursue my search for Zargisu or mount a horse, a camel, a donkey or aught else that moves and make swiftly for Samarkand, leaving all this burdensome perplexity behind me.*

All that remained was to meet with Barmak on the morrow, but in such a guise as would render me unrecognizable as the dapirpat who had fled the scene of the crime the day before.

But a dapirpat, I thought, remembering the two murderers, *is a man without a face. Ink bottle, brushes and kalam serve as his face, so that with no such paraphernalia about me, my chances are more than fair.*

For all that, though, I also thought, *I seem not to want to take myself off whithersoever. I want to stay here. Here I have business in hand.*

Because, having been forced once again to flee away, I was now becoming irate in good earnest.

8

THE ROSE OF IRAN

"You cannot even imagine, my dear Maniakh, the marvelous place I am taking you to," he who had once reigned in Balkh said, coming toward me with a beaming smile. Only kings can radiate benevolence so lavishly in their every movement, in every crease of forehead or cheek, while at the same time reckoning to a nicety how many steps they will deign to make toward you, be it two or the high honor of three.

Barmak of the House of Barmak was garbed in light-colored Iranian trousers of the broadest cut that were enveloped in the folds of a cream-colored muslin cape. His silken white beard was carefully combed, and although he manifestly did not share the Arabiya's predisposition for heavy perfumes, he did give off a spell-binding fragrance that may well have been mint and verbena.

"The cook still lives – I made it my business to inquire – and he is a remarkable man," he continued, taking me by the arm. "It's a great art. First you slice the orange zest finely and boil it in milk. Then you soak saffron in the same liquid. And then... Well, I don't know what you do after that. But into that liquid, in due time, you pour rice, and that is how they cook pilaf to such perfection in these parts. And what fruit they serve! How well chosen! But I think you'll need something more substantial. Sheep's liver cooked over hot coals? Yes? Maybe only a taste? They serve it with red Mervian wine, and I'm sure you know how delightful that is."

I shuddered a little at that, but Barmak was already leading me down a path through a garden marked off into squares by well-trimmed rose and gardenia bushes. The couches for the guests were arranged singly, each in a place of its own between those waist-high green walls, so that all one need do was recline into the pillows to be secluded with one's companion amid sweet-smelling greenery and flowers. There was a thrumming of instrument strings, a singer's mournful voice that gave a gentle caress to the soul, and boys running to and fro with bowls and large platters. I sighed.

"Permit me to regale you as you have regaled me in your home often enough," the teacher prattled on, unruffled yet slightly winded from the walk. "I haven't unloosed my own purse in so long... Now what is the name of that Mervian wine whose price by the pitcher would buy an entire camel with money to spare?.."

He marked something in my face then from the corner of his eye but made a show of disinterest.

"Then tell me what befell you, Barmak," I said, having at last found space to put in a word. "Are you truly happy to be teaching some dark-skinned urchin? You are Lord of Balkh, Barmak. A king. A maliq. An ikhshid. Had you grown weary of wielding power, you could instead have done nothing at all..."

"But life's happiness does not lie in doing nothing," he replied, with the broad, sly smile of a camel's calf. "You are young, very young, Maniakh, but a time will come in your life when you ask yourself what you have truly wished to do, all your life long. Very well, two summer soups and that slightly sweet bread made of layered dough, if you remember still how to bake it here, with such a crust... And that sheep's liver..." He had paused to bestow a cheering smile on the youth fawning before us. "And what to bring me, I need not tell you. So then, Maniakh, power, as you surely know, is no joy. There are, in addition to power, so many other interesting things. Not least your great forebear and his remarkable story. Don't frown, now. I know you cannot abide hearing his name. And you do not wish to acknowledge yourself his direct descendant. But you must agree that a thousand years gone by is time enough to look on the destruction and death he wrought with equanimity. And in another thousand years, he will be a hero, no less, both to the men of Roum, who call him... What do they call him?.. ehh, Alexander, and to us, who call him Iskandar the Two-Horned Lord."

"But in the meantime you, I hear tell, have deciphered the real name of a woman whom I would be pleased to recognize as my ancestor," I said with a sigh.

"And how interesting that is!" Barmak exclaimed. "The woman who halted the bloody hand of he who visited ruin on Sogdia. She is not simply a name in an old scroll. She truly is numbered among my ancestors – and yours too, Maniakh. Have you ever thought that you also have a claim, albeit not a primary claim, to the throne of Balkh? True it is that many stand ahead of you in that line, but even so... I and your esteemed grandfather spoke of it often enough. And chuckled as we did, of course."

"So tell me now something other," I said to turn the conversation, as I sank my teeth into the best food I had tasted in the past month of my life. "The Kingdom of Balkh is no more? But who caused its demise, the Caliph or Abu Muslim?"

"Nay, nay, why so?" He waved a dismissive hand. "I have, after all, a son and have passed the power to him. Not that I would have him overly absorbed by it. Today, as you surely know, there are places of greater import than Balkh. And as for me... Such a pleasure it is to travel, to speak with the owners of old books and other documents... But you didn't let me finish," he said in a suddenly reproving tone. "I learned all I could about the woman we know as Rokshana. And, you're right, I learned that she was really called Roushanak. Or, in the ancient tongue of my land, Vakhsh-ona. And in my tussle with her, I came up against a curious episode in the life of our hero. One that you, of course, have heard – that Iskandar the Two-Horned Lord is said to have ridden across the sky on an enormous bird called a griffin. And that a share of his victories was won for that very reason. At which point, I began burrowing into the old books in good earnest."

"But Barmak, what do they not say about Iskandar?" I protested. "People don't ride birds. There are no such birds."

"Ehh, how hasty you are, Maniakh my friend," he said with a sunny smile. "There are no such birds *now*. But this was over a thousand years ago. What do we know of those ancient beasts and birds? I began to dig not in chronicles but in legends, interested to learn if such a bird was mentioned other than in connection with Iskandar. And yes, there is something. Indeed there is something. In fine, then, that bird would explain a great deal – all those victories of his, one following another. Imagine a general able to rise to the height of a bird on the wing above the battlefield. Seeing armored cavalry flanking him from the rear under cover of a hill or copse. Waving his hand from on high. Sending a detachment of war elephants against the foe."

"Then why not mount archers on a dozen such birds and let them shoot the enemy as he approached?"

"Maniakh, you're letting your fancy get the better of you," he said, reproachful now. "Had that been so, the chronicles would have contained a word, if not more, about such archers. But they contain nothing of the sort. They're very clear: one huge bird, for the general alone. And that being so..."

His eyes, raised to the sunset sky, grew warm and thoughtful.

"Are you teaching all this to the boy?" I inquired, as I finished my soup.

"That and the wisdom of Aristotle, king of all philosophers, and the Indian science of numbers that so interests his father" – who was, I recalled, treasurer of the House of Abbas – "and the language of Iran... But I am not, of course, trusted so far as to read the holy books to him..."

At that point, having already devoured a sizable amount of the sheep's liver, worrying my way through it like a wild wolf of the steppes, I turned my gaze to the bowl of food in his hands.

It held rice with a vegetable sauce poured over. And from time to time he neatly directed a slice of fruit into his mouth.

"Barmak," I said. "You eat no meat. They have good reason not to trust you to speak to the boy about the holy books. You still revere him to whom we... my God in heaven, 'we'! . . to whom in the Celestial Empire they give the name Teacher Fo. And in Ind, Prince Gautama. Tell me, then, why did you hand your monastery over to new gods? Did the conquerors threaten you with death?"

He smiled a long, dream-filled smile.

"Teacher Fo cares not what words are addressed to him by the manikins below," he said slowly. "What language it is he cares not. He understands them all. The manikins create their own karma. They are beyond help. But you and I, Maniakh, we are people to whom karma, in this incarnation, has brought singular gifts... Wealth, knowledge, intellect... You must know that in any age, in any people, scarcely one in a thousand thousand can boast such knowledge, such abilities as we possess, you and I. The rest" – he leaned confidingly toward me – "do not know and do not want to know aught but their little town, their groves of fruit trees, the road that passes on, beyond the horizon. And what lies on the far reaches of that road is naught to them... So tell me, how are you, the richest man in Samarkand, disposed toward such people?"

Irritated, I swallowed another mouthful of meat.

"What do you mean, 'how'? They're my fellow-countrymen. And... when they feel pain, I pity them, whoever they be. How else can one be disposed to them?"

I saw then a sincere warmth in Barmak's eyes.

"Quite so, my dear man. And, furthermore, we are held to account for them. And that is why I gave over my monastery peacefully. Because we – you and I – have not received our wealth without cost, Maniakh. There is a price to pay, and sometimes one pays dearly. Sometimes it falls to us to change this world of abundant suffering. There's none but we can do it. And that's no merry pastime."

Casting a glance at my more than humble attire, I had to agree: *Yes, such can be the way with us. We pay. And sometimes most unexpectedly.*

"Our monastery was needed because it brought healing or comfort to the sick, the suffering, the fearful. And what difference does it make which of God's names we, the keepers of the monastery, utter as we dispense those things? Balkh exists to this day. It has not been ravaged as has my much-beloved Samarkand. And besides, there were no prospects for resistance, as you may know, with land that lies flat and naked all around and a mere fifteen thousand warriors. Merv was already conquered... But we survived. And there's naught more important. So now the time has come to change our whole world once more."

Again the singer's low, serene voice came floating through the bushes.

"At this time, though, the world is changing us, Barmak... But, my God in heaven, who's that singing?"

"I was wondering when you would notice. I've known a few who have sat as you've been sitting all evening long and have even left without sensing that something unusual had transpired. And then – the following day, the week after – they come running to me in great distress. 'What could it be, sire? I cannot forget that voice,' they say..."

I could not see the singer through the dense array of bushes. And I did not want to crane my neck and seek her with my eyes. I wanted only to listen and smile.

She was not trying, like other Iranian women, to display her art for all to hear, with astonishing trills and warbles. Quite the reverse, in fact – she did not even sing sometimes but almost spoke, in tones hushed and serene. But her voice – low, pure, sure, and powerful – made every word she uttered improbably meaningful. A rapturous chill ran in a wave along my back.

It was, of course, simply music for an eating house, now mirthful, now mournful. But her mirthful songs brought a prickle of tears to the throat and her mournful songs made the soul smile with newfound wisdom.

"Divine her looks, Maniakh," Barmak said, watching with sparkling eyes my vain efforts to crane my neck and swivel my head, little as I had wanted to.

"She's no chit of a thing," I responded on the instant. "Possibly even thirty years of age. Very tall, a figure long and ill-balanced. Proud, self-assured. Her face... Hair light and softly waved. Maybe that... you know, that large Iranian nose, like the beak on a bird of prey, but breath-takingly so. A mouth too wide. A proud face with much meaning in it, which holds the onlooker rapt."

The voice fell silent, while Barmak gave a thin-lipped smile.

"Yes, my young friend, that is not at all a bad description. Proud, self-assured? That woman, you know, spent her evenings year after year singing in an eating house, this and others. For food and for whatever the patrons would give her. There was naught especially proud about her then. But later, she began to collect from old women the songs of bygone years. The music played at the courts of Sassanid sovereigns. Songs of battles lost a century ago and of sweethearts long dead. And suddenly, Maniakh, suddenly and not very long ago, something happened. A golden rain began to fall on her. People now come from other cities to hear her. Those old songs have proven to be exactly what they need. What people these Iranians are! Over ten decades have passed since their last sovereign was killed just there, on the banks of that river, and they cannot forget that time. They still weep over it. And they will never forget."

He turned to a small, stout old woman seemingly molded at haphazard from clods of clay who had appeared at his side, then reached under folds of cream-colored muslin for his purse, and drew from it not a silver dirham but a small Umayyad dinar with a golden glitter. The old woman, though, only glared at the coin.

"Yes, Maniakh," he went on, eyeing the dinar and placing it, at last, in that plump, outstretched hand, "you have been fortunate. You have heard a great woman here. Do not try to remember her name. We call her the Rose of Iran. She warms our souls. But in matters of money, she's a niggardly sort."

He took out another dinar and, with a sigh and a disapproving upward glance, placed it in the hand of the old lady who stood motionless by his side.

The Rose of Iran gave a broad, happy smile, vouchsafing a portion of it to me, and tripped away down the walk.

Barmak was ready with his summation. "Sometimes God places a soul in the wrong body," he said.

A SWEET SORROW ELICITED BY music and well-filled bellies hung over the courtyard. The yoked black crescents of swallows flitted between the cypresses, across a turquoise sky that was darkening into sunset. "Chree, chree," they told us from on high.

"Oh, how good it is," a satisfied Barmak said, drawing his snowy beard through his fist. "That orange zest with saffron in milk has no equal the world over. But know this." Here he lightly slapped a palm against his knee. "A worthy evening must be worthily ended. Boys, as I recall, hold no interest for you. So a pair of girls, sixteen or seventeen years of age, will be just the thing. A stroke of the hand across an ample rump, and who can say but what something good may come of it? Don't refuse me, Maniakh."

He was about to assure me that he, of course, would bear the cost, but instead he saw something in my eyes, and his face became instantly immobile.

"No, but this is quite interesting," he said, in a changed voice. "What do I see? The master of Sogdia's grandest trading house sitting beneath the wall of the fortress of Merv in the guise of dapirpat. Naught unnatural in that, since the man's name is, for all that, Maniakh. Who came for that very purpose, yea even from the Celestial Empire. I, you know, was not even greatly surprised because the time bids fair for such... And therefore the highly modest black attire that you never put off must come as no surprise either. It is most apt for what you are doing. But this, now, is interesting indeed. I need only utter the word 'money,' and the master of that trading house comes all unstrung. Is the miser's sickness upon you, Maniakh? That can happen with the very rich. But I now deal every day with one so afflicted" – he chuckled into his beard, while I tried to imagine whom he was speaking of – "and his conduct is not quite the same. On hearing the word 'money,' that man becomes a touch... ehh... gloomy, and then he inquires long and carefully into the amount of money in question and what it is to be spent on. So. Maybe your family has somehow stripped you of the wealth that is lawfully yours? But what, then, of your fame as the commercial genius of the Celestial Empire? And why, even if, as we assume, you are now bereft of all connection with your renowned trading house, would you have come to the most unquiet place in the world – to Merv, and to this fortress into the bargain? This won't do. No Maniakh, you simply must satisfy an old man's curiosity. Something of exceeding interest is transpiring in your life, and I know naught of it. How can that be?"

It would probably have been more prudent to maintain a mysterious silence and then to make some joke about those plump girls. But at that time I was, to say the least of it, inexperienced. And when all was said and done, I hungered no less for conversation with one of my own kind than for wholesome food. The wine and the music had been so wonderful. And the bright eyes of the overlord of Balkh were radiant with such merry fellow-feeling.

"Barmak," I said with a sigh. "While you were busying yourself with teaching, and uncovering along the way some interesting facts about great war-birds, strange things were indeed occurring in my life. First, there was a rather unpleasant journey, especially on the stretch between Bukhara and Merv. I had to travel in haste and, in passing, I found myself without money. Second, as a result of that, I now earn my bread with a kalam. A dirham a day, if all goes very well. Or nothing. Third, it's good that I hold the brush in my right hand because I have difficulties with the left after being unfortunately – unfortunately for me – stabbed with a knife. So at present I spend my nights in a hospital, for which I am very grateful to the good healer. He could have driven me away, since I can pay him naught save with my services."

My genial host's eyes were round with sympathy. "So, so, so. And precisely what knife was that?"

"A thin knife with a wooden handle that transforms into a case," I responded promptly, and only when it was said did I wonder if I should have told him that.

"Oh my," Barmak said. "My, oh my. And then, oh dear. So now we draw our conclusions, Maniakh. You quit Samarkand for Merv in a great hurry – although your return from the Empire is of interest in itself. And you were pursued on the road or were waylaid, due to which your money was lost. But all that is easy to understand. What is not to be understood is that you were unable to find money on your arrival in Merv. That is, there was no one to whom you could apply here. Furthermore, your family could simply have sent you money, but that also has yet to come about, although the journey to Samarkand is not a long one. Aha, but if unpleasantness befell you on the road, then such unpleasantness could also befall some other sent from your House... Maniakh, do you know what you have just told me? That the ties between your right worthy House and the people it once had in Merv have been broken. So you are seeking to reestablish those ties. This much is obvious. But your enemy, accordingly, is trying to prevent it... Finally, that dagger. It means that the people who have sequestered you here are none other than... And, in essence, to put the affairs of your House in order, you will have to take them to task – the very people whose daggers... Well, say only that their daggers lie hidden in a wooden case. How interesting! How very interesting! This is, do you know, the best news I've heard these several weeks. Because so much is easier to understand now."

Shaking his head, he again thrust a hand into the folds of his impeccably clean garments, drew out a long, thick leather purse, and handed it, unopened, to me.

"The girls can wait until another day," the tutor to a rising generation said ruefully. "This will serve you for the time being. You understand that neither is the sum so great nor is the occasion such as to warrant any talk of repayment. Besides, you will shortly receive more, a great deal more. And that will not be my money, no indeed. There will be as much as you will need to... In short, deal with that riff-raff, Maniakh, for it seems there is none but you can do it."

The former ruler of Balkh had said all he wanted to.

And, as occasions went, this was certainly no occasion for me to argue or protest.

Book II

The Book of the Poets

I swear by sparks arising from a heart set all ablaze,
By these deep sighs of mine whose smoke rests softly on your hair,
And by the thirsting soul that pines in yearnful search of you,
And by the flesh undone in this inferno of despair.

9

TELL ME TRUE!

I was resting, resting with great gusto and in great earnest, and gazing thoughtfully over a plane tree's broad crown at an evening sky that gleamed like burnished copper and teemed with the coal-black crosses that were kites on the wing.

Two weeks had passed since my unforgettable supper with Barmak. I was sitting on a rug spread over the firm wooden floor of the veranda in my new home. In truth, I was not even sitting, but reclining, rather, propped on a careless elbow in a heap of well-stuffed cushions whose one side was rough to the touch while the other offered the caress of satin. And from time to time, I idly surveyed the oval enclosure within the fortress of Merv, stretched out now beneath my feet, where I had but recently earned my livelihood with a kalam.

Separated from my residence by a respectful distance, the crowd below buzzed – the women with braids wound in ribbons and glinting with silver ornaments and the men whose red beards and locks rose above a sea of motley garments. Between myself and all that magnificence were the heads and shoulders, clad in chain mail as if swathed in gray shawls, of Abu Muslim's warriors. For I was now settled in that part of the square where the ruler of Khorasan held sway.

It was tranquil here, and it was good.

My head was adorned with a tall – a forearm's length in height – yet weightless kalansuwa wrapped in fine, delicate silk with a scarce visible pattern woven into it. This was no Sogdian cap, soft and most often made of felt, but its Iranian kinsman, nonsensically, haughtily tall and ending not in a cone but in the semblance of a small flat table that would likely hold a whole peach, if not two. The whole edifice was secured to the head with a broad, twisted strap, much like an ordinary headband, that kept my fine piece of headgear from soaring heavenward.

I was also wearing a short, narrow kuftan with bulbous sleeves, made of soft black cotton and trimmed with silk that was also black. Black too were my sardwil trousers as vastly roomy as ever Barmak's were and my cloth slippers with their long, curved toes. Which is to say that I would have been dressed entirely in the color of the Merv rebellion were it not for the band around my head, for which, out of sheer perversity, I had chosen a silvery fabric, in order to stand out even a little from the throng that surrounded the general. Although that throng, as I had remarked while sitting among the dapirpats, was already also allowing itself some flashes of color on otherwise identical garments that were the color of gloom.

Black too was my horse, for again I owned a horse, having had my fill of donkeys and camel packs, and a strapping Iranian giant he was. I had named him Shabdiz, for his midnight hue. He was a beast of calm and proud demeanor, although in truth I had not yet burdened him overmuch, in that I took from his stable outside the fortress wall only in order to make an unhurried turn about the city every day after breakfast.

As to breakfast, and indeed any food whatsoever, I did not venture too often to Barmak's favorite eating house but had explored the surrounding squares well enough, obedient for the most part to the dictates of my nose.

The aroma of Khorasan, the aroma of Merv... How good it is to wander of an evening through the dark streets of a strange city, amid lights that glimmer through foliage, and seize on the tastes borne by the smoke. The smoke was not here as it was in Samarkand, being somehow viscous and sweet. And even the aromas of meat and bread that it carried were different, and tantalizing and fragrant beyond measure.

It was, however, thanks to those very aromas that I passed the greater part of the time in my new residence beneath the shady southern wall of the fortress of Merv – the time between breakfast and dinner, between dinner and supper – nibbling any of a variety of breads torn into bite-sized pieces or munching on the astounding local nuts, either with some sweetmeat or alone, or drinking, having pledged to myself that I would stop when my new jacket began to split at the seams.

My two unfailing shadows did much as I did, which was, I fear, almost naught but study the merits of the local markets and kitchens. The first of those shadows was the now recuperated but still quite lethargic Nanivandak and the second, one Makhian of Samarkand – also once a soldier of none-knows-whose army, whom Ashofteh and I had, by our combined efforts, delivered from the burning in the belly and the queasiness of stomach that had fastened on him after three months spent healing from a pair of arrow wounds.

They did, however, take turns guarding me by night, which is to say that they simply barred the way up to the second story of my new home.

What was now one of the walls had been a brick facing that over untold years had transformed into a sand-colored hillside dotted with burrow-like depressions and orifices. The flooring and, for that matter, the house in its entirety was secured both to that facing and to a gnarled old trunk like to hardened clay crowned with thick and tangled branches over which the foliage plashed in the quiet of the night.

I had come by all this happiness with astonishing ease.

Having received that weighty leather purse from the good Barmak, I spent the entire following day and evening in the quest for and ingestion of savory food, and in considering the fact that a person in possession of such a purse should surely not be sleeping among snoring, groaning bodies, or be gallivanting about the city for that matter. Only take from it any single coin, and you, the coin and the purse from which it came would be fixed for good and all in the memory of the whole street.

For the streets and markets of Merv were, as I had begun to remark, crowded with a ragtag company from a multitude of places both near and far. My brief turn as dapirpat had told me all that had befallen these people. These children of Iran or Sogdia – they or their fathers – had once owned land or other property, but a hundred years of warfare and of brigandage by tax collectors had not gone for naught. Deprived now of everything, all these people knew was how to wage war, and that not always well.

And far from every child of the Arabiya, whether cast unwilling to the easternmost outskirts of the Caliph's empire or born here, had prospered in all things, as a result of which they manifestly felt themselves to be more a part of the local landscape than its conquerors and had, to boot, taken a liking to the garb of Iran and had begun to speak its language and to dye their head's vegetation in various shades of red. So that their provenance could be judged, if at all, by their dark faces and a certain set to the nose.

I own that I could well have observed this selfsame picture every day in Samarkand. But to me, Merv had always been the city of our conquerors. It was from here, from inside the walls of this fortress, that the cavalries of Qutayba ibn Muslim had ridden out in their thousands, time and again crossing the river that ran gray beneath the fortress walls, in the first year descending on Panjakent and returning back again. Then on Bukhara and back again, then on Samarkand... And it was to here, to Merv, that tens of thousands of slaves had been driven and spoils looted from all Sogdia had been brought.

Now I could – even here, in the erstwhile lair of the enemy – watch the chaos gradually overwhelming an empire that over mere decades had seized territories all the way from Chach and Fergana in the east to al-Andalus at the western ends of the earth. While the Prophet's descendants were conquering their world, all was well with them. But as soon as they were required to be able rulers of their conquests, everything fell out of joint.

So that Abu Muslim, as I now knew, had only to send forth the now-famous call from the village of Safizanj to bring thousands flocking to him. And more thousands stood ready even today to swell his, or anyone else's, army.

I was not entirely pleased by all of this, though, especially because cities packed with paupers make but a poor market for sellers of silk.

And further, I was disconcerted – although less displeased than confused – by certain particulars of my own present situation.

On the one hand, I had been given money that it would cost me no trouble to repay to Barmak forthwith on my return home. But on the other, I seemed to have promised to do something in return for that money. Or, more properly, I had lacked the strength to say him nay. And I had not even noted how that had come to be.

Today I would instantly have understood where the conversation with my grandfather's good friend was tending so unexpectedly. And would just as instantly have grasped that I was in dealings with more than a king who had quit his throne. Today I would easily have divined that the game being played by the erstwhile overlord of Balkh with such assurance and so tastefully would surely amount to more than a visit or two to Merv's best eating houses.

But at the time, even with a heavy purse made fast to the sash at my waist and beating against my thigh, I did not yet fully understand what had just befallen me and what Barmak's words of farewell had signified.

"Well, you'll require a week to collect yourself," he had said, "to find accommodation, even the most down-at-heels bodyguard, and all the rest of it. But then you and I will need to afford ourselves some of life's pleasures again and speak seriously about everything. And let us meet often too – no less than once every three days, and why not? Send me word. I shall look forward to that, dear young friend of mine."

And it was not until the following morning that I understood how awkward it would have been to refuse so kind an invitation. When the sure and sorrowful voice of the Rose of Iran had first caught my ear, I was in desperate straits yet, for all that, still relatively free. But when that grand evening was over, my freedom was not what it had been, although by then I was a beggar no more.

But even on the day after my supper with Barmak, I was in no great haste to make a change in my life. My thoughts instead revolved around money, murderers, horses, guards, and a solitary female figure on a garden walk, as my fingers worked the shoulder of yet another wounded Sogdian soldier, whose name – Awlad – he shared with a character in a Rustam tale. I then brought to his lips a bowl containing an herbal decoction. Meanwhile Ashofteh, his eyes as red as a rat's, watched me impatiently and counseled me, and two of the girls, scarce daring to breathe, rinsed his hands, which had the greasy glister of blood, over a copper basin, and a third touched a cloth soaked in a healing potion to the great man's tired, blinking eyes.

And so, on the following day, I passed with sprightly step, still wearing the black garments given to me at the hospital, between the two towers of the fortress of Merv. I skirted the place where, beneath a layer of dust, there remained but a hint of the blood shed by the elderly horseman killed here two days earlier and marched on, light of foot, to where, under armor that hung heavy on their shoulders, the towering warriors of Abu Muslim stood.

"Maniakh of Samarkand, from the House of Maniakh, seeks audience with the sovereign lord of Khorasan," I said to one of those black-garbed figures.

He found the needful person for me, evidently a secretary, who let his eye slide over my humble attire while his face took on an expression that bespoke his weariness with life in general. But, since that was only to be expected, I added, "I am known by sight to Barmak of Balkh."

At that point, others came to look at me, and yet others, and all at once it was somehow very clear to me that I would soon be again at close quarters with the young man who not so long ago had trembled under my hands as he battled the savage pain.

They seated me on a rug by the entrance to a rather modest courtyard, and I, fetching a deep breath, began to repeat in my mind what I proposed to say to him or to any one of his close confederates.

Although what I had to say was little enough; others had surely come with requests of greater moment than mine.

As I sat and waited, I took to musing on how the rebel received his visitors. It was, as everyone knew, customary to come before the sovereign lord of the faithful, to the Caliph in his Green Palace in Damascus, after a final ablution for good measure and in clean garments, under which was to be worn the quilted tunic called a jubba, lest the odor of the guest – if any odor there be after so much washing – offend the Caliph. And custom also dictated that one emit a fragrance of rose, violet, cedar or something other. At present, I was not exactly meeting those requirements, although for days now I had never slighted any chance to launder my clothing, or at least parts of it, in fresh water and with equal care to wipe a damp cloth over my body. More than that, I had been doing the same for my – yes, *my* – patients.

But on the other hand, the Leopard of Merv was not the sovereign lord of the faithful. Much, including the ritual of reception, would have to be fashioned anew for him.

Further, he who faced the Caliph had to do so from a small prayer rug set opposite he who had dominion over one-third of the world, striving not to appear taller – of which I ran no risk – and to speak quietly to him, using the familiar form of address, that being the simplest and the most sincere.

If food had been set before him, it was considered respectful to stretch out one's hand and take a pinch or two of it between the fingers. There was naught there resembling such Sogdian – or even Iranian – inventions as the two-pronged fork, especially since the food of the Arabiya did not lend itself to being conveyed so from plate to mouth.

It was almost the same as the ritual at the court of the Radiant Emperor and head of the House of Tang, except that in his reception room there was certainly no food, and any form of familiarity would have been less than proper.

But an audience with Abu Muslim was wholly other.

Here, a young man with loose ringlets of hair that flowed from beneath a simple headband came flying, like a disembodied specter, round a corner. Two soldiers in thick leather jerkins, and some others too, were trying to overtake him, but in vain, for he moved fleet-footed and low to the ground, his aba flowing from his shoulders in gossamer waves. His movements were smooth and precise. It came to me that in battle, whether afoot or ahorse, this was one best avoided.

A secretary dressed in black began to speak in low tones, but Abu Muslim gave him a look of polite reproof, causing him to fall silent in mid-word, and began eyeing me with great curiosity. He was endeavoring to remember. Back then, with elbow torn apart, howling with the pain and his eyes puckered against it, he would scarce have glanced at the man who held him, but later, once himself again, he had looked well into our faces, both mine and the healer's.

A frank and childlike smile appeared on his lips.

"Maniakh can wait, Ziyad my friend," he said, again brushing his secretary away. "First, here is a man who not very long ago did me a good deed. And now, no doubt, wants to do more. I said I would not forget you, my dear man, and I have not. But you are here on the healer's behalf? He was with me two days back and said that my elbow is as good as new. The skin is knitting too. What else can there be?"

"I am here on my own behalf," I said with a courteous smile. "And I have come on a wholly other matter. Ashofteh has no need of my services as regards your elbow and, for that matter, I am as much his patient as you, o sovereign lord of Khorasan. At that time, I happened to be needful to him, for none other was nearby."

Abu Muslim's belated attendants arrived at last and formed a half-circle around him. And it was with some surprise that I saw among them a man whose face was covered with a translucent white fabric, like the women of Byzant, and alongside him, a fine fellow of a warrior with a nose like a battle axe. He it was who had ridden across the fortress courtyard two days earlier, followed by another horseman who had soon found himself skewered on a murderer's knife. I was instantly on alert. *All too comely to behold*, I remembered, had been my verdict on him then.

Ziyad again began muttering into Abu Muslim's ear.

"I understand naught of that," Abu Muslim replied with a hint of plaintive petulance, again turning half toward me. "You're kin to the family Maniakh? Of Samarkand?"

"I am no kin," I said with due modesty. "I am head of that family. Confirmation of which may be had only from a most respected person by the name of Barmak."

At this, the young man swung around to the fine fellow, calling him by name – Khalid – and they exchanged some quick, quiet words.

"I came to Ashofteh," I went on, "wounded almost as you were, in the shoulder. A knife wound. You know there are such here as will... No more than a day or two ago, they found them another victim two hundred paces from here... But with me they had worse fortune. I was only injured."

In all honesty, I could have forgone explaining to Abu Muslim who had wounded me and why, but I wanted, I must confess, to make an impression on him.

And in that I had, it seems, succeeded right well.

The young general again traded glances with the magnificent warrior and waved his suite away, at which they moved back as one. Then he strode the short distance to a blind white wall, made a half-turn toward it, and raised both hands to his face, as if in prayer. And stood motionless.

A profound silence reigned. No one so much as stirred.

At last he swung around and approached me close. Again I smelled attar of roses.

"The head of the House of Maniakh is here? The head of the House of Maniakh has come to me, and in black garments too?"

"At this time I need no other," I replied in some vexation.

"And what do you want?" he asked, while merry sparks shone in his yellow eyes.

"I wished to ask the sovereign lord's leave to take up residence for a time hereabouts," I said, waving a hand in the general direction of the small houses. "It is safer somehow. And also to keep some chakirs about me."

"Your own hireling soldiers, no less? Here? In emulation of a prince of Iran?" He seemed now to be strangling on his laughter.

"No, just ten," I said, only to name some number.

He promptly tired of the subject – since ten chakirs, whether armed or not, manifestly held no interest for him – and began to think hard.

"And you come to me with this?" he whispered at last, with almost no expression in his voice.

"To whom else may the head of the House of Maniakh go?" I replied, just as quietly, but in a tone of sincere bewilderment.

It was not just anyone, after all, who could settle into one of those little houses behind the line of guards. Therefore permission was needed... but from whom? At the court of the Radiant Emperor, I was accustomed to going to the highest-ranking official who could decide whatever question I may have had. All in all, it would have been peculiar if one from the clan of Maniakh had humbly applied to an official of the second or third rank on any matter whatsoever. I would simply not have been understood. And so on the eve of this visit, I had given little thought to what I should do, and had done as I would have done even had my family's money not been the spark that lit the flame of rebellion in Khorasan. And never mind how impudent it would have been to speak aloud of that money at this time.

Abu Muslim's face began to spread into a smile that I did not wholly understand. Then he came a half-pace closer, clasped me abruptly to his heart, and turned me with him to face his suite.

"This man – Maniakh, head of the House of Maniakh – is my friend. Forevermore. He shall live here," he said forcefully, as if anyone dare contradict him. But all, naturally, were silent.

Next he told me, wasting no words, that we would meet again and more than once, before the hem of his aba whirled again into the torrid air of Merv.

The rebel general passed out of sight through the gates of the house where he had granted me that audience. And now it remained only to exchange a word or two with the man named Ziyad – Ziyad ibn Saleh in full – as to which house was vacant, and so forth.

From that day on, although I, along with the whole enclosure, had seen his fleeting figure a time or two, I had spoken no more with Abu Muslim, not that so much time had in truth elapsed since our last conversation.

But on that serene evening of which I was speaking earlier, it was not any possible encounter with the Leopard of Merv that occupied my mind, but something other and of greater import.

I was making ready to write a poem.

Which is to say that I was sitting on cushions and gazing on the colorful crowd below, while my fingers drummed out a rhythm on my knee.

Before coming to Merv, I had never written a poem in my life.

My life as a poet had begun but two weeks earlier, and it happened in this wise. On the morning after my visit to Abu Muslim, I walked, stopping to rest along the way, to the house that Barmak had named to me, which was quite far from the hospital, in the fashionable Western suburb near the Madjan canal.

He greeted me in his courtyard, mounted on a docile mule, and was long in apologizing that he was constrained to depart forthwith, while I was equally long in preventing him from dismounting from his mule in order to converse with feet firmly planted on the trampled, hummocky, yellowish ground.

I quickly told him where I was proposing to make my home, and he opened wide his eyes of softest blue and clicked his tongue in delight.

"A fine ploy!" he said. "By the by, inquiries were indeed made of me yesterday as to whether I knew you by sight. That was a quandary for me, but I decided to admit all and describe you to the life. Now I understand what was afoot."

That was my time to make my request.

"I've been reflecting, and if I understand even a little of what has transpired," I told him, "you would appear to be correct. They of the daggers have somehow placed a stranglehold on the road through Bukhara. Though I don't understand how, since hundreds of travelers journey along it."

He responded instantly, laughter glinting in his eyes. "It's all quite simple, if at the same time they have a hold on your private caravanserai there and on certain points in Samarkand. They pass information among themselves. Which also means that they are great in number."

"Then another... point of ours, here in Merv, is in the same situation," I went on. "And, to be on the safe side, we must add the hospital also. Although of that I am uncertain, since dozens of people enter and leave the hospital and now I understand how well that suits. Yet this is not for me to puzzle out. I have no plans to return to Bukhara. But come what may, I must now find a way to send a letter to my brother."

The erstwhile king again responded on the instant. "Yes, yes, to Aspanak," he said, and fell momentarily into deep thought. Then, after a very brief time of reflection, he spoke again. "So. You have portrayed the situation with utter precision, but you are not, to be sure, the one to unriddle it. Well, you can, of course, give the letter to me. I shall send it through Balkh, and it will arrive surely and very soon. But still, do what you can to make it... harmless." And with that, he had no more to say.

And so, having obtained from Barmak what I had come for, I made my way back to the hospital, bound and determined that this would be my last night there.

On the way, I acquired a new brush and two more sheets of papyrus, to replace those I had abandoned in my recent flight.

But how am I to make the letter harmless? Sogdian merchants are well familiar with the encoding of missives, and a whole epic poem could be written on how my brother sends and receives letters hidden in the most unexpected of places – in a horse's hoof, in the bottom of a pitcher smeared again with clay and again put to the fire, and so forth. But I have neither coding tables to hand nor any experience of my own in tucking letters into strange places.

And then the word "poem" that had, to all seeming, but flitted through my mind just now guided me to a diverting idea.

What if I were to turn poet? A letter in verse... Not so bad an idea in a world where all and sundry were songsters and writers of poems.

The meaning of the missive I was about to write was clear. I was to begin by informing my brother that I was in Merv and still lived, although the arrival of the letter would of itself signify as much. Next I needed to recount to him that our affairs were in utter disarray and on every hand, at that – in Bukhara, at Adijer's vineyard, and in the hospital that was no longer receiving our money. I also had to explain that I myself needed money, since I naturally did not propose to live much longer on Barmak's largesse. And I must offer my brother the pleasant opportunity to reply and to tender apology after apology.

And, most importantly, I needed to learn from Aspanak who Yukuk was and if he really was working for him here, in Merv. Because to attempt anything in Merv on my own would have been rank insanity on my part. As much so as trying to travel home alone. But with a tall warrior at my side, I would feel at least a little more tranquil.

Yet right well I remembered that back in Bukhara I had determined to be the most cowardly of the world's cowards. *Yukuk saved my life? But there could be any number of reasons why he did so. He says he's working here for my brother? Then let me have my brother's confirmation of it.*

And so, all that remained was to set it all down in verse.

I had little reason to count on achieving the fame of Li Bo, whose soup the Emperor himself had stirred, but in my beloved Celestial Empire, anyone at all, or at least any individual with a modicum of education, could compose a simple verse. And not only there. Here too, in the Caliph's empire, rocked as it was by revolt, everyone was writing or had written poetry – the vagrant Arabiya in the marketplace, and the generals of the vanquished Shahanshah, and the no less vanquished governors of the sovereign lord of the faithful.

The world around was full of poetry. If aught distinguishes man from beast, it is that he is a poetic beast.

Writing poetry is a simple matter, I told myself soothingly.

I imagined the slow, fanciful rhythms of the street songs of Iran, since a letter from Merv had best be written in Pahlavi. I drummed my fingers on my knee. Good, now the rhyme. The simplest would be, in imitation of those street songs, to take lines ranged in pairs and find

one word to end them all, such a word as might be intoned long and
dolefully in song.

And that word came into being at a stroke. Because for what did
I wish to ask Aspanak other than for money? Why, for a reply to my
question about the man who answered to the byname of Owl, about
Yukuk. To tell me if I could trust him or no.

Tell me, brother: that was the meaning of my question in chief.

And so, as I lay on a flat and pitiful cot that smelled of the hospital,
there was born the first draft, the no less pitiful snatches of lines that
rendered me inconsolable.

Bukhara now is grieved, oh, tell me true!
The wine pitcher is shattered and will not be whole again,
    oh, tell me true!
The physician's eyes are sad, oh, tell me!
And shall I trust the owl, oh, tell, do tell!

Maybe writing poetry was harder than I had thought? "Bukhara
now is grieved" was a fair beginning. But what exactly had grieved
her? That there could be no riding out of her without being tailed by
a fresh pair of murderers in place of the murderers who had just been
cut down? What sense could be drawn from such ravings, though, and
how was it to be couched in verse?

Very well, but to determine where the watchers were hiding, why
the gates of our trading yard were guarded, and why those who had
followed me had even so been killed there was no job for me. My
brother would make a better go of that than I.

It was also not my business to make out what to do about Adijer's
vineyard, or who had arranged that raid and why. All my brother had
to know was that things were bad there too. That the physician was sad
not for no good reason but because of money – this too must be writ
down. To speak of money was important, because I was also in need
of funds. And regarding the owl, all was clear: things can be no worse;
I sit, I mourn; I hear an owl because it's nighttime and there is naught

else to be heard, save donkeys maddened by a bad dream. In sum, the utter wreck of all hopes, as pins fall from thinning hair... But that was from a different poem.

Then I remember thinking what a good idea it would be to make a poem containing only the names of cities, long dead or scattered to dust before our eyes and transformed into sleepy villages amid the ruins. Where were the proud Volubilis, Septem, Hispalis, Caesarea Augusta, and Panormus? Soon naught but their names would remain.

"Bukhara is now grieved" I repeated, not without pleasure, then sighed and completed with no great effort what I had begun.

Bukhara now is grieved, awaiting not your steeds.
How to evade the unkind eyes that burn you all to ash, do tell!

The wine pitcher is shattered, ne'er to be whole again.
How to contend with such a loss, oh, do thou tell!

The physician mourns and gazes long into an empty purse.
How may I comfort him when poor myself, do tell!

The owl of night alone is friend to me,
But may the owl command my trust, do tell!

Proud of what I had accomplished, I rose from my dismal pallet the following morning and again crossed the city to Barmak's home, promising myself on the way to go the very next day and pick out a horse.

His little house was close to what had once been Nasr ibn Sayyar's spacious residence that now, of course, had opened its gates to Abu Muslim. To the attentive eye, though, it too was ample in size, and indeed it accommodated the entire peculiar company – the treasurer Abu Jafar and his nimble boy, who occupied one room together, and the two bodyguards whose exacting eyes followed me as I entered, and the slave with the pock-marked face. I found the sovereign lord of Balkh in a far corner of the courtyard, sitting in the cool shade.

"I think that such a letter will need no special concealment," I said, handing him the scrap of papyrus with well-hidden pride.

He appraised my work with uncommon speed.

"The blood of the first among the Maniakhs is no trifle. Yes this can be carried anywhere and no one will cavil," he told me admiringly. "Such a low-minded, melancholy little street song it is, or, rather, a fragment thereof. Splendid!"

Then he glanced at my face and seemed to understand that he had spoken amiss. And hastened to drown his blunder in a flood of words.

"I shall copy several such short verses directly, so that my man will take along a whole pack of them, openly, neither hidden nor sealed. Such as this:

Pour, then: I wish to hear the pitcher's sigh.
The sound of strings has stolen souls that we once fancied ours.
But if that be so – pour then! And all my sins and sorrows
Are like to this black wine, soon to o'erflow the cup,
And shall never be redeemed.

"Yes indeed. I'm retelling it to you in the language of Iran, of course. And I'm no poet, to make a translation worthy of the author. The rhythm's uneven, there's no inner music. I merely conveyed to you the images. In the language of the Arabiya, however, the sound of it is simply magnificent. But it will be yet more magnificent to you when you learn who wrote it."

"Who?" I asked, still a little taut but already beginning to soften.

"Al-Walid! The Caliph and sovereign lord of the faithful. What a man he was! You'd be amazed to read all he wrote. Unbridled, simply frenzied... But you've heard, of course, the tales of the caliphs of the House of Umayyah – about Hisham, who drank wine on Fridays only, and Abd al-Malik, who drank once a month but drank deep. And Yazid the Wine-Bibber, who drank every day and trained a monkey to amuse him in his cups. But this one, al-Walid, the second to bear that name, is almost our contemporary. I myself met him. And, although he drank only every other day, he drank famously well. Yet when they say that he swam in a pool filled with wine and swallowed so much that the level could be seen to fall... You and I know that cannot be. People do not drink so much. Yes, but we were speaking of poets. So, a most entertaining story once befell one of them, either al-Akhtal or Jarir or al-Farazdak. But not Jamil, although... his love is pure and exalted, and the songs he wrote for his gentle Buthaina are sung to this day. Or more likely Umar ibn Abi Rabiah – he wrote volumes about love and the ladies who traveled to Mecca, in words so fresh and so passionate. But this is the story. It was in Kufa, not Damascus – because you know that all the philosophers and poets for some reason idolize the life in Kufa, for all that it's a grimy sinkhole, not a city at all but a chaos... So, our poet wrote a mournful ode to a lady with whom he wasn't even well acquainted, beseeching her to send him her image as he slept, to comfort him in his solitary nights. Touched by those lines when they reached her, the lady asked to have it relayed to the author that he need not suffer so, and that instead he should send her some small sum – namely, three dinars – and she would come in her very own person and give him all the comfort he could wish for."

Thoroughly calm now, I bade farewell to Barmak, promising to tell him where my impending move would take me.

The reply from Samarkand came with astonishing speed. I was by then living in the fortress but, true to my word, was not neglecting the hospital. And one evening, during his daily rounds of my patients, Ashofteh, with a slight wrinkling of the face and many a glance around, thrust a small page at me and timidly took his leave. Then he stopped and turned.

"Money has been sent to me," he announced through gritted teeth, making a point now of not calling me "lad" but still not saying my name. "And to you too."

The crumpled page contained, to no one's great surprise, a verse.

The ladylove's sorrow scorches the heart – deliver up your sorrow,
And for that sorrow, 'tis you I thank.

The ladylove's tear is like crystal – let me drink a tear,
And for that tear, 'tis you I thank.

The owl's grizzled plumage is both joy and hope,
And for his loyalty, the owl I thank.

"That slimy toad," I said to the twilight of the hospital courtyard, which at that time was filled with languid movement.

My mood was bad now and had rarely been worse.

First, because my accursed brother had made a woman of me, which I would have to remain until our correspondence ended, unless I could find some way out of it. Second, because those lines of his about my tears and sorrow contained an especially subtle mockery. And third, because it could not have been more clear that his verse was quite plainly better than mine, so simple and polished it was. *What a mangy dog he is!*

As for the meaning of his missive, that was obvious. The first two verses, for all their mockery, were at once an apology and an expression of gratitude, and no more. Well, but not completely: following the logical assumption that the lines of the response traced quite precisely the lines of my letter, which had begun with Bukhara and then gone on to Adijer's vineyard and the healer, weeping and all out of funds, then my brother's reply could have been couched far more briefly: Thank you, all is understood, trouble yourself no more, this is my business now.

But even to the eye, the third verse differed from the first two. The rhythm was slightly broken, there was no "ladylove" here, and the key word, in this case "owl," was not written thrice, as "sorrow" and "tear" had been. Which meant that this verse bore a particular and more than manifest meaning. The man who went by the name of Yukuk was called loyal and I was being told that he was my joy and my hope. And so my central question had received a clear answer.

And all would have been excellent, had that answer not been so manifestly well-written

"The owl with grizzled plumage..." And I pictured to myself the tall warrior's temples, slightly gray, and then an owl perched on a branch in silvery moonlight that had a greenish cast.

A slimy toad in truth and naught else.

My mood was not even improved by the arrival of a right familiar object that resembled a long, thick, leather cable. Ashofteh, still glancing around every instant, had popped up again to bring it to me, and I almost dropped the thing, for gold is pleasant enough but very heavy.

As I was tying that cable around my bare belly like a belt, I pondered gloomily the two daunting tasks that lay in store for me.

The first would be to inform myself in no uncertain terms what I was going to do next. Because my brother had contrived to ask me no questions, but, without even counting the money he had sent and judging from its weight alone, it was clear that the sum was far greater than I would need to return home. It was, of course, more my money than his, and no one in this world could bar me from hiring two or three bodyguards among the patients from Samarkand whom I had helped heal – for are there better bodyguards anywhere? – and setting out for home, thus rendering to my brother what was my brother's and to me my trading enterprise again. Even so, the size of the purse was a certain sign that he had respectfully left the choice to me, and it only remained to make that choice, to make it now and never again.

And the second daunting task would be to write a poem in reply that would have my brother choking on his own envy.

"The courier will tarry for your letter a day or two more," the unhappy Ashofteh told me in a whisper as he accompanied me to the door. "And if I understand aright, I will again be without one who can heal with his hands. Just as you were beginning to shape up."

I didn't consider my reply for even an instant.

"I shall continue as before, every evening," I said. "Because I truly do want these people to live."

10

IN SLEEPLESS CITIES' DUST

"Greetings to you from Samarkand, Yukuk," I said to the tall warrior who sat opposite me beneath the hospital wall.

Naught could be read in his face, expressive though it was, save that the look in his light gray eyes was as attentive than ever it had been. This was seemingly a man not given to much blinking.

"And in what terms are those greetings couched?" he asked at last.

I knew what he meant, and the terms appropriate to the instance were weighing down my belt with the imposing heft of pure gold. I suspected that the closing of the road between Merv and Samarkand had presented the warrior who had been my savior with difficulties comparable to those of the healer's, and never mind that Yukuk was evidently the one more accustomed to difficulties. But, plunging a hand into the pouch that hung from my belt, I allowed myself the pleasure of answering him to the point.

"Well, you know, our letters are sparing of words, but as to you, the words used were 'reliable' and 'faithful.'"

Yukuk dipped his head in satisfaction. And raised it again on seeing before him my hand, clenched almost into a fist to hide from prying eyes a stack made up not even of the dinars of Caliph Abd al-Malik but of their elder brothers, the denarii of Constantine's Empire. A time there had been when the appearance in the Caliphate of those latter coins' golden twins – and shamelessly called by almost the same name – had sparked yet another war between the two empires.

There were ten denarii, which made one hundred dirhams. A very, very impressive sum, which had even had me pensively nibbling at my fingers the day before.

"This is for what is past, for all the unpleasantness that is now behind you," I said.

Yukuk sighed, took the money, bowed. And, evidently to help me launch now into a serious conversation, said, "And so, you have succeeded in restoring communication with Samarkand?"

I replied with another such sigh.

Because for me the most complicated part of the conversation was yet to come.

But to delay it, I asked him something else.

"I have. And now I think of it, you also tried to do something of the sort? You were in Bukhara, were you not, when you were chasing either me or those two?"

The corner of Yukuk's mouth twitched. "But what could I do alone? All I came to understand was that the trading yard was close surrounded, with no entering and no leaving. They who departed the city were also under watch. So I needed time for some watching of my own, and then I had to think hard on what to do. At which time, a man appeared who was causing a stir around him. As one example, that pair were following him. And I thought I would do well to observe what happened next, where that man was going, who he was, what the murderers would do..."

"I already know the luck I was having," I said, and fell silent again, preparing to pass on to the heart of the matter.

If someone is born, as I was, into a family in which, on the whim of even an adolescent, a sprig of that family, tens and hundreds of people depended, that adolescent would very soon become versed in the hard-won and subtle art of command. He would, for example, be apprised of the knowledge that giving direction to others affords not the slightest pleasure but is, on the contrary, the price to be paid for wealth. And that most of the people around you are older, more experienced, and wiser than you, and, what is more, that you depend on them exactly as much or even more than they on you.

So from the very outset I knew well enough that even those ten gold coins would not ensure me any power over one who could trail murderers through a desert, could instantly change his appearance – by bandaging his whole face, for one thing – and could hew enemies down in one indiscernible motion. And, all told, apparently do any number of things to which I would never rise even after years of training.

Thus, if I wanted Yukuk to work again for the House of Maniakh and for me personally, there was no profit in making myself out to be worldly wise and awe inspiring. Or to invest overmuch hope in the ability of even denarii from the lands of Room to effect much change in that.

No, I had to be piercingly honest from the outset.

"Yukuk," I said. "Let us begin with this. I am a silk merchant. Our trading house is very large, and strange as this may be, some of its owners actually do trade in silk. I am adept in trade. But I am adept in naught else."

"Ah," he said, and his face took on a look that seemed to bespeak a sincere interest in me. Which meant that I had most likely calculated aright.

"And I am here," I continued, "for one strange reason. We have already spoken of it. The fact is that none of our people know what I know. They do not know by sight the woman I very much need to find. They have not been acquainted with her as long as I. Add to this, Yukuk, that I cannot and will not restore everything here that my family has done, aside from the trade in silk. Let others busy themselves with such matters."

I was already growing accustomed to the way this man would make a very brief but strained pause before answering – which he then did tersely, expending no more words than he must – while sitting absolutely motionless, his face a stony mask.

"Yes, I remember our earlier conversation well," he said, after just such a pause. "That woman... From what I've heard, she's very, very dangerous. And that raises a question: You want to find her, but then what will you do?"

And that was in truth an excellent question. Now it was my turn to pause.

"The correct answer would be 'I don't yet know,' " I said at last. "As matters progress, I hope, that will come clearer. But I can say that the first thing I must do is... talk with her."

"Oh," Yukuk said.

"Since we will evidently have much occasion to speak of her again," I continued, "there is something I must say at this time. I've known her since we were children. We grew up together. Yukuk, my family is such that the greater part of Samarkand's dehkans speaks our name with envy. And the lesser part too. Our clan is more ancient than many. It has also boasted dozens of dehkans, but it simply transpired that trade is more pleasing to us than owning land. And that means that all our family's children have received a superlative education."

Yukuk was silent, his face expressing nothing.

"And so," I went on, "our father approved my friendship with that girl of a rather poor family of fugitives from unhappy Iran, not least because she, like her mother, was surpassingly well educated. Ancient, ancient blood – no worse, and belike even better, than our own. And my father wished my brother and I to learn from her. A good upbringing, Yukuk, is not simply the knack of keeping a quiet tongue and not brandishing a well-sauced bone at the table. It's also the knack of remaining beyond reproach even when in difficulty. Especially then, in fact. And that woman, whose real name is Zargisu" – here Yukuk nodded, as if to say that this was information useful to his task – "not only said the necessary words at the necessary time, which many are also able to do. She... We always knew that from her could and must be expected conduct that was beyond reproach. Always and in all things. That we took for granted... And now we are hearing the utterly unthinkable of her. The signs are that something strange has befallen her, and the person who was once the best of all those who worked for us has, suddenly and on the instant, transformed into a demon who is visiting her ire on us as well as on others. And the tales of what she does to men... It's a conundrum, Yukuk. And for that reason, if for no other, I must begin by talking with her."

Yukuk's reaction was instant astonishment. "She worked here for us? That woman?"

I was equally surprised. "You knew naught of this?"

At that he tried, but without success, to hide a faintly patronizing smile. And again took great pains to explain to me things that would, like as not, be plain as day to a man of his profession.

"In this work it is best that one know naught of another. I see that you hoped I would tell you much of what has happened here, to ease your search," he said. "But I, alas, have been attending only to what was transpiring to the west of Merv."

I could guess what that was. "Caliph Marwan," I said. "His armies. His intentions."

"Yes, just so. I have spent much time riding westward... And unfortunately – or otherwise – I've seen naught of that woman. This and that I've heard, no more. I've been working quite apart from most of the others. And so, possibly, has she. But I'll warrant that she knew many things and many people. Because the operations of the House of Maniakh in Khorasan were destroyed or hamstrung at a stroke, and that is all."

A very simple thought then came to me.

"Yukuk, can it be that only you remain?"

"There remains," he responded after a pause, "the physician. But he's a physician. He also had some people at the hospital. Although, now I think of it, he had no notion that they too were working for us. And others as well. But they were killed. One by one. What happened at the vineyard, you saw for yourself. I learned the details later... But you do even so want to restore if not all, then at least some of your house's operations?"

"No," I replied after a long interval. And then, gathering my strength, I added: "Because I don't know how. I must find that woman. All the rest, as I have said before, others will do."

He nodded. "That makes matters easier, then. So, to find her... and to talk with her. That's possible, with ropes strong enough. And after that?"

"I don't know," I said again. And then, understanding why he had asked that, I spoke very emphatically: "Yukuk, unless I order it so, nothing must be done to harm her."

That, now, was a very important moment. Because until then, it was only a conversation between two free men whose old accounts had just been settled. But when I said "unless I order" – not words to be bandied loosely about, whatever the situation – that must have made everything clearer than clear.

Yukuk was silent for quite a long time, then slowly bent his head. And I tried to catch my breath as stealthily as I could.

"Good," he said at last. "Three orders could come in this situation. One" – and he sliced a hand eloquently through the air – "That's simple. The second... The contrary – to speak with her and let her go."

"Yes," I said quickly. "That too is possible."

"But very dangerous," he replied in a hoarse whisper. "Dangerous beyond compare. And the third... Is there a third?"

"I don't know," I said yet again, now almost in despair. "Yes there can be a third. Two of that third, in fact. One is that she'll come with us. Will come home. Until I know what has befallen her, that must not be excluded. And then again, she may come with us, but against her will."

"That's still not the most dangerous," he said, so low I could scarce hear him. "Six days traveling in a sack... Ah well, others have done it."

And he fell into thought, before asking me about something that, to my utter astonishment, I had almost entirely forgotten.

"And then there are the murderers. What would you have done with them?"

I was hard put to hold back a bark of laugher, for the problem had always been, rather, what they were going to do with me. And also because if the word "pairidaeza" meant anything, the murderers and Zargisu were somehow bound up together.

Yukuk sat up straight, expecting the conversation to turn now to the murderers. But I was suddenly aware that my throat was dry, that I wanted to stand and take a turn about, that my head was ringing and spinning with the strain, and that, all told, I was not my brother, to speak at such length on topics so unfamiliar to me.

"What to do... For that, we need to know a little more. For example, their number." I remembered then what Barmak had said: *They are great in number.* "But even so, we're not in search of murderers, Yukuk. We're in search of a woman."

He fell into lengthy thought this time, and then slowly bent his head once more.

And I knew that I had got from him all I had wanted.

The details followed. As to horses. As to Yukuk coming to live with me in the fortress – or some such arrangement that would leave him with freedom of movement. As to how much would be paid to my chakirs, my hireling soldiers, and how much to him. And, finally, that some serious work must be done with those chakirs, since it was still to be known what kind of soldiers they would make, and idleness has a way of spoiling a man. I was immeasurably happy to agree to all of that.

"One thing only," Yukuk said, to bring the conversation to an end. "You yourself told me when last we spoke, and I've also heard it from a patient or two, that they call you... the Hawk. Tell me, are you truly he who..?"

He did not finish. But I, thoroughly weary of this conversation, sighed and confessed, "Making a long story short, yes."

And a very strange expression appeared in Yukuk's eyes.

Aspanak had indeed done himself proud, if the legend of the Hawk had spread so far.

I now believe that with that "yes" I altered the net balance of the whole conversation. Before we spoke of the Hawk, Yukuk had seemingly drawn certain conclusions about me. And afterward, those conclusions changed. In my favor, let me add.

He was evidently beginning to suspect that I was not so unlettered in the family business as I had tried to have him believe.

I took my bag – yes, I now carried a real physician's bag, although it was most often left at the hospital for the night – and returned to my charges.

"You have to stand and take even a few steps, rest, and then try again to walk," I admonished yet another poor wretch, a Sogdian who went by the foreign name of Omar. *But if it is Omar, then Omar it shall be*, I thought, looking at his greenish Sogdian eyes. *I care not in which temple you beseech your God for His protection and aid.*

I knew already, I felt, with my fingers and with some other sense, that he would soon be on the mend. It needed only...

"Why should I?" he asked bluntly.

"Why should you? You should because I want us to return home, you and I, to Sogdia," I said, still staring into his sorrowful eyes. "You should because others I have cured are already living in my home. They too asked me why they should. You have a choice, Omar of Sogdia. The same choice that was given to them."

I TURNED AROUND AS I left him, to see one of the girls hastening across the courtyard, carrying a pitcher in which medicine lapped from side to side. Then she caught sight of Yukuk moving toward the gates with the graceful step of a large animal on the prowl.

And the girl began to make a right diverting transformation.

The pitcher was shifted to the curve above her jutting hip. Her waist was suddenly all pliant, bending as if of itself somewhat more than was needed, while the hips swayed most delightfully.

But Yukuk, deep in thought and oblivious to her efforts, walked on toward the cracked wooden gates.

Some prosper more than others in this life, I thought.

And off she trotted to the tents, the pitcher now pressed to her chest. She hadn't noticed me at all.

BUT WHEN I REACHED HOME, thinking that I would be long absolved of complicated conversations with difficult people, my chakirs, who had been leisurely gaining both strength and weight, were there to inform me that a courier "from a friend of my grandfather's" had come and that I was being asked to present myself, preferably without delay.

Cursing, I turned the horse I had acquired that very day toward the Western suburbs.

Barmak greeted me with "All I beg you is not to be angry, my young friend. Just speak here with a certain party. And by way of reward, I will not permit you to dine within these walls. You won't like it here... But for tomorrow I've found an eating house where they make a formidable chelo kebab. Are we agreed?"

And he pushed me toward the room occupied by the treasurer of the House of Abbas.

Where I came upon a scene that briefly stopped my heart. There sat the treasurer Abu Jafar, clasping the dark-skinned lad with his long, thin legs and equally long, bony arms and laying his sparse beard on the boy's shoulder, and the both of them, improbably serious, were studying an enormous book that lay open on their knees. It was, like as not, the book that had so enraptured my brother and the explanation of which had never been entrusted to Barmak, by reason of his stubborn devotion to the doctrines of karma and the transmigration of souls.

"The Prophet has said that we are to seek knowledge even in the Empire of the Chin, your beloved Celestial Empire," Abu Jafar told me after the first, and very speedy, introductions had been made. "And Barmak tells me that you live ever in that Empire's capital. Say then: What kind of city is it? Is it truly the best in the world?"

And he fixed me with two coal-black eyes.

I looked into his face. This was, of course, a man of the Arabiya, all his unsuccessful attempts to dye his beard notwithstanding, but even for them he was surprisingly dark of face. His thin, square-cut countenance seemed to have been carved from very hard wood, or out of an old piece of tanned saddle-leather that was rigid as any stone.

Like Barmak, he spoke to me in the language of Iran but either had a poor knowledge of it or could make shift with only the simplest of words.

I began to gather my thoughts: *What does that mean, the best in the world?* Yes, I had seen the magnificence of Constantine's city, and remembered a close-set array of fortress towers and below them water, heavy as oil, and emerging from that water, wet stones overspread with light-green velvet. And beyond that expanse of water, more towers, rising from the sea on the other shore and clambering up the steep hillside there. And the smell, the smell of that sea – damp, redolent of fish, dizzying...

What passed for refreshments were brought to us then. It was only water, but I wanted naught else at that time. And I began to explain that I had yet to see many cities such as the flourishing Damascus, but Chang'an was the best I knew because... because nowhere else did life feel so serene, measured, sated, happy, and commodious in every regard.

Abu Jafar gave an energetic nod. "Exactly so!" he said, in a voice that was surprisingly resonant but unpleasant and grating too. "There is the thing we must discuss. How is such a city made? That word, for example, 'Chang... An...' It means peace?"

How is the city made? Surprise silenced me, but then I again collected my thoughts and nodded my assent.

"Yes, 'Chang'an' means long or everlasting peace."

"So, then, noise is forbidden of an evening and by night?" was the next unexpected question. "Crashing and clattering and all manner of music?"

That did, I own, bring me alive and move me to unwonted eloquence.

I told him that in Chang'an it was quite to the contrary. That the peace was in the soul, at which he nodded vehemently. That to forbid much would be a bootless undertaking. The first emperors of the House of Tang are said to have forbidden all they could bestir themselves to forbid. The simple folk, for example, were not to wear silk in the same colors as the high officials, which prohibition at least was still observed. And a whole host of other things, such as carrying a weapon, although whoever needed one carried one, save that in the city there was no need, for there was no one to defend against. And a long-departed emperor had forbidden foreigners to ride horses, which order had never been revoked. Yet I rode mine every day. Why? Because I brought herds of horses into the Empire, to exchange them there for silk, and furthermore I played an Iranian game fashionable at the court of the Tang, in which men mounted on horses propel round balls across a field with mallets. And everyone knew that this was permitted me. But others also had the same permission, and so the foolish order was not rescinded but simply forgotten.

The next question came in an instant: "But is every neighborhood locked shut at night?"

"Of course" I replied. "And the city is very peaceful and safe. Even petty thieves are few. Although if you have a great need to pass from one neighborhood to another by night, you can do so. You know, Abu Jafar" – I was affable with him now, for I had discerned that this was a man younger than me although with no better a look about him – "I think it senseless to forbid anything unless people wish to comply. No emperor can ensure that a prohibition is followed when all others are opposed. And a city is a place where all live as they wish."

The treasurer, again quick to move on to another topic, was now asking, "Does the Emperor have an interest in the true faith?"

"He's interested in all faiths at once," I replied, "including yours – the true faith, that is. And good it is that you have asked me this. In Chang'an there are temples of all the prophets and all the gods. I too have oftentimes thought on this, and to me it seems that a city, a real city, is a home for travelers. A crossroads. A large caravanserai. A city is great and flourishes when it is well there for men of all nations who venerate all prophets. Such was Samarkand too until there came... those I need not name. Your brethren. Samarkand stood all those ages because it was needed and gave shelter to all – to the Turkic peoples of the Great Steppe, to Iranians, to men of Byzant and of the Celestial

Empire. And now all of Samarkand is moving by degrees, as indeed have I, to Chang'an and to other great cities of that other Empire. And, tell me, Abu Jafar, who does well thereby? Caliph Marwan?"

"Ah-hah, ah-hah," he said thoughtfully.

But I pressed on. "What did you especially seek in my country, in Sogdia? Why did you have to destroy so many of our temples and burn so many of our books? The caliphs have oftentimes repaired at their own expense the temples of prophets foreign to them. Where was that, now – by Damascus, was it not? Then why did we warrant such ill treatment?"

"Because, my dear, dear man, you resisted as none other ever has and no one knows what to do with you as you are," Barmak, sitting close by, put in venomously.

The treasurer kept his own counsel before continuing his interrogation, wanting to know how many books were in the homes and palaces of Chang'an, in what languages and on what subjects. And how many could read them.

And then he brought the conversation to a remarkable end.

"Well, then, it is probably time for you to return home and dine... We shall surely speak again, but now... Ehh, quite simply it will soon be Friday and there is something I should by now have inquired into, and must do so swiftly."

What has Friday to do with it? But no matter.

I had already been warned that the supper here would not be to my taste. And so I drank up, under Abu Jafar's approving eye, the water with naught added – *So that it need not be poured away*, I said in my mind on his behalf – and, bowing, began to rise.

The lad, who had been silent all this time, gave a loud sigh of relief. I looked at him and, to my own astonishment, I managed a slow and hard-won smile. And nothing befell me as a result; my heart, or my head, had not played me false.

"An interesting man, your Pinchpenny," I said quietly to Barmak, who was accompanying me out.

Barmak gave an affectionate smile. "Abu-d-danik? Then you've heard his pet name? Yes, if you must know, speaking with him of money, which he and I discuss constantly, is no easy matter. He's very plainly a gardener's son. On the other hand, to learn from others is a great pleasure, because the idea of already knowing everything makes one downright lonely. And from him I learn that he is a man who will disburse any amount of money in a good cause but not a danik more than is due. There is one mistake you must not make, Maniakh, which is to think that a gardener is a simple peasant. The garden is extensive enough, and no family that stands in kinship to the Prophet can ever be simple... An utterly remarkable woman once spoke a few words to me about him, to my good fortune, and she also it was who introduced us."

That "woman" made me sit up. "Who was she?" I asked.

"Arwa! Princess Arwa of the royal house of Yemen! His wife. And the mother of my ward, that pop-eyed little tyke. She married our gardener on the one amusing condition that he would have no other wives while she lived. And, do you know, he keeps his word."

I was astonished. "A princess? Married to this Abu Jafar?"

"To this very one." There was a wily sparkle in Barmak's eyes. "To Abu Jafar. Although we call him a little differently – by his childhood nickname, Mansur. Which means the Victorious."

"And over whom has he been victorious?" I inquired.

"Well, he has a frankly unpleasant way of winning every game you can imagine. So you may draw your own conclusions, Maniakh." Barmak had naught further to say.

As I rode, kicking up the dust of Merv, the shades of Chang'an followed after: a forest of black bamboo poles in canals and lakes that shone blindingly bright in sunset's silver; the bountifully expansive and stainless avenues of early morning; the august officials with thin beards, their robes falling in elliptical folds to lie over the thick soles of their curl-toed slippers; the walls of neighborhoods, fresh painted in scarlet and white, and crowned with ridged gray tiles... So far it was, so very far away.

Yet what I saw around me now, what had remained of vanquished Iran, was lovely too. Here, the sharp-tipped torches of poplars lunged, like tongues of dim flame, into the sky and through the gardens between the little houses, long galleries of dark wood capped with green grapevines ran in every direction.

Should I buy a little house in Merv, forsake it all, live here a year or two?

My chakirs, now a mere three in number – for I had added Awlad, named for a character in a Rustam tale – were sitting in a circle around a copper bowl that contained a good deal of meat in a thick, reddish-brown sauce and intently dipping hunks of bread into it. I, the weary and dust-begrimed, was quickly handed a plump, soft, downy round of the principal food in those parts and invited to join them. That was a gesture of respect, for usually I declined to share in the common repast, having eaten my fill – sometimes twice over – in town, but this time my lads of Samarkand had divined my need.

Supper was consumed in a gladsome silence, after which I took great pleasure in casting all this long day's endless conversations out of my head.

At last I could do something of note.

And so, garbed in black, sated and happy, I propped myself on a heap of cushions and began to drum a finger on my knee, measuring out the rhythm.

My brother must have another poem.

I had never in my life known Aspanak to write poetry. But this time he had, because my challenge had stuck in his craw. And how had he contrived to carry out his intent so ably?

My brother had always been set in the old ways, in literature as in other things. And there, I must own, lay his strength – which one could always, of course, seek to turn to weakness. I began trying to recall what he had said about the poets and musicians of Sogdia, which was exactly nothing, if memory served. But artists, now... He was made uneasy by the abundance of celebrated wall paintings in which the bodies of fabulous beasts, warriors, mages and dancing girls not only twisted and turned in the strangest poses possible but also grew impossibly long, as if made of sky-scudding clouds. My brother valued simple, powerful, vivid colors in painting, where an elephant resembled an elephant rather than Azhi Dakhaka, the ancient dragon of Iran, and a princess carrying a parasol was a woman, not an ifrit, a demon of fire.

And yes, he had spoken of poetry once, observing that no amount of writing would ever produce aught better than these mere two lines whose greatness lay in their astounding simplicity.

And all he said was, "Leyli, Leyli,
Leyli, Leyli," while weeping inconsolably.

Very well, but if that was so, why all this "let me drink a tear, and for that tear, 'tis you I thank"? First a long line split in half, the stresses falling first on three or four syllables and on three in the half that followed. Then a short line whose rhythm was altogether other – three unstressed syllables with two heavily stressed syllables following after. *Why so intricate, dear brother? Why so intricate? And how can I now lay you low with something utterly simple?*

Or, by contrast, with something so intricate that naught can outmatch it?

As for the meaning of this new letter of mine, that should indeed be simplicity itself: he must give me something on which to hang my search. I needed to learn the cities and villages of Khorasan where Zargisu had ever been, the names of those who had known her. A trace, a trace of any kind.

Where was it, that trace? In the oval enclosure within the fortress of Merv where a motley crowd milled? In the weightless downy dust of quiet streets that today bore only the imprint of hooves, the large, split circles that annihilated the elongated ellipses of a woman's little shoes?

Had I galloped today on Shabdiz past her tall, slim figure, her face hidden from the sun by a light shawl? Or had she ridden down those same streets a day earlier, her heavy, dull-gray armor rattling and clapped on her head a round iron helmet from which streamed locks the color of a golden dawn? *Tell me any small thing, brother. Give me the slender thread that will guide me on.*

"Bukhara now is grieved," I whispered. "And for that tear, 'tis you I thank."

Then the lines flew to me out of the darkness of night.

Awake, o my Samarkand, sleep no more, Gandhara and Merv.
Must you toil and moil forever, and weep for lack of bread? . .

Perhaps poetry was not something we make. Perhaps it existed before ever this world began and even then was moving over the waters and the dry land of chaos, amid the insubstantial towers and fortress walls of the clouds. Perhaps a poet is no more than one who can hear the music of those words in heaven's ether, can seize the lines that have hovered long above an earth drenched in blood and grime, waiting and waiting there for us.

But what was I to do with those words that had flown to me out of nowhere? Why would I awaken cities already asleep at that hour of the night, not to mention that they had bread aplenty, in both peace and war?

I shook my head and began to jot disjointed words onto a scrap of papyrus.

Show me, let me find a trace
Of a lovely woman... an incorporeal trace on earth,
To seek in cities, on sleepless streets
The scent of warm skin, a forgotten scent... the unheard sound of a voice
The trader who sold her an apricot... whose hue was like to radiant hair...

And then I remembered that I knew neither the scent of Zargisu today, now a grown woman, nor of her youthful self. I simply had never been that near to her. What strangeness had befallen me, what hunt was this for a woman whose naked skin had never come so close, had never clung so fast as to become one with mine, if not forever then at least for an instant?

Whom or what what was I seeking, in very truth – and why?

"On sleepless streets," I whispered soundlessly, and all became simplicity itself.

The traces of her feet I seek in sleepless cities' dust.
In lilac smoke of evening, I scent a fragrance fleeting
Through lane and alley, garden court and grove.

Oh tell me where she be, thou wind, with flutelike cadence greeting,
Amid proud poplars, soaring towers, their summits skyward thrust,
And bearing still the fume of fire and clay-clad stove.

Who gave to her an apricot, so luscious in the eating,
The color of her hair, dressed metal's hue repeating?
Who served her steaming pilaf scented with the clove?

Who gave her refuge even once from fiend and stormy gust,
Safe haven in the vines and quince, and screened from all mistrust
Where birds of turquoise dreams their measures wove?

Say e'en a word to me, each name shall be my sweeting,
Sweet too the names of roads on which,
    'mid heaven's hot shafts retreating,
A trace of her remains this day in sleepless cities' dust.

"There you have it, my dear man," said I, laying down my brush.

And it seemed that Zargisu glanced over my shoulder, read the still damp lines, and gave an uncertain smile.

11

MANSUR'S TEAR

Morning is no time for poetry. Morning is the time when visitors come for the sole purpose of causing vexation. And so I was unpleasantly taken aback by the sight of Yukuk at the foot of my stairs the following morning. It had somehow never occurred to me that a new, a wholly new, life would begin so soon.

"An excellent house," Yukuk said, having dropped a swift bow. "There's only one way up to you. Sentries on three watches by night, and you may sleep peacefully... You said you have consent to keep ten chakirs?"

"Aside from you, Yukuk, nine. Ashofteh allows me to remove two from the hospital perhaps tomorrow. They're willing. Evman and Kevan, the first once a scrivener now an infantryman, and the second... but now I think of it, Kevan has owned himself no great swordsman. So I'm left to seek five more. I could choose so many from among my patients in a week."

"You shall therefore be guarded by men whom you have healed, and with your own hands," Yukuk said, spelling it out for me, and his face showed that he was well pleased by the idea.

"With your leave, I shall begin my work with them tomorrow," he said crisply, eyeing with no evident pleasure my chakirs, who were squatting on their heels in the shade. "I shall bring strong staves – not the worst weapon for a beginning... Now, again with your leave, I'll spend some time at the hospital. I'm known there."

I allowed myself an unsavory smile and was instantly ashamed, while Yukuk's cheek did not even twitch.

"A hospital is a very good place," he went on impassively, "since it always contains an abundance of wounded men. Soldiers, that is. With naught to do but speak of this and that. You talk with one, with another, and learn much of interest. What I would tell you is" – and here he looked me hard in the face – "that I have heard somewhat of that woman of late. At the hospital among other places. And it all resolves in this wise. She appears on horseback. Sometimes her face is covered, at other times no. She is never alone. She travels with a group, always the same. Some five they are, and all men. Armed. One has a very long nose and is a skilled archer. This band is, belike, of no army. It stands apart somehow. Then come tales of every kind. You know what they are. That this company often arrives on the battlefield, and then... all that about the wounded. The wounded men. Some patients dream of that woman appearing to them as they lie dying in their next battle, and mounting them. Her name is supposedly Gisu, but there's also a byname, the Consoler. Now all I must do is have some long, long talks with the wounded, to know what particulars, what trifles they have to tell. And compare. And find those who have truly seen her, not only heard of her from others. Learn where and when. It will be long in the doing but... so it is."

"In two weeks I'll have something from Samarkand," I told him.

"Most timely," he nodded and, with another ill-natured glance at Nanivandak, Makhian and Awlad, my three idlers, he left.

My next vexation of the morning was, of course, Barmak. His ability to find good eating houses was estimable, to be sure, but at table this time his talk was of something beyond my ken, for he must speak of weaponry. He wished to know how I proposed to arm my little guard.

"Set it not at naught, dear young friend of mine," he said. "Because very serious events draw nigh, and to puzzle your way through them..."

At which point he disgorged upon my head a torrent of names, mostly Abu this, Ali that, al-I-knew-not-what, and the like.

The burden of it all was that the House of Abbas would soon be moving of a piece from one place to another, whose names, I understood, were not for me to know – nor did I wish to. That the House contained several of an older generation and several of a younger, those latter being the Mansur I had already met and his brothers.

And that the rebels against the Caliphate were far from exhausted after count was taken of the descendents of Abbas, cousin to the Prophet, for there was also the Prophet's son-in-law Ali and his posterity. And between those two rebellious clans "all was complicated, most complicated."

But the chaos seemingly extended far beyond the rebel ranks, for Caliph Marwan, as I was now told, stood at odds with his own capital, Damascus, which was therefore no longer his capital save in name only. Marwan had betaken himself to the city of Haran, in Jazira, "a strange place for the sovereign lord of the faithful to inhabit, where no one knows what the local people believe, who is their God and who their prophets." And that had transpired because Marwan, styled the Donkey, had been too long governor of the North, of the mountains and valleys between the two seas of Gorgan and Buntus, where live people of a haughty and sly demeanor, known by the set of their noses and the oily gleam in their eyes. From these erstwhile wards of his, Marwan had mustered what was for all purposes a new army and not a bad one, either.

From all of which I understood very little, other than that the Caliph's empire was in vast disorder and that Zargisu must be brought away from here, come what may.

"You do understand," Barmak continued, pushing toward me a metal platter that held the year's first cherries, which had barely appeared in the markets, "that when matters hang thus, they cannot remain so long. One will perforce attack another. Either the Caliph will at last begin a great war with Abu Muslim, or the reverse. And those mysterious murderers simply complicate the case beyond measure. And is there aught new with you?" This sudden turn was unexpected.

"Somewhat," I said, all business but with a mind full of malice. "In two weeks, Samarkand will send answers to certain of my questions. I know there's some connection between those murderers and a certain woman who has been the butt of some unpleasant legends. I'm on her trail" – at which my mind was filled again, this time with admiration of my own effrontery – "and there's much said of her among the wounded at the hospital. But I'm far from knowing who of them has something to tell and who is but prating on. And if that Abu Muslim of yours ever summons me to come and talk, I'll ask him outright what he knows of that woman and those murderers, and we shall see how he replies."

Barmak flung himself back into the cushions and looked long at me with eyes that betrayed an entirely childlike joy. Then he composed his lips into that smile, the smile of a camel's calf, and spoke.

"Ask him only of the woman," he said, and that pleased me, of course, because the murderers seemed less important now. "Tell him that this is very personal to you. Because to speak to him directly about the murderers... after the events you know of, which transpired in this very fortress enclosure, under his very nose... could be deemed indiscreet. He is, as you surely know, very sensitive."

And Barmak ended our meal in a manner that, once again, contrived to annoy me to the limits of forbearance.

"My dear Maniakh, I want to apologize again for having distracted you with that conversation with Abu Jafar, he being Mansur, he being... Well, but you know all his names. But there was much profit for you in making his acquaintance, as you will know in time. And he is most beholden to you for speaking with him. So beholden that he now invites you to hear him preach. Now, I know that you, unlike your brother, have no great love for the Prophet's temples but you yourself have declared unimportant the temple in which a man speaks with the God Who is the same for us all, wherever in the world we be. So, then, come to this city's chief masjid before tomorrow's sunset. It will be Friday, a day of great importance. You will sit a while, listen a while, take your ease... And besides, you know, while you live here, in the fortress, your appearance in that temple is simply a matter of good manners. It will be well received. Everyone knows that I am an inveterate and incorrigible worshipper of wholly other prophets, but even I will be there..."

A feeling had arisen and was growing ever stronger in me that the work do be done, compounded by various other accessory affairs, was increasing apace. And that a great variety of people was quite simply compelling me to perform that work, and that I had but a poor understanding of why I should yield to them.

And especially of why I should attend a foreign – a very foreign – temple, to give my ear to this Abu Jafar. For all that "Mansur," one of the names he went by, betokened him Victorious.

THE MANNER WITH WHICH MANSUR mounted the wooden dais set in the middle of the quietly humming hall was in no way stately. Indeed, at first it even seemed that he had merely chanced to set foot on the first step and was now looking about, wondering how he had happened there and how to come down. And although, according to custom, he had slapped his hand against that dais thrice – first when he approached it, again when he began his ascent, and a third time when at last he loomed over the rows of worshippers seated on their prayer rugs – the congregation, while favoring him with a kindly glance, continued to mutter one to another until he intoned, in his nasal way, the inescapable "Bismillah." And even then, dozens of voices still hummed quietly in the spacious, shadowy hall where rare dust motes swirled in the golden rays.

" 'Read,' he said!" Mansur cried, in a sudden, shrill voice.

An astonished whisper passed along the rows then, and silence reigned. Most had evidently just grasped that this gaunt and ungainly fellow was up there on the dais for some good reason. Even so, this was a most peculiar beginning for a homily. But what followed was stranger still.

There was a pause, and then, abruptly, "But read what?" The matter-of-fact question hung in the hushed room. And, with an awkward wave of the hand, he continued on, speaking fast and with scarcely a break between sentences.

"Yes, that was how it all began. And yet how splendidly it all began! A glowing angel, bringing to us, bringing to this earth of ours, immersed in ignorance, the simple word – Read! And it was not only the Prophet, peace be upon his name, to whom he spoke that word. For what of us? We, the unfortunate ones. We, still unable to comprehend which word of our Lord he had brought down from the heavens. Well, but it is no great wonder. It is 'read' in the sense of 'tell your tale, speak!' And the Prophet, peace be upon him, did so, bringing to men the wisdom of that heavenly word. But there is also 'read' in the plain sense of reading! And that is said now no longer to the Prophet. It is said to us. How many books there are in our world! A hundred thousand... hear me, a hundred thousand in the library of the Emperor of the Celestial Kingdom alone! And we? Where are our books about distant lands? Where are our books about the healing art? Where are our books about the sages of old? Other peoples have them in abundance. But we, the faithful, also need those books!"

In the eyes of those who sat on the rugs, especially the Iranians, appeared an unfeigned interest. This was not at all the kind of talk they were wont to hear within these walls.

"The Prophet, peace be upon him..." Mansur continued, louder now, then hesitated, shook his head, and ended in quiet and somehow confiding tones.

"For Muhammad, blessed be his name, was the nephew of my great-great-grandsire."

The silence in the prayer hall was now the silence of the dead. Everyone had heard that people from some House of Abbas had come to Merv, but few had caught so much as a glimpse of them. And only now were many beginning to understand exactly which Abbas that was.

"In our home, in the house of my father and grandsire, we would often sit of an evening remembering that man and the days when yet he lived, when it was possible to stroke his warm beard or to give him a ripe fig with a scrap of bread. What manner of man was he? Well, he resembled me not at all."

Quiet chuckles ran around the corners of the room.

"Not tall but very robust, with a powerful chest and a thick beard. Strong. But the point in chief is that he was a kind man, so he was. And merry, which was sorely needed when times were hard. 'Is there aught to eat in the house?' he would ask when unhappy souls gone all astray, lost in a benighted age and without the strength to leave it, forbade the selling of even a crust of bread to the Prophet's ummah, to his people. 'Aught to eat?' he would ask again. And, on hearing no answer, he would smile. 'Then today we fast!' he would say. No subtle jest it was, but somehow it made things easier to bear."

Mansur paused again, dropping chin to chest.

"But he is now gone from us!" The strident voice shocked the air. "Yet we are here! And we have no one to ask what to do, how to escape the wasteland of our grief and woes, of our foolishness and doltish ways. For see, now – already one hundred and seventeen years have passed since the Prophet quit this world, but what have we done with the legacy he left us? What?"

I could not tear my eyes from him. Never before had I encountered a man able to speak as he did. And he, meanwhile, was casting his wrathful words into the faces raised toward him.

"Three caliphs, and every one a righteous man, died by murderous hands. And then came these, of the Umayyad clan. Soon they will have ruled us for a hundred years. Half the world is in their hands, from the Western sea, where the land ends, to the snowy mountains beyond which rules the Emperor of the land of the Chin. All is yours. Then why not live in peace and righteousness? Yet... are you happy, my brethren of Merv? Is your life good and is it righteous?"

Sitting there in my corner, I almost laughed aloud. The earlier enchantment had passed, nor could it have lasted long. I knew very well what would come next: having shaken up the assembled company right well, that gaunt, gangling bookkeeper with the sparse and unkempt beard would now begin to enumerate all that had gone awry in the Caliph's unhappy empire

And in that, I did not err.

"Yes, Caliph Muawiya created an invincible army and fleet," Mansur said, confiding to his congregation truths they already knew. "Yes, the new mosques, schools and hospitals were spacious, and there were other hospitals for those whose illnesses returned time and again, never really departing from them. But what is this, o my brethren? Here Medina, city of the Prophet, was burned and pillaged under Caliph Yazid, ere the body of the Prophet himself had crumbled to dust. And then they turned to Mecca, where a madman proclaimed himself caliph. Two months the city lay under siege, the mosque of the Ka'aba burned to the ground, and to this day the sacred stone is streaked with black soot from that blaze."

He halted and drew a heavy breath.

"Remember also Karbala!" His voice swelled again. "The crowd shuddered with horror on the day when the bloody head of the Prophet's grandson was cast at the feet of Ubaydullah, and the hardest of hearts melted. Remember Hussein!"

The silence lingered, while I held back a sardonic grin, recalling – and none too soon – my talk with Barmak on the previous day. There could have been no avoiding mention of the hard-fought battle at Karbala in a sermon delivered in this rebellious city, although the House of Abbas would, like as not, long hold back from speaking against the House of Ali, since none yet knew in which family the Prophet's blood ran thickest. And that raised an interesting question. How did our household, mine and my brother's, regard the House of Ali? Surely we had not staked so much on the House of Abbas that no other stakes had been made?

"These are the matters of bygone days, you will say," Mansur interrupted himself, evidently sensing that he must now put on different airs. "But our days too are fearsome indeed, and full of sorrow. Bitter is our laughter; salty are our tears. In whose hands lie the Prophet's mantle, staff and ring? Why, in those hands, in the hands of the erstwhile Caliph who is called the Donkey."

The *erstwhile* Caliph? Strong words, especially since that "erstwhile" ruler still led the most powerful army this side of the Mountains of Heaven. On their other side, the Emperor of the House of Tang commanded an army just short of a million strong, but that was very far away. And in his Haran alone, the Caliph, as I had heard tell, had to hand some two hundred thousand, and if he were in addition to reconcile with the army in Damascus... But most importantly, the Emperor was far, far distant, while from Haran to Merv was less than two weeks' journey.

But Mansur had attained what he had sought. His congregation was livelier now, laughing at his impudence, shaking itself alert.

"How many Caliphs have there been in the world these past five years?" Mansur asked with a derisive snort. "Count with me. Caliph Yazid died having spent not even half a year in the Green Palace, and then there was a rebellion in Homs, which had found its own Caliph, he being Hakam, son of Walid who would jump into a pool filled with wine and drink of it so much that the level of wine in the pool could be seen to fall. That is one Caliph. And his army moved on Damascus. And was broken there. Meanwhile, in Palestine at that same time, Yazid ibn Sulayman was proclaimed Caliph. That would already be two. But then also Marwan – the very same, our Marwan – determines the time fair for rebellion. And moves on Damascus. Yet before you know it, he has recognized Yazid as the overlord of Palestine. But God, Who sees all, promptly gathers Yazid to Himself. And so we have a new Caliph, Ibrahim. And yet another is declared in Homs. How many now? Three? Just try to untangle it. Well, that is more than our Donkey can bear. He says he will raise to power Hakam, son of Walid the Drunkard. In sum, Marwan vanquishes all others, and what then? He simply executes all the sons of Walid, that being Hakam and all the rest. And enters Damascus and says 'Now I shall rule.' Is our Donkey bad or good?" Thus Mansur called on his congregation but answered himself forthwith.

"No, he is in no way bad. He is a skillful warrior. Except that he knows not how to count money; his treasury is empty. But see now how all this ends. Here is mutinous Homs. Marwan marches there and crushes the rebels underfoot, like snakes. And Damascus again rebels. Its inhabitants have found themselves another Caliph, though they remain ever unquiet. And Palestine too rebels. But Marwan quiets them all with his weapons of iron. Then Sulayman, his cousin, mutinies. Marwan was victorious there also, and his cousin fled to Homs. Marwan goes to Homs – Homs again! He is victorious. But there he learns that things go ill in Iraq, where Said ibn Bahdal has raised a revolt. And the Kharijites are mutinying there too. So Marwan comes to Iraq from the fresh-routed Homs, and there himself routs all and sundry. Then he goes to thrash the Kharijites. He is victorious. But the Kharijites have a new general, one Shaiban. Marwan now moves against him. For a year, he belabors him, and does so well. Then a certain Abu Hamza captures Holy Medina and holds it for three whole months. And now Marwan frees first Medina, then Mecca. At which time war begins here, in Khorasan and also against the Berbers. And al-Andalus is restless too..."

I sat in my corner, quietly biting my lips. What Mansur had said here signified, in short, that Marwan had quite simply won victory after victory and none could outmaster him. And that even the fiery Abu Muslim had best think well on that. But this perturbed our orator not one whit.

"Does one hundred years not suffice? This is no kingdom of eternal tranquility. It is a kingdom of eternal chaos, where every day one of the faithful comes athwart another. And still the horror never ends, never ends! What was the wish of the Prophet, blessed be his name? Was this what he wished? That the blood of his children, his grandchildren and great-grandchildren should be endlessly spilled?"

Mansur took a breath. The audience sat in attentive silence.

"What are we now to do?" And he flung his arms asunder, revealing a patch inexpertly sewn under one of them. "Here sits a son of Iran, a well-respected artisan of Merv. His brother was a soldier of the Caliph but perished when, alongside others who mutinied against injustice, he ushered our city into a new age. Shall we return to this man his brother?"

People began to glance around, seeking out the injured party, but Mansur thundered on.

"And here sits a trader from Samarkand, and such a one... from a famed trading house. He is here, he is with us, he is our brother. But as a youth he too sallied out, sword in hand, with an army commanded by the sovereign lord of the faithful, and was victorious, and himself came away alive and without a scratch on him, while at that same time a detachment of the Caliph's troops was waylaying a caravan in which rode his wife and two children, a boy and a girl, and many more peaceable, unarmed people, and for no known reason killed them all."

I wanted to raise my hands and cover my face, to leap to my feet and flee that place, but neither hands nor feet obeyed. I was at the bottom of a deep river, but that screeching voice still carried through the oozing green water.

"Know you that since that time all that trader's intimates fear even to utter the word 'children' in his presence?"

A pause then – a long, booming pause.

"Know you that all the women of his city dare not even dream that he will take them to wife, while to this day he takes none? And what are we now to do, to ease his grief? Can that grief be wiped away by my tear, the tear of one who is kin to the Prophet?"

Dazed now, I saw naught but Mansur's long, dark face and the two trails of tears that streamed down to his sparse beard of orange hue, passed through it and dripped from it.

"What, then, shall we do now?" came the quiet question from the pulpit. He was no longer looking in my direction. And then even more quietly, in a near-whisper that could yet be heard in all corners of the masjid: "We shall build a city. We shall build the best city on this earth."

The astonished silence lingered, and I suddenly felt able to breathe again.

"Hearken, oh, hearken, my brethren of Merv!" Mansur cried, again in a sudden, shrill voice that resounded beneath the dome. "There must be a place somewhere on this earth where a true believer may see men living in tranquility and righteousness. May see and may try to make a city of his own at least remotely like to it. Somewhere there must be a repository of peace and tranquility, and with those words we shall name our city. No, we shall not return to life the guiltless who have perished. But our city shall be our atonement, an atonement of our forebears' guilt for the souls sent flying heavenward to no good purpose.

"And how shall it be?" came the quiet question. "I see it as well as if I stood now by its mighty walls. It will be round, because the best cities I have seen, the cities of Iran, are all round. Because Gor is round. Because the lovely city on the Tigris that is no more – your capital, my brethren – was round. Because none can make cities as lovely as yours, o ye people of Iran."

From that moment on, I knew, the Iranians would be wholly and forever his. And I, sitting among them, scarce craned my neck to watch the last tear hang from the tip of his beard. And I did see it, and heaved sigh after sigh.

"At its center will be a temple of the true faith and a green-domed palace," he went on. "Four gates will lead to the other cities of our world, and from the north-eastern gates, the road to illustrious Merv will make its start. On the river's smooth back, vessels from all the world will be carried to our city. There will be markets and temples, bath-houses and shops for the traders of books in which wisdom is found. There will be golden gates faced with marble. There will be housed there people of all tribes and nations, who shall revere whatever prophet they wish. And between them there will be neither enmity nor rancor. Because, as our Holy Book says, 'O mankind! We created you from a single pair of a male and a female, And made you into nations and tribes, that ye may know each other, not that ye may despise each other.'

"And by building our city, we will inaugurate an era of righteousness.

"It shall know no end.

"And that city, a city we shall share in common, will stand forever."

The bookkeeper of the House of Abbas then made an awkward turn, extended a bare, sandal-clad foot, from beneath his roomy garments, and began carefully to descend from the dais.

Again an astonished silence, and again it lingered. Not until all had thoroughly understood that the lovely tale was ended did the faithful of the city of Merv, giving voice to their wonderment, talking among themselves and all smiles, begin to disperse from the dark of the masjid into the sweltering heat of a summer day.

And still I could not rise to my feet.

Feeling nothing, nothing whatsoever, I stared at an empty cavity with tapered top carved into the bare wall, which looked toward the Prophet's distant city and through which God observed me, unseen.

12

THE SHADES OF ELEPHANTS

From that time on, my life began to transform into a string of scenes, fragments, and episodes that flickered by faster and faster. There even came a time when I began to think that I was dreaming of running in place, that my feet were mired in clay, while everyone around me already knew that something untoward was happening to me, but I still did not.

So it was that ever after I remembered those few weeks, all the way to the unexpected outcome – as a succession of scenes hewn into pieces.

HERE YUKUK HAD LINED UP my lazy chakirs – who were seven in number now, Vanaspar and Muhammad having joined them – by the staircase leading up to my abode on the second story. And, leaning on a long, knotty stave, he treated them to a brief speech, in this wise:

"Listen, now, and listen well! Life shall from now on be a serious matter. We shall address our lord as serdar, chief. Or, to be short, as ser. I shall divide you into relays. One will guard our lord. The others, when not sleeping after a night watch, will study the art of combat with me. With such a stave as this, a man can do more to a fully armed warrior than can the unlearned wielding a sword. Horsemanship, now. The mounted formation. You all have something to ride? Excellent.

Finally, disobedience to an order is punished by expulsion from the chakirs. If the serdar so decides."

At which, Yukuk fell silent and stood stock-still, straight as the stave on which he leaned, and with his chin, adorned by grayish stubble, cocked.

The rest were silent too.

I raised my eyes, to see them all looking at me. And waiting.

This began to anger me, for I do not like being forced to do anything before I am ready.

"I cured you and will cure you again if need be," I said at last, and knew when I said it that this was not the best way to begin. "But that is a separate matter. Because a healer does not heal in order to have something back from his patients..."

I faltered them, bent my head and glared at the toes of my boots, hating every instant of this.

"The money you receive from me is naught but money, because people must eat," I went on, feeling that I was still raving incoherently. But the chakirs were interested in earnest now, for why else did they serve me?

"Now to the heart of it. To each of you I once said 'I want you to live.' I can say the same thing today. And I can add that I need you to serve me because I myself want to live and to return home. To Samarkand. With you. But first that for which I came here must be done. It may be dangerous. And after that, homeward. Where we will all find employment, and where life will be what it should be. This I promise you, and you all know who I am and what my word is worth. But to carry it off, we must hold together and keep our heads. You were all soldiers, and of which army is naught to me. You should know better than I what that means."

Thus it was, in less than grand style, that I ended the first speech I ever delivered to warriors in their ranks – and that had, let me say again, afforded me no pleasure whatsoever – after which I looked them over, with anger still in my eyes.

But my speech, and, for that matter, my stern countenance, seemed to please them well.

IN THE NEXT EPISODE, YUKUK was reporting on the results of his long and patient conversations at the hospital.

"Ser, much of interest is transpiring there. You are healing one Omar of Sogdia. He and Mihraman, a friend of his, conduct themselves most strangely, for all that you wish to take them as chakirs. There must be some unriddling here. In short, other people are speaking with them also. They come as I do, and the conversations begin forthwith. To my understanding, they speak of God, of how to vanquish death. Of the demon and the angel that stand to the right and left of them. And so forth. When your two future chakirs make mention of it, their eyes grow strange. As if they dream. In sum, I do not like it. Because the people who are to be made into murderers must be found somewhere. So why not in the hospital, where the misfortunate lie side by side with death, at leisure to reconsider many things? But against whom are those two being turned – what if it's against you? Oh yes, and about the woman there's much talk, even too much, but all retelling what I have already heard from others. And what I already know. My work continues."

THEN THERE WAS THE TALE of the armor.

"Divine, my dear Maniakh, what gift I've brought you," was Barmak's greeting when I came to him to make my regular, and for him disappointingly brief, report. "Let me help you guess: Where does the fame of my kingdom of Balkh lie?"

"In camels, of course," I responded without much thought. "And that's a very simple riddle, because of the crush today in your courtyard and outside your gates too. Why such a press of camels? There's no breathing because of them."

"Yes, yes, we are famed for camels above all," he smiled. "But what else? Something as famous as the camels? So you can't remember, and there's no need, because here it is."

And he led me to the nearest two-humped mountain, which was smiling repulsively and mumbling its thick lips.

Two taciturn and well-knit bodyguards panted as they began to relieve the animal's tufted, dun-colored side of an improbably heavy pack. They then unrolled it, and I saw at my feet a lake of metal, its surface rippling with fishlike scales. Next to emerge from the pack were long, scarce-crooked objects like curved sticks.

"Armor, of course," I said. "The chain mail of Balkh. Renowned throughout the world. And swords too..."

And I knew what was happening.

"A gift? Barmak, you're determined to present me with real Balkh chain mail?"

He spread his hands. "You and your chakirs both. And swords, assuredly. And another pair of weighty gifts for each of you. Helmets of all kinds, you know... Because, you understand, how could I leave Balkh's praises unsung? Take it. It's all yours."

And he waved an arm to show the caravan that was spilling out of the yard.

What was this? Before me was a mountain of iron, the dream of any warrior. And costing, when I thought of it, far more than the sum Barmak had given me after our first evening together.

"Barmak, I don't understand... I can have only ten chakirs, and I can't yet enlist the last two I've found. But this is a whole caravan."

"Yes, well, I had a small unpleasantness," he replied despondently, while his white beard raised up and wagged sprightly from side to side. "I knew they were to be ten, with you to make the eleventh. But you have studied the Indian science of numbers? The one where ten of a thing is written with a single digit and one of those empty little circles that signifies naught?"

"Naturally I've taken an interest in it. And many in our trading house can already work with it," I replied, bewildered now and trying all the while to escape the heat by sheltering beneath a tree.

"Yes, yes. But I'm evidently too old for such scholarship, for all that I teach it to that very young person of your acquaintance. Imagine: I was deep in thought, I was distracted, and then came the mishap. I wrote that naught one too many times, but instead of signifying twice naught, it multiplied all by ten. And here is the woeful result..." He waved a plump palm in the general direction of the camel herd that groaned under its burden. "But no matter, my dear man. I'll send to you now as much as is needful, and the rest will remain here, in some cool and hidden place within this sizable house of ours. There's plenty of room for it. It will, come what may, be yours when you have need of it, and right quickly too. Because we can't send our famed camels back bearing such a burden!"

And, with another despondent smile and shaking his hoary beard, he set off into the depths of the courtyard to give his orders.

I could have taken to musing on what was transpiring here.

But all I could think of was how much I hated the gray that gleamed there in the sun – the color of the desert viper it was, the color of war and senseless death.

Yet for Yukuk it was the color of joy. Unrolling the chain mail without the slightest effort, weighing the swords one after another in his hand, he gathered the seven chakirs into a circle, and the captivating conversations began, of the steel from Bhilamalla, known in the Celestial Empire as Pilo-mo-lo, which lies to the south of Kashmir and where a finely forged sword is made that can cost up to fifty dinars, of the hanafi swords that drag along the ground even if the hilt is worn above the left shoulder, of whether or not the large Iranian bow can hit a target at five hundred paces, and of other useful and interesting matters.

I kept my distance.

NEXT CAME THE LETTER FROM my brother.

Once it was read, I should have known joy beyond measure. I should have whispered to the empty room, "You've buckled under, Aspanak." But instead I feverishly scanned the short, arid lines written by a poet admitting his defeat and tried to understand what his words could mean.

A gloomy garden that all men abhor
Where tracks are lost behind the dusty door
Go seek, to have its truth to you revealed.

Unhappy Safizanj, whose howling sore
Spreads o'er the dead, cold earth for evermore,
Find there they who recall, and leave no mouth unsealed.

Two names that now in silvery accents pour
For those that transcend death and peace implore,
Through these at last their sorrows shall be healed.

That "howling sore" would not have been bad, had it not been so mournful. But the "go seek" would to my mind have spoiled any verse, although a simple "seek now" would have been another matter altogether.

Yet how to understand it?

"Ah, he's ciphered it in verse," Yukuk nodded, with a manifest lack of interest in the poetry of it. "Good... Well, this is already something. Unhappy Safizanj, so much is plain. No, ser, this is not about Abu Muslim mustering his first army in that village, for there was no howling sore at that time. Safizanj grew unhappy later, when battle was joined there – later, when the outright slaughter of like by like began... And there are two hills there. It is a dead, cold place indeed, and well bathed in blood. And the verse, belike, hints that this will be no easy tale to untangle. Now, the garden. Except it seems that he who wrote you this doesn't know where the garden lies. He's only heard of it and he advises us to seek it out. But the image is clear. This is a garden of ill repute and feared by those who live nearby. That's already something, because are there not ten such gardens here? The door's a mystery, though. Tracks disappear behind it, and what of that? Say, then, that our men came to this door, but once the door was breached, there was the end of it. Maybe they never returned. Yet I remember no hint of any such thing when the work here was going as it ought. Then there is the designation 'those that transcend death.' For them, that garden and that dead, cold ground are the comfort before the end. A mystery, this. But do you remember my conversations in the hospital? The very same designation I heard there: those that transcend death. And we even saw them, you and I – the ones with the knives. And what befell them in their last moment. That, then, is what they call 'transcending death.' Excellent. I have here something to work with."

And I, strange to say, understood more than Yukuk. because the word "pairidaeza," which means "garden," still rang in my ears. My brother had told me naught new there save that the garden existed and that all abhorred it. Aspanak was only advising me to seek it out. But Safizanj... That, now, was something new indeed.

The twilight was creeping into Merv along shadowy streets, rousing night-blooming flowers behind garden walls. This was the very time to write my brother a reply, showing all the mercy I could to the vanquished. But instead I delayed in sad reflection. *What world do you live in, brother?* I asked him in my mind. *In a world of gloomy gardens, in fields of bygone carnage and murders, in a world of unfortunates who think that by dying they will defraud death? It's no wonder, then, that you're being worsted in this contest between poets.*

Then Yukuk broke into my reflections.

"As for the garden, I shall have to journey a while and look at a place not far from the city. It's on the highroad to Rayy. I once heard that people have shunned it for many years, that the garden there is overgrown and is of ill repute... Because a beginning has to be made. Then, to Safizanj. All in all, there's traveling to be done."

"I'll go with you," I said, to my own surprise.

With a slight tilt of his stubborn chin, Yukuk made a magnificent pause then, such as could only be wrought by a veteran commander who hears his chief proposing to perpetrate a folly but who as a military man is constrained to obey. And he ended that chill pause ever the man-at-arms, irreproachably respectful, but with his voice pitched lower than usual. And all he said was, "Yes, ser."

AND, A DAY AFTER THAT conversation, the bustle, the clatter of hooves, the flapping of fabric, many-hued but still for the most part black, the dry smell of dusty ground stirred up by all the horses. An event of great note it was, this hunt on the outskirts of Merv. Intent, fretted, his face as swarthy as any of his race, and with a beard freshly dyed red, Ziyad ibn Saleh was lecturing me in deplorable Iranian, by which he meant to say: "The sovereign lord of Merv may summon you for conversation. Probably after the hunt. Or he may not. But doubt not that he has long wished to speak with you. So, do you intend on taking game today?"

I showed him my empty hands.

Ziyad sighed in relief. "That is excellent," he said. "All the less trouble. Then just gallop, with many others or alone. You may flush the game for others and for the sovereign lord. The first deer is his. Then whoever wills may kill, all is yours."

I was intrigued. "The first deer's his? What is that – a hunting ritual of the Shahanshah?"

"Come now, Maniakh! Although all is gradually tending that way. But explain to me, rather, what you hunt in Samarkand. The tales I hear of your city are wondrous... I swear to God, could I be there even once..."

But then Abu Muslim in all his glory laid eyes on Ziyad from afar and called out to him something in the way of "Who conspires there?" – and my red-bearded companion's face turned grayish as he betook himself in great haste to where the mount of the Leopard of Merv was impatiently prancing.

Meanwhile, one of the Iranian princes had come up and was peering into my face with an amiable smile.

"The head of the House of Maniakh, as I have heard? Here?"

"But there are descendents of ancient families here too, and may the head of the House of Maniakh not hunt alongside them?" I replied, giving unfeigned pleasure to this hook-nosed man who was manifestly ill at ease in so strange a cavalcade. "I'd rather you told me his true name and who he is by birth," I told him them, my eyes following the general as he galloped away, his curls streaming behind him like a banner. "Is he Iranian, at least?"

"No one knows," the prince replied. "He was supposedly born in Isfahan. But of which race... He was certainly once a slave. And with slaves, as you must know, such matters can be hard to determine. His age may be twenty or it may be twenty-two. And his real name's another mystery. He can't read. But then again, what's that to you or I?"

We stood almost side by side, observing Abu Muslim thoughtfully, as if he were a stallion presented to us for sale.

"I too find it hard at times to know who is who or who hails from which people – at home in Samarkand also, although we've been suffering this indignity there for less than forty years. And so, my esteemed neighbor, do you think that Iran will rise again and be as she was before the conquest? Although a hundred years have passed?"

At this the prince drew himself up, glanced at me from his slight vantage of height, and said crisply: "Even after two hundred. We shall regain all."

I was readying myself for the compulsory rant about lizard-eating Arabs and about they who had taught the conquerors to supplement their diet of lizards with rice and to wear trousers, but, happily, the moment passed, and instead, to temper his recent words, my worthy companion invited me to visit at my leisure his castle, which lay a day's travel away. And I likewise invited him – to my home in Samarkand.

The hunters had begun to arrange themselves by rank. I had noticed, though, that the array contained rather too many people with excessively serious, almost surly, faces, and that they were all keeping their distance from the general.

Yet it was not only the people that held themselves aloof. The horses too were shying away from Abu Muslim's steed, a silvery Damascene of supernatural beauty. They shook their heads, jibbed, and champed on their bits. And even my own Iranian mount came near to rearing, and balked at going any closer.

The reasons for these oddities were very soon made plain, when the long trumpets gave a raucous blare and the hunt began all of itself.

Our young man's horse sped along the arid ground alone, throwing up rock-hard clods of earth that fell back with a dry rustling. The beaters clustered about the bushes, waving their flags, while the rest of us stayed no less than ten horse-lengths back.

That tactic soon served its expected purpose by flushing the first deer – a fallow deer it was – from cover. But then another arrow, the color of the sandy earth, flew out from beneath low-hanging branches to the right. Certain of the hunters, princes of Iran and proficient hunters all, should have known what to do at such a pass, should have spread out in a chain to keep the quarry confined The general could then have chased alone after the game to his heart's content, as it flew forward in broad twists and turns, its antlered head bent despairingly low all the while.

Shaking my own head, I followed close behind the leader of our hunt, until, with a short cry and a smooth tug on the bridle, I sent my swift Shabdiz slightly leftward, for I had seen that we three – the deer, Abu Muslim and I – were racing directly toward a fold in the ground that resembled the bank of a tiny river.

The deer could of course have scrambled slantwise up that slope and escaped us forever, but its speed told against it. And when it began to discern the pounding of my Shabdiz's hooves to its left, it did the only thing it still could, which was to swing sharp to the right and tear along the earthen crest that blocked its way.

But the sovereign lord of Khorasan had already sent his fleet gray beauty to intercept it at a speed that matched its own, for he had guessed the meaning of my maneuver. The young man was, I saw, holding neither bow nor spear but was instead bending over a long, soft object that resembled a rolled rug and had lain all this time across his saddle.

A falcon? I thought. *But why keep it swaddled?*

And the reward for my curiosity was a unique sight of which I had heretofore heard only legends.

At first I thought that a full-bodied, spotted snake, mottled gray in hue, was sliding down from Abu Muslim's saddle. But snakes never fly and this creature, having scarcely touched the ground, was indeed flying, its long, high-stepping paws barely grazing the earth. A few bounding strides carried the smooth, spotted back over wispy grass and thorny brush, and the unhappy deer was checked, knocked off its feet, and tumbled onto the cracked ground. And with a growl, the huge, long-legged cat plunged fangs into its flesh.

And there we have it. They call Abu Muslim the Leopard of Merv, I thought as I trotted closer, steadying my restive horse. *And now we know why. Except that what he carries on his saddle is no leopard but some other cat. Leopards sit quietly atop a cliff and pounce on their prey from above. They don't run over level ground. But this is a... what to call this rare creature? Well, no matter, but a horse that can be trained to tolerate a ravening beast lying across its unprotected withers – that, now, is a wonder indeed.*

The young Abu Muslim sprang from the saddle, vanished for a moment into the dust, and then reappeared, his white teeth sparkling and his happy face raised toward us as we milled at a respectable distance on our frightened horses.

His arms were clad to the elbow in shimmering iron gauntlets. His right hand clutched the collar of his cat, whose tail flicked back and forth and whose maw was bloody. The creature's shoulder came to the height of the general's knee.

The princes of Iran howled their admiration. A miracle had been made before their eyes, and a true hunt of kings had been born anew from the pages of forgotten books.

I, meanwhile, was thinking that I now better understood the flocking to Abu Muslim's side not only of the city's poor but also of the denizens of proud castles left untouched by the conquerors but withdrawn now into scorn of those same conquerors.

The mystical farr, the divine light that descends from on high to rest on a true sovereign – is that what they saw now surrounding a young man whose only present care was to replace the sack over his spotted hunter's head?

In all the heat of the chase, Abu Muslim had noted and appreciated the maneuver of mine that had allowed him to check the deer before it could swing farther to the right. This I learned later, when another hoarse blare of the trumpets announced that the hunt had entered its second stage and all the rest of us were now at liberty to bring down whatever we could. I learned it after six departed deer had been brought to the camp of tents that had arisen on the instant and through which there already floated the aroma of meat juices dripping onto coals with a merry hissing.

"You did well," was the greeting I had from a weary Ziyad ibn Saleh. "Go, then. He is calling for you. He will tell you how excellently you accomplished all."

Abu Muslim was lying in his tent, with the look of one who had just surfaced from a barrel of cool water and was smiling with the pleasure of it. Large drops glistened on his young face; his curls gleamed moistly too, as did his not very long and not very even beard. And was that the rose oil I knew so well?

Then he smiled from ear to ear, and the face changed. While his teeth glistened with a preternatural whiteness, there were also creases on his forehead that sat ill with his age, and a gentle affection filled those strange yellow eyes.

"Lie alongside me, if you will, Maniakh," he said, patting the carpet by his side and inviting me to do the utterly inadmissible. "You performed excellent well in driving that stubborn beast toward me. But the rest are cowards. Yes, yes, cowards. Tell me, Maniakh, is there nothing you fear? Then why so?"

This was a most unexpected beginning to our conversation. What, in truth, did I have to fear there?

"Perhaps because fear can grow wearisome," I said with a smile of my own.

"No, no, tell me more." Abu Muslim still reclined, but his face was eagerly upturned and a new fire blazed in his yellow eyes. "Let all be as it may, you know who I am. I am speaking to you now as a familiar; you don't take that amiss? But what you don't know is what it means to be born a slave. That's not your world. It's an entirely other life. There, a person's worth is known, but in dirhams only. There the meaning of the place called As-wan is known. The people driven from that place are black of face and already castrated. Or the place called Pra-ga, a city that lies halfway between here and the lands of the Franks, and its monastery, a monastery dedicated to the Prophet Isa the Anointed. Ah, castration there is so gentle, so quick! But do you know, Maniakh, what happens before it is done? The night of the slaves they call it. It comes when you know that tomorrow you will be put to the knife and after the knife you will go into a barrel filled with warm water, to quiet the worst of the pain. And during that night of the slaves" – his voice fell to a whisper – "each seeks to give pleasure to each, and no matter that sometimes there's not a woman to be had, because this will be the last time. Again and again, with hands, with mouth... And by morning all are so spent that none care what is to be cut or where... I was fortunate. I was never cut. Yet I am forever slave-born, Maniakh. And they outside this tent, they know all. And they fear me. But you were born to Samarkand's best family, Maniakh. You keep your own slaves. And that I know. But you're here and you're not afraid. Explain to me why."

By the end he was whispering so low, I could scarce hear him.

No conversation imaginable could possibly have been more unpleasant than this. And the only way out of it was to attack rather than to defend.

"I will not apologize for having been born to that family, my lord," I said in an equally tense whisper. "As I will not weep that I shall soon be in my fortieth year and will never – never! – be a twenty-year-old general who leads a hundred thousand men and does not know what defeat is. That I will not be, for all my family's money. Never... in... my... life!"

And, having acted out my scene, I sat straight-backed and turned slightly away.

But in response to the silence that ensued, I looked again into eyes that burned with an amber flame and saw his smile.

"So that's the way of it. It is all so strange, is it not?" Again he was whispering. "Well, now, the hour of our ordeal will soon be upon us, Maniakh. Don't disappoint me when it comes. And then, when all is over, lay Samarkand at my feet, bold man. For there is much you can do. And if we band together, you and I, naught shall stand in our way. A general? Maybe you will not be a general. But a king? Why not? Look at yourself – you were born to rule. You're not as I am. Desire it! That's how all must be done, here and now, simply and free of guile."

And still I played my game, looking steadily into his eyes. Yet all this was frightfully sad.

You poor boy, I thought, and no longer in pretense but with an acute sense of the approach, if not soon then later, of my fortieth year. Because many truths come to your mind in the presence of an all-powerful general almost half your age.

And so, boy, you are but twenty years old and command an army a hundred thousand strong. Merv, Balkh, and even Nishapur lie at your feet, as may – who knows? – Samarkand and Bukhara too. A large and lovely world. But your eyes, the eyes of that world's overlord, ask the question, This world is now mine, but what of it? *Because no armies and no riches will of themselves bring to you what, say, Barmak's pupil, the dark-skinned lad whose name is Muhammad, possesses every day, that being a father's long arms and legs clasped about you and a huge book serving as the lock that seals the whole structure up tight.*

So you were not castrated as thousands of your fellows were. But a young man of boundless wealth who holds an entire world in his hands and can make no use of it because he cannot even read, is he not more wronged by life than any castrate?

And naught can be done. It is too late.

Or is it?

"And it shall be Nanidat Maniakh, ikhshid of Samarkand," I said slowly, tasting the words on my tongue. "Avarkhuman, Tarkhun, Gurek... and now Maniakh. And if such is the case, good shall be returned for good. Now I shall say what Samarkand can give you. It will give you a world that is not yours today. Qutayba the beast destroyed many books and drove many wise people into slavery, as you yourself were driven. But there are still books, in many languages. There are teachers most wise. There are poets and musicians. And all this we shall give into your keeping. If Samarkand is ever as free and flourishing as once it was, you'll be surprised by how many of those people will appear in the city, as if springing from beneath the ground. But even today, we – our family – know the best of them. You still have time. What is four or five years? Not only Merv, Nishapur, and Balkh but the whole world shall be yours, if you learn to speak its languages. With the sword, one can only destroy the world or force men to fear. With knowledge, you will force the world to smile on you. Another life will come, and that life is wholly possible. Do your comrades in arms look on you today with dread? That's because they can't imagine what to expect from a young man into whose hands such strength and power have suddenly fallen. And who doesn't even know what is known by ordinary boys in Sogdia's trading families, who from the age of five are taught the languages of Roum, Iran and the Celestial Empire... But we shall have them looking on you with respect and admiration. As the most enlightened of emirs in the Caliph's empire. The swords of your warriors will never give you that. But we can. So make your choice, Khorasani."

The effect of my words struck me more powerfully than the words struck him. Again and again he shuddered. And finally, he lay supine on the cushions, his eyes squeezed shut in torment and his face upturned to the tent's translucent canopy. From the folds at the corner of his eye, through the ashen dust of the hunt and down to the cushion's black silk, a happy tear traced its way.

"Another life, a new life... I know that you say this sincerely. And I shall not forget, shall not forget," he said at last, his face still upturned.

But my sadness was none the less for all this. Why, then, all those thousands of warriors galloping down many a road and leaving behind them the greasy smoke of conflagrations and blood soaking into the dust of those roads? Why, when two people can shelter from a midday heat that hums with gnats, and speak in quiet voices and change, really change, the world with their words?

"I hear tell, Maniakh, that you are seeking someone or something?" Abu Muslim, his eyes still shut, said suddenly, in a different voice.

I remembered then some sage advice I had once been given: *Never scruple to ask aught from a man with such power, even if he is almost half your age.*

Never, ever ask for anything. Let them make the offer and you'll have the best price, another voice objected in my head, this one similar to my father's, which I had near forgotten.

Next Barmak was cautioning me to *Say naught of the murderers, for that may displease him.*

"I thank you, my lord, but it's a trifle that I shall grapple with in time," I replied at last. "I am searching for a certain woman. She is greatly needed by our trading house. A woman, who... Her name is Zargisu... It's a long and tangled tale... Best take no trouble with this matter. But if... if she should fall into your hands..."

"You need that one woman alone? Only her?" Abu Muslim asked at length, with manifest mistrust. "The one who... is so well known to all here? But do you need her soon?"

"I have time," I replied manfully.

"Then if such be the case..."

And Abu Muslim clapped his hands thrice and thrice again.

I was actually frightened by what happened within my breast at that moment. Because it would have been utterly foolish at my age to fall flat to the carpet, my face gray, and not to rise again.

No, no, it cannot be that in an instant, as simply as may be, she'll throw back the tent flap, and you'll have all you've wished for. She's here? She's coming in?

But although the flap was indeed thrown back, the one who entered, thrusting forward his head, was a man. Or, judging from his gait, as much a youth as Abu Muslim himself. But such a youth as covers his face with a gauzy veil, like a woman.

Then I had yet more cause to fear. He straightened up and flung back the veil, and again I almost cried aloud, to see a familiar horror – the singed, disfigured face, the eyeball bulging out of pale pink flesh bereft of eyelashes... That savage, ghastly scene at the winery, the crunching of the great winemaker's breastbone, the soldiers helping each other unloose their trousers...

"See now, Hashim, what it is to be the scion of a good family" through the beating of my heart, I heard the young voice behind me say. "His cheek did not so much as twitch when he saw you. Maniakh, before you is a man who wanted to know too much. But witchcraft leads to no good. You think he fell face forward into a fire by some mischance? No, here before you is a man who has studied the secrets of alchemy. He poured two liquids together, leaned over to see if any tiny minions of the demon Iblis were crawling from the mixture, and the foam flew into his face... Now he wears that womanish rag when the sun shines bright, else he will be burned quick as a wink... And he occupies himself for us with the affairs of which you spoke just now."

I was silent.

"Hashim, what say you to handing over to my friend Maniakh later, in a little while, a woman by the name of... What was it?"

"Zargisu. Or simply Gisu," I said, trying to keep my voice from trembling.

Hashim's horrible eye met Abu Muslim's gaze. The two seemed to be conversing soundlessly together.

The young general gave a sudden, ringing laugh. "Hashim and I understand each other well without words, not so?" he asked. "Well, the time will come, if we all have great good fortune, that you shall have her."

"Alive and unmolested," I specified, unable to tear my eyes from the demon's face.

"He also wants to find his way to a celestial garden, Hashim," Abu Muslim said, with a peal of happy laughter. "Well, all in good time. And now, my friends, hasten away, the both of you, and someone other

will hasten in, since I was once deemed unfit even for castration...
Again, Maniakh, thank you. Thank you, my friend."

I went out into the scorching sun, a din of voices, a clang of metal
and a clatter of hooves.

What had just happened? What had I been promised? No more
than should Hashim and, if I understood aright, Abu Muslim's secret
chancery that Hashim headed ever uncover the entire network of
"those that transcend death," I would receive what I had requested?
Not a bad prospect, that.

The question, though, remained: How was it that this hideous
man had descended upon Adijer's house with his band of ravishers the
moment I came there?

I shook my head in perplexity and looked around.

An Iranian princess, young, eagle-nosed and seemingly all abrupt
angles, was approaching Abu Muslim's tent with a firm tread. Making
a show of not noticing the dozens of avidly admiring gazes cast upon
her, she stopped, gave a nervous shrug of the shoulders, and bent to
throw back the tent flap.

And on quitting the tent, Hashim, by contrast, dropped the gauzy
strip of fabric over his fearsome face.

AND ONE LAST SCENE, THE strangest of all. A long journey in
debilitating heat. The silence of Yukuk, who was demonstrating by the
entire look of him his opinion that the head of the House of Maniakh
had no business taking upon himself work so unbefitting to his rank.
Long conversations with peasants that I barely understood, while
Yukuk calmly addressed them with rasping, incomprehensible words
that are evidently heard only in Khorasan. And at last, a long, winding
path among dry bushes, with Yukuk ever and again halting his horse to
listen, and ever and again looking close at the ground before him. The
silence was complete; not a word was spoken.

Then the bushes parted to reveal a clearing.

No, this was not a garden. This was something else altogether.

Amid an unending drone of flies, we led the horses at an easy pace past an entire grove of green trees with lush foliage. Then came a very large and spacious paddock rank with dense, dusty weeds and even slender young saplings.

And in that paddock it suddenly seemed that Yukuk and I had instantly become shorter of stature.

Because the old gray logs that fenced it in, cracked lengthwise with deep chasms, were unaccountably thick. And were, furthermore, secured at a standing man's eye level. No less thick and powerful were the posts that held up a roof, once straw-thatched but now more earthen than aught else, over a long and ample lean-to that stood at the other side of the enclosure.

It seemed that a race of giants must have kept its enormous horses here.

"This is a very strange garden, Yukuk," I said, dreaming that I would now awake.

"It's not the garden we need, sire," he said, slightly subdued. "But it is feared, and the reason is there."

And he pointed with his whip to some hummocks in a far corner. I looked there and saw movement on one of the bald, sandy humps, like the streaming of metal.

"There have long been no people here, but the snakes have multiplied," Yukuk said, betraying no particular alarm.

"But what is this, Yukuk?" I asked him. "Where are we? This is no garden. And what was here earlier?"

"This... Well, of course... Elephants. A century ago, the war elephants of Iran's Shahanshah were quartered here. And for good reason. Khorasan... The eastern frontier..."

The flies sang a wordless song to themselves in the searing heat. And I cast a questioning look at Yukuk, whose gray eyes stared steadily at those powerful logs.

"An elephant cannot be allowed to trample a man," he said in his hoarse, halting voice. "And so their trainers had to... break them. But when that was done... Metal spurs on their legs, pointing forward.

Archery towers on their backs. They moved across the field in a wedge formation, and they couldn't be stopped. And the earth trembled."

He fell silent then, narrowing his eyes and looking off into space. And I watched as he absent-mindedly stroked the warm, gray skin of those old logs. And, for the first time I could recall, a smile quirked the corner of his lips.

13

IN FRUITED GARDENS,
IN THE WIDE-FLUNG SHADE

Before coming to Merv, I had thought that I not only knew the language of Iran but knew it well. Yet in the village of Safizanj it became clearer than clear that while I might be understood there, I myself understood almost nothing. My ears rang with an endless flow of seemingly familiar words, either from Iranian or from my native Sogdian, that never came together into anything intelligible.

But I never spoke much anyway, as I was acting the part of Yukuk's groom. And also of a purse on two legs. During one of his wearisome conversations, the tall warrior, whom the peasants met and saw on his way with admiring looks, silently reached out his hand to the left and a little behind, in my general direction, and wiggled his fingers in peremptory style.

Understanding the signal, I placed into that hand the almost weightless circle of a silver dirham.

The gaunt, gray-haired old woman watched the dirham taking a journey that ended beneath her nose, and squeezed her lips tight shut.

Yukuk again reached out his palm behind and to the left, and I gave him another dirham.

There was now panic in the eyes of the old woman, who possibly had never before in her life seen two dirhams in her hand at one time.

Then I heard Yukuk's hoarse baritone, honeyed now as he calmed and soothed her. I recognized something of what he was saying – "consoling angel," "it's of great importance to me" and "help me, mother mine."

And the old woman, with another glance around, began to speak, but I could make out only small scraps of what she said, on the order of "she dismounted," "heavy iron," and "they cry out."

Then again I heard Yukuk pressing her to do something. The old woman gave a shamefaced snort, and, groaning, dropped to hands and knees and began to move her hips back and forth.

I averted my eyes.

And she said something further, in which I discerned the word "pairidaeza," and thrust an imaginary knife forward and down, as if plunging it into someone's breast.

Yukuk emerged from the old woman's neglected and weed-choked yard gloomy but on the whole content.

"It's all true, sire," he said, addressing me as he rarely did, as "sire" rather than with the more neutral "ser." "She appeared here after a battle, that woman of yours. With two attendants, both men of the Arabiya, and all in full armor and carrying weapons. Like as not she took no part in the battle. She walked the field, hearing the cries and seeing the hands reaching out to her. She would approach some who lay there, would speak, and then would pass on. But others... well, you saw it all. The old woman could not have invented such a thing – not that person, not at her age."

"Did she see her face?" I had the presence of mind to ask.

Yukuk gave an approving chuckle. "No, but she had a fine view of... other body parts." He slapped himself on the haunch. "The old woman, you see, was herself all but engaged in the fray. She carried arrows. And later she went in search of slain kinsmen."

"Who was fighting whom?" I asked then.

My inquiries seemed ever more pleasing to him.

"That, now, is an entertaining story. The battle was between supporters of the Bihafridi doctrine and the soldiers of Abu Muslim. A year and a half back."

"The Bihafridi doctrine?"

"I can't tell you exactly what their belief is. Or used to be, because Abu Muslim slaughtered them almost to a man. But it related in no way to the true faith of the Prophet Muhammad. And so, that woman of yours did what she did only to the Bihafridis. And they were waiting for her. Sire, I did not believe the story. Until today. Because I myself have been wounded twice and the last thing I wished for then was to be mounted by any woman. That is, I may have wished it, but the pain was somewhat of an inconvenience. And the thing that is a man's adornment cannot, after all, be forced. How is she able?"

"Imagine a man who for three days has been tormented by an ever-increasing fever occasioned by a wound," I replied after some thought. "And suddenly a scene unfolds before his eyes... He witnesses its beginning, and something befalls him. The fever and the pain yield, if only for a time. From somewhere comes the strength, through not the will. Who knows what that man might be induced to do?"

I faltered then and was silent, while Yukuk looked at me with unconcealed interest and said, through clenched teeth, "That may be so."

"But I have learned more," he went on, "not from that old woman but earlier – remember the urchin who brought water in a copper pitcher? . . So, before your woman came, Abu Muslim's soldiers were harrying the vanquished through all the groves and fields around. None of his men were therefore left in this place save some five who had stayed behind, belike to seek their wounded. And that woman with her two companions descended on them like a kite on the wing. Her friend – he had a very large nose – shot one of them with an arrow."

A very large nose? Yukuk had said that same thing once before, and something familiar was now glimmering in my memory. *This is not the Celestial Empire, and no nose here, including my own, is small, but very large... Where have I seen such a one, and recently too?*

Yukuk was still speaking. "The woman," he said, "had a long, light sword, much like mine. And with two strokes of that sword she destroyed two cavalrymen who were bearing down on her from right and left, after which the others fled. I had heard that she is dangerous, and this confirms it. And what else have we learned? That she was seen in this village again, in very recent days, no longer in armor but with the same pair of attendants. She was on her way to Merv. She asked for water. And she galloped away. So, then, the meat of the matter: we have long known, in sum, who the consoling angel is. It is she. But here we've learned two more things. About the garden, for one. Sometimes it's frequented by those warriors who have transcended death, which is a great happiness to them. In that garden, they know the joys of paradise almost every night, and all with that woman, or with others too. And from that garden, if they're deemed worthy, they're dispatched to the true garden of paradise, where the same entertainments await them. But for those who prove weak, something other is in store – a demon with a singed face."

There. This, now, was fine, very fine.

"Yukuk, do you also know whose singed face that is?" I asked pensively.

"How could I not?" he replied morosely, taking the horse's bridle from me. "Everyone knows him here. He is the demon who destroyed the Bihafridis without reckoning and without quarter. And many others too. But something sits ill here. It is one thing to be a demon so as to put fear into the denizens of that garden, but something wholly other to be Abu Muslim's right hand, a man who brings to light all and sundry enemies and spies. Which is, if you know this, his labor in chief, ser."

That I did know. But, again remembering the man with no face in the home of Adijer the winemaker, I determined that I now understood nothing. It was all rather too simple, that Hashim should play the part of a chastening demon. But while the woman by the name of Gisu was elusive as the wind, Hashim was seen every day in company with the Leopard of Merv himself... Who had of late made that very Hashim promise me that when he caught Zargisu, he would hand her to me. And what did all that signify?

But Yukuk was ready to be done with the subject. "Of him, I hear only talk," he said. "And soon comes the time to draw all these conversations together, to make of them a picture that will help us know what must next be done. Today we have no time. Because we must both away to the hospital, to the worthy Ashofteh. You for the same reasons as ever, but I have been promised an introduction to the fellow who is having those strange conversations with the patients. And thereafter we must make our way back to the city, and in this accursed heat too. We shall return and fall asleep, and there will be an end to it. But tomorrow will be the time to sit and talk."

ZARGISU'S FACE, WHICH THE OLD woman had not seen, rose suddenly to the surface of my memory, at a stroke and of a piece, as if she had been long gone and had just returned. Almost all the women of Iran are beautiful, and their principal pride is a splendid nose, not only arched but also often of no small thickness. Yet even the most lavish noses are balanced by a no less lavish and prideful lower jaw and also by the capricious pouting of the lower lip, as a result of which the smiles of those women can flatly dazzle the eye. When Zargisu gave her waspish smile, she was downright lovely, and lovely too were her honeyed eyes, filled with a bashful suffering and set beneath the arch of gilded brows whose only wish was to grow together. Yet the suffering was more often than not feigned, as it is with most women, while the smile was wholly sincere and unwontedly memorable.

Did she smile as she thrust her dagger between the ribs of a warrior who lay pressed to the ground by her body in its ringing chain mail?

And what would I read in her eyes when I looked into them at last?

THE MEASURED THUDDING OF TWO horses' hooves on the dusty road. Cypresses casting sharp shadows on either side. A scorching sun that made even the cloth about my head hot. This was an endless, fear-ridden summer.

I glanced back. The road was empty behind me.

"A person acquires his second shadow most often in the city, in a crowd," Yukuk said, noticing how I had turned in the saddle. "Here any movement would be heard from afar. A horse cannot go quietly."

His second shadow? At first, I was surprised, but then I understood and smiled. *An apt expression, that. I should tell my brother. He'd be well pleased by it.*

THEN YUKUK HIMSELF BECAME a shadow.

For several days, serenely, languidly, and moving with no great ado, like a fleck of gray, between the rows of sickbeds, he had lain in wait for he who came to solicit converts. And who had spent most of his time with Omar and Mihraman, who were mine, or very near to it.

How that long-legged man toward whom turned many a head – mostly of the female persuasion – could go unnoticed, I did not know. But Yukuk, portraying now a drunken vendor of sweetmeats and now a sober patient who came to the hospital day after day seeking treatment for some suppurating sore, had observed the soliciting from the corner of his eye and had later followed the solicitor as he traveled about the city.

"It's also very important to be able to see over a good distance while keeping the head still," he had said, reluctantly sharing with me one of his secrets. "And not to hurry, never to hurry. Your man has gone away from you, has hidden his tracks, but you must make no stir, must not reveal yourself, for tomorrow you'll begin again."

And the result of all this was that Yukuk was able to discover the place where the solicitor ate by day and of an evening, and the hovel where he slept, and to find at length the house he sometimes visited. And that house was where all those patient efforts tended. It lay in the city's northern purlieus, where the waters of the Murgab River, scarcely discernible on the horizon, grew crimson toward nightfall, in a goodly cluster of quite modest, almost rustic, dwellings.

It was learned to be the home of a holy man – though how holy remained to be seen – who could not be approached in casual style. For one wishing to come to him, his very existence must first be known, after which the sizable crowd of his admirers and dependents must be persuaded to grace the supplicant with their slightest notice, to say nothing of conducting him to the master of the house.

A lengthy dispute with Yukuk ensued. Should I go just as I was, straight from the street, to that strange house? I told him I had a name and the position in Merv of one who from time to time had converse with Abu Muslim himself. And that I could therefore present myself at any house and make a public announcement of my name without reserve. Besides, I would have come on business, that being to wrest from their clutches my two future chakirs. None of this was out of the ordinary.

After arguing long and hard, Yukuk agreed to let me go, but only in the company of Nanivandak – "he has a good mind and a cool head," he said – and left unanswered my inquiries as to what he would be doing in the meantime.

That somehow disagreeable home on the outskirts resembled a hospital, albeit a small one, in that there a number of people also sat or lay on the ground, swaddled in broad, shapeless wraps. And oil lamps cast a bobbing light on the figures that stirred hither and thither in the darkness.

I was, of course, correct. To come there and give my name was simple in the doing and entirely successful in the outcome. I did not have long to wait.

In my lifetime I had known any number of people who could be called big, especially when compared to my own relatively modest proportions. This man, however, was very large and very hairy, and his beard was beyond thick, spreading far to the side of his fleshy cheeks and reaching almost to his shoulders. Standing in his garden by night, he had the look of a steep-sloped mountain topped with a headscarf, whose base nestled unseen in dark valleys.

No one had troubled to tell me the man's name, apparently believing that I would not have come to this place without knowing it.

"You are here because your soul is sorrowful, Sogdian," this mountain of meat and hair greeted me in a delectably deep bass voice. "Yet who is merry in this world of many sorrows? Tears stream from your eyes when you lie alone in the night. Take thought, though: how many more pillows are dampened with such tears as yours at that same night-time hour? You are not alone, Sogdian. And how good it is that you are here. How good that you are with us. But even here with us, you shall long wander the paths of error until your eyes are opened to the light that brings clarity of sight."

The reddish reflection of the lamps played on his round cheeks and his forehead. All was quiet save for a whispering and a shuffling of feet in the corners of the garden. Somewhere far away, a horse neighed. Today I think that the sound helped me know that I must take care lest that deep and sympathetic bass voice quite simply lull me to sleep. I must say something, do something, make some argument, and that with all speed.

"Clarity of sight?" I replied with a bitter mistrust that I did not even have to feign. "Am I the only one who thirsts for it?"

"Do you wish to know how to see clear?" he asked, smiling at me in the darkness from beneath his head scarf and drawing long, deep breaths. "Then are you familiar with these words: 'Verily, man is in loss, except such as have faith'?"

He looked at me questioningly and, receiving no response, continued: "But not only they who read the book of the Prophet come here. No, not only they. Because there have been other sages who also knew how to tell the light from the gloom. Yes, we are in chaos. We are between Ahura Mazda and Ahriman, and every one, every one of us must know for himself which of the strong and the weak of this world sits on the throne of his own error and which directs the steeds of his fate to the feet of the Lord. To spill the blood of the first is but to shower rainwater onto the cracked ground. But what will be if each begins to shed blood as the heavens shed rain? What will be is what transpires this day. No, only the chosen shall hold in his hand the sacred weapon..."

"These names you speak I heard as a child," I chided the bearded prophet, for I was beginning to tire heartily of this conversation. He was telling me about my own mother's gods! Next, if all went on this way, his tale would be of the God of Blue Sky, the God my father had worshipped...

He spread his meaty hands. "But did I not say that they who come here worship many prophets? And what of it? Was he not correct who said that man himself decides the side to take, that of the light or that of the gloom? If only all who read this book or that could choose aright."

"In that kingdom there would be neither cold nor sweltering heat..." I responded with a dash of irony.

"...nor old age nor death nor envy most malign," my nameless mentor finished for me with supreme confidence.

And then we looked at each other.

"In this house you are no stranger from the Sogdian land," that bewhiskered tun of meat said, his voice pitched lower. "You come timely, for decisive days are upon us. Another age. And he whom men call the Mahdi, the redeemer, is here. He is already among us, yet we in our foolishness pass him by and fail to notice him. But wait a while, for it is ever thus. You sit in the gloom, and suddenly there comes a blinding light!"

About to reach out his hand and strike me on the forehead, he stumbled against the look in my eyes and thought better of it.

"As for your sufferings, bear them. At least you're rich. Your name is renowned. But what are the poor people to do? Their burden is heavier."

I had not lived almost forty years without learning to mark when someone was beginning by degrees to encroach upon my money. But, to his credit, he left that sensitive topic there where it lay.

"Determine what you need," he said by way of conclusion. "The ease of your soul? Here you shall find it. Your life grows unbearable? Then you shall also receive the thing for which you thirst."

Not a word about Zargisu, I thought, preparing my departure. *Not a word. His kind is more dangerous than a snake. One other word, though, I shall speak.*

"The garden," I said. "The garden where it all ends... I would fain betake myself to that garden, of which so many here speak."

Again he began to draw deep, pleasurable breaths. And then, with a sly glance at me, he almost sang out: "We shall be in fruited gardens, in the wide-flung shade, by water that flows constantly and with fruit in abundance, neither cut away nor forbidden us, recumbent on spread carpets. And the houris, perfect in creation and ever virgin, shall belong to those who stand on the right hand... Ye-e-e-s... But bide your time. Then the garden will come to you and you to the garden. To the garden of eternity where streams flow. There you shall abide for evermore."

"O sage..." – standing now, I forced myself to say it, for I had to address him somehow – "do you know what trifle brings me to you? Now I am even ashamed to mention it, but on the other hand, two human fates are no trifle..."

His shaggy head tilted questioningly in the darkness.

"Two Sogdians, one by the name of Omar, the other, Mihraman. Your envoy has spoken with them in the hospital that they must soon quit. I wanted to take them into my home. But now I don't know how to proceed. Are they needful to you, the two of them?"

For all that the fat man's face was not full in my view, it was apparent that another two candidates for clarity of sight were of no great importance to him.

"But are you certain that it is for you to chose their fate?" he asked testily.

"I am a physician," I said, with some pride. "They were healed at my hands."

"Then, let them make the choice themselves," the fat man replied with a nod.

I was led from the courtyard with all the deference due.

And it would have been a lovely courtyard and he a right remarkable person, if...

I looked around, to where some of the gray shadows – five, six, ten or more – must have settled themselves for the night. The rest were lost in the gloom, amid invisible foliage.

Desperate people these, who had lost land, money, their near and dear, and then, evidently, found themselves lacking the health without which they could go no more a-soldiering. This, now, was their fate – to be gray shadows lying in that courtyard, from whence, if it pleased the preacher, they would pass directly to the mysterious pleasure-garden, there to receive that sacred weapon, to go to their places and to await the signal. How simple it was!

Too simple, I added in my mind.

Had Zargisu, proud daughter of Iran, lain in that garden along with the others, until she made her choice between the gloom and the light?

In the deserted street, amid cypresses unseen in the dark, a solitary silhouette loomed. It was Nanivandak on horseback, holding my mount by the reins.

Nothing beyond could be seen in the murk, but I was certain somehow that the tall warrior Yukuk was close by.

14

SHE'S BRAINSICK, SIRE

It was such a pleasure to discard for good and all the black jacket and broad trousers I had worn to travel many a highway and byway on the outskirts of Merv in the company of Yukuk, for they were already beyond laundering. Then I promised myself that on the morrow I would take to my bed promptly after supper. But today I had to straighten my leaden legs, load myself onto my horse once more, and make my way to the quarter where pleasures were to be had – not such as one thinks of at such times, though, but simpler. The pleasure, for example, of a bath both leisurely and thorough.

"A dyeing for us today?" a hairdresser who sat in the shadows by the bath-house asked, not expecting to be rebuffed. And pursed disapproving lips submerged in luxuriant red vegetation on hearing my languid "no." A Sogdian must, come what may, remain a Sogdian, especially when he is half-Turkic. And, all in all, my yellowish Sogdian hair, my eyes of a light, indeterminate hue and my stiff, short beard sat well with me.

With the long-awaited lightness of a head well-shorn, accompanied by the lightness of arms and legs that comes after a bath, I then rode to an alley near the Northern Market and spent entirely too long in a perfume vendor's dimly lit store amid his hundreds of small pitchers and tiny bowls. I selected a fragrance with a rather frivolous note of rose – a token of respect to the Leopard of Merv, that was – strongly seasoned with jasmine.

Then I passed on to the Northern Market itself, where I acquired new everyday attire in the form of a shirt and vest, both inescapably black, but with broad gray trousers to wear with them. I also took a liking to a headband whose wide stripes, though black yet again, were interspersed with a light green.

While returning to my roost in the fortress, it came to me that I was behaving like one of the Celestial Empire's artists, intentionally drawing out the time as I prepared myself for a serious, a very serious, conversation with Yukuk. This was exactly how an artist of the Tang Empire would concentrate his mind prior to committing his genius to a scroll.

At such times, the artist mounts a donkey and journeys a day or two, into the most lovely of the surrounding mountains. He wanders from the east toward the sunset, amid peaks crowned with twisted pines, at whose feet bamboo groves cluster in pale green clouds, as a cool mist rises from toylike waterfalls.

Then he pours wine from a small pot and sips it thoughtfully while nibbling on something fitting, lies on the woven mat that he has brought, lowers his head, topped with its knot of hair, onto a porcelain neck rest, and falls asleep to the din of rivulets and the cries of nocturnal birds.

And in the morning he takes a chestful of fresh air, again casts his keen gaze upon those very same mountains and waters in their new guise fashioned by the slanting rays of dazzling light, and turns his donkey homeward.

Once home, he sheds his dusty garments, sits long in a barrel to wash himself clean, and dons clothing new and fresh, including a new headband. And, stern and intent, he approaches the scrolls of silk or rice paper, and dissolves the dry ink with a slow hand.

His servants, if such there be, have scattered ere then and hidden, trying to make no more noise than a mouse in a government rice repository. The respect shown by the Empire's inhabitants to a person who has taken brush in hand is vast. But never mind him, they have as great a respect even for a scrap of paper on which a brush has traced so much as a word or two. To this day I remember how a warm breeze once carried from my low desk in the trading house in Chang'an just such a scrap of paper, which bore not even the Imperial calligraphy but uneven lines of Sogdian script. I lazily stretched out my boot to bring it back. And an Imperial lady, whose name was Tender Petal Huang – not of the lower orders, she, but the wife of an official historiographer – and who sat facing me, sprang from her place in horror, darted over to pick up that shred of paper, smoothed it, and held it out to me in her two hands, while I, a mere lad at that time, was only confounded by the scene I had just witnessed.

And so our artist, clean and attired in something fresh, simple and austere, having dissolved and diluted the ink and having touched each brush in turn, draws a deep breath in and breathes it out again. He takes a brush in hand. And as it slides uninterrupted across the scroll, those same peaks emerge from a damp mist; there is an intimation of bamboo leaves weightless as a dragonfly's wings; streams spring up; monkeys appear, motionless on the knotty boughs; and downy clouds fly high above. And all this in no more than the time it takes for the water to boil for an infusion of tea.

I cast my eyes over blind house walls the color of sand, breathed in the aromas of spicy food still unfamiliar to me, and turned toward the tethering posts hard by the fortress that soared into the sky. The conversation with Yukuk could be postponed no longer. *Very well*, I told myself. *At least be glad that you never had cause to become a soldier, which could well have been your lot in those strange days that transformed imperceptibly into strange and bitter years. You are now the Hawk. And a good Hawk you shall be, by returning again to your beloved Empire. No more than two months' journey eastward... But for that to happen, a long and difficult conversation must first be had this day.*

"We have learned much, ser." Thus Yukuk, sitting stern-faced before me, began that conversation. "How they work could be no clearer. They find wretched people, utterly unprepared, and select for them the simplest method of murder. For without the need to save oneself, anyone can kill whomsoever he wishes. All that is required to begin is for everyone around to take those murderers as a normal part of the landscape, to cease to notice them. The murderers themselves have their heads turned by all the gardens, the eternal life and the women who come to console. All in all, it's a simple matter. The important thing for us is that we don't need to uncover all the murderers, as you have said. All we need do is find one woman. But you already see that this woman is a puzzlement, for where she is, there also are the murderers. And in search of her it's easy enough to be rendered headless and even fail to notice it is so until struck with a desire to turn that head. So no part of the picture can be left aside. No matter, though. It's crabbed at first but later much will be simpler."

"Wise is the man to loves to learn," I observed. "Which is to say that the occupation holds no shame for me. Then let's begin at the very beginning... but where, now I think of it, was that beginning?"

"Belike in Safizanj. Abu Muslim raised his famous rebellion in that village two years ago, sent secretly there by certain pretenders to the Prophet's mantle, staff and ring. Them you know better than I. But a few months after the rebellion began, the head of his secret chancery destroyed in that same village the devotees of a strange doctrine of which we know naught."

I was indignant. "How can we know naught? What of my talk with the preacher?"

But Yukuk was quick to correct me. "No, no – we don't know if it's that doctrine he's preaching or something other," he said. "Likely he has devised something other. Because if all the Bihafridis were destroyed and he is truly one of them, he would not be sitting here. We only know that by then your woman was already familiar to the adherents of that doctrine of earlier days and had almost certainly joined herself to it. Thereafter, as you say, she found herself in a difficult position and had to pass into the clutches of that preacher, and so forth. Which means that they gained her and much else in legacy from the Bihafridis, but they have also devised much that was new. It is, all told, good that you went to see him. But back to the meat of the matter. How is it that he sits here in Merv, out in the open, and naught untoward has yet befallen him?"

At this point, I raised my hand, commanding him to silence, and knit my brows. Something indeed was sorely awry. Zargisu, never having even worked in our trading house and unversed in all its ways, comes to Merv... What had my brother said? That she had left to come here when the rebellion had scarce begun. So, then, the timing was such that she came here and at once found herself among those Bihafridis, whoever they may have been? That could be so if my brother had sent her here for a reason. If he had long been working with them. Else how could he possibly know that here those people were already being struck down to the last man? That was where the unpleasantness began for him, and not with Zargisu's purported disappearance at all.

But she... There had been naught for her but to fall into the clutches of those who had resolved to gather up for themselves the remnants of the Bihafridis – so much I now understood. For an inexperienced woman flung into the flames of war, this was a great stroke of luck. She could otherwise, without so much as a by-your-leave, have been killed at the very outset.

That was, quite simply, the only answer.

Which, now I thought of it, meant that the information she had sent to so delight my brother had never had the value he thought it to possess. And small wonder that shortly thereafter...

"And shortly thereafter," I said, having first unclamped my lips, "not only in Merv but in Samarkand too, unpleasantness began to befall our trading house. When did those murderers appear, Yukuk?"

"Less than a year ago," he replied in a firm voice.

"Several months therefore elapsed after she first appeared on the drear hills by Safizanj. And, like the big-nosed man and the others, gave her allegiance there to new masters. Who are to be thanked, first, for the appearance of the murderers here and next, for the unpleasantness that beset us, who had sent her to Merv." My case was made.

But Yukuk gently corrected me. "The one thing did come after the other," he said, "but how all that is linked and even if it is linked, we do not know for a certainty. Although from the looks of it, the logic is good. So. What did you learn from the preacher? On the one hand, a great deal. That there is a doctrine that holds a Mahdi to be already here, already among us. But until he reveals himself, the chosen will still be able to vanquish death, by killing as they lay down their own lives. But that isn't the meat of the matter. At risk of repeating myself, there are many doctrines and a prophet on almost every street corner. But not all prophets have money, and this reeks of money. Solicitors. A preacher with a tolerable house. And then there's that garden – every garden costs money. And, as I have said, this band goes near unmolested. And so we have still the same problem: To whom is this needful?"

"The roster of the slain," I said with heavy heart, knowing that naught would come of it. "Two of Abu Muslim's judges, then one of his commanders, that last before my eyes. But earlier, Nasr Ibn Sayyar, the Caliph's governor of all Khorasan and of Sogdia besides, and three of that governor's intimates, at our very door, in Samarkand, and in Bukhara. And the two failed attempts against Sogdians of the Maniakh clan – meaning against us. Who support the rebellion. That is, they are killing now on one side, then on the other. They are killing everyone."

"And this is interesting," Yukuk remarked gently. "Not everyone is killed in a crowd. Some are killed secretly. Nasr for example... It bears more thought..."

"Yukuk, that matters not. What matters is this: You asked to whom all this is needful. My brother says that some third power is at work here, neither the Caliph nor the rebels."

"But we already see for a certainty that one of Abu Muslim's own people is helping that third power," Yukuk prompted softly. "Let us call him by his name – Hashim. That preacher of yours would not last a day if Hashim, the man without a face, had not given his consent to it. So, then, a plot within a plot? Abu Muslim has heartily wearied someone among his own confederates? Among the princes of Iran?

And the Caliph has wearied those very same people? But here we know nothing, save that we must approach this woman of yours with great care, because she is the murderers' consoler. She is part of this story. If we err... as I have already said, we might pay with our heads."

"Abu Muslim made Hashim promise that he would give her over to me," I began. Then I fell silent, realizing that this was worth naught, like so many other promises in this world.

Abu Muslim has wearied the princes of Iran, I repeated to myself, and old Barmak's serene face wreathed in clean, snow-white hair rose up in my mind. And he was not even a prince. He was higher. And wiser too.

I grew ill at ease.

"Now then, Yukuk," I said. "Give me all that's known about Abu Muslim. And Hashim."

"They're friends," he shrugged. "Both young, both merciless. Abu Muslim... was born either in Isfahan or in a village by Kufa. He was formerly a slave, and his armies contain a multitude of slaves, both former and less so. First he told them that they could rebel because they were downtrodden. But later it transpired that this would quickly put him at odds with the princes of Iran, for all that they adored him. Because if every one of the downtrodden was to rebel... So the slaves in Abu Muslim's army may be free this day yet still they live in a goodly camp in the settlement of Shawwal, not far from the road to Rayy. Well protected it is, too. And what else? What prophet does the general believe in? Naught to wonder at there, for his battle cry is 'O, Muhammad! O, thou who wast aided by God!' And something further regarding the need for the power to pass from the usurpers to the Prophet's family. All in the usual run of things. What else? He kills people not in their thousands, but in numbers even greater. And now he is killing his own, since the Caliph's men – Nasr ibn Sayyar, that is – are no more. Do you know how many of his own former confederates he has destroyed? Some thirty thousand, I hear tell. But that I cannot believe."

I remembered speaking with a certain boy, watching a tear slide over the plane of his cheek, but now I understood how improbable it was that he could never be made over into an enlightened emir. Ah well...

"Hashim, though, is rather more interesting," Yukuk went on. "He's a local man, from some village between Merv and Balkh. A soldier's son. A cloth-dyer since childhood, he suddenly took up with the sciences, apparently for the purpose of making better dyes. He's reputed to be a sorcerer since the experiments he conducts are none other than wizardry. Although that cost him most of his face... He leads Abu Muslim's secret chancery. He also kills indiscriminately. And he cannot be without a new woman at least once a day. Or more often. That's the manner of man he is. But, ser, this of itself sheds no light on the matter of the murderers who lay low ours and yours alike. As you have it, Hashim stands behind it all. Yet Hashim can murder whomsoever he wishes, and he kills without cause, openly. So why must he have secret murderers in his employ? But those friends of yours who are to be thanked that we now have the best chain mail in all of Merv – do you yourself know to a certainty what they seek, why they come here?"

"I know only what they tell me," I owned, to which Yukuk nodded his approval. "Yet there's something in what they tell me... They very much want me to find my way through this matter of the murderers. They – how was it said? – they hinder them greatly and make a muddle of everything. Or so they tell me," I ended, quite forlornly.

"Very well. Then we have more thinking to do. And now let's return to your woman," Yukuk said dispassionately. "We've just ascertained that she's to be sought with the greatest of care, which is to say with a good understanding of all that's transpiring around. But we've also learned something about her own self. That she's no shadow, because she's been seen, and also that she comes with attendants and that one of them has a long nose, that she's called as you said she was, since everyone responds to the name. But now something else is clear."

Here Yukuk heaved a deep, sad sigh. And again my heart shrank. I was silent, waiting for him to continue.

"She's brainsick, sire. Today she's not at all the person she was in the days when you were growing up together. Something has befallen her. Which is no surprise, for something has befallen us all in recent years... There's altogether too much brainsickness all around us. The preacher's brainsick too, you say. And those murderers who thirst for death, are they in their right mind? So your woman... Do you know what the old one in Safizanj told me and others have confirmed? That your woman would leap on the wounded, no less than four in succession, and then finish them off. Is that a woman in her right mind? I've heard that such women, insatiable women, do exist, but they're deemed sick... And this one's boundlessly cruel too. She loves blood, she loves weaponry. She tortures captives, I hear tell."

"Talk, Yukuk, it's all talk and naught else. Where does she capture them? Why does she torture them? I know what such talk is worth. There's such a one called the Hawk, and much is said about him too, but I know who's spreading those rumors and why, and how it's done... We've already heard the talk of how she ravishes helpless warriors on the field of battle, but now it emerges, look you, that she's consoling them. And even the dagger blow is a last act of mercy, wherewith she sends them to paradise. I'm not saying this is good. But it's not the same as taking pleasure from a dying man against his will and then dispatching him without cause."

Yukuk was silent. I was finally beginning to distinguish around me the familiar sounds of the enclosure within the Merv fortress, which had emptied with the approach of night.

"You forget that I'm a physician, Yukuk," I said at length. "Albeit a novice still. But there's something in the art that's stronger than I, and you know this too. The sick can be cured, Yukuk. Everyone deserves a chance in this fearsome world. The chance to be healed, for one. I shall begin by giving her that chance. And the rest will follow."

"Yes..." he said in gloomy tones. And went off to teach my chakirs mounted swordplay.

Now that the conversation was done, I pondered a while and sat down to write a letter to Samarkand. No poetry this time, only the brief jottings of some commercial document, with lines running pell-mell and seemingly unconnected.

Then I rolled a cake of dried dates in that papyrus, as if it were a thing of naught. And I handed it to the courier at the hospital.

I only hoped that my first attempt at crafting a letter coded otherwise than in verse had come off well. Taken as a whole, what I had produced was, it seemed to me, a very brief account – lacking names, to be sure, but clear – of the conclusions we had reached thus far. And there was also a request to change the courier's route, since the hospital, which was much frequented by the solicitors and whomever else, was now rather less to my liking than it had been.

And at the end of all, a short line containing two superlatively serious questions that had not occurred to me before.

The burden of one question was, in rough measure, thus: "Where did you send the money – to Merv or farther west?" It was, I now thought, very important to know exactly how our family had financed the recent revolt in the Caliph's empire. Who exactly had been receiving the money. Because if the whole picture of what had transpired must be known, it must be known well.

That papyrus also bore, in larger letters, one other immensely pertinent question. written all crisscross, and looking like naught more than the testing of a new brush. If all went according to plan, I would have my reply to that query, and all else, in two weeks.

THIS TIME BARMAK WAS WELL pleased with my report, which he was wont to call a friendly conversation. I had rarely before seen his face so serious yet at the same time even handsome, with two long folds that came from who knows where to run across his forehead and lend an odd eloquence to his nose.

"This is now something," he said, with a satisfied sigh. "Although, of course, of Hashim and his distinctive face one would wish to learn more. Because it's one thing if this is simply one of the sects that are now multiplying without number here, and another matter altogether when such a man as he is entangled in it. Precise knowledge must be had of him, be it yes or be it no. Yet perchance he has naught to do with this, Perchance it's all to the contrary, and someone is throwing a dead rat over the wall at him, to see what he'll do. Which is, come to think of it, a common stratagem, the dead rat."

But now I had a request to make of him. "Barmak," I said, "tell me about all these doctrines, schools and the rest of it. Have you heard of any that cultivate murderers? Maybe if we understand whence it all comes, it will be simpler for us."

"A good idea," he replied with an energetic nod. "The problem, though, is a surplus of information. You can imagine for yourself, no? Naught but doctrines and preachers on every hand. Most revolve around Ali, who was married to the Prophet's daughter. They had a son, Hussein, in whom the blood of the Prophet ran. And pure it was there. Not a whit worse than the blood of the House of Abbas or possibly better, let it be said betwixt the two of us. But to proceed... They have such an accumulation of legends, of the imams who preach openly and the secret imams who will supposedly come soon... And, aside from the imams, there is also a certain Mahdi, but that is sheer mysticism."

"Yes, I've just now heard something of that, of the Mahdi," I said.

"I doubt it not... But to go on, then there are the Kharijites. Who favor purity and poverty, a return to the doctrinal wellsprings. In your homeland of Sogdia, your Harith ibn Surayj was a Kharijite. Then also there are the Mutazilites and Qadarites. And there was too a Jew known to all as Ibn Saba, who taught that Muhammad would return to earth again, in the way of the Prophet Isa. But that aside, several years ago, the House of Abbas sent here, to Khorasan, a man by the name of Khaddash or Khidash – who knows? They sent him to muddy the waters and raise the people in rebellion, naught so hard to understand about that. But once he began, what did he preach? That there was no need to fast or make the hajj to Holy Mecca and that every wife belongs to every man. His days were, of course, numbered..."

"But Barmak, don't you know of any doctrine that enjoins a man to kill his enemy, after which he will fly forthwith to paradise?"

"How could I not? There was an Abu Mansur al-Ijli and a Mugira ibn Said. The former taught that the enemies of the true faith must be killed only with a noose and the latter, only with a wooden club. Not until the coming of the Mahdi would the use of steel be permitted. But they began to quarrel between themselves, whereupon all were able to rest easier. But as for doctrines with gardens and daggers, both large and small – no, of that I have never heard. But this, then, is the agreement we shall make between ourselves: I'll have plenty of time now to think over this entirely pertinent question of yours – which is simply to say that you are on the right path – while you... For you it will be easier to keep your eyes on Hashim, while at the same time seeking that garden, with its blossoms, maidens and what not. For it does exist, and it is here somewhere. Let's meet some three weeks from now – in a month, say. And then we shall compare our findings."

"In a month?" I asked in surprise.

"We depart soon," he explained briskly. "But I shall leave behind a most interesting person for you. Abu Salama, my friend, come here. I want to introduce you. Maniakh of Samarkand may come to you at any time, and if it's help he needs, help he must have."

A man of thirty or so, impossibly solemn in appearance and plainly a pure-blooded denizen of the conquerors' lands, with a head overgrown by coal-black vegetation, approached, embraced me, filling my nostrils with a powerful odor of cedar, and uttered the needful words regarding the importance of my family "to us all." When he at last departed, drawing Abu Jafar whose byname was Mansur into a corner of the courtyard for a long conversation, I turned again to my benefactor.

"So, Barmak, the most reliable of my chakirs once gave me sage advice – that when you're looking for something small, you need to survey the whole picture at once or your head will come off. Then does it not seem to you that it's time for me to understand in full all that's transpiring here? Where, for example, will you be gone for a month? And, now I think of it, why do you come here at all and what do you do here? Because there is, without a doubt, some close link between those murderers, every one of them, and the affairs you're conducting.

Speak, then, Barmak. Or I'll go on groping my way along and will run up against some great unpleasantness. I feel it already."

While Barmak pondered, I turned my gaze to the two plotters, Mansur and Abu Salama, and to the dark-skinned boy under the ever-vigilant eyes of silent bodyguards.

"You're right. It's time," Barmak reluctantly admitted at length. "In short, everyone here is awaiting a decision on a campaign against the Caliph. Caliph Marwan races frantically from one group of insurgents to the next. His quarrel with the army in Damascus never ends. We have before us a Caliph who does not trust the most battle-hardened of his own forces, nor they him. But, though this be happiness for us, it cannot last forever. So we and the sovereign lord of Merv are striving to decide on where and how to mount our campaign. An offensive must be set afoot and power must be seized. There are his forces and there are those in Kufa. Kufa, if you don't know this, is a most down-at-heels little town, one of those military camps that arose as if of themselves, from the very mud one might say, in the days when the Prophet's heirs were beginning to conquer the world. They would capture a territory, a town, and beneath its walls would set up a jund, a military camp. And before you know, that jund would be a town in its own right. Such is Kufa, which lies in the south of Iran's westernmost province, in Iraq, almost to the sea. So, we too have something of a host there, although – strictly between us, now – one that is far and away less imposing than Abu Muslim's. It's stationed, though, not in some far-flung wilderness like Khorasan but within easy reach of the principal highroads of the realm. Our idea is to strike with two armies, the army of Kufa from the south and the army of Abu Muslim from the east, so that Marwan will not know which he must repel first. And it is time too to say outright that the House of Abbas will then take the power into its own hands. I'm speaking of the proclamation of a new caliph, a true caliph, Maniakh. That's why the matter of the murderers is so important at this time. We must know who is doing this, and why. Because they can kill anyone they care to. And who will be the next they care to kill? That's the question."

I weighed this carefully, then asked: "A new caliph? Muhammad of Humayma, who was wooed by a certain apothecary and fragrance trader, is dead, yes?"

"Four years or more," Barmak affirmed.

"Then who is now head of the House of Abbas? Surely not..." And I glanced over at Mansur.

"To know that secret will not profit you at this time," Barmak said, very seriously. "But in the main, yes – the next caliph will be a son of Muhammad of Humayma. Mansur is also a son of Muhammad. Although the old gardener had brothers, who are uncles to Mansur and his brothers. The family of Abbas is large. The rest of it, I say again, you had best not know. Such are the matters before us. Now we must perforce journey again. A week to the west, a week to return, some days there. Yet, for all that, it's merrier on the road."

"HEALER," I SAID TO ASHOFTEH when he had tired of trying to teach me the art of working my will on jagged wounds, "I have a serious question. Imagine a woman who... This is the story: her favorite horse is old. He runs no more. He eats no more. You know what good husbandry advises in such cases. But this woman, then not full-grown, allowed none to approach her darling and cared for him to the end. She slept there in the stables and passed with that horse its last night. And now hear what they say of her today. That she lays people low not only with ease but with pleasure. That she... satisfies wounded warriors on the field of battle. And then she dispatches them with a dagger blow. Is this possible? And if it is possible, what has befallen her? How is she to be helped?"

"How to help a woman who has suddenly begun to take pleasure in killing?" Ashofteh snorted. "And who has wrought such things upon men? Where all may see, if I understand you aright. You may make a true healer yet, Maniakh my good sir, if these are the questions you ask. But I have no easy answers for you. It may have escaped your notice that we are in a war. The world has been upended yet again, and has still to regain its feet. In times such as these, there are in the streets and the marketplaces more people than before, several times more, who need help. You can see it in their eyes. But I swear by all the gods of this world, it's simpler to sew up a wound than to cure a brainsickness. They do not ask for help; sometimes it is even the other way about. So now I shall name a man very well known to you..."

He looked at me with heavy eyes, sighed, and continued: "Note how he speaks when you are alone, for I hear that you have spoken with him more than once, and note how he conducts himself when many others are about. Those are two very different people. With you, in my understanding, it behooves him to be most open-hearted and even easily swayed. But when others appear... He stands very straight, throws back his head. And slices the air with his two hands, like this. And then the hands clench into fists. He has a constant need of someone to defeat. He chooses his opponent and defeats him. To the death. If he has an audience, he has much to say. Such as he must always be in the company of others, must be greatly admired. And how will you help him? That man is very, very sick. I can imagine what he will become in some five years, if he lives that long. But in the meantime, others are dying at his hand. All this" – and he waved an arm to take in the tents from which carried the groans now so familiar to me – "is his handiwork. He cannot stop..."

Indeed. But I had already understood all regarding the Leopard of Merv from my earlier conversation with Yukuk.

"The woman..." I reminded Ashofteh at length.

"What of the woman? I would need to observe her," he said reluctantly. "Her eyes, her face, the movement of her hands... They tell all. Yet how will you fetch her to me? Will she ask you to bring her?"

"But healer," I said, unwilling to yield, "there are herbs... Now that I think of it, is it possible to dose her with potions of such herbs for six days or so? So that she could also endure a journey, strapped to a camel's flank, say, and would only be a little drowsy? And that no harm would come to her from this?"

Ashofteh looked at me long and sadly. Then he grudgingly agreed.

"I shall give you such herbs, Maniakh my good sir. But you should understand that I must first see her as she is, not drugged And then... Then I may well tell you that it is too late. Are you certain that this is the outcome you want?"

Now I began to smile, because for the first time I had a tolerably clear notion of what could be done. Bind her. Deliver her to the hospital. Hear the verdict. Send her, drugged with herbs, to Samarkand. Assign her a bodyguard. Consign her to the best physicians .

Give her a chance.

Who if not I, a man with all the resources of Samarkand's richest family behind him, could do so much? I asked myself. *Is it mere coincidence that I, all unbeknownst to myself, am becoming a physician? Or is it a sign from on high? Maybe my whole life to this day has been like a tree preparing itself to bear sweet fruit, and from amid the thousands of the lost, to save but one woman?*

And I will succeed! I will succeed in all!

"I'm certain only that I want to try," I said at last, trying to master the joyful curling of my lips. "And do not doubt that I shall try."

Ashofteh sighed again.

"I feel you'll not be my pupil long," he said gloomily after a pause. "You've got yourself into a distasteful business. And a pity it is, for you're a good pupil. And be mindful that I don't speak thus to everyone."

"Well, if I have to leave, I promise to buy a girl and present her to you so that you may teach her any trade," was my flippant response.

ON THE ROAD TO THE fortress, I followed the healer's method of inhaling and exhaling very slowly, several times, but the fear that had settled into the pit of my stomach did not pass. It had long been seated there, but I had never before ventured to own to myself what it was.

I was no longer afraid of the murderers.

I was afraid of losing my mind.

Brainsickness is all around us says Yukuk? In time of war and revolt, the brainsick multiply, say you, worthy Ashofteh? But what will the two of you say to the fact that war itself is a brainsickness that is conveyed on the air, that flies in on the wind, like the disease that leaves round pocks forevermore in the skin of those who survive it? And why is that iron-hued ailment claiming ever more victims on every hand?

She's brainsick, they tell me. And am I sound of mind?

And for the first time in recent months, my thoughts returned to the most infinitesimal details of all that had transpired at Adijer's winery, to what I had seen there and done naught to prevent or to stop. Ere now I had driven those memories from me, but there must come a time to draw them out.

What if that ailment, that clouding of my reason, had not left me but was only biding its time to break loose from the secret crannies of my heart?

Walking now through the fortress enclosure, I glanced about, to see striding toward me a grand old man whose hoary beard was framed with a border the color of carrots. Maybe it was too long due for dyeing and was growing out? Then all was as it should be, no brainsickness here.

Yes, but that, that... For several days now it had seemed to me that close to my home, on the edge of the enclosure, rather too many women had gathered. There they were, sitting in a tight little circle, selling fabrics of some kind. Their faces were close covered with translucent veils, following the enchanting custom that had been born in the eternally seething minds of the denizens of Constantine's city in lovely Byzant. True enough, if you ride all day through the desert and your face is not enveloped in something, it will become a tanned hide, and what woman would be pleased with that? So faces were perforce covered elsewhere than in Byzant, but there it was now also a matter of decorum.

Who would not want to tear that piece of cloth away from a woman's face or, by contrast, leave the cloth and tear away all the rest? And these women seemed choicely limber, and the movements of their legs and shoulders were both strong and gentle. One would gladly gaze on them ever and again... *Then am I sound of mind or brainsick? Will the day come when I demand that one of them be brought to me by force, without regard for the consequences? Will my chakirs obey the order of a brainsick man?*

The tramp of feet grew louder behind, and my hand jerked of itself toward a dagger that was not there.

But it was only Yukuk coming after me and panting as he ran.

"You were at the hospital today?" he wheezed.

I only nodded.

"And it seems you know nothing. The hospital has grown. By two corpses. That's in the way of things, yes?"

"What corpses?"

"The very same," Yukuk said almost soundlessly, coming closer. "Omar and Mihraman. You asked the preacher to give them to you, but it so falls out that both of them have just been found at the back of the courtyard, dead."

"Daggers?" I asked, wasting no words.

"That's the thing of it. No. Arrows. Arrows to the head."

Yukuk shook his own graying head, visibly ill at ease.

"They let me see all," he said. "Two identical arrows. With iron tips and fletched, in the way of the Arabiya. The two corpses lay almost side by side. Say one man is hit by an arrow, but then the other doesn't stand still. He tries to flee. Which means he should lie at some distance from the first. But here someone drew his bow twice with furious speed and each time hit square. And it happened just now, while you... while you were speaking with the healer, were dispensing remedies... Yes, and your prophet's solicitor has vanished. He hasn't been seen these two days. And there it is."

We were silent.

"And so, sire," Yukuk said at length, and yet more preoccupied than before. "It's a bad business. Where there were daggers, now there are bows. Maybe this is the preacher's answer to you, or maybe some other knows that you are on the trail. And is paring that trail away, leaving you exposed. You went to the preacher undisguised... I beg you to choose your two remaining chakirs from among your patients with all haste, since for those two it was not meant to be. Because, as the preacher himself said, decisive days are upon us. And you and I stand scarce prepared."

15

A BLINDING LIGHT

I was riding as if to my own execution. Even Shabdiz trod the hot earth somewhat diffidently, glancing back a time or two at the great bulk of the fortress of Merv beyond the river, as it dwindled away behind us. He had indeed been a fortunate find for me. He was so... taciturn, if such may be said of a horse. But reliable. Like a Yukuk with four hooves.

Two of my chakirs, Evman and Muhammad, were following me a short distance behind, their faces wrapped against the sun that shone full in our eyes.

An all-too-familiar hill stood to my left now, while ahead of me, the road to Bukhara led away into the molten gold.

As I rode, I turned over in my mind some well-weighed words, unsure though I was that any words could properly be addressed to the girl I had so signally failed to defend when... At that point, even my thoughts grew mute.

But I could no longer avoid a visit to Anahita for at least two good reasons, they being a man by the name of Hashim and also a certain garden.

And I was overjoyed to discover that the wall, the gate and the roofs behind them were still in their place.

The pungent odor of wine, detectable even in the courtyard, also told me that Adijer's enterprise had not vanished from the face of the earth over the past months. And the people running hither and thither only confirmed me in my conclusion.

"Oh, you've come for your donkey?" It was a woman's voice, and it came from down by my stirrup. "He is weary of waiting for you. You're well? You have a fine mount? And even a bodyguard? How good this is..."

And all became simpler, clearer, easier then. I was led into the shade, all the while trying to keep the smile of an idiot from my face, as servant girls brought an entirely unsurprising pitcher of wine.

"A summer wine, this is, and light as can be," she said. "My poor father struggled through six long harvests to find that faint, refreshing tartness."

I attempted a courteous refusal, but in answer I heard: "I'll have none of that. You are, after all, a welcome guest in this house."

I was dumbstruck. And Anahita, with a slight, sorrowful smile, modestly diverted her gaze to the toes of my right manly, soil-spattered boots.

"The shame is gone as if had never been..." she went on. "But you hail from Samarkand and likely understand none of this. I can only imagine what you have thought of me since that time. Know you, then, that when..." – roundly mortified now, she finally found a way to say it – "... such a thing befalls a woman here, in Khorasan, it means naught. But in some villages to the west of Iran, in Iraq that is, her kin may even kill her for the disgrace it brings upon the family. Here, though, there exists an old custom whereby the shame may be washed away..."

She allowed a tactful pause.

"And so my shame was lifted from me... Such customs there are even now, for all that earlier, when the Shahanshah reigned, centuries passed without war. But here the old ways are all remembered and have stood us in good stead. Is there not, in your home of Sogdia, the custom of a darkened room that several men and women enter once each year and where, in the darkness, all is permitted them?"

Yes, that custom was indeed still observed in parts of Sogdia. I filled my chest with a deep draught of air. Those most savage scenes and images, which had brought a flush of humbling regret to my face day after day, flew from my head, and I could at last look upon her calmly. And see that she was an ordinary and not very beautiful young woman with dark, clever eyes and also with a good head for business, given that her father's enterprise had not foundered in the months past.

And now I could broach the matter that had brought me here.

But first I must delight in the truly light wine that was winging its way around my mouth. Then my donkey was presented to me.

"He wasn't idle here," I was told. "First he bore vine trimmings, then water, and soon it would have been the harvest. Then he would have known what work is, but instead you'll take him?"

The donkey looked at me superciliously and bared his strong, yellow teeth as a sign that he recognized me, brief as our acquaintance had been. Upon which he became wholly Anahita's, because the last thing I needed in my home on the flank of the fortress of Merv was a donkey.

And I heard her account of her continuing difficulties, inasmuch as all that had been done proficiently while her father lived was now achieved by dint of laborious effort. And the vultures were closing in: already five offers had been made to buy.

For that, though, I had come prepared.

I drew five gold dinars from the heavy purse at my belt and slowly laid them, one by one, on the low table.

"So that you'll sell to no one," I said. "This is earnest money that you may spend as you will, earnest money in consideration of a future transaction between us, whose price we shall discuss at another time. This will make our house a conjoint owner, with a lesser interest. The greater interest will lie with you, Anahita, or with your husband, should husband there be. And you will make the wine. And our family will buy it – not all, of course, but as much as before, at a little over your cost."

This was now a festival and she the guest of honor. She scurried hither and thither, calling others to witness, then solemnly dropped one of the dinars into a goblet of wine and in view of the assembled company drank the wine to the dregs. And her eyes began to shine.

"And now, Anahita," I said, not refusing the refilling of my own goblet, "now that all have left us, I have two matters to discuss. The first is: Why did the man without a face kill your father? Because of me?"

She shook her head sadly. "No. I had my part to play in his death, did I not? It all began two years ago. My father was among the most respected of the Bihafridis. That is a very ancient doctrine of these parts. And then they were all killed, by Hashim of the fearsome face. But he let my father live, ordering him to tell him all, to obey his every command."

And then I understood. This was how all my ill-fated brother's dealings through that house had come to the knowledge of Abu Muslim's secret chancery. Moreover, the thread might surely have run to our trading yard in Bukhara not necessarily from Zargisu but like as not from these very gates. And from Bukhara, evidently, on to Samarkand, since those two with the daggers must have been installed as servants in our home by someone. *I shall have whereof to write to my brother now, and couched in no verse either*, I thought.

"Then you appeared," Anahita continued. "And the two who followed after you must surely have taken themselves at a dead gallop to that... terrible man. My father likely thought he would still have time to... And besides, he had first to confirm who you were and then decide whether or not to tell Hashim about you, yes?"

Well, true – he did not know who I was, but my pursuers did, and they were not about to wait. And ere he died, poor Adijer had had time to say naught but "What is this, and so soon? I'll go and explain all to them..." And he had saved me, saved my life by stuffing me into that jar...

But that thought only stabbed me to the heart, because behind it was another thought, yet larger and more important, which was that there now remained no doubt as to who was behind the murderers and who was trying to injure my brother's affairs.

And so our family's friendship with Abu Muslim proves some impediment to you, Sorcerer Hashim? And Abu Muslim himself has grown superfluous?

I said the needful then to the great wine-maker's memory. Anahita, her face turned to the sky, also whispered some words, And I proceeded to the second part of my errand.

"My family needs not only a winery here," I said, "but also one or two good orchards. Help me choose them, Anahita. I expect you know everything here, not least the prices that are named to strangers. Here it is, then: I need a large garden reasonably close to Merv – say, no more than two days' journey away. Surrounded by a sturdy wall. Not in a village, but best in some distant place, almost like a castle. You know, I recently tried to strike a bargain on one such garden that the local people downright feared – someone had died there or the like. Yet the price was simply formidable. And picture this, Anahita – we would have needed to lay down new underground water conduits. And until we did, it would be hard even to know if the ground was good. So, are there not other such gardens, even such as were abandoned after Abu Muslim came, even such as are still haunted by the souls of the dead, provided only that trees grow there?"

"Hmm. Yes there are. Of course there are," she began slowly.

When she was done, though, we had to search the house for a Sogdian brush and a scrap of parchment – there being no papyrus – to list them all. And I was striving not to show my joy... nay, my very delight.

"Yes, Anahita," I said as I took to my horse, putting the precious piece of parchment away, "since the day of my arrival, no little time has elapsed and a great deal has changed. I am no longer foe to the man without a face. I now live in the fortress of Merv and see him almost daily. You may send a courier to him here and now, and tell him everything about my visit, omitting nothing. I shall have no objection."

She began to titter then, all abashed, and to blush. Her face was a picture of frank relief.

"Tell him that I want to buy a share of your enterprise and take your wine at a good price," I reeled off. "That my plans for trading in Merv are earnest. That I may long remain here. But as for my needing an orchard – best not speak of that yet. Because Hashim has more on his mind than war here, and before you know, he will have come in and purchased the garden in my stead."

Anahita looked at me with some doubt and nodded.

A week, I told myself, running over the points of the list in my mind. *A week and I shall find my garden.*

"Anahita!" I called her from the saddle. "What was the name of that general whose warriors brought your special vines here?"

"Crassus," she replied, wrinkling her brow. "Marcus Crassus."

Not until I was nearing my home did I suddenly understand my folly.

Bihaf... oh, however that strange name was said.

Adijer, Anahita's father, had been one of them.

And Zargisu had some connection to them.

Which meant that Adijer, and possibly Anahita too, had seen her, had spoken with her.

I came close to making my mount rear as I turned him sharply around, before telling myself that it mattered not, that I would return on the morrow or in the week following. Nothing would happen in that time.

And I almost laughed aloud. I was so near, so near to my goal!

BUT YUKUK WAS ALMOST RUNNING toward me across the fortress enclosure on those long legs of his.

"I found the native village of the man with the large nose," he began, forgoing all salutations. "And there I learned that he who followed after your woman" – at which point he rattled off some name – "lies dead."

A dead man who still strikes unerringly with his bow – that at least was an interesting beginning. But what followed was more engaging still. Yukuk, as he had already informed me, had journeyed to that native village, where lived such as were well familiar with the doctrine of the Bihafridis... Ah, mince no words – where lived the surviving adherents of that doctrine. And he was told that when the mother of the big-nosed man learned that her son had dealt a blow with a wooden-handled dagger there in the enclosure within the fortress of Merv and, with the word "pairidaeza" on his lips, had gone to find his garden, she donned her finest attire and darkened her eyelids with kohl. But then came the tidings that he had, rather, come away alive, upon which she sprinkled sand on her head and tore her face, and ever after told everyone that she no longer had a son.

But we already knew where the tale of the murderers had begun and that the sorcerer Hashim had simply pilfered the idea from those he had all but annihilated while retaining in his service the two or three still left alive. And since many murderers were required, he had begun to groom them from among those who had lost their taste for life – the wounded, the destitute... And sure it was that our trading house had, by a strange coincidence, hampered him greatly. Wherever he might go – the hospital, Adijer's winery... – there were Maniakhs.

"While I think of it, ser," Yukuk continued, "we now have one riddle the less. I've been ever pondering why most of the murders must be committed in plain sight of a crowd. At first it seemed to me that it was because the murderer must cut his victim down and say naught thereafter. But now I see it's because they must be as much as possible heroes to their own kind, even if only to their mothers. It was probably an interesting doctrine, that teaching of the Bihafridis. And even more interesting is that with this secret army one can hold an entire land in fear... Or no, not even one land but many..."

I could only agree.

"But this, now, is interesting indeed," he went on, with a shake of the head. "Do you know which murder is spoken of in connection with our big-nosed man? The one that happened over there, in the enclosure, as you watched. That was committed by those two self-styled dapirpats who sat beside you below the wall. One murderer was cut down on the spot and the other, he of the big nose, was, in the event, captured. A rare case, was it not? And it proves to be rare for a reason. I spent a quantity of your dirhams to come at him, but imagine

– he was no longer in the prison. He had, I was told, 'vanished.' But do you know the look of the prisons that lie almost below our feet here, in the fortress of Merv?"

Yukuk made a smooth motion with his two hands, as if caressing a woman's contours.

"A sack of earth, they are. The walls meet above, so it's impossible to scale them. None may 'vanish' from such a place. A man can only be taken out of it. And this means that, one, he has friends of consequence in high places. Two, he's no ordinary murderer, whose path leads directly to paradise. He's an important member of their company. Evidently, in certain special instances, one murderer does the deed while the other is there as surety, watching but attempting no knifeplay of his own. And three, if such be the case, the murder of that warrior here, in the fortress, was an important one. This I've often pondered: What if only some of the murders are the real object and the rest a distraction? And used, furthermore, as a training exercise? Then, last, that big-nosed man is now killing the overly loose of tongue with arrows from his bow, but ere this was seen in the company of that woman of yours..."

"Stop, Yukuk," I said, with more than a modicum of pride. "As for friends of consequence, that much is plain. I know to a nicety everything about Hashim who is in want of a face."

And I quickly recounted my morning conversation, after which I brought out my booty in the form of the list inscribed on parchment, and asked, "Now, what about these gardens?"

I watched Yukuk's lips moving during his brief perusal of that record.

"This is not the one, nor this... But this – how did I not guess it earlier?"

"What is it, Yukuk? You've found one you know?"

"But it's not only a garden," he said pensively, jabbing the parchment with a finger. "It's a small palace. In the desert. With a very good garden. Your girl erred, though, since it's not for sale. It's a rustic residence of the sovereign lord of the faithful, the one closest to Merv. I've also seen several such close to Damascus."

"The Caliph's palace? Here, at such a far remove?"

"I know that place, sire. No caliph has ever been there, it's true, but that's of no matter now. The holdings of the sovereign lord of the faithful in Khorasan have surely all fallen to the rebels. And are now at the disposal of none other than Abu Muslim. Ah, how did I not think of this before?.."

"Or, rather, at the disposal of the head of his secret chancery," I summed up for him. "So I'd do well to take me to that palace. How does tomorrow suit, Yukuk?"

At that, he began a lengthy explanation of why I had best not show my face there. And I made no objection, although... although I had for several days been unable to put off the strange sensation that time was growing very short.

At this time, for one thing, I should have been resting after my journey, but I was ill at ease. I began to loiter, aimless and nervous, about our closely guarded section of the enclosure.

Abu Salama, whom Mansur and Barmak had left here in their absence, came to me and, from the vantage of his stature and his majesty, told me that "they of the Prophet's house" had been expected in Merv that day but as of the morning, when the illustrious Abu Salama was last at the house, had not yet arrived.

We spoke of the art of the Iranian kitchen and of how the Arabiya had adopted it along with the attire of Iran, yet still could not take on the ability that ran in the blood of every Iranian to govern, to collect and count money, and so forth. And how every caliph this century past had learned for himself that if the scriveners in whichever of his chanceries were children of Iran, his affairs there would be well ordered.

All this I knew without help from Abu Salama, and I found him inexpressibly tedious.

Ziyad ibn Saleh came to me next, for no reason other than to express his good will. He made long-drawn-out inquiries regarding the fountains of Samarkand, ascertained the truth of what he had heard of their standing in streets and gardens, open to all, and of the copper basins of those fountains being cleaned weekly. And so I told him about the fountains and the clay pipes that ran below the ground throughout the city bringing water, to those fountains among all else. Ziyad also informed me that Abu Muslim had departed for a few days to visit his troops.

"Do you feel that preparations are in train, Maniakh?" he asked.

A shadow fell on us then as a rider approached, the one whom I still deemed too handsome, too perfect not to be feared – Khalid. Composed, amiable, smiling, he sprang from his horse and embraced Ziyad. And then, after a scarce discernible vacillation, embraced me also, at which I felt the iron-clad breast beneath his cloak and saw at close range the magnificent nose that resembled a battle axe.

Then he passed on, into the depths of the courtyard.

While I caught my breath.

And felt my legs now leaden from all that senseless walking to and fro. I remembered the wine I had drunk that morning and was suddenly overwhelmed by a weariness of no small consequence. Evening was drawing on, and it was time to return to my roost in the shadow of the foliage and eat something. Although, possibly due to the heat, I was not hungry.

"Yukuk, what's amiss?" I asked him at haphazard. "I don't see…"

"Amiss?" he repeated slowly, as his face grew hard and pensive. "All is, I'd say, as it should be. Our matter takes its course. The garden we shall find by degrees. Much is already understood: Who the murderers are, whence they come, how they operate. We know who stands behind them. We know that Hashim must perforce conduct his operations in secret, which means he is still weak. But let me say this to you, sire. I do indeed know what's amiss. It is that there have long been no attempts on anyone's life. What does that mean? For we know how they work, after all. They send out far ahead of time such as wish to transcend death. Remember, there has been but one instance of two murderers pursuing a man yet going astray. That instance was the one that befell you, sire. At that time, their masters learned that these murderers are in general ill-suited to such sport. They are mostly sick men whose wounds have yet to heal, or some such. They have nowhere else to go, so are dispatched to the heavenly gardens. Very well, but now understand this – all the future murderers have long been in place. They're stable hands in someone's service. They go to the temple every day to pray. They're chakirs." And here Yukuk could not but glance around at my guards, while a chill gripped my own heart. "And so they sit, every one of them, and wait. But for what?"

Yukuk was abashed then, which he was very seldom. He was long clearing his throat before saying, his voice hoarser than usual: "I crave your pardon for my forgetfulness. An envoy has been here. Your friends have arrived and they ask you to attend them this day, at any time."

"Oh dear," I said, most feelingly, and betook myself to Mansur's home in the far west of the city.

But no joy awaited me there either. The recently arrived Mansur was sitting on a rug and digging into the earth with either a dagger or a simple piece of iron. Digging and drawing to himself, and the furrow deepened with each stroke. The boy, with his ever-present bodyguard, was playing alone, casting dice onto a board.

Then Mansur abruptly laid the iron aside and engaged me in conversation on poetry and poets, which conversation conveyed no more to me than that this haggard and weary man, all else aside, was truly well-read in poetry and wished to be more so.

Next, at his request, I gave him the lengthy tale of how Gao Xianzhi, general of the Celestial Empire, had two years earlier won what was as yet the Imperial troops' only victory over the army of Tibet, and not on a plain either but in the small and mountainous kingdoms of Balur and Gilgit. He had done it by working deceit on his own army more than on the Tibetan forces, for had his soldiers known that those who met them were not local guides but Gao's own men in disguise, had they guessed that they were not merely performing maneuvers but going into battle, there would have been no victory.

Mansur nodded time and again, but I could see that his thoughts were far away.

And I could feel on my very skin the precious time passing fruitlessly by.

Barmak, when he found his way to me at last, listened most attentively to all I had to say, including my questions, which were: "Why have there been no recent attempts on anyone's life?" and "Can I myself be in jeopardy?"

"Only for now," he said, uncommonly terse, in answer to both queries, and frowned. "You, my dear man, are still of interest to all and present no serious danger to anyone. You're right, though; that too may change. But that naught is occurring – you yourself, you see, are discomposed by it. As am I," he added. "And so we all indeed must sit and wait, and wonder when the next blow will fall. Although should you come but one step closer to the answer to this riddle, matters will run far and fast, make no mistake... For you and the truth are close as can be. Because you work excellent well."

Thus inspired, I was shown the door, unfed as always, and told that I had been troubled for naught today. They were awaiting important tidings that, for no known reason, had yet to come, but tomorrow we would converse in earnest.

To this day I do not understand what, other than bad humor, prompted me to forbid Yukuk from going on the morrow to survey the Caliph's rustic garden-palace, while adding that something was possibly in prospect for the morning.

After one of his characteristic pauses, Yukuk bowed his head.

But had I not done that, it is unlikely that I would be alive this day.

I slept badly. And when I half-woke I could not rid myself of the sensation that I knew all, positively all, and only had to rouse myself fully and I would see, in the morning light, the whole picture, the exact picture – and that it would be such as to heartily displease me.

WHEN ON THE FOLLOWING DAY I presented myself, still heavy from lack of sleep, at the home of Mansur and Barmak, I knew at once that something was indeed amiss.

Mansur sat with fixed gaze. The boy Muhammad clung to him in silence, which for some reason brought to mind that I had only heard his voice from afar but when adults – I, for one – approached, he would fall silent. *He has good breeding*, I thought.

"Ibrahim has been arrested," Barmak informed me through tight lips.

I stared at him, bewildered. Ibrahim? Who was Ibrahim?

"The man whose name I could not tell you three weeks ago," Barmak hastened to explain. "Mansur's brother. It was he whom we wished to declare the true caliph. The head of the House of Abbas. Or the former head, since Caliph Marwan's berid will never release him now. And so it is, Maniakh. Only yesterday we were saying, you and I, that all was very quiet. Now it has begun."

"Where was he arrested?" I asked, still perplexed.

"What does that matter, my dear man? Although it is a good question. He was arrested in the village of Humayma, where, as you know, it all started. It started with Muhammad of the House of Abbas, who sired three sons – Ibrahim, Abu al-Abbas and Abu Jafar, nicknamed Mansur. And to think that only shortly before setting out for this place we were at peace, for we had finished moving the entire family to Kufa, on the very eve of the decisive days to come. Ibrahim, as I understand it, had simply returned to Humayma for a day or two, to perform some errand. And they were waiting for him, the men of that renowned messenger service, the berid. Which we had already discounted as worthless. They had never been to Humayma, not once in all the years it had served as the base of operations for the family Abbas. We did wrong to think so little of them. Very wrong."

"Who knew that, although the family had moved to Kufa, Ibrahim tarried still in Humayma?" I asked. The question had come quickly.

Barmak looked at me, his head atilt.

"Another good question, this. But even Mansur didn't know. Nor did I."

"I must think," I said in a feeble voice. Barmak nodded despondently and spread his hands.

And again I returned to the fortress, to await I knew not what. Because I had nowhere else to go and naught else to do.

I settled in my roost, from which I could see the whole enclosure. All was as it ever was. A circle of women, upward of ten – the same ones, their faces covered – who were at that moment giving food to an aged beggar. Beyond them, the rest of the crowd. The mail-clad guard motionless in the heat, barring the crowd in the public enclosure from the depths where we resided. People moving languidly, also by reason of the heat, about our domain, whence was governed unruly Khorasan, along with Balkh and Nishapur. *Naught of consequence here*, I thought. *A fortress enclosure like any other.*

It came to me then that we had found the garden that lay hidden, if it was indeed hidden there, in the Caliph's former palace. The palace that was officially owned not even by Hashim, but by none other than the Leopard of Merv.

"They're friends," Yukuk had said of them.

But what if all that had happened here was not a plot hatched by Hashim against the House of Abbas and against his own master, Abu Muslim? What if it was a plot in which the presently absent general, Hashim's friend, was much pleased to participate? What of that?

Well, then, much would become clear that earlier had been utterly otherwise. For example, the true role that I – and my brother too – had played in it all.

I had no further need to wait for the letter from Aspanak that should name for me the recipient of funds from our grandfather, then our father, and today my brother.

Because my brother had spoken of money given to the House of Abbas. Which was tantamount to it going to Mansur. And none at all to Abu Muslim.

But suppose, only suppose, that Abu Muslim had wanted to depend somewhat less on the family through whose veins coursed the blood of the Prophet and whose treasurer went by the unpleasant byname of Pinchpenny... No wonder, then, that Abu Muslim must, among all else, break the thread of money that ran from our trading house through Merv and thence westward, to the House of Abbas. And do it in such a way that he would at first remain beyond blame and even above suspicion.

What should next transpire was... all that had in fact transpired. Two daggers, one for my brother and one for me, the utter destruction of the network of spies that answered to the House of Maniakh in Merv and even in Bukhara. And Hashim of the singed face arranging that raid on the winery of Adijer, his reluctant agent, as punishment because one by the name of Maniakh had appeared there and Adijer had not sent timely notice...

But already my memory was obligingly hinting to me that, although Abu Muslim knew of murderers being operated under his very nose, I had never seen him guarded in any way out of the ordinary. The murderers were quite simply killing his enemies but no others. Yes, he had killed tens of thousands of his own, but did he perhaps have friends that he feared to do away with openly, lest he thereby stir up the rest of his comrades in arms – men such as Ziyad?

Which brought me to the solution to yet another puzzle. "Tell me, Maniakh," he had asked, "is there nothing you fear? Then why so?"

How must he have marveled to see me before him, seeking his leave to live in the fortress, on his very doorstep. "The head of the House of Maniakh is here? The head of the House of Maniakh has come to me, and in black garments?" But how simple it was: he had thought that I had resolved to play for all or nothing, by staking my life as the gage of our alliance. And he evidently still deemed me insanely bold and therefore worthy of his respect – nay, his admiration. And, what is more, a man capable of casting Samarkand at his feet.

Had not the unctuous preacher told me "How good that you are with us"?

Which meant that there was naught to fear from my extensive knowledge of those who wished to transcend death. And that I would be tolerated as long as I was "with them," although, for safety's sake, Omar and Mihraman had been treated to an arrow apiece in the head. Because it were best I did not know too much too soon.

In torment now, I twisted my head from side to side. *Brook no distractions!* I told myself. *A little more thought, only a little more!* So. What sense was there in Abu Muslim's wresting our house away from the House of Abbas, yearning for an alliance with us, if the goal of the Merv rebellion was to replace a caliph from the House of Umayyah with a man in whose veins ran the blood of the Prophet?

How this accursed heat hampers me!

But suddenly I was cold. *For decisive days are upon us*, I heard in my head the deep bass voice of that mountain of a preacher. *And he whom men call the Mahdi, the redeemer, is here. He is already among us, yet we in our foolishness pass him by and fail to notice him. But wait a while, for it is ever thus. You sit in the gloom, and suddenly there comes a blinding light!*

And that light at last shone upon me.

Because why would Abu Muslim need people with the Prophet's blood in their veins, if he himself was the Mahdi who was already here among us? Only one more province conquered by an army a hundred thousand strong and he would be able to discover the blood of the Prophet flowing in his own veins and declare himself a god into the bargain. *With such preachers in his employ*, I thought, *it would be the work of a moment.*

There began in me a trembling.

"Put the chakirs on full alert, Yukuk. Have the horses saddled. Station two chakirs with them to await the signal. Armor must be worn and weapons carried."

I was feverishly trying to tie the thick money belt under my jacket, while my eyes fixed on the brush that lay on the rug along with my other writing accoutrements. Would I really have to abandon them yet again?

The enclosure that had been slumbering in the searing, quivering heat came alive. With astonishing dexterity, my boys from Samarkand – nine of them now, they having been augmented of late by the last two, Muslim and Devgon – donned their heavy chain mail, while two of them sped through the crowd toward the outlet from the fortress.

The outlet through which... now entered, as on the day when I had first come upon Barmak, a small caravan consisting of Mansur the Pinchpenny, the dark-skinned boy, the slave with the pitted face, the bodyguard and Barmak himself, majestic in clean, bright garments... They halted before the line of guards, hard by me, and toward them came the black-bearded Abu Salama, as dignified as ever was. He spoke a while with Mansur and vanished again.

"What's afoot, Barmak?" was my agitated question for him, once descended from my roost at a dead run.

"Serious matters are afoot, my young friend, as you well know... Now we're going to speak with Abu Muslim and make those decisions. Ah, so this is your modest abode? Agreeable. Most agreeable."

I understood none of this. How could they speak with Abu Muslim, when Ziyad, his secretary, had just told me that he was gone for a few days to visit his troops? Who, then, could have summoned here, on this day and at this time, these people from the House of Abbas? And why?

"Barmak, tell me quickly: Who is Abu Salama? What does he do for you in Kufa or Humayma or wherever else he has work to do?"

"Well, since you now know so much, why not say it? He commands all our troops in Kufa, where the family Abbas has betaken itself. As I have already told you, those troops are not over-numerous, but in Kufa, where none has known these several months with whom the authority lies, he is a man of note..."

Commands all the troops... Then what does the family Abbas command? And what is to prevent that commander of the unruly army of Kufa from reaching agreement with he who commands the unruly army of Merv, without regard for any Ibrahims or the like?

"Wait Barmak, for the love of all the gods and prophets. Did Abu Salama himself tell you that Abu Muslim awaited you? That he is sitting there now and waiting for you? Yes? Then I have another question for you: Could Abu Salama have known that your Ibrahim was not in Kufa but in the village of Humayma, where he could easily be seized? Suppose, now, that although you didn't know that, Abu

Salama did, and he told Abu Muslim. How easy it would have been for him to send a courier directly to Haran, to the Caliph's palace. A few days' journey at a full gallop... They may not have believed the courier, but all the servants of the berid had to do was travel to Humayma and look into it..."

Barmak looked at me with silent, stony curiosity, until Mansur, who had dismounted, along with the boy, from his camel and moved into the shade, called him. Barmak glanced at me, his face most grave, and shook his gleaming white beard. Then another summons came and he must away.

I, though, remained at the foot of my stairs.

No, I was in no peril for the time being. How often had I had it hinted to me, subtly and far less so, that decisive days were approaching and when they came I must neither miscarry nor misguide... From which I somehow understood that I was being required only to do nothing. If anyone was to be killed soon, it would not be me. I would not be the next to follow the departed Ibrahim.

I glanced around fitfully, seeing the treasurer of the House of Abbas seated now in the shade, the boy, his bodyguards, Barmak, the group of women, the beggar and the crowd.

Abu Salama was gone.

And none other than he had appeared.

Because there was no need of it. The only need now was to strike down the victim there, in the enclosure, and so depart, or even go off to be with the army, feigning stark surprise at all that would then ensue.

I was alone, at the center of no one's attention.

And only paces away, marked for slaughter, sat Mansur, whose name means Victorious – a black, gangling shadow alone beneath a tree.

We shall build a city. We shall build the best city on this earth. The words resounded in my head.

16

THE FLIGHT OF THE HAWK

Those who would run must first fall forward but then extend a leg to keep from falling.

As if losing my footing, I began to fall toward Mansur but my legs, first one then the other, held me up in that endless fall.

And I was running, dodging around the line of guards while one thought pulsed in my head: *All's out of joint. I'm making a terrible mistake.*

Yukuk's words were also pounding in my mind. *The murderers are in place,* he had said. *They're ready. They're waiting.*

Then where are they? They should be here, now, no farther from their victim than a dagger blow can reach.

I was running and watching Mansur beneath his tree, as he raised his black eyes to me in astonishment. He was alone, utterly alone beneath that tree. Many paces lay between him and those closest to him in the enclosure. Then where were his murderers? This was indeed a mistake.

The two bodyguards! The two bodyguards who had never, in my recollection, moved so much as a step away...

... from his son, the dark-skinned lad, the pupil of the lordly Barmak.

Yukuk was running toward me, sword in hand. I gestured him toward the two bodyguards, one standing beneath a wall the color of sand while the other was already halfway between that wall and another tree, where stood the dark-skinned boy who was just beginning to turn and look at the place where something was transpiring that baffled his understanding. From whence people he did not know were rushing toward him.

The boy seemed about to take a step toward the bodyguard, knowing, when all came to all, that such must be his refuge, hastily sought, when unpleasantness arose. For that, the man was made.

But the guard was running too, leaning hard forward, his face bereft of reason and his right hand already sliding from the folds of his garments.

Between him and the boy was no one, nothing. The only person closest to them both was I. But my hands were empty and even at a run, I would not have reached either one in time.

And so I did the one thing I could do.

I flew.

Three bounding leaps and a plunge through the air, head first, my aim the patch of rust-yellow earth where the murderer should be in a fleeting instant.

I cannot know the look of my flight, which lasted for a mere five or six strides of my not very long legs. I think that to an observer it must have resembled the curved trajectory of a sack flung by a caravan driver from a camel's back, to fall to earth with a heavy thud and a signal lack of grace.

But today that brief flight is to me one of the finest pages in the book of my life.

And so I flew, and saw the bewildered expression on the boy's swarthy countenance, and the woeful eyes of Mansur, as he stood motionless, his arms raised, and also the black circle of his mouth, agape in a soundless cry. I flew, like a hawk to its prey, and during that endless flight I thought that every child enters this world to see the turquoise blue of the sky by day and the scattering of stars by night, to live out his days to the full and to say with pride at the end of all, *I was here, my life changed the world if only minutely, so speak my name and remember me.* And I knew that whatever this boy with the inquisitive eyes would become, whatever he would bring to this world, be it bright light or dark sorrow, never, never, never is there reason enough to kill a child.

I landed painfully on a twisted arm and shoulder, and the sunlight above me was for an instant eclipsed by a black, batlike shadow, as the murderer, his garments fluttering, swooped over me and fell, hitting his head on the ground. The two of us raised a cloud of gilded saffron dust.

I was already regaining my feet, while the murderer, shaking his head, was also trying to rise and not only that but also to reach the dagger with the wooden handle I knew so well, which lay at his fingertips. But Mansur had already clasped his son to his breast, at risk of stifling him in his unreasonably long arms, as Yukuk, with an instantaneous sweep of his sword, felled the second murderer by the wall, while turning to the first and crying, to whom I know not, "Alive, take them alive!"

"Ooo-ooo," said the air above me in a dull drone, and there appeared in the back of the murderer's head the fletching of a gray arrow, protruding like a pin that secured his white head wrap.

"Flee, flee this place," I wheezed to Mansur, and he dragged the boy away in his tight embrace through the crowd that had begun to gather.

In my mind I thanked that crowd. There was now less cause to fear the big-nosed bowman's arrows, the fellows of the one that had just brought down the murderer, flying in from the left, from the gallery of a home like my own.

"All chakirs to horse!" I called to Yukuk. Hearing that cry, Mansur turned his dark-gray face toward me and nodded silently. Barmak, stumbling and sullying his white garments with dust, was struggling to catch up. And so we sped through the shrieking crowd toward the outlet from the enclosure between those two glum towers.

Then behind the backs of Abu Muslim's guards came a snorting and a pounding of hooves. They scuttled aside to make way for ten horsemen in black, some with swords and others without. The crowd also parted.

Nanivandak and Muslim were meanwhile splitting the crowd from the other side, coming in through the gates. They were leading my horses by the reins, and Mansur and the boy were already clambering onto one of them.

The hoar-headed Barmak was still bringing up the rear.

And here I had the delight of witnessing a scene that lasted but two instants but was none the less remarkable for that. I saw a king turn horse thief.

Barmak, panting still, tugged on the reins of a gray nag taking its ease beneath the wall, while men of respectable mien and with blazingly red beards howled at him and one began to pluck at his dagger's hilt.

Barmak's arm in its capacious white sleeve made a flowing motion from left to right. Golden sparks flickered in the air, and several coins fell silently to the ground between him and the nag's owners, who stood stock-still as if fearing to overstep the dinars at their feet.

And so we all – I on Shabdiz, Yukuk double-mounted with Nanivandak, and Barmak on his gray beast – cantered toward the outlet, while the black cloud of horsemen rushed toward us from behind through a crowd now run mad.

Then a dream seemed to descend on me, as, with catlike movements, the women with covered faces leaped up one by one and ran athwart the riders in black, holding strange objects that resembled harnesses interlaced with stones. One woman dropped into a squat, her haunches almost touching the ground, and hurled that length of harness at the nearest rider. The leather straps skimmed the earth before wrapping around the horse's legs and bringing it down with a crash and a snort.

And the aged beggar, who ere now had been sitting peaceably on the rug with the women, ran to me, raising a peremptory hand, while Yukuk, mounted behind Nanivandak, turned the horse in his direction, his sword arm lifted to the side.

"Maniakh of the House of Maniakh, stay that fine fellow with the heavy jaw!" the beggar called to me in an astonishingly youthful voice, his green Sogdian eyes glittering. "And give me a place on your horse!"

"Ashkend of the House of..." I began, then stopped, reaching one hand out to him and waving Yukuk off with the other. "Ashkend, what are you doing? They're women. Clear those women away before they're exterminated!"

"Soon enough they'll be the ones clearing all away and exterminating all before them," the husband of gray-eyed Khalima called out in a happy voice, stepping painfully on my foot in its stirrup as he clambered onto the horse's croup. "Have you forgotten Samarkand's coterie of women warriors? All shall remember them now. And your mother, who was not least among them, would gladly have joined this skirmish. Consider, then, that it is she who has protected you here."

I glanced around, seeing the array of black warriors now a formless heap, as those behind ran into those in front, who then fell, together with their horses. Hooves twitched in clouds of sunlit dust. The women stood in a neat half-circle around that chaos, and the forward ranks, having taken small bows from beneath their clothing, were unhastily training them on the floundering horsemen. The translucent fabric over their faces was thrown back, and I caught a fleeting glimpse of the light hair and merciless blue eye of one who stood in profile to me, firm on straddled legs bent slightly at the knee.

With a shout, the crowd moved away from us as we sped toward the outlet.

"A message," I heard Ashkend say behind me, as he began thrusting something beneath my arm.

Trying hard not to fall behind, I unrolled the small piece of papyrus, almost tearing it in the process, and saw two lines written there. It took but an instant to read the letters that leaped before my eyes, give a joyful laugh, crumple the papyrus and fling it over my shoulder without a second look, for, come what may, no man in this world could have understood what was written there.

Or could have given me my due for having divined the answers to both my questions without help from my brother. Both the question of whether the money disbursed by our House had been going to

Abu Muslim or to Mansur directly, and the other, which had now, if anything, lost somewhat of its importance.

Our small squadron – including all my chakirs, their Balkh chain mail sparkling – was galloping westward along the Madjan canal, toward Mansur's house. No one pursued us.

Again I heard Ashkend's voice, wound tight with sheer joy, behind me. "You and I can fall back now, go to ground, and then travel east. Plans have been made, and thorough ones too. Bukhara is ours again, thanks to you, Maniakh. The road is open."

"Eastward, no," I called to him over my shoulder. "Westward, yes. To Kufa. Send word to my brother, Ashkend, or tell him yourself, but Abu Muslim must be kept in Merv, if only for a few days. If you have here miscreants and murderers you can spare, let them rebel. Let them do what they will. We must have none on our trail."

"I knew it, I knew it! There are indeed such men. And we shall set something afoot in Bukhara too," Ashkend shouted in my ear. "There's a certain Sharik in Bukhara who need only be told and given his money. Then, while the street is deserted, let him have at it... We shall begin this very day."

And so our cavalcade clattered its way to Mansur's house, which was all aflutter. We were expected there, some astute person having sent one of our party ahead to forewarn the household, so that we were met by people waving their arms and urging us to take our place at the head of...

At the head of a great assemblage of heavily loaded camels that filled the street.

What was in those packs that were so heavy even to the eye?

At first I thought that the camels were simply there to shield us from behind, but then I saw two pairs of strong hands removing poor Barmak – *How old is he?* I wondered. *Sixty? Older? How can a man of his years possibly be equal to such hard riding?* – from his maddened dray horse and not loading but cramming him into a camel pack.

And I knew that we would be going nowhere at a gallop that day.

Then my arms were grasped and raised to the torrid sky, while an iron rain of chain mail was poured down over my shoulders, the weight of it causing me to slouch in the saddle. Next, they slung over my head something resembling a shawl or hood but also made of jangling rings. And atop it all they clapped a helmet rounded as an egg and fashioned from forged metal plates. Last, they hung from me a baldric and sword. "Drop your left shoulder and with a sw-e-e-e-ping movement of the right a-a-a-rm, you draw your sword from behind your shoulder, bringing it in a half-ci-i-i-i-rcle before your face" – thus I remembered Yukuk bawling at my chakirs during their training.

The worst, I now knew, could well be yet to come.

The chakirs evidently needed to hear my command for their comfort. And so, bowed down under my armor, I treated them to a mounted inspection – Nanivandak, Evman, Vanaspar, Muslim and all the rest in their glittering metal, with swords and bows, all fully armed at enormous expense. I motioned two of them back, positioning them between the unarmed and the camel train, and commanding them to call out if they caught sight of any pursuit. Yukuk rode ahead, with me.

The company set off toward the western egress from the city, but slowly, so very slowly. I saw Yukuk's face grow grave.

And pursuers did appear in short order, but they were only two horsemen in black, who looked at our drove scarce creeping along, then turned about and fell back. There would be more of this.

And indeed there was, though it came not from behind but stood on the road ahead, blocking our way out of the city.

It was a flicker of black headbands in the swirling dust, their ends fluttering in the breeze. These warriors for the most part wore no armor but then again, they had no need of it, so many of them there were. And such a multitude of swords.

One of those who stood athwart our path rode forward.

And a fine fellow he was, with a proud nose like an ax blade and wearing the same Balkh chain mail as we. He raised a hand to his eyes and began indolently to survey our ranks.

This is the end. Now I understood. I had known, I had known all along that the most to be feared was neither Hashim nor Abu Muslim, but this man. *Here it is, the thing to fear the most.*

But since it had come...

A time there was, thirty years and more ago, when a detachment of Sogdian warriors had ridden to the aid of my Samarkand, close on its capture by Qutayba ibn Muslim. Those young men from the best landowning families had ridden to the city walls armed to the teeth, and such of the Arabiya who survived the battle spoke long thereafter of how they had felt on seeing the intolerable brightness of their mail, their helmets, their iron gauntlets, and their horses' harness. The invaders had been ready to lie prostrate in the dust in supplication to these bejeweled beings the like of which they had never seen before in all their lives.

But no miracle transpired, and all that armor had done naught to aid Samarkand.

And now my turn had come.

All that remained to me was to hope that the incomparable brilliance of the metal we wore would at least give our foes pause. And then we could sweep the unarmed from their camels and into our saddles, and break through at a full gallop. Which would give us time to devise something better.

Amid the snorting of horses, the thudding of hooves and the rumble of voices, I raised my hand and cried, "Warriors of Sogdia, remember your home!"

And they, clad in their indestructible metal, began to flow toward my raised hand, whereupon I arranged them in a row, all ten of them together and leaving none at the back of our train, to face the warriors in black who swirled athwart the road.

"Strike on my command!" I called "None shall break ranks!"

The face of Mansur, as if carved of dark wood, looked down on me from his camel.

And, chilled by the belated insight this brought me, I ended, straining a voice that could now strain no more, with "Defend your Caliph! Safeguard the blood of the Prophet!"

After which it remained only to speak the word, the last word.

"Attack."

What I saw then was strange indeed. My charges were nowise perturbed by any of this. Indeed, Mansur and his boy gazed calmly ahead, disregarding even the warriors before us, although the lad was examining their swords with some curiosity. But Barmak, with no care for aught else and fetching hard breaths, sent his camel forward with a tap of his stick, toward the fine fellow.

Once side by side, they halted, put their heads together and exchanged a few words, following this with an odd gesture in which they reached out their hands and touched the tips of each other's fingers. And Barmak, tapping his camel with that same gnarled stick, returned to us in leisurely style.

There was movement behind him then. Ten of those unknown horsemen were ranging themselves across the road before us, but with their backs to us now. They were manifestly preparing to travel in the direction we seemed to be taking. The rest flowed around us on either side, to gather on the road behind, between us and the city. Yukuk, I noticed, was no longer in the least agitated, and he was never thus without good reason.

And so our small cavalcade set off behind the ten horsemen, leaving the fine fellow motionless on the roadside, his head proudly atilt and a smile on his face.

"But that is my own son, Khalid. Khalid ibn Barmak," the erstwhile king said with an easy tenderness, drawing abreast of me on his toplofty camel. "His own forces here are but small, a mere two hundred horsemen, far from what we have, he and I, in Balkh. But you see how timely they came here. He did well, that boy of mine. Besides, he needs no troops. He manages something of greater import for Abu Muslim, that being money. He is the treasurer for Khorasan, pays the soldiers their wages and so forth. And so, young friend of mine, all here was wrapped up very tight. But we shall speak more on this presently, just as soon as we're a little farther from the city. And now I think of it, what was that you were shouting about a caliph? It was all most handsome on your part, but your understanding was unsound. Or, more accurately, was almost sound. All will be somewhat other than that, provided we reach Kufa in time... But for now we must diverge a jot from our path. Where a small surprise awaits you, my dear Maniakh. Belike it may even please you."

THE SURPRISE RESEMBLED AT ONCE a city and a small military encampment, and even from a distance it stank of horse urine and human feces. Powerfully built men – yet with not a single woman to be seen – loitered here, working their jaws and eyeing us with no particular interest. Beyond were stables and kitchens, and then all that chaos ascended a hill and vanished behind it.

Khalid's ten horsemen began complex negotiations with the warriors who were most obviously guarding this great assemblage of men – though for what reason, I knew not. Then assenting hands were waved at us, and the slave with the pitted face rode from Barmak's camel to the tail of our heavy-freighted caravan.

"Here's what I've been thinking, Maniakh," said the proud father of that fine fellow Khalid, his blue eyes gleaming. "I've been thinking that greed leads to no good. Why should we carry all the way to Kufa this great mountain of iron that I presented to you, as you remember, solely by mistake? As it is, the camels can barely drag themselves along, although mine and Mansur's can at least go at a trot or better. So, since I've given you a hundred sets of arms and armor, someone had best wear them. Take those reinforcements under your command, Maniakh."

And then I knew that I could smile again.

"Yukuk, you told me once that there's an encampment of slaves from Abu Muslim's army here," I said to the tall warrior. "Then we're now in Shawwal?"

"Just so," he nodded with gloomy satisfaction. "And there's more, because hard by here..."

We were distracted then, as the first of those eager to wear chain mail from Balkh began to approach, causing an abiding rackety, din and clangor that beggared description.

Yukuk, self-possessed, sure and calm, was a rush of activity as he followed a profusion of commands, including one of my own. For my part, I had instructed him to take only Sogdians, since I needed to be certain that they would understand my orders. And so each of my chakirs, to his own surprise, became commanding officer to ten men. Following the Sogdians came men of the Turkic races, which is when I knew that a thousand warriors could never defeat this detachment of ours. There was much exchanging of suits of mail and hauling from the camp the old, familiar arms, to compare them with the new. There were spears, short for the infantry and long for the horsemen, and leather quivers holding a fan of arrows. Next came the horses, and a very serious matter that was, because Yukuk was also demanding replacement mounts, for which the entire caravan of camels, relieved now of their burdens, would remain in the camp by way of recompense.

But I was tired.

I wanted to quit this clattering nightmare for some low hill, and there raise my head to a sky strewn with myriads of rhyming lines. "A trace of her remains in sleepless cities' dust"? That was good indeed, but now new lines were sounding in my head

O thou pale sky and thou black-hearted heights
Impaled on cypress dagger in my sight!

Just a little more, just a few more lines. Three, even. And they need never go to my brother. They need only remain here, in what is now our world.

At which point I remembered that my brush, my papyrus and all the rest had of course been left in Merv. My luck with writing implements did indeed leave much to be desired.

And meanwhile, evening was beginning to descend on us.

So I found the treasurer of the House of Abbas and took him by storm, with "Vegetables, Mansur. We must have vegetables, of whatever kind. And no less than one sheep for every ten men, for these are robust warriors. You may pay them for their service when the journey is over. But they must be fed, and well fed, this very evening."

His grip still firm on the boy I had rescued for him, Mansur gnawed a finger nail and put to me some astonishingly apt questions regarding the procuring of cooking vessels and bread. But there was surprise in his eyes as he looked at me and... and I might even have said that this man with the motionless face was somewhat abashed. Barmak, meanwhile, gave a tight-lipped smile.

"We can pass the night here at our ease," Mansur said, answering my unspoken question. "They took a good lambasting from those girls of yours. And another when the youngster Khalid met us and conducted us here. And yet another when, on his command, our detachment came to number in the hundreds. And with such weaponry too. They've surely had their fill of tossing caution to the winds. Hashim will wait now for Abu Muslim, who, as you informed us true and timely this morning, is away from the city. So this night we may sleep easy."

But there was no sleep for me. Because when the cooking pots found I knew not where began to bubble over their fires, Yukuk came to me and sat, having first saluted the slumbering Mansur, Barmak and the rest with hand on heart.

"Sire, I began to speak earlier and was interrupted. To continue, then: Do you know what lies hard by this place?"

"The road to Kufa, of which I know naught," I replied. "We shall travel the length and breadth of Iran, Yukuk."

"I know that road very well... The garden, sire. The murderers' garden. We could be there before dawn."

And Barmak, lying flat on his back, opened one eye and scarce turned his haggard face to us.

"And if it's the wrong garden?" I asked, plumping myself down. "How are we to know..."

"Two have already departed to that place on the best horses, by your leave, sire," Yukuk said impassively.

Barmak opened the other eye.

"We are safeguarding these people's lives..." I began.

But already frantic plans were spinning across my mind like tumbleweed through the dust.

To take her alive and without a scratch on her. To bind her. To bring her with us westward, along the highways of Iran. No, to send her back with two of our men, to Merv. To give her over to the healer. To find Ashkend. To give Ashkend a supply of herbs that induce sleep. To carry her to Samarkand. To give her over to my brother. It would work! It would work most excellently!

On that, my thoughts came to a standstill, for Mansur was now sitting bolt upright – or no, leaning slightly forward – and holding in his ashen fingers a knife with which he was slowly gouging a deep furrow in the earth, drawing it toward himself.

I looked at his face and understood once and for all time that no one, should ever, ever in his life, have that man for an enemy.

"I shall go," he said, in a voice that grated like sand.

"And you'll leave the boy with me?" the recumbent Barmak asked quietly.

All was still. Yukuk sat motionless with a face of carven stone. He seemed to be the only one able to look at that moment into Mansur's ghastly eyes.

"Leave the perpetrators to us, sire," he said at last in a low tone. "We shall not kill them in haste. We shall do it slowly."

Mansur, staring at his knife, scarce bent his head and began to gnaw a nail on his free hand, while we awaited his decision in silence.

"First we eat," he said at length.

After our meal was done, Yukuk's two scouts issued forth from the rays of the setting sun. And the talk we had with them was long and earnest.

Next we posted guards to cover every direction. We demonstrated the alarm signal, having purloined for that purpose several copper bowls and pitchers from our new-found kitchen. We were given to understand that Mansur would stay. We issued our instructions to Nanivandak and Devgon, who were to remain in the camp: in the event of an attack, two groups of ten would fight, while the remainder would hoist the family Abbas onto horses and gallop fast away, surrounding them with a wall of iron.

"We need ropes and something in the way of camel packs," I muttered.

"It's not a castle, ser. Its walls may be scaled with a leap from the saddle," replied Yukuk, understanding me in his own way. "That garden does not defend itself with walls. It lies in the desert and cannot be taken by mere stealth, for all is in the open. And it's said in the villages around to be inhabited by ghouls. Peasants have been found there dead and drained of almost all their blood. But that's easily done. With a thrust of the knife here and here, the blood gushes out and then you cart the body away and throw it onto the dry ground... Hashim would have had no difficulty making it so. But I would have contrived it better."

THEN THE CRIMSON STONES OF the desert, their long, black shadows pointing toward the lilac east. Somnolence in the saddle, strings sounding, a woman's voice. "It is shameful to be of no purpose on this earth. Without my carpets, Samarkand would still be Samarkand. But how happy you are, Nanidat. Your silk unites the whole world. It's stronger than any war, any revolt. If I could but have raised a son and made him to be like... Oh, forgive, forgive, forgive me... You see, again I do more harm..." "You're the only one who never needs to seek my pardon. Because I will forgive you anything. And for that very reason you are not without purpose. You are needful, because without you this world would be empty, Zargisu."

And then a line that flew to me from parts unknown: The moon above Bukhara, a slice of sweetest melon... A line that flew away without a trace, and with naught to follow it.

The snorting of a horse whose head was bound lest it neigh. Horses' hooves, wrapped in rags, to go unheard in that deepest darkness. Yukuk's malignant muttering – "And if we've strayed from the path..." And a yellowish spot of light on the horizon.

"You and you, gather all the horses and hold them when we climb over, and answer the signals by rapping the basin thrice. Three raps mean all is calm and you are alive," Yukuk said in a strained and very distinct whisper. "If two raps come twice in response, bring the horses to us. If nothing comes, stay in your place. You and you, vault to the top of the wall and bide there with drawn bows to give cover. The fourteen of you who remain, go over the wall and proceed by turns, one to the right and one to the left. You and you, block the gates, allowing no one out. The rest of us will scour the garden and enter the house. Leave no man alive, but the women you must take only alive, wounding none gravely. No talking: we do everything swiftly and silently. A mouthful of water each, then follow me, and in haste because at a hundred paces horses' hooves can be heard even when they are wrapped."

AND THEN, RISING UNEXPECTEDLY OUT of the gloom, a line, level and utterly black. It was a wall the height of a man, and above it the knolls of treetops, lit sparingly from below by a pinkish light. And small towers barely taller than the wall.

And the wild flickering of torches amid the foliage, a bewildered wail that broke off with the sound of a blow. The riotous scent of night-blooming flowers, a sweet, dizzying smoke that crept through the garden. A figure, unmoving and with head cocked, blocking the path. A girl, her hands bound behind in her own very meager garments. I look into her black eyes where the torchlight dances, say "No," and she is led away.

The din of a veritable battle before the towers that mark the entry into a house that resembles a toy fortress. Yukuk dashes in that direction, then come clipped howls and I hear his voice: "I said to right and left. Go now, at the double!"

Rooms scantily illuminated by oil lamps. Low doors, a high-domed ceiling. Four corpses on the floor, one of them ours. The floor's smooth tiles and on the walls, a delicate mosaic showing sinuous vines, running animals, musicians with flutes, and women with wide, sorrowful eyes. These are, I see, women of Constantine's city, enveloped in the same costly silk and their eyes the same too, as round as any owl's and full of sweet promise and mad pride and an unexpected, lustful cruelty.

"The craftsmanship of Byzant," Yukuk muttered. "Wrought by masters from thence. How far they were brought. Slaves, of course."

Then a room where the contents of a large, iron-clad chest, also the handiwork of those same masters, were scattered at our feet. The wooden blocks fell with a soft thud and rolled about the floor. These were the murderers' knives – ten, twenty, and even more...

And after that, nothing but a few frightened women, none known to me. *Stupid, all this is so very stupid...*

I went out into a spacious courtyard that was now full of torches. We had one killed, three wounded. I wandered, lost, looking into the corpses' grinning faces. There were no women among them.

Then from a low structure attached to the house flew a horse, alone and riderless, that made a sure half-circle around the courtyard toward me.

And alongside the horse, like a shadow in the trembling folds of a long shawl, a woman's bowed figure came into view, took beautiful flight, and settled, a weightless phantom, in the saddle.

I took several paces out into the emptiness of the paved courtyard. There was naught in my hands, for throughout that frenetic battle I had never once drawn my sword.

"Zar-gi-su!" I cried, and at once she turned her head, swathed in a light cloth, toward me.

"Zargisu," I said again, stepping forward into the emptiness – one step, another step, and yet another. "Speak with me, Zargisu. Look at my face. Remember my name – Maniakh. Remember your garden, which awaits you. You are safe with me, Zargisu."

The horse halted while the woman on its back bent her head uncertainly toward me, as if listening to something, then urged it forward at a slow walk. Glittering crimson in the torchlight, the blade of her sword dipped lower.

"No, no, no!" Yukuk's harsh voice came from behind me, followed by the clump of his feet. And I saw two horsemen like black clouds hurtling toward her from right and left, and as one turned his head to her, I caught sight of his long nose. Together they took her horse's reins and all three sped deep into the courtyard, directly toward a blind wall.

He who led reached out from his saddle to push aside an ivy-wreathed contrivance set in the wall and, bending his head, plunged first into the darkness that opened behind it. The limber shadow in its billowing shawl followed after at a full gallop, vanishing as he had. The big-nosed man went last.

The fitful clatter of hooves across the desert. Cold stars in the soaring heights.

Book III

The Book of the Victors

The monarch of the realm is generous of heart.
He willingly gives gold to enrobe the deadly dart
So that the slain may have a shroud when they depart
And wounded men buy herbs to ease the stinging smart.

17

THE IRANIAN SKY

"It was I who solicited aid and protection for you from your brother," Barmak told me apologetically at the conclusion of our morning converse, which was so necessary to both of us. We had met beyond the naked rocks that surrounded our camp, already aclang with iron and reeking of smoke. "It simply seemed to me after we spoke once that there is rather too much recklessness in your ways. Balkh armor is, of course, a fine thing, but you had made your home in their very lair. And although you seemingly feared nothing, there would come a time when armor alone would not suffice."

He pursed anxious lips, then smiled at me.

"On the other hand, you could do no other. You did have to force some reaction out of them. And time was short. I felt that then, and today, as you see, my forebodings have proven correct. That's why I sent a courier to your brother Aspanak, to convey the notion that he must afford you a little protection here. He sent me no reply, in truth, but what could be better than the answer we received yesterday? And your pale-eyed girls saved my old hide too, while they were about it."

I looked at him in silence. Then, with a sigh, I acknowledged the obvious, which was that naught could have been more apposite.

"And in reply to your countless unspoken questions, events will now unfold in this wise. They will start thinking on what to do. That poltroon, as you may have noted, resolved to put himself at a good remove from the events in chief at a key juncture. And his subordinates, Hashim and the rest, are now set all atremble by their failure. And they're loath to make contact with my son Khalid, when all is as it is – taking into account that there are also the princes of Iran, Ziyad and other neutral parties, who could well be aggrieved by an internecine feud, especially when it is not the first."

"Where's Abu Salama, Barmak?"

"We've directed him to Kufa, where we ourselves are going, but he will travel alone. We left in our deserted house a messenger bearing an order to that effect. He's trying to overtake us, like as not. But what would we do with him then, with that Abu Salama? No, better he should travel apart from us, for we'll be the sounder for it. Now, don't interrupt me, Maniakh. Let an old man speak... So the Poltroon of Merv will determine what to do. And the chances are good, you mark my words, that he'll determine... to do naught at this time. As if none of this had transpired. Here it is – when such a reversal as this befalls, be these linchpins of the House of Abbas or not, it matters not a jot. The murderers have struck again, and that is all. Such a state of affairs has never been known before, meaning that one may explain it to one's followers however one wishes and proceed thereafter in any number of ways. But if the matter has gone amiss, then amiss it has gone. So all smile on one another and continue working for the common cause."

"But you knew all this, Barmak," I said, my voice expressionless. "Long, long ago. And when did you give me the armor? But if this is so, then what need have you had for me?"

He chuckled drily into his beard.

"What does that mean, 'I knew'? I guessed, but that does not mean I knew. And besides, what were we to do with my guesses? The situation had to be brought to some resolution, if only to draw it from the dark into the light And whom would you have do that? Khalid could not have done it. He had no facts, no more than I. And who would have allowed him to gather those facts, when he's ever in the public eye? So, then, why not acknowledge you to be no worse than Khalid, and in some wise even better? No, all came about as it should. It came about most excellently. The murderers are no more and will never be again, Maniakh. Had they been in some castle on a cliff, that would have been a different story. And it matters not how many you let slip yesterday night. Because do you know what they – our Poltroon and his Hashim – will do now? Drown their donkeys. So indeed they say in Balkh, the sense being that even dumb livestock that know much, silent though they may be, cannot be allowed to live. I'd hazard that your stout preacher of all the prophets and those unhappy suicides yet to be... and everyone, everyone... are disappearing as we speak. And, like as not, they've understood all and are hiding with might and main. But why so sad, dear young friend of mine? Are you weary after yesterday's battle?"

I was silent.

"Some wench, of course," Barmak surmised with confidence. "But no matter. If you didn't meet too often, she'll be the least of Hashim's concerns. And if she's clever, she'll know to vanish. So, then, let's think of the good..."

She's clever enough, I said to myself, glancing at the enormous crimson sun as it rose above the earth. *She'll vanish.*

Barmak was already striding back to the camp.

"One thing more," I said, running after. "Why did the boy... have to be killed?"

"You've lacked the time to consider that?" he snorted, wheeling about and narrowing his eyes. "But then again, you probably don't know the customs of the Arabiya. Both father and son must be taken out of the game, and their whole family with them. Picture it for yourself..."

Then he faltered and eyed me, his head atilt. And looked back at the camp, where the dust was already rising, as camels and horses were loaded.

"Nanidat my boy, grandson of my good, old friend," he said at length, coming close, "forgive me for saying to you now that of which none other ever speaks. The story, the one that Mansur mentioned so ill-advisedly in his sermon... I told him all later, and he rued it greatly. The story of the family you once had... No, no, my lips are sealed. I only ask you to remember what befell your father afterward. He took all that fearsome burden on himself. And rightly so" – his voice rose then, and there was an unlooked-for harshness in it – "for his was the responsibility to defend the family, the family of his elder son, to think all through, to provide bodyguards. No blame, none whatsoever, could have been laid at your door. You were in battle, but he should have... He carried that burden for the few years that still remained to him. And you remember what he became... Well, then," Barmak said, his voice quieter now, as he gently patted my shoulder, "what your father suffered, our Mansur would have suffered also. But these are not men of Sogdia, as you are. They are a people wholly other. If a father of that people were unable to defend his little son, allowed him to be killed before his eyes... and if after that he did not fling himself headlong on Abu Muslim with a knife or even just a stick... then what price the blood of the Prophet, what price the House of Abbas? He and the rest of his family would have won not an iota of pity in any quarter. So the reckoning was correct. And meanwhile he, now I think of it, sits by a campfire there, not knowing what to say to you and how to thank you. Ha! But we must make haste."

We almost ran back to the camp. While still a distance away, I waved to Yukuk, calling on him to report if all was ready, if every man had his weapons about him and had broken his fast, if there were any fevers among the wounded. Mansur, I had time to note, was not, in fact, sitting deep in thought by any campfire. He was, rather, carrying the boy pickaback to a camel.

Barmak touched my shoulder again. "The last thing I will say before we depart," he said, "concerns money. It has, regrettably, always been a matter of money. If you remember, Abu Muslim was first at Bakr's beck and call, while Bakr answered to Ibrahim of Humayma. But the heart of the matter was that every conspirator had to give one-fifth of his income, and to whom? To the House of Abbas, of course. But later, when Abu Muslim found himself with an entire country under his command, and no small country either, with the sizable revenues it yielded... In due time, the utility of the House of Abbas must have come into question. And of yourself, who are linked with it. Yet on the other hand, how were they to make shift without the descendents of the House of Abbas, who have within them the blood of the Prophet and all the rest of it? And so matters became strained. Abu Muslim began to wonder if he could do it all alone. I, of course, had given him my son Khalid and all of Balkh into the bargain, and Khalid, as I told you yesterday, is responsible for collecting and counting the money here, since that requires a man who can, among all else, read and write. And Mansur, being first of the House of Abbas where money is concerned, has also been a constant visitor here. Which not everyone found pleasant. But matters could not hang thus forever. You could have known none of that, nor was there need, but I understood right well that those murderers had arisen for good reason. That was naught but Abu Muslim's last resort, it being too soon for him to act openly. And besides, I say again, he's a poltroon. And a slave."

To that I could only agree, sad as it was to acknowledge.

"But hereafter... hereafter we must to Kufa with all haste. For it is there that all will transpire. Now after these two or three days that you have granted us, the race must begin, to see whose forces can come fastest to Kufa. Else, just imagine – we arrive there only to be met by our friend Abu Salama, who informs us that there are five thousand warriors from Khorasan in the city and a caliph has already been named. We would be vexed then, would we not?"

And, uttering not another word, the overlord of Balkh struggled up his camel's side while I greeted Shabdiz, led to me by Yukuk, as if he were my own flesh and blood.

And so the race began.

From Merv to Kufa, as my friends in the Celestial Empire might have said, is a distance of three thousand li, with every li comprising a thousand steps. That ground could be covered, changing mounts, in five days, or a week at most. But camels are not horses and an empire torn apart and roiled by revolt is not the best place for a military detachment in a troubled relationship with both the Caliph and the mutineers against him to be sauntering about.

We began with the solemn ceremony, pleasing in the eye of God, of giving the slaves their freedom, which Mansur himself conducted. Then riding to and fro before the assembled ranks in my much-hated armor, I had my own say.

"They call me the Hawk and I am a coward. Because I want to remain among the living. These unarmed people – the old man, the boy and his father – want the same. And our task, yours and mine, is to bring them alive to Kufa. And to remain unscathed ourselves. Thereafter whoever wishes will go home. If any here requires martial glory, let him seek it elsewhere, for you are now free men. Because we are an army of cowards. We shall not join battle even once, if it be not needful for the protection of those people and our own survival."

Strikingly, the only word of that not very commonplace speech that all remembered well was "Hawk." This was respectfully reported to me by my erstwhile chakirs, who, while not yet elevated to the rank of emir, at least had their own squads of ten men each. Our new recruits, meanwhile, had spent the night giddy over the Balkh armor and weaponry, and were still so.

As the race began, we moved westward toward Nishapur, across the desert and amid rocks between which swirled columns of dust any one of which could at any moment reveal itself to be an ifrit or a djinn.

Then, having approached and traveled past the mirages of mountain lakes, we saw on high the blessed, cooling mountain snows. And on the ground, the serried ranks of something that resembled anthills, chains of hillocks that ran downslope to close-sown fields of wheat and rows of poplars and palms. Those were the irrigation systems left to us by the greatest of the great – Cyrus, Darius and Anushirwan.

Next came villages, where children played by the walls, swinging on ropes secured to sturdy branches, but ran away when they saw us coming, our iron all aglitter.

And on we went, between brown folds of earth, along the valleys of the Zagros mountains, one slope of which might be dun in color and another pale yellow with gorse. Along the wayside, mountain flowers bent their ponderous heads to us and the petals of large poppies quivered.

And overhead, a gentle light, something between ice and turquoise, spilled across the vastness of the world. No other country on earth boasts such a wonder as the eternal, limpid, radiant Iranian sky.

Our detachment made the turn to Nishapur through Tus with no difficulties, for we were at home here, journeying still through the lands of the Leopard of Merv. But all changed when we struck hard westward, toward Damghan and passed through those parts where all roads led to vast Rayy, which lay behind a singular quantity of fortress walls, both old and new.

But that city, with its spacious warehouses, its renowned potters' stalls, its incomparable library on the banks of the Surkhani Canal in the Rudha neighborhood, with the world's best chelo kebab, and with silver pitchers and dishes too, was no place for us. Because for the local inhabitants, a hundred armor-clad warriors from Khorasan could only be the vanguard of Abu Muslim's long-awaited assault. And while the city sentries might not even think to challenge us, that did not mean that they would not call out a detachment of the local garrison that numbered in the thousands.

I began to learn from Yukuk the art of sending out advance guards and devising signals to exchange with them, And in the next hamlet, I visited the apothecary and at my own expense, so as to waste no time in dispute with Mansur, purchased a goodly quantity of liquids, herbs, oils, needles and thread for the healing of wounds.

Otherwise I spent all my time with my former chakirs, who were now commanders in their own right. And I learned that Nanivandak, clever, free-spirited and sprung from a Khorezm family of fair repute, was without equal when advance guards and raiding parties were needed, and that his entire command had taken up that work, which no army could well do without. That Awlad, his belligerent name notwithstanding, would rather have been – imagine this – trading silk, for which I promised to lend him both money and support. And that

Makhian had been a miller once and had in mind to rent several mills when the war was over and thus supply all the environs of Bukhara with flour.

But when we reached Rayy – or, more precisely, its outer edge, which was called Tehran – I knew that we must not travel on without rest. Barmak, that miracle of endurance, might be persuaded to hold out a while longer, but no such understanding could be expected of the horses and camels. And we would also do well to replace some of the camels with fresh ones. And so it was that we occupied the whole of a caravanserai in Tehran, posting guards on every road that led to it. There, while some busied themselves with the change of camels, others – by which I mean Mansur and I – found ourselves a choice and long-awaited occupation.

We went to the bath-house, a small neighborhood bath-house, where we were left alone after being waited on with much ceremony. Having neatly folded his well-patched garments and crowned the stack with his black headband, Mansur wrapped his sinewy loins in a threadbare rag, took another under his arm, and waved me on, as if inviting me to enter his palace.

I breathed in the familiar aroma of dampness tinged with iron, lay on a warm reddish stone, and cast my eyes across the flaking vault of the ceiling, seeing there griffons, the same fabulous birds that had borne aloft that great general and greater cut-throat, Iskandar the Two-Horned Lord. I set myself a riddle as to when a drop would fall from there full on my nose. And I awoke, already drenched in clammy sweat, to Mansur's languorous murmuring: "... and in every village there will be a new masjid and a good bath-house, because the time must come when someone shall occupy himself with such simple things. One cannot be warring forever."

Then, running his fingers over my hot shoulder, he motioned me with a silent gesture to the stone bench by the wall, while he went to the other wall and tidily poured a saucer of cold water over his head and its plastering of thin, saffron-colored hair.

And, after a moment's thought, another.

This man is paying for the upkeep of a detachment of a hundred men here and for an entire conspiracy there, in the west, I thought. *He could buy this bath-house outright, with all its water and griffons thrown in.*

Mansur had now come to the much-anticipated time to show himself grateful that his son yet lived. Slowly, solemnly and carefully he wiped a soapy cloth over me, unbending with the utmost respect my every joint, as though I were a living deity.

This is one who can never speak his thanks, I thought.

"You know, Mansur, I've been thinking: your little Muhammad cannot possibly have understood what transpired there," I remarked, incidentally, as it were, with my face turned upward. "Maybe he need not be told? Why burden him so, at his age? Who knows, one day he may rule this whole empire... Tell him later, if you wish."

I saw Mansur's damp, dark cheek give the slightest twitch. He looked at me and nodded.

With that the civilities ended, and it was my turn to play my part in a bathing ritual as ancient as Iran and the Great Steppe themselves. Save that not everyone who entered a bath-house knew what I had learned at the hospital in Merv – all the dozens of points on a man's body that will render him weary no more.

Mansur moaned, groaned, and made sounds in his throat, and could not hold back the question at last.

"It's true, then, that you studied daily the physician's art?" he asked.

"Who would refuse to study under one who hails from Gondishapur?" I replied.

"What is Gondishapur?" The query was returned on the instant, and I knew then that yet another lengthy conversation lay in store.

THAT NIGHT I FLOATED OVER the drowsing earth, touching it ever and anon with the toes of my boots. And before me swayed the silhouette of a horse that sped around and around, and Zargisu, in a whirl of light cloth, flew up from behind the horse's flank time and again, weightless as a shadow.

As we left Tehran, we found our way blocked by a wall of horsemen. These could be none other than soldiers of the Caliph.

Yukuk rode forward to converse long and peaceably with their leader, while I numbered them. Five hundred there were, if not more. I also kept watch on Yukuk but for some reason was not in the least perturbed.

"I served in the same jund with him once," he explained to me on his return.

And the wall of horsemen parted.

THE SMELL OF MUCH-WORN CLOTHING now also smoky with a fire's fume. I had made Mansur pay for all the soldiers to visit the bath-house in the closest village. We checked the weaponry, tightened the straps on our small, round shields. The baldric of my sword, which I had yet to draw from its scabbard, had chafed my shoulder to bloody bruises.

My erstwhile chakirs and I spoke of everything. Muhammad, I learned, very much wanted to see Mecca one day and questioned me avidly to learn if such was our heading. I assured him that there, in general, we were indeed bound and that he would see Mecca. Muslim, another who had converted to the new faith, kept close and drank in our every word. Devgon, the other of my two last chakirs, now greatly resembled my brother Aspanak to me, being as well-fleshed as he and much given to happy smiles. He had become adept in the use of the huge Turkic bow, and the Turkic soldiers, who were numerous enough among our freed slaves, were treating him with growing deference.

A long detour to avoid the crossroads in Hamadan took us through fields and around villages with their gardens and their dove-cotes like to fortress towers. And this we did because a considerable contingent of the Caliph's men had gathered at the crossroads and was tarrying there in expectation of some event.

"No matter. We shall soon be in Nihavand where naught is lacking," Yukuk said to me at one point.

But in that he was wrong. The following evening spent by our campfires was the last we would pass in peace and contentment.

Those whom I had sent into the city returned with the news that Abu Muslim was ensconced in Merv, where he had suppressed an unforeseen flare of rebellion. Furthermore, in the no man's land of Bukhara, which belonged now to neither the Caliph nor Abu Muslim, had appeared a rebel by the name of Sharik, to be yet another unpleasant surprise for the Leopard of Merv.

At this, I gave a tight-lipped smile and thanked Ashkend in my mind. Barmak noticed that smile and raised his hoary brows in understanding.

But the news did not end with that. Because twenty to thirty thousand of Abu Muslim's horsemen were now pressing westward in two columns, one hot on our trail and the other bearing south, toward Isfahan, whence led the road to Kufa. The southernmost column was commanded by Qahtaba ibn Shabib, and Yazid ibn Omar, governor of Iraq, was moving to engage it. The one close behind us, to the north, was led by Abu Ayun, and Abdullah, son of Caliph Marwan, was preparing to throw it back.

And there we were, in the very heart of a land roiled by approaching war.

All the more precious, therefore, was that last peaceful evening by the campfire, when, having supped well, we sat in a circle while Barmak taught his dark-complexioned charge.

"Muhammad," he said, "were we not, you and I, at the point where the history of the sovereigns of Iran ended?"

"The unfortunate Yazdegerd was killed in the home of a miller on the banks of the Murgab, in Merv. The greed of the last of his courtiers was his downfall, since he was carrying with him his crown and his treasure," the boy rattled off, as his eyes glistened gaily in the darkness. "Yes, that's where we were, master."

Mansur gave a slow, satisfied nod.

But Barmak had only begun the lesson. He continued by asking what had brought peace to the Kingdom of Iran, to which little Muhammad confidently told us: "God in place of idols and bloodstained sacrifices, a government that presides over a diversity of peoples who live in peace, a philosophy of toleration toward others, justice, and art second to none."

Then the sovereign of Balkh, his brows knit, began to trace our route in the night air, recounting to the boy the places we had kept our distance from and what we had forfeited thereby.

"Northward of the path we chose, where that path began," he said, "lie Tabaristan and Dailam, now behind us, which are all rice, cotton, oranges, sugar, tigers and panthers. To the south, Isfahan, with its renowned melon gardens, its sky that casts a pure, soft light, and its walls with hundreds of towers, will soon be left behind. And yet farther south... There, my boy, is Persepolis, with its tall, slender columns, like spears pointing up to the sky. And with huge winged bulls made of stone, The great capital of a great realm. A piteous ruin.

"And farther southward still, Shiraz, where are the world's best cypresses and plane trees, and all the fruits of the world, and also nuts – ah, such nuts! A little beyond is the round city of Gor. But when we come to Kufa, not far from there are the ruins of another capital, the last capital, which was Qataysfun and ere that, Ctesiphon. Oh, Muhammad, it did indeed eclipse al-Konstantiniyye, the city of Constantine, with its enormous arches and the grandeur of its palaces! But a silver camel, modeled life size, we shall no longer see there, nor a horse with emerald teeth. Think on the fate of that realm, my boy, for once it stretched from the land of the black-skinned people to the Empire of the Chin."

The campfire crackled quietly. The breathing of horses and the jangle of metal could be heard in the darkness.

"Do you know, Muhammad," Barmak went on, "that to your credit you have never once questioned me as to the meaning of life? But I would have given your good question a very poor answer. The meaning of life is to travel all around this enormous and lovely world with the goal of discovering what is to be done with it. And the trick of it is that no man can travel all around the world, which is all to the good, and what is to be done with it can never be known, yet while gadding hither and thither, what pleasure you shall have."

But since the boy was, of course, already asleep, the three of us then went on to discuss in low tones the peerless book that Barmak had once seen in the possession of a man who still dwelled in the ruins of Ctesiphon – a book about twenty-seven shahanshahs, with twenty-seven portraits showing them on the day they died, and also with chapters on the sciences and history, on palaces and horses. Mansur swore to God that one day he would insist on having a copy taken of that book, while Barmak drew some crumpled papyrus sheets from the folds of his garments.

"Here it is. Listen to this, friends," he exulted, poking a finger at a badly creased page. "Oh, what a delight! Here:

> Walid had a passion for horses and one day, when the rider of the front-runner was thrown in a race of a thousand four-year-olds, the Caliph overtook that riderless horse on his stallion and at a full gallop leaped into the saddle... (Oh, no, that's not it... Yes, yes, here it is)
>
> One of the first acts of Walid after becoming Caliph was to invite from Mecca a singer by the name of Mabad. He was led into a vast hall with two pools in its midst, in one of which was water, and in the other, wine. Behind the pools, Mabad saw a light, transparent curtain drawn full across the hall, and behind that curtain sat the Caliph. Mabad was asked to seat himself at the edge of a pool and sing. And he began with a song about love.
>
> And the song so touched the Caliph (Maniakh, young friend of mine) that he sprang up, flung the curtain aside, and tearing off his perfumed garments, leaped into the pool of water and fell thirstily upon it. The slaves swiftly ran for fresh clothing, which they sprinkled with fragrance as they returned, and Walid again took his seat and asked Mabad to continue. Again the strings made their plaint, and he sang:

And I shall summon clouds of spring
To shed their frigid showers
Until I see these joyless stones
Bedecked with fragrant flowers.

"Bring a purse containing fifteen thousand dinars!" the Caliph cried when the song faded into silence. And when given the heavy purse, he poured the gold like rain into the singer's bosom.

"But sing that song once more, o prince, o thou lovely prince of mine," Walid asked. "Sing it for the sake of my ancestor, Abd Shams!"

"In the name of God and of another ancestor, in the name of Umayyah, sing again!" he cried when silence fell. And again and again the singer touched the plaintive strings while Walid recited his lineage.

And then, when the tally of his kin was spent, the Caliph wept. "And now, the last time. For my sake. For my sake and for my soul's sake," he said.

And when the song again faded into silence, Walid ran down from his place of eminence and, falling on his knees before Mabad, began to cover every part of his body with kisses. At which the singer crossed his legs, lest he be kissed on his privy parts. "No, no," exclaimed the Caliph, "and here too, and here, I must, I must, o thou lovely prince of mine!" At last, saying "oh, happiness, happiness!" he again tore away his garments, cast them over Mabad's shoulders, and stood naked until more clothing was fetched.

Then he ordered that another thousand dinars be brought and given to Mabad along with his own mule, saying, "Leap into my saddle and vanish from my sight, for you have lit in me a fire hotter than tamarisk coals!"

"That's all. Mansur, are you sleeping? Oh, Maniakh, what a story! It can only be truthful, down to the last detail. Such things simply cannot be fabricated. And how fearsome it is to imagine that this record might ever go missing, be forgotten, be lost…"

"But remind me, Barmak, what befell that unbridled overlord at last," I inquired somberly.

"Everyone knows what befell him. His head was impaled on a spear and carried to Yazid, who would later be Caliph, whereafter none in the caliphate has known any peace. Which is why we sit here, you and I," the sometime overlord of Balkh sighed. "But, oh, what a stupefying scene this is, my good young friend!"

Falling asleep, I wondered if anyone were looking down on us from the heavens and if our campfire seemed to him a lonely star in a high black sky.

WHAT CAME WITH THE MORNING was dire indeed, for on that day and on the following too we were compelled to battle through an eddying mass of horsemen, through the din and the howling and the bloody scraps flung hither and yon.

And for the first time I saw Yukuk's celebrated sword-strike, sweeping down from the right toward the left ear while his opponent, with a grin, raised his sword to parry it. But there was more to come, because Yukuk next drew the tip of his sword in an upward slash across the face of his foe, who then raised both hands to the place where that face had been only a moment before, dropping his sword and unable to believe that such a horror could have befallen him.

But the merciful Yukuk ended his own sword's leftward movement by dealing a death-blow. And so the space before us was freed.

"Forward, forward!" Yukuk cried, dragging me behind him as I turned, to see which of my men could still be saved.

Many lay prostrate on the battlefield and to many of those who were still in the saddle I later gave decoctions of healing herbs and sewed up their wounds, to dull their hurts.

Then another day of pursuit and affray. My chakirs, although scratched and hacked about, were all intact except for Kevan, who had taken a hard blow to the head. I had thought him dead but after

I had rolled away from him a light-haired warrior from the Caliph's forces and of an unknown race, I found him still breathing. But the Caliph's warrior died, muttering, in a language unfamiliar to me, "Despota Iesou Christe…"

We lost more than twenty men in that battle but were joined by a whole detachment of fifty or so that had received no salary for a month.

A rest was called, during which Yukuk, who feared nothing and was the victor of all victors, broke a tooth from biting down on a goat bone. I will never forget his distracted, surprised, woebegone face. "So soon?" it said. Because teeth, once gone, cannot be replaced. The loss is forever, and the time is nigh when there can be no thought of tasting again even the softest meat. And so the end of life begins.

Next our path was barred by a veritable host that was thundering down to meet Qahtaba's column of Khorasanis. My detachment thus found itself between two armies, and we had to force our way through a formation of infantry – Whose? We knew not – that was denying us the road. Barmak's camel fell beneath him, and we hauled the unfortunate old man, his feet dragging along the ground, onto a ready-saddled horse.

This was followed by another senseless fray with a detachment of soldiers who themselves did not know whose side they were on, because neither did their commanders. And when we were done with killing each other, our column, which had left a long and bloody trail behind it, was increased by another two hundred horsemen.

Each time we stopped to rest, Barmak would no longer eat. His lips had turned blue. I made him drink at least, while my fingers sought to breathe life into that exhausted body.

Then there was a smooth descent into a defile between mountains, and when we had traversed it, a satisfied Mansur said, "All's done."

And we ambled on.

BUT WHEN IT BECAME CLEAR that the frowzy clusters of houses amid refuse and sickly greenery were about to grow into an equally frowzy city, I drew my troops into relatively orderly rows, commanding those whose Balkh armor was still sound to put it on, the infernal heat notwithstanding, and move to the fore, ahead of the camels that carried Mansur and Barmak.

Here, though, we were met by Abu Salama, that paragon of dignity, on a mule and accompanied by two wary attendants.

"Abu Salama, dearest young friend of mine," I said to him in Barmak's sugared voice, "here we are, together again. And I had such misgivings that my troops would find no place in Kufa, nor water, food and much else, for seven hundred men is no jest. But now all can be done that was planned, not so?"

And Abu Salama, his widening eyes taking in my warriors as their metallic silhouettes rose out of the dust, made no objection.

How the now-enlivened Barmak, not to speak of Mansur, greeted him I do not know. I passed on at the head of my detachment, closely examining the myriads of tiny houses on the plain and dreaming, like any true soldier, of bathing and of much else no less simple and needful and after all that, of enjoying a good long rest.

But that very evening, I learned that a column of horsemen had proceeded from our camp into the center of the city, to the governor's palace. And at its head rode... no, not Abu Jafar hight Mansur, but his brother and the brother of the unfortunate Ibrahim – the youngest of the three, Abu al-Abbas. A rumor was abroad that he would now quarter himself in the palace and that something of note would transpire on the morrow.

That day came – it was a Friday – and I was again in the saddle at the head of a metal ribbon of men from Samarkand, towering above the sea of human heads around the high, reddish walls of the principal masjid, while people poured on through the gates, filling the spacious courtyard.

And within, unseen by me, Mansur's brother had mounted the dais to announce an end to the sufferance of tyrants and declare the House of Abbas to be the tool of divine vengeance.

"Therefore prepare yourselves," he said. "I am he who spills. I can spill untold bounty down upon you but I can also spill your blood. So choose!"

At that, Mansur's brother began to cough, and he coughed and coughed amid a sympathetic silence until his Uncle Daud, standing on the step below Abu Abbas, took the burden of the speech upon himself, and cried out for all the temple to hear, "There is in the world no sovereign lord of the faithful other than he who now stands at my side!"

Then the residents of Kufa stood in an endless file before the coughing man, so that each might for an instant take his hand and thereby lay at his feet the tribute of due fealty.

I saw none of this spectacle as I sat bowed over in my saddle by the heat. Only later, that evening, did now one, now another of my warriors come to bring me ever new details of the great event. For example, that the new sovereign lord of the faithful had promptly been styled as-Saffah, He Who Spills.

And so there was in our unhappy world yet another caliph. How many was that now? I knew not and had no wish to know.

My wish was for something other – to sleep for a week or even two and then quietly, unnoticed by all, to quit the city, taking but three or four with me. Although I was certain enough that I would do nothing of the sort.

Yet that – how best to rally my strength and flee – is what I was contemplating at the moment when couriers from Mansur burst in on me with the news that my detachment, now numbering a thousand men of Samarkand and Khorasan, would set out in two days' time. A man from the House of Abbas hitherto unknown to me – Abdullah, yet another of Mansur's uncles – had already taken charge of assembling the siege train.

We would go up the Tigris to meet the army of Marwan – "The true Caliph?" I almost asked – which was moving southward, while from the east, to cut him off, came Abu Ayun and his Khorasanis. But, although the forces of Khorasan had already dealt Marwan's son a good drubbing, the Caliph and his army were, for whatever reason, intent on trouncing not them but us. Foremost in all this, though, was the determination to prevent Abu Ayun, he being Abu Muslim's emir, from laying sole claim to the victory.

What victory? I thought.

And all that I remember after that of the nonsensical city of Kufa was the voice in the night.

I lay, unmoving but sleepless in the tiny room I had been honorably assigned above the bazaar, hard by the angular balcony on which the muezzin stood and rent the air at sunrise and sunset. The night could not have been blacker, and in that blackness, either from behind the wall of unfired brick or from somewhere below, I heard the exhalation of a woman's voice, plaintive in her happiness.

"I am Fadl's habibti, his beloved. Oh, my sweet Fadl!"

And again there hung over Kufa a silence full of distant footsteps, laughter and scarce-heard conversation.

18

THE WALL OF SPEARS

From the very beginning I sensed, with the qualmish feeling that is apt to beset an experienced commander, that this was a most peculiar campaign, that the bearded and swag-bellied Abdullah was ill-suited to play the part of qaida to an entire army, that he might be able to command at best a hundred men, and that had he not been a respected member of the House of Abbas, he would never have seen the inside of an emir's pavilion.

The army's departure from Kufa was a chaotic and shameful spectacle; against that general background, my men of Samarkand looked positively splendid. The Army of Cowards had held together, while their armor and weaponry, carefully preserved by one and all, were closely scrutinized by all the vagabonds in Kufa, who came running to see. They had pledged themselves first to one diwan and then to another, and only later had begun to wonder what they would do for weapons, how they could supplement their own swords in a shoulder belt with an outfit of chain mail, preferably sleeveless and reaching to the waist, and pair of iron Iranian trousers to go with it. Meanwhile, any who had not kept possession of his father's and grandfather's treasured coat of mail was also pondering how to acquire at least a leather jerkin of several layers sewn together, since the campaign would, he had heard, be taking him northward, into the cold. The only thing that everyone seemed to have was a small and worthless round shield edged with leather.

How one was to distinguish in this rabble the harbia or infantry, with its spears, swords and shields, the ramya or squads of bowmen, and the fursan or cavalry with its long spears and battle axes was a mystery to me.

Then more chaos, as the catapults, the battering rams and the heavy arrows wound about with oiled rags that would be lit before being loosed over walls were loaded onto boats. And all the while, no one had gathered us commanders together to tell us what fortresses we were preparing to capture. Not Haran, assuredly.

Later we learned that the boats with their dreadful cargo had sailed up the river, but exactly to where was unclear. So we were left with our battle camels and horses but without our siege engines and also lacking no end of other useful things.

It also emerged that no one knew precisely where we were going and whether Marwan was moving on us or on the Khorasani army that was coming from the east led by Abu Ayun. And a question of especial interest was what would befall us should we meet with Abu Ayun – would we clasp his soldiers in a firm embrace or join battle with them?

My indignation during the two long weeks it took to move that poorly armed herd northward along the Tigris ran high. I was, furthermore, striving with all my strength to hide my feelings from Yukuk, who, of course, was of the same mind.

Once, after a long and manifestly senseless day's march, after the horses were unsaddled and the meal was ready – and where the enemy was and how we were to find him was as unclear as ever it had been – Yukuk and I looked at each other and burst into laughter at the same moment.

And, as a sign of sincere respect, he spooned from his bowl into mine some long shreds of especially tender, long-boiled meat – likely water buffalo, since that was seemingly the chief source of sustenance in those parts.

I had laughed because I now well understood what Yukuk had been thinking as he saw me for the first time in my life commanding ten chakirs, himself included.

And he had laughed because he had read my mind, which he had also likely done when I was passing Abdullah's latest order to my thousand men. That order was to proceed along the banks of the River Zab on the following morning, as far as may be to the east, to forage for our own supper, and to set up camp in such a way that we could distinguish the faces of the soldiers in other detachments.

Abdullah might as well have said, "We are simply strolling with our army along this little river and what we shall do next we know not, so divert yourselves as best you may."

"Have you been in these parts before, Yukuk?" I asked.

"Here too," he replied, for he had seemingly been everywhere. "To the north of the river lies the road to Haran, Marwan's capital, where all his army also is. So we are trying, without embroiling ourselves in a fight, to hold at bay on yonder side of the river those of his detachments that are said to be threatening to make a crossing and strike at us. But since Marwan knows well that we have here a mere twelve thousand or so, we hold little interest for him and his one hundred and fifty thousand. And half of Marwan's army will suffice to face Abu Ayun of Khorasan, who is trying to menace him from the east. But trying right gingerly, for Abu Ayun has some twenty thousand but no more."

"It is as if a well armed, powerfully built warrior stood before two brawlers from the marketplace," I observed. "One to his right and one to his left. Both are feinting and capering hither and thither, while he simply stands and waits, since he understands that he can easily dispatch both at once. Nor would it be any great imposition for him to buffet them one at a time, but he can't be troubled to."

"Not quite so, master," Yukuk drawled, as military men are wont to and as he always did. "Our two brawlers are not of the common run. Both very much want to strike the first blow and spring back, leaving not even a scrap of fame to the other. But that is the least of it... Who's warring with whom, master? Like as not, all three with one another.

Have you heard even once during your military councils of the need to send a courier to Abu Ayun, advising him to strike Marwan wherever he be, so that we may then come from the south and draw him away? Are any couriers at all going back and forth between Abdullah and Abu Ayun?"

"Nothing of the sort," I admitted. "Would you had seen Abdullah gnawing his entire fist when he learned that Abu Ayun of Khorasan had vanquished a detachment commanded by the other Abdullah, who is Marwan's own son. One thing only is clear at those councils, which is that our Abdullah is mortally afraid of the victory going to the Khorasanis. But what victory can there be if we and Abu Ayun together have half the strength of our foe? And so we stroll about these plains without rhyme or reason. Our advance guards are worth nothing, the signals we have are as good as having none. All in all, it's to be well expected that we shall meet one of Marwan's larger detachments and retreat, well trounced. You say you've been here before? Then you should lead the detachment when we flee, for you know where best to run. But what will be left of our detachment then is another matter. And while I think of it, Yukuk, Evman has two men sick. I'll go and look at them now. The one good thing is that it's not hot."

"Indeed," he said, wrapping himself in a horse blanket. "There can be snow here in winter."

And so we parted, having warmed each other's soldierly souls.

The following day was as different as could be from the one before. Horsemen galloped far and wide, throwing up clumps of frozen earth, and Abdullah had at last posted an advance guard. Then, toward evening, we watched as wounded men were borne past, strengthlessly embracing their horses' necks. But still most of our detachments had not moved from their places and were busying themselves with no one knew what.

Wearied by the uncertainty, I sent out several men, who returned by evening bringing tidings. Abdullah had for some reason dispatched by night five hundred cavalry to the other shore, where they had met with a detachment of Marwan's cavalry and been badly beaten. It was being whispered that few of our men had escaped with their lives.

Abdullah was, it seemed, played out. Next he would order us to pull up the stakes, strike the tents and move southward, leaving Abu Ayun's army open to Marwan's attack. And so the sport would go on and on.

I understood then if I did not send out patrols on no one's authority but my own, then I must sit and wait for whatever may come, until one of Marwan's detachments appeared and beat us with no great trouble, no matter what our numbers might be.

But those bold plans were to remain so, for I was instead summoned to Abdullah. I remember striding to his pavilion in vexation, thinking as I went that all a qaida did was hinder his commanders from doing well what was theirs to do.

As I approached the pavilion, which glowed peacefully from within with a fleshy pink light, like a tiny lantern from the Celestial Empire, I heard many agitated voices. Next, one voice alone, saying words I could not make out. Then a strange, a very strange, pause came and lingered, until it was broken by Abdullah's dry, cracked voice asking "But where shall we bury them all?" and by the veritable storm of hilarity that came in reply, a glad guffawing from a dozen throats.

Still understanding nothing, I bent and entered the pavilion, which smelled of garlic, onion and fragrant oils past their prime.

The merriment within was somehow unwholesome. Everyone was strangely overwrought, and Abdullah most of all. His beard jutting testily forward, he greeted me with great and unaccountable glee.

"I'll teach you to come betimes, and in ways you won't soon forget! But now to business. Omar, I will need one of your detachments, the halest lads you have, on heavy mounts. They should have wooden crooks, long spears, and axes. Let them stand behind the lines and await the signal. And may the merciful Lord cloud the reason of our bald-headed foe, let the erstwhile Caliph commit but one foolish act, since the Lord has already laid the river at our feet. And has hung the sun in its rightful place in the sky."

Understanding nothing, I lowered myself onto the carpet, while Abdullah continued:

"As you've already heard, Omar, you will be on the right flank. Where you will absolutely not need all your troops, some of which do not even understand your commands. So the men of Samarkand and Bukhara and the Turkic soldiers you shall give to he who was tardy. Not so, Maniakh? Take this new cavalry under your command. You will stand with it on the left flank, where there is at least room for the horses to run. So you shall have in total..."

He was then distracted by one speaking heatedly in the language of the Arabiya, which was not intelligible to me, although belike he was being advised to cross the river then and there, by night, and strike. When their talk was done, the general again turned to me and ended with "In sum, you will have three thousand, and not badly armed, either. But mind you don't disgrace yourself with them, emir. Such as by not coming betimes."

And again the pavilion rocked with a riotous ha-ha-haing and hee-hee-heeing.

Three thousand. I am an emir. Did I dream?

"And I shall take my seat at the heart of the host," Abdullah said, his booming voice betraying his displeasure. "Because it is at the heart that our donkey will strike. He always does."

Our donkey? Could I have heard aright? Abdullah was at such a pass as to have come upon the vanguard of Marwan himself, and still he was not saddling the horses, not striking camp now, in the watches of the night?

"He will have at the very heart, while we... We shall form a wall of spears. Shahrud, it is you shall form it, so heed me well. You will lower your eyes, kneel and front the enemy with the tips of your spears. You will be a field of black stones until the enemy comes close. Then the spear shafts are thrust into the ground, the tips are pointed toward the enemy, and after the first shock, you rise and advance step by step. So. Now, Maniakh, you will be in an open field, so do what you will once there, the point in chief being not to permit them to come around us on your flank, while we are holding our wall of spears steady. That is your task, that and naught more. And you, Omar, stand with your detachment armed with the crooks and the axes, and await the command. When I wave my hand... Well, you already know all."

Then all of us, myself included, fell prostrate to the carpet and offered up a prayer.

I must own that even as I left Abdullah's pavilion, I did not fully understand all that had happened and what awaited us. Until into the trembling dome of crimson light cast by our campfires strode Yukuk, a figure carved of gray stone.

"Master, is it true that one hundred and twenty thousand men stand on the other bank, with Marwan himself at their head?" he asked.

I began to feel queasy then. This could be no vanguard.

"You were speaking of it a moment ago, at the council. You were there," Yukuk persisted.

"But... Well, yes – 'Where shall we bury them all?' " My mind was suddenly clear.

Yukuk, though, understood me in his own way, and I thought I saw a new respect in his eyes.

And already the formless figures of horsemen were issuing forth in the darkness from amid our campfire's sparks. These were the commanders of all the detachments assigned to me from the right flank.

"We are the left flank, Yukuk, and we now number three thousand," I told him, with a touch of malice.

He seemed to grow instantly in stature.

In assembling them all in their ranks, in giving the new arrivals and their horses to drink, in counting them all anew, in letting the Hawk's healing hand rest on every man's shoulder... Thus I spent my night, as people rushed in a clatter of iron from one fiery dome of light that shot sparks into the blackness to another, driven to despair by the chaos all around that was, although painfully slowly, becoming order. I issued one command after another, looking into the white-hot coals and asking myself why I did not lie down for a while or at least quit this confusion and go alone into the blackness and cold of night, where I could see at once all the stars above my head.

And say to them: "O God of the Black Sky and God of the Blue Sky, the mild and the merciful, the redoubtable and the invincible, whosoever you be, may your clear eyes look down. Do you see the pitiful constellation of our campfires, that scattering of puny fireflies in a shoreless gloom? Three thousand warriors of Sogdia, three thousand living bodies – warm, defenseless even when clad in gray iron, that will soon be sought by the thirsty barbs of sharpened shards of metal? Are we – grains of sand in an endless time, blind mouselings on a boundless plain – aught to you?

"And if you cannot save our lives today, then surely you can make it so that this will be the last battle, for ever and aye?"

I must, despite myself, have fallen asleep where I stood, and when I woke, there was nowhere to hide from the pitiless gray of the sky, from the dark and dirty columns of smoke that now rose up to that sky from where the gleaming, warming half-spheres of fire once had been.

Chewing hungrily on a piece of flatbread and wondering whether I would have time enough to put fresh wine in my flask, I rode out with Yukuk to survey the place where the light mist that lay hunched over the unseen river was beginning to glow pink. To the north, like a mountain range, were layers of slate-gray clouds gradually turning lilac.

"The sun will be in their faces. That's very good," he said dispassionately, coughing a little. "But look there, 'tis a rare sight. I've never quite seen the like."

At first it seemed to be a huge sheet of chain mail spread over the hills across the water, which covered the horizon and crawled slowly toward the river.

But I soon knew that this was no chain mail.

Next I discerned in the mist that lay over the Great Zab, a strange strip of grey scales that also crept toward us from one bank to the other.

"So they're already here," Yukuk's voice came rolling in from my right. There was an odd satisfaction in it. "Look there."

I followed where his hand was pointing, and on our bank of the river, exactly where the gray strip that I had just seen in the mist was making landfall, dark squares with indistinct edges were already stirring across the earth. And there were none to hinder those squares from separating into parts and spreading by degrees all along our bank of the river.

"They will be striking not only facing the sun, but also upward from below, as they scale the bank. Abdullah has done well, for all that," Yukuk said, his voice at last betraying the strain within.

It's over, I thought. *Whether Abdullah has done well or no, his calculations are sadly awry, for we are one against ten. They are one hundred and twenty thousand in iron mail, on horses and camels, under the command of the best general on this side of the world. Thus ends the dalliance among allies – in catastrophe and certain death.*

But what now? Turn the horses around? Lead three thousand warriors through the mountains of Iran and plunge them into the bloody chaos to which our homeland will now surely descend? They will be hungry by midday, and what then? Plunder the villages we come upon? No. It's too late, too late. All is senseless.

And then I suddenly remembered: I had been at such a pass before. But in those days, at the Iron Gates, the steppe grasses smelled so sweet, in those days I knew that naught could befall me, untested novice though I was, for I was pressed tight by the iron ranks of our Turkic cavalry. Besides, death did not befit a young man of the House of Maniakh. I had come there for victory, and victory was nigh; we were carrying the day, and how could it be other?

And at that time, somewhere far away, at the edge of another plain traveled by a peaceful caravan, on the far horizon of that plain, a puff of dust was rising. And a woman's voice that I had long forgotten whispered: "Fear not, child. Naught will befall us. They will gallop past."

And my ears rang with the neighing of startled horses...

An iron gauntlet lay on my arm.

"Shall I order the gong be rung?" Yukuk asked.

I shook my head. "No, first bring the standard bearing the image of a hawk."

THE GONG HISSED INTO SILENCE over the serried ranks of my cavalry. First, wreathed in all the sanctity bestowed by the black bird on my banner, I rode up to Karzanandj, one of the Turkic warriors, and we looked each other long in the eye. He then turned his gaze to the hawk and at last nodded to me.

"You have more than a thousand horsemen," I said to him. "You are an emir. You shall stand here on the flank and a little to the rear of my Sogdians. Permit no one to strike Abdullah from behind. Do as you will; I shall give you no commands. But lay about you in such a way that it will ever be remembered."

He nodded again and began directing his detachment, with a wave of his hand, into its battle positions.

The newly arrived Sogdians I placed in the cover of my thousand combat-tested men. I rode slowly along the cavalry ranks, looking full into every face. Then I turned my eyes to the center of the army – to the heart, as Abdullah had called it.

To the rear of the dense black rectangle of that heart, I distinctly saw two small men afoot and carrying something like to a beam of wood. They laid it on the brown earth and began to roll it out. I remember marveling that not even a thorn bush grew in that place, river bank though it was.

The two little men were now throwing cushions onto the square they had made, and Abdullah himself – I had the aggressive jut of his beard in good view – was now swaying his way toward it. He tramped across the carpet, set himself clumsily down on it, rested his head on his hands, and sat stock-still, staring at his soldiers' backs.

I looked farther left then, over the heads of Abdullah's warriors. Detachment after detachment of Marwan's army was slowly crossing the river. I could now see them leading their horses across a tottery bridge made of a multitude of boats lashed side to side.

And then their horsemen were again in their saddles and had dispersed to the right and left of the bridge. Our bank fairly swarmed with them, while Abdullah sat alone on his carpet.

I passed in front of my formation now and moved slowly along it, looking into my soldiers' faces. With naught to say that could comfort them, I simply looked in their eyes, speaking to them silently: *I too am here. I am where you are.*

All we could do then was dismount and wait, wait until Abdullah had allowed that endless host to cross and marshal itself little by little into more orderly squares along our bank. But across the river, the hills still stirred and glittered with the sparks thrown off by well-honed metal.

Then the gray squares on our bank moved forward, unhurriedly at first and then, in the center, ever faster. And I knew that my hopes for a miracle had been in vain, as had all my mental shifts and preparations for flight. Naught now remained but to give the signal, the upward motion of the hand that would tell my men to mount.

But it was yet too soon to be ahorse, because the gray metal squares positioned ahead of us were no longer moving. Only to my right, in the center, a grimy wave flew forward across the dark earth, devouring it on the instant. Fierce sparklings of metal rode the crest of that wave.

The first and second rows of our center resembled nothing so much as a beard thrust stubbornly forward, for they bristled with spears. And, as the earth began to quake even beneath our feet, the rolling surge of the Caliph's cavalry crashed into that wall of spears.

At first all was hidden from sight, though sound there was, a dull groaning and roaring like to naught else. But time passed and all was as it had been, as if a swell had dashed against a cliff and forgotten to ebb back.

But that stillness was, I now saw, more improbable than aught else.

For the wall of spears was holding.

And over it hung a cloud of arrows that flew from our ranks. No other movement was there on that field.

Marwan's cavalry began to pull back and form once more into even squares, and again a wave studded with metal flowed toward us over the unhappy earth.

I looked over the river. No, even so there was no hope, none whatsoever. On the other bank, hundreds of gray squares were still crawling in our direction. The check of that first strike had signified absolutely nothing.

But yet another tossing wave receded from the heart of Abdullah's army.

Yukuk's overworked voice reached my ears. "Look, look master – there, across the river. You can see now that this is not the army of Damascus but something far inferior." And I knew then that a dull roar had hung all the while over the field but I had not heard it.

Again I looked over the river, following the direction of Yukuk's hand, and what I saw there was strange indeed, for one square of warriors had stopped moving forward and begun bearing sideways, trampling a fellow square. Both of those living hills then stood immobile until a long, broad snake encased in metal passed between them, away from the crossing, causing chaos wherever it went.

"Marwan is in a bad way," Yukuk called to me, drawing out the words to make me hear. "He... is... being... dis-o-beyed..."

Yet warriors still flowed across the bridge of boats, and on our bank we were outnumbered almost two to one.

And then I saw movement far to the right, along the river's very edge and in the deep rear of the detachments that had already made the crossing to our shore, where dust was rising as a throng of people, though few in number, was converging inexorably on the crossing. A general broil was under way there. Shortly thereafter what I saw I could not believe, for a detachment of Marwan's warriors on the other bank, also few in number, had separated itself from the rest and was at work on the bridge.

What had transpired I did not understand at the time and did not learn until much later, when the soldiers told their tales, and it was this. While the marauders were hacking through the cables that secured the bridge to our bank, a detachment of panic-mongers among the Caliph's troops was for reasons known only to themselves doing the same on the other side. Had Abdullah's cavalry, by breaking through a field choked with troops all standing stock-still, struck fear into them? Who could say?

Gently, making never a sound, the road of horses and soldiers that had been cast across the river canted slightly to one side until it was no longer pointing directly at my chest but was slewing toward my left shoulder. And then the entire iron strip drifted leftward at an angle on the river's current.

People began falling into the water, but I already knew full well how a soldier dressed for battle would fare once submerged, how hard he would try to unloose the sodden leather straps of his heavy armor. I turned away.

All at once, the sun glanced out from behind the clouds. *And how has it contrived to rise so high*, I wondered, *when just now it was dawn?* And the world changed, gaining distinct contours and brighter colors.

The field of battle on our side of the river was also a different place. Abdullah, a tiny, motionless figure, still sat bolt upright on his carpet, but the heart of his army had begun to bow outward. A surge of infantry struggled over the strange hills that had risen in front of the place where the wall of spears had been, and with a sudden jolt of horror, I fancied that those hills twitched and cried out under the soldiers' feet, that those feet were slipping in blood.

There had also been a change in the portion of Marwan's army that stood on our side of the river, cut off now from the far bank. It had brought itself back into order and was again moving forward in a body. And beneath the feet of the cavalry that had to that moment stood unmoving in front of my Sogdian detachment, the earth seemed to seethe.

Facing forward still, I gestured with my hand several times, as if suspending a great weight from that hand. My Sogdians, though, knew it as their signal to mount.

The wing of Marwan's army was, however, not closing on me. It was instead moving slantwise to the right, to where our center was bulging outward, turning the entire battle array into a half-moon. And thereupon, as I watched, the heart of our army advanced yet farther, disengaging finally from my left flank. The cavalry was about to drive a wedge into that widening fork between flank and center

I could by now make out the faces of those moving, like a flow of thick lava, from left to right – their big dark eyes, their black moustaches, their short beards. A strange and unfamiliar people, this. Were these my enemies? Were they the ones who had been putting my Sogdia to the sword these four decades, carrying off money and goods stuffed into thousands of traveling packs, driving before them throngs of slaves? But if they were not, then let them gallop by my ranks and gallop on, as far as they may.

Then a disquieting thought began to thrash in my head. *Do you think you're watching a spectacle in the marketplace?* it asked. *If that be so, the enjoyment is now ended for you. And something other begins*

The lava flow of cavalry clattered by my ranks, and still I sat unstirring in the saddle.

Until I slowly turned around.

Hundreds of eyes were fixed on me, with Yukuk's, mournful and gray, the closest of all. There was no escape.

Slowly too I raised my hand.

"Attack," I said. Only my lips moved, but all in the iron wall behind me heard.

My hand sank down. I turned my face to Marwan's cavalry and, not even drawing the sword that sat useless in its sheath, sent my horse unhurriedly forward, hearing a voice in my head that said, *This is happening, but not to me.*

Several moments, insanely long, passed. The earth slowly heaved and sank beneath me; the flanks of horses and the fluttering garments of Samarkand glimmered in the dust.

The first to perish was Awlad, who had gone forward at a full gallop and fell hard on one of Marwan's cavalrymen, before slumping down his horse's side. And, although horsemen and their mounts then hid him from my sight, I knew that he would never trade in silk.

Nanivandak too fell from his horse, after clinging long and fitfully to its neck, his face buried in its mane.

And Muhammad, his face bathed in blood, went crashing down too, having never once laid eyes on Mecca.

Muslim fell next, and after him, Kevan, who had yet to learn to wield a sword as he ought.

Then... The crowd that spun madly around me yielded no more dark-eyed foreigners, only our own men in their round helmets, who gathered wearily under the banner with the image of a hawk that was borne behind me by a horseman I had never seen before. There was no one to beat the gong, nor, for that matter, was there a gong anywhere to be seen. Only Yukuk, unscathed, his face stony, sat in his saddle and gazed on me in silence.

Is this victory? I wanted to shout. *I need no such victory. Rather give me back my friends and brothers.*

But there was none to answer me.

The dust was settling. We stood hard by the river bank, and the field around us was in utter chaos. Horsemen were not fighting each other as much as they were speeding senselessly to and fro. A blurred black mass in the center of Abdullah's forces was sprouting and growing, it seemed, as the heart of his army took to horse. And the gray specks that were Marwan's men were taking new positions on the field, mostly spreading to either side, along the river.

One of those formations was close to me. Too close.

Shaking my head to awake from this fearsome dream, I motioned those at my side to betake themselves a little farther uphill, so that all might gather beneath the hawk on my banner.

And no sooner had I done so than a fist struck me from behind on my mail-clad right shoulder. Vexed by this, I tried to shrug that shoulder and discovered that I could not do it, that someone was holding the shoulder and the arm along with it.

Again the sun is passing behind a cloud, I thought, *and the world is growing gray*. I lowered my eyes to study the glittering, reddish point that protruded from somewhere below my armpit and spent some time languidly devising how to flick it away with my left hand, since my right was proving undutiful.

A cry came from behind. Yukuk was flying toward me with outstretched hand and open mouth, until an arrow's fletching jutted crookedly up above his shoulders and he began to lean forward, resting his face on his horse's neck.

No more, I thought.

The world filled then with a din punctuated by the deep-throated slap of Turkic bow strings. A solid wall of Turkic cavalry was sweeping aside all who stood in the way, dispersing the last of the resistance.

And the sun went out.

19

THE BERID

A fly was tickling my nose, and right odiously too. I tried to move my head to drive it away, but my head just lolled to the left.

And when it did, in place of the low-hanging gray tent-cloth I had been observing, I saw rows of people, lying motionless or stirring and close by me, a girl with a foolish face sitting cross-legged and holding a bowl in her left hand and a scrap of bread in her right. She dipped that bread into the bowl and then tried to thrust it into the mouth of an unkempt old man with sunken cheeks.

Without a trace of feeling, I recognized that old man as Yukuk.

And I closed my eyes.

I remember next a dull-edged, nauseating pain, my head floating skyward, the smell of vomit and blood, and again the flies, the swarms of flies. Day after day, week after week. And even when the pain had passed, I was firmly convinced, I knew not how, that never again would I be able to stand and take even a few steps.

But everything changed one day when, between my head and the tent's gray sky, a man rose into view, holding in his two hands a platter bearing a heap of rosy, angular pomegranates.

The pomegranates, the physician told me, had been sent by the Caliph's brother, by Abu Jafar hight Mansur himself. And I believed him with all my heart when I discovered that they were not of the finest quality and that two of them had even rotted on one side. Yet their quality was of lesser importance, because from that day on, the physician began to appear at my bedside at least four times a day, bringing to me, and to Yukuk too, more fruit along with small cups of wine and herbal infusions. And I began to return to life, which fact afforded me no joy whatsoever.

Because news was now reaching that field infirmary, where more heroes of the battle by the Zab died with every passing day.

While we who had been wounded at the Zab were being loaded onto row after row of litters, while the dead were being hurriedly buried on the battlefield, Abdullah's army, enveloped in a cloud of dust, was approaching Haran, where Marwan would fain have immured himself. But instead, having numbered the remnants of his army, the sovereign lord of the faithful bolted to Damascus, whereupon Abdullah entered Haran uncontested, having come to peaceable terms with its governor, Aban ibn Yazid, and even having allowed him to remain as governor.

But he did not linger there.

The army that attacked Damascus was not what it had been, for the veterans of the Zab had been joined by fresh detachments from Kufa and also by Khorasanis sent by Abu Muslim. And when, on a gentle spring morning after several days of siege, that host streamed through a breach in the walls of Damascus, murder and pillage ensued that scarce abated with the sunset.

And so I knew that the Green Palace, home to they who had ruled one-third of the world, and the crooked streets where, like a scattering of precious stones, candied fruits of many colors sparkled, were places that I had best not see in the years near at hand. Because the smell of blood dissipates fast, but old stones long retain the memory of it.

To this day I do not know, and do not care to know, the truth of the tale in which the victor of the Zab gathered together no less than eighty princes of the House of Umayyad soon after the battle, to share a banquet of reconciliation, and began to have them killed as soon as all were seated on their rugs. That done, he bade the still-trembling bodies be covered by leather horse blankets and the dishes be placed thereon, and then set about his food.

It may not all have been quite so. But not one prince survived, save the fortunate son of Caliph Hisham, Abd ar-Rahman al-Dahil, who fled with a detachment of soldiers far to the west, to Córdoba in al-Andalus, where the land ends.

Day after day, Abdullah's men sought the remainder, and their kinsmen too. And found them all.

And when none was left alive, crowds began digging up the graves of the sovereign lords of the faithful in Qinnasrin and Damascus. The body of Caliph Sulayman was dragged from the ground in Dabiq, although only his spine, ribs and skull remained. They were cast into a fire.

When the body of Caliph Hisham was disinterred in Rustafa, it was found to be incorrupt. Only the tip of his nose had vanished. Abdullah himself gave the corpse eighty strokes with a whip, after which he had it burned.

Naught was found at the bottom of Walid's grave save handfuls of black ashes that could not even be burned.

And only the righteous Omar proved worthy of being left in peace. Only his bones were not hacked, not burned, not flung abroad in streets and desolate places.

But Abdullah, now Emir of all Syria, set out from Damascus to Fustat, in the land of Misr, where stand pyramids tall as any mountain. And when the mild summer on the banks of the Zab ended, he had run to ground – yes, had run to ground in Misr the last of the Umayyads.

Marwan, nicknamed the Donkey, was killed in some small town called Busir, at no great distance from the Fayyum oasis. After a brief battle, the old man, who had hid himself in a temple dedicated to the Prophet Isa, was swiftly beheaded and his head sent to as-Saffah, to He Who Spills.

Then they went for Marwan's wives and daughters, who by that time had also taken refuge in the temple. On their way, those murderers came upon one of Marwan's eunuchs, whose sword shook in his hand.

The people in black twisted his arms behind and began to question him.

"Marwan ordered me to cut off the heads of all his wives and daughters, should he be killed," the slave said. "But spare my life, because if you kill me, I swear by Holy God that the legacy of the Prophet will decay away and leave no trace."

He was duly warned to be more heedful when speaking of such things.

But he led them outside the town, to where the sands began, and told them to dig. And so were found the Prophet's striped mantle, his ring and the staff on which the Prophet leaned when he preached, all of which Marwan had buried there. Amir ibn Ismail, who had killed Marwan, sent those relics to Abdullah, who in turn sent them on to He Who Spills. And where the headless body of the last of the Umayyads is buried, no one knows.

Abu Salama too received his just deserts. He returned from as-Saffah in high spirits, clasping to his bosom a suit of ceremonial attire, his gift from the new sovereign lord – all complete, from a long, black cloak with gold thread and a short jacket-like kaba to a tall kalansuwa topped with a turban.

He was allowed to die happy in consideration of the great services he had rendered in times past, and in recompense for his acts in latter days, he received no more than a knife to the back in some alley. "A long, thin knife," my long-forgotten informant told me, while I only nodded, for Abu Salama had, at least in part, well earned his fate.

When further tidings came, neither I nor any other of Abdullah's warriors still remained on the banks of the Zab. Some had gone to their eternal rest in the earth, while others, in a slow single file, had quit that mournful place. Only now does it seem to me that all the news of the death and destruction came to me together, at one time and in that one spot, amid the cries and wheezing of the small multitude that lay beneath the sagging tent canopies.

Probably it is just that I knew what would follow. I knew that Abdullah's turn would come.

Four years would pass before that cough ceased to rend the breast of the unhappy as-Saffah, and his brother at last took his exalted place, amid cushions trimmed with black silk. And the name he assumed on ascending the throne was that which all had long called him.

Thus did Mansur, the greatest Caliph of them all, rise to power.

And Abdullah... In those days, that fat, bewhiskered man who at the Zab had vanquished the best general on our side of the world was mustering an army from Khorasan to mount a campaign against Constantine's city. An army of Syrians too had rallied to his aid. And to this host the merry Abdullah suggested that the uncle of the recently deceased Caliph – he himself, that is – ought rightly to inherit the Prophet's mantle, staff and ring. Why should they descend instead to the lean bookkeeper with the thin beard who at that time was making the hajj and was therefore far from Kufa?

And so the soldiers, with joyful cries, saluted the new sovereign lord of the faithful.

But Abdullah ought never to have misprized his nephew. Because Mansur was making the hajj with the one man who did not fear Abdullah.

And that man's name was Abu Muslim.

Few people in this world can imagine what the Leopard of Khorasan was feeling at that time. Fear? Guilt? The hope of now atoning for something known to Mansur and very few others?

Abu Muslim had in due time yielded to Mansur's blandishments, thus depriving Abdullah of his army, which hailed in the main from Khorasan.

And so it was that Abdullah's army fell all to pieces; so it was that the Khorasani soldiers left him to return to their best beloved.

The Syrians who had come to the camp did still remain. But then the Leopard of Khorasan spoke again, saying that he would now journey to Syria and there be governor.

Thereupon the Syrians ran back to their homes, not wishing Abu Muslim of Khorasan to plunder those homes while they sat, awaiting they knew not what, around the tent of a disconsolate, bewhiskered man.

So that man had naught left to him but to flee to his brother Sulayman in Basra, far to the south, where the land ends. To flee and there to await the end.

The end that came to the victor of the Zab was not the most hideous – merely a swift smothering. And the slave girl who had lain with him that night was smothered also. They were then placed side by side with their hands entwined, for the executioners sent by Mansur pitied them.

The house was then torn down over the two bodies, making those ruins their tomb.

And Abu Muslim departed to Khorasan, swearing that he would never again leave the ancient fortress of Merv.

Much later, though, in a distant land where rivers and canals take the place of streets, where the vine-draped trees are thicker than the houses, where a wall of rain renders even the trees outside the window invisible, I would learn from Iranian seafarers that Abu Muslim too had at last received his due.

The sovereign lord of the faithful had sent courier after courier to him with assurances of friendship. Courier after courier, and all for naught.

But at length he was enticed from the fortress, and they met in the Caliph's pavilion, in a camp near Rumiyah where they were girt about by Khorasani warriors. This latter circumstance afforded Mansur no joy, but Mansur was no coward and never would he forget the knife that had almost found its way to the dark-skinned boy's breast.

"Take care," Abu Ayyub al-Muryani, Mansur's secretary, said to him, "for if you touch even a hair on his head, you will thereafter have to kill again and again."

On the first day of their meeting, Mansur treated his general right kindly and sent him to bathe and rest, whereafter he berated Abu Ayyub soundly for his excess of caution.

And he summoned his most trusted guardsmen, turned to he who was the best of them, and asked, "Will you do all that I order?" "All," that man replied. "Will you kill Abu Muslim?" he asked then, and the officer looked long at the ground in silence. "What troubles you? Why do you not answer?" the sovereign lord of the faithful inquired, his voice low. And at length the guardsman quietly said that yes, that also he would do.

The Caliph sent Abu Ayyub to the soldiers in the camp, to spy out their mood. Abu Muslim, as it transpired, had spent most of his last morning with his friend and kinsman to the Caliph, Isa ibn Musa. Isa, though, decided to wash before visiting the Caliph, so that Abu Muslim entered the pavilion alone.

What follows... is known mostly from what Mansur himself would later tell the shaken Abu Ayyub, to the very point at which Abu Muslim was groveling on the rug before the Caliph and seeking to clasp and kiss his hand, while Mansur numbered his sins. And then, when the Caliph clapped his hands, the guardsmen burst in, rained a hail of blows upon the general, slit his throat, wrapped the body in a rug and left it in the corner of the pavilion, it being as yet unclear what was to be done with that body. Because the ring of Khorasanis around the tent lingered there still.

Then at last came a freshly washed Isa and asked, "Where is Abu Muslim?" to which Mansur replied, "He's bundled up over there."

And a horror-stricken Isa murmured, "We have come from God and to Him we shall return." After which, turning to Mansur, he said, "Sovereign lord of the faithful, today is the first day of your rule."

But the story does not end there. The soldiers in the camp were informed that their general, Mansur's dear friend, would live henceforth in the Caliph's pavilion. And the guardsmen began to add a new section to that pavilion, bringing in fresh rugs and carrying out the old ones, including one that had been rolled into a wide tube. The body of the Leopard of Merv was pushed with no ado into the Tigris, so that he had no more of a grave than did Marwan, last of the Umayyads.

On the following day, Mansur sent splendid presents to Abu Muslim's commanders, and gradually a large number of them made obeisance to him. But many said, "We have sold our master for trinkets made of silver." And they quit the camp.

Old Barmak's voice rang again in my head: *His name is Mansur, which means Victorious, because he has an exasperating way of winning any game you may care to name.*

But all those solemn speeches and lengthy particulars were, of course, concocted in later times by court poets, whereas in life it was as it always is, lacking any resonantly poetic words, swiftly done, witlessly done, with loud cries, labored breathing, and the harsh, hollow sound of blows.

Be all that as it may, though, but today it seems to me that even then, as I lay amid dying soldiers on the banks of the Zab, I already knew all that would come to pass.

And I also knew that it was time to dislodge myself from there and go home.

But before setting out, I had to close the chapter on a certain story.

"Yukuk," I said one quiet summer evening to my savior and constant aide, who sat next to me, well-shaven now and thus more human to look upon, with whom, though I do not remember when, the familiar form of address had become customary.

And he, interestingly, understood all on the instant, although I had thought my voice to be free of emotion. He simply sighed – a long, abstracted sigh.

"I've been thinking," I continued, "that now would be the best time to talk. Because we lack the strength to cut each other down. But we do have the strength, should we so decide, to simply stand, the both of us, and go our separate ways and forget one another. Our legs falter but still they carry us. Correct?"

A long pause ensued.

"When did you begin to divine it?" he asked at length in a voice that would ever after be aught but strained and gruff.

"The elephants," was my terse reply. "That abandoned paddock for war elephants."

Yukuk was silent.

"It was near the only time when you showed real feeling for me to see," I explained. "Before that – and after too, for that matter, in skirmishes, in battles – there was little enough. Quite astonishing: a man of iron. But these... not even elephants but the shades of dead elephants, the shades of imperial majesty and might... At the time, I wondered: What manner of man is this, for whom these shades have such meaning? And in general, what manner of man is he, what is important to him and what less so? And so my thoughts progressed, on and on..."

Yukuk's lips began to curve into a smile, stretching around his near-toothless mouth. His hoary head still bent, he gave a quiet nod and held his silence.

"But all I did thereafter was write to Samarkand," I went on. "As you remember, greetings had previously been sent from there to one named Yukuk, which made me calm. But after our visit to the elephant paddock, I determined to confirm it all once more and wrote a letter to inquire into the appearance of that man. And the answer made all clear. The man who went by the name of Owl looked naught like you. He was short and plump."

There was quiet then, until at length the man I had known as Yukuk said, "I am an official with the messenger service."

What messenger service is that? I wondered. And it came to me. "Oh, *those* messengers. The berid. The berid of Caliph Marwan. Now I understand all. Although in our family, truth be told, what they do likely goes under the guise of silk trading rather than of bearing messages from place to place... You came away safe after what that scoundrel Abu Muslim did to the berid?"

He shook his head. "No. None came away safe. Six thousand men throughout Khorasan he slew. Ordinary postal workers and others such as I. Without distinction. Their kin and their friends. He killed them every one, for safety's sake, to risk no error. And I was sent from Haran afterward, to gather up the pieces. So I came, and saw that there was naught to gather. And another thing I saw, which was that the Caliph would need a very large army if he was to do aught in Khorasan

– if aught could indeed be done there. I could have turned back at once," he sighed, "but I thought that if I returned to Haran, I would be sent again to Merv, to prepare the Caliph's campaign. So I had best stay where I was. How to send my reports... I would find a way, I would manage. And I began to unriddle all. I heard tell of those interesting folk with their daggers and understood that all was not so very simple there. But then I stumbled upon something else. Others proved to be at work in Merv, but they were being gradually destroyed, or at least their network was being dismantled into its separate parts. That, now, was interesting to me. Your network, it was. There was a man by the name of Yukuk who did a foolish thing, by accepting a proposal from Hashim. That Yukuk did not live long, since Hashim used people for but a short time before destroying them... But something that Yukuk did tell me. The poor wretch would have stopped at nothing, including fleeing to Haran because the way to Samarkand was – or so he thought – closed to him. He told me something of what had transpired in Bukhara. And I went to Bukhara, there to puzzle out who was working for whom, who had cut off your House's communications. And on the road to Merv, I encountered a man on a donkey and two I knew, who were hard on his heels. And, thought I, I needed that man alive as long as may be, to see what happened around him. The rest you know. And while I was puzzling still in Merv, it became ever clearer how senseless it would be for me to return to Haran. And now, after the battle, even less so. That's all."

I had never known Yukuk to speak so long.

A cool breeze blew. Gray shadows moved awkwardly, shuffling their feet, beneath tent canopies that hung down to the ground and among figures that lay motionless or stirring. The rows of supine figures receded into the darkness, where small lamps were beginning to burn. In a corner, disobedient fingers were trying to coax a trill from a four-stringed Iranian oud whose sounds were drowned by a hollow, hacking, hopeless coughing.

"No, that's far from all, Yukuk," I said, breaking the silence. "Life goes on. What should I now feel toward you? Nothing but gratitude, in truth. What was I? A good trader. Even very good, they do say," I added, unable to keep that to myself. "And look now at what I have become. If not for you, there would quite simply have been none of this."

"I never saw a man learn so much so fast," Yukuk said reluctantly after a brief pause. And I was truly glad of that.

"But now the training is ended and I must go home," I went on. "And you... You are a renowned commander in a victorious army. All know this, while the berid... I need only whisper one word to old Barmak, and he will value you yet more than he does now. So choose, Yukuk – a pension from the new Caliph, a command numbering no less than a thousand in his army, or the old, familiar work for that same Caliph. Or you walk out of this place and vanish. If you have money concealed somewhere, a small abode, well... The least I can do for you is not stand in your way. So much you have earned, from that first sword-strike there, among the wounded."

The distant cough grew quieter and the sound of the oud more sure.

"And those are not your only options," I continued. "There's also the House of Maniakh. Work can also be found for you in Samarkand. One man of your acquaintance will recommend you right earnestly. And more – that man, here and now, is eagerly advising you to choose this way. None in Samarkand will fault you for having been not the least in the berid. On the contrary, in fact."

Yukuk, his face utterly motionless, fixed his gray eyes on me, while something worked on him from within. And I knew that he was trying to compel himself to do that which was not in his nature. He wanted, seemingly for the first time in his life, to ask something of me. To ask for himself.

"Speak, then," I quietly prompted him.

"I have been more than twenty years at war," he said, with much effort in his rasping voice. "And, speaking with you, I have often thought that this is a man who, if he is spared, can go where... Where... But I shall never see that place. And a pity it is."

"What place?" I urged him.

"The great Empire, sire," he sighed at last. "Its canals and rivers. Its palaces and their gardens. Chang'an. Its silk. What need have I to serve as commander in yet another army? Better to be a simple stable hand but to see even once that magical land..."

My ears filled then with the gentle sigh of strings plucked on the Imperial orchestra's multitude of qin, and I reclined on the cushions in a long silence. And then again I turned to my left.

"A simple stable hand? Tell me, Yukuk, could you learn maybe two hundred phrases in the language of the Han?"

"Not two hundred but more," he responded on the instant. "I know seven languages. In my youth I learned languages with ease. That's how I fell in with the berid, since they take... they *took* people with particular talents."

Seven languages? I knew then that my small idea had come to me with a purpose. And I began to lay it out.

"Soon I shall journey home. With attendants, of course, and you could be of use to me in that. Since I must travel through Merv, care is in order. And thereafter... Yes, I will at last return to Chang'an. But not straight away. Because when my work is done here, I will go back to Merv, for I have business there still. My own business, on which I will expend my own funds. And I will need aides. So here is my offer to you, Yukuk. You help me find her. We return to Samarkand, of which we have spoken already, and there start all afresh, Yukuk. And then you will journey, with or without me, to Chang'an, to our trading house in the Imperial capital. But as no simple stable hand. And not as a poor man, either. Because, your imminent departure for the Empire notwithstanding, you shall have received ere then a small home in Samarkand. On a hillside. Hundreds of lamps will burn before your window of an evening on the slope opposite and will sway on the black waters of the canal far below. It cedes naught to Chang'an. Say yes, Yukuk."

"That woman..." he said, his voice low, as it was that first time, in Merv.

"Have you not learned by now that I'm a very stubborn man? I may back away for a time but I never forget. I shall return and shall find her." Thus my soft-spoken affirmation.

Yukuk looked long at me, and I seemed to see sorrow in his eyes. Then, slowly, he nodded.

20

GOD-GIVEN

"Now here is our pet Hawk of the House of Abbas, and I was just beginning to wonder who I would dine with." Thus Barmak, fresh and rosy of cheek, greeted me in what had once been the palace of Kufa's emir, which buzzed with many voices. "Remember how you ate at our first meeting in Merv, with such restraint, dignity and elegance, but in extraordinary quantities? It was a joy to behold. This, then, is what I propose. Since spring is here, there shall be a soup of young goat meat, know you, that is green with fresh herbs. And I remember you speaking once, by the Zagros mountains, of candied fruits from Damascus, so I have all this while been keeping a small store for you, of the greatest variety. Quince, Palestinian apples, dates from the Jerid and even candied currants. Each fruit in its own papyrus basket. You must eat, eat, and eat it all, here and now. And you will not have to go after it, for it will be brought here. And if you resist, I shall send you to dine with our mutual acquaintance, who has just sat himself down to eat, and that you will regret. There's naught tasty there. He doesn't even like sweetmeats. And while I think of it, I had a talk with him just now. He believed the name of your city, Samar-kand, to mean 'sweet harvest.' But I put him out of countenance when I told him that in the ancient language of the peoples of Ind, the meaning was quite, quite different – 'a place of battle,' it was. A battle long forgotten..."

My eyes creased with pain. "Dear God, Barmak, when will it ever end? How can one be done with your accursed battles and have only sweet harvests?"

"On that you must speak with our victorious one. Be mindful, though, that he's in ill humor with all the world, now that people are coming to him for their reward. So many heroes... One came once, and Mansur scraped together the money for him. He came twice, and again Mansur could not refuse him. But you know yourself how little is to be had from Mansur even when he is in fairly good humor. And, imagine this, that man counted the money, was crestfallen, and came a third time. 'And why do you present yourself once more?' our mutual friend greeted him, with a right good grace. 'To learn from you the prayer you spoke of,' the man replied, knowing then that he had overreached. 'Trouble yourself not,' Mansur answered him, 'for there is little to it. I only beseeched God to let me see no more of you in the near future, but He did not heed me.' So there it is, my young friend. But you are not one that would make such a mistake. To get money, for example, from Mansur, you must first offer him money... So do let me show you to him now. Doubt not that he will be glad of it. Here, around this turn. Ah, what ill luck! He's sitting with his back to us... Very well, he'll send for you later, have no doubt of it."

Through the doorway I caught only a fleeting glimpse of one seated in a place of honor, on a prayer rug facing Mansur, with platters and bowls between them. He was small and prim, of middle years, with a straight back, gray eyes and a trim, light beard. Red spots burned on his cheeks, and he had a generally offended and unhappy air about him, hard as he tried not to show it.

"Look and remember, Maniakh," Barmak whispered, taking me by the shoulders and leading me from the dining chamber. "There you see Doctor Bukhtishu himself, he who holds in his hands the threads of our lives or at least sees those threads right well. And you have observed him at a difficult pass. Because he has just been informed that no wine is served at Mansur's table. Imagine, he was well in the way of explaining that he is a votary of the doctrine of the Prophet Isa the Anointed, which doctrine declares that wine symbolizes the divine blood and that it is, to boot, of great medical benefit, by aiding the coursing of the blood and the digestion of food, and in sum, that he had never in his life sat down at table without wine. But on the man I need not name this produced no impression whatsoever."

I was intrigued. "And what will the great healer do now?"

"Well, it remains only... To begin telling Mansur about the curative properties of water from the Tigris, unless he has utterly taken leave of his senses. But for you, Maniakh, a modest pitcher of tolerable wine will be found, since your need is great... And, while I think of it, you have just seen the man who is, in a certain sense, your savior. Bukhtishu it was who advised that horse doctor at the Zab to feed you pomegranates and to give you wine and herbal infusions to drink, a drop at a time. He himself wrote brief instructions regarding what to give you and when..."

I stopped. "I was healed by Bukhtishu himself, was I? Then I'm now assured near-eternal life."

Barmak shook his head. "That's a vast exaggeration, my young friend – yes, as vast as can be. In any event, the great healer has promised me no such thing, not even for all the treasures and all the camels of Balkh. But something quite other he has promised. This uneven pulse, this creaking and wheezing... Since there is no eternal life, know you... But let me read you one charming passage. I have it with me, about my person... Here it is: 'When passing by a cemetery one day, the righteous Caliph Omar asked his attendants to await him behind the fence. They saw him standing over the graves, his lips stirring. "What were you saying there, o sovereign lord of the faithful," they asked him, "and what did you hear in reply?" And Omar said to them: "I was walking between the graves of those I loved and repeating their names, but they did not answer me. And then the earth called to me and said: 'Omar, do you know who I am? I am he who erases beauty from the face, who strips away shreds of skin, who spreads the bones of the hand like a fan.' " And having said that, Omar wept until he almost swooned away. And few enough were the days that remained before he himself descended into his grave.' Yes indeed. But would it not be interesting, Maniakh, to be born into the next life as some animal from warm forests where streams flow in abundance, and fruits and nuts hang from every bough?.. And you will soon be homeward bound?" Such was the unlooked-for ending to Barmak's lengthy discourse.

"How did you guess?" I replied, without even the hint of a smile.

"One of the persisting joys of my position is that I have dealings, for the most part, with clever people. And you, Maniakh, have afforded me such joy in greater quantities than many, many others. You have done excellently, simply excellently, and now it remains only to close the book. For which you shall have a surpassing good opportunity a few days hence... And then, of course, you will be homeward bound. But you yourself understand all that right well."

And I was indeed able, as Barmak had evidently known ahead of time, to close the book a few days thereafter. Because, as promised, Mansur, treasurer of the House of Abbas, sent for me, the courier without preamble informing me that that I and the brother of the sovereign lord of the faithful would be setting out on a journey. A short one, he added.

Mansur was even more drawn and fretful than usual, and wasted little time on embraces. But he did take me by the arm and lead me, amid a multitude of scurrying people, deep within the courtyards and chambers of the governor's home, which was now the palace of the Caliph.

I had noticed that Mansur's path was now constantly crossed, as if fortuitously, by anxious people who seemed to care for one thing only, that being for him to notice that they had much to do and were manifesting therein a singular zeal, rather than whiling the idle time away.

"I must still beg leave to make this journey," Mansur said, hiding a wry smile against his shoulder.

And all at once, the people around vanished. We traversed an absolutely empty little courtyard and halted before a carved door that stood open.

Behind that door there was naught to speak of, save a small, sickly garden. And there, sitting in solitude on a prayer rug laid beneath two shade trees and leaning his back against the wall, was a youth with sunken cheeks, wearing a simple black cape and a black turban. On his knees lay a book so huge that it cost the youth an appreciable effort to turn the soft parchment pages in his search.

I suddenly saw that this was almost an exact copy of Mansur, tall like him and with a long face. Furthermore, the disparity in their ages was not great; only to the outward eye was Mansur by far the older. They were both gangling and thin, but thin in different ways. The sinewy treasurer of the House of Abbas could, it seemed, be given an entire camel pack to carry and he would stagger morosely on. But the youth with the book would fall beneath such a load, never to rise again.

Mansur stood and waited, holding me by the arm.

The youth raised his head, looked at us with a slight smile, nodded, and coughed. Then he bent again over his enormous book.

Mansur tugged my arm. We turned and went back whence we had come. Behind our backs, there was another cough, this one harder.

"And that's..." I began, but stopped. I had wanted to say: "And that's all? For that there was the Zab, and my wound, and a year gone furtively away, and my friends slain..." but the words caught in my throat.

Mansur, though, understood me in his own way.

"There should be somewhere on this earth where, to everyone's knowledge, that man may sit in peace and quiet to read a book," he said. "All the rest falls to us."

IN FRONT OF THE GATES that gave out onto the dusty street, a string of camels, lying aloof on the gray ground and ready loaded for the road, awaited us. The ever-present pockmarked slave – at last I knew his name, which was Salam al-Abdrash – waved us over to the head camel. Then, having looked me over with doubt in his eyes, he lifted a stone of no small size and put it in the bag suspended from the camel's left side, after which he bade me climb inside. Paying no attention to any of this, Mansur went by habit to the bag on the right side. Once the packs were equal in weight on either side, the camel driver dolefully called on the camel to rise, and, after some reflection, it reluctantly began to unbend its legs, the back ones first.

Our journey was indeed short, and the greater part of it came when we had bid farewell to the camels, after which we traveled on boats down a broad canal lined with palm trees, and ended where the canal met the wide, tranquil river.

"It will be here," Mansur said to me as he scrambled along a steep, sandy path up the river bank.

"What will be here?" I asked, trying to wave a cloud of dust away from my face

"The city!" he replied in vexation. "*That* city. Madinat as-Salam, the City of All-Encompassing Serenity."

And for this he has brought me here, when we could have stayed in the palace, to converse there at our ease?

I looked at him in surprise and began to survey the plain around us.

This was no desert. The sawad, the black earth of those parts, needed only thin trickles of water to grow green and flourish. But here there was as much water as one could wish, in the lavishly broad, glittering ribbon to my right, on whose bank, at a point where the river was crossed by a chain of boats lashed together, a tumbledown castle stood.

And water also sparkled over all that boundless plain, in fine threads of mica that ran amid the green of trees and the low, square houses set amongst them.

Standing atop our hill, we likely looked to those below like two playthings whose garments the warm wind was vainly trying to wrest away.

Mansur pointed downward and to the right. "There is naught downriver from here all the way to Qataysfun... Ctesiphon as was," he said. "The city of kings... Now mere heaps of stone. But excellent stone. That may be loaded onto boats and brought here. Farther downriver is Basra, and there, the sea. The whole world. Or go down this canal to Balis and from there it is no distance at all to Damascus, Antioch, Jerusalem. Across the Euphrates, of course. And then to the south... But you've already been there, Maniakh. In general, here it is: the crossroads of the world."

The wind tossed another helping of dust into our faces.

"Rivers. That's good," I said. "But there must be people too. To build."

"People?" The word was a grunt. "People there shall be, and no end of them. Imagine, now: you're living here, you're building the city. For that work we pay" – and this with a dismal determination – "a dirham. A dirham every... every twelve days. That's enough." His bony hand reached out to me, although I had made no objection he could hear. "But the building is done. You receive here land and pay naught for it. And that land is pure gold. It will feed you for the rest of your life. Because here there will be a vast city and here will live the sovereign lord of the faithful, emirs, qadis, scriveners and altogether the richest people in the world. And they will all need to eat. And some to eat well," he added with mild disapproval. "You will be able to bring your goods to the city markets on foot, if you wish. From here, here and here."

I followed his hand as it pointed into the void, at the plain with its miniature houses and green treetops.

"A round fortress three parasangs wide. Four gates, to Damascus, to Khorasan, those being your haunts, and... Streets leading in from the gates. Along each street, markets. There are plans to place a dome over the palace, a green dome. We shall see about that. But this is enough for now. Thereafter, all will grow of itself... A beginning must only be made. There are no complexities here, Maniakh. Everything complex may be divided into many simple... well, bricks. A brick is this" – and he sliced out a fairly voluminous portion of air with his hands – "which two men can lift. From these gates" – here he jabbed a hand again into the void – "to these there is a wall, first the lower course, a hundred and sixty-two thousand bricks. And as it rises higher, the wall narrows, so that the upper courses are only a hundred and fifty thousand, and the highest of all a mere hundred and forty thousand. And what is a brick? Earth, clay... It costs nothing. Although true it is that in addition to the wall there will be towers, three hundred and sixty in all."

I looked at him askance. Those who wish to build a house or a palace or a city and speak of it with spluttering enthusiasm are far, far more frequently encountered than those who actually begin to build, and even they seldom finish the job they have begun. The difference between those people and this man was that this man could be expected to succeed in all he did.

I broke the silence at last. "And what do you say it will be called, your city?"

"Ma-di-nat-as-sa-lam," he said, spelling it out for me as though I were an idiot.

I shook my head. "I see... And you wish that name to be repeated around the world? Maybe something shorter, then. What name has all this now?"

"None" was Mansur's dour reply.

But I would not leave it be. "What about that little village, the one nearest to us? Surely it has a name?"

"Ah," he said indifferently, striving to shield his face from the blowing dust. "That village... It once had a temple in which stood an idol... their god... and so the village is called Gift of God, God-Given. Baghdad."

"Now that's a good deal easier to say," I observed. "And, you see, it's the name everyone will use in any case."

Mansur looked at me and said again, expressionless, "The city's name will be Madinat as-Salam."

I chose not to argue.

Because a far more serious conversation lay ahead.

On the river bank, at the water's edge, rugs had been spread for us, and attempts were being made to hang an awning to shade us from the sun. It kept wresting itself out of the boatmen's hands, though, and threatening to fly off into the glittering water.

"And now you must be properly fed," the treasurer of the House of Abbas said, with a wry smile. "As Barmak has reminded me."

The wheat stew known as harisah, bread that could be fresher, water from the Tigris and something more, prepared especially for a convalescing veteran, I thought. *Maybe even something with a faint fragrance of meat.*

I erred in one thing only, which was that instead of a humdrum harisah, we were served a light pilaf with fruit, mostly dried, that had been brought from nearby.

I knew that while we ate, I must reach an agreement with he who would one day be the sovereign lord of one-third of the world, as to the fate of my own country. Because here, on a bare riverbank three weeks' journey from Samarkand, there was none other to do it in my stead.

"You need money, Mansur, and we can give it to you," I began, after a long, lavish pause filled with food, and by the expression on his face, I knew that this had pleased him well. "Because you will impose no special tax on the merchants."

Regrettably, we shall not, I read on that face. *But we shall still turn the abundance of merchants to good account.*

"My trading house is to take an entire street in any and all of your markets," I continued. "We will be the first to come there. We will be the first to send ships from the southern shores of the Celestial Empire. If all is well with us, others will follow. And so, a street on the southern, shady side, by the Khorasan Gates, goes to the House of Maniakh, yes?"

"You're an astute man," he responded, and right promptly too. "Yes, of course."

"But another small question remains. And it is that there must always be money in Sogdia to purchase goods and pay for the caravans," I went on. "The plundering of my country will ruin you, Mansur. Because there is almost naught left to plunder. Do you have need for impoverished subjects who will try their utmost to find trade routes around your lands? That we can do. Indeed, my family was renowned for exactly that many decades ago. The rest we have spoken of. The best of the best have already fled Samarkand for Chang'an, and how has that profited you? And those who have not left... Do you really wish to have throngs of the dispossessed applying to our mutual acquaintance in Merv?"

He said nothing, though he smiled disagreeably.

"I am no ikhshid of Sogdia nor am I your emir in those lands," I continued. "But you've seen the men of Samarkand, in battle and elsewhere. One need not be an ikhshid to remind you that in our golden age, the lands of Sogdia were under the power of the khagans and there was another authority besides. And to that authority we could never accustom ourselves. All would have been different had Samarkand not vied with Bukhara and Bukhara with Chach. But as it was, when each city had its own overlord... We cannot make shift without an empire, be that to our good fortune or no. Besides, if Samarkand prospers, your power will be secure. If it does not, you will have greater Merv and naught else. But then... Then you will lose us. On this I need not reach agreement with you. It behooves you to reach agreement with me. In short, Sogdia is as deserving... as Iran. That you must have. That we must have."

Mansur sighed and looked away, to the river. Then came an unexpected question: "Will you be journeying soon to your beloved Celestial Empire?" he asked.

Whatever else that signaled, it did not give me leave to turn the talk to trifles. The answer was mine to guess, and I seemed to guess it well.

"That, in any event, would be my wish... Not immediately, for I have business still in Merv. But to answer the question you did not ask, yes – if Sogdia continues as it has these many years, someone in Chang'an may begin to take an interest in any lands that lie ill-attended. That lie, furthermore, to the north of its eternal enemy, the Tibetans, and to the south of the Great Steppe... And then there will be problems aplenty."

"Which of the Emperor's commanders is most powerful of all?" he interrupted me brusquely.

"There are one or two," I sighed. "Note that they are all from foreign parts. The Han, the natives of that place, have an outright hatred of war. Well, there's Geshu Han. He's Turkic. His defeats outnumber his victories, but he is experienced and careful. He's more famous now for his musicians and his wine than for his military prowess. Of the rest... Well, there's only Gao Xianzhi, he who deceived two armies, the Tibetan and his own, and so carried the day – you remember I told you about that? He's no Han either, but hails from Koryŏ... Yet he's now governor of a large province in the Mountains of Heaven, to the east of us... of you, I should say. In sum, to the east of your, and therefore of our, frontiers. And yes, Mansur, I shall keep watch on what is transpiring there, in the Celestial Empire. And my brother, who reads the same book as you, shall keep watch on Samarkand. And there are things that we shall tell you. Although, let me say, the Radiant Emperor will hardly consent to the risk of a campaign against the West. It is enough for him that the Imperial envoys are as snug in Fergana as they are in their own homes. And to venture beyond, to Samarkand... No, no, that would be too foolish... But it all leads to one thing, which is that you need a new emir of Sogdia. One who respects the House of Maniakh and other such houses, so that they will lend him their aid. And one who knows who Abu Muslim truly is. What of Khalid, son of he who tutors your young? How timely he appeared on that road..."

Mansur shrugged. "We need Khalid here," he said.

"Then Ziyad ibn Saleh," I persisted. "He will be simply overjoyed to find himself as far as may be from his general. He wearies of fearing him."

Mansur thought and gnawed a fingernail.

"But then he'll kill him."

"Of course he will," I sighed, understanding well enough who would kill whom. "But maybe not. And someone is needed there, regardless."

Mansur nodded. We were silent.

From the river rose the plash of oars and the conversations of boatmen plying the river.

"This will soon be a noisy place," I said enviously. "Just think – an entire city with markets, hallooing voices, the sounds of the oud and the tanbur."

"And what's a tanbur?" Mansur asked with no expression.

"You know what a tanbur is," I replied, equally glum. "And you also know that the life your city lives will be not yours but its own, just as your nimble young son, Muhammad, will not be exactly as you are. Yes, yes, I can speak of children without fainting away... He's your child, but he will resemble his father only in half-measure, if even that. And you can change none of this. Perhaps he will not only tolerate music in his city or his palace but will even extend his patronage to musicians. Because music, you know, is naught but the sounds of our life, given harmony and order so that we unfortunates will understand how lovely that life is. Bass strings, for example, large gongs and drums always put me in mind of a cavalry detachment flying across the steppe. That's how you feel it – not with your ears, but with your feet, when the earth trembles and quakes."

"Hmm," Mansur said, as he shaped his fingers to scoop up another mound of rice, glistening with oil and sparsely dotted with greenish, waxen raisins. He inspected that mound with a look of displeasure and quickly directed it to his mouth.

"I rue that I cannot inscribe music in symbols on a page," I went on, looking at the pilaf cooling on the platter. "It's distressing that when I am gone, my music will also vanish. It always begins to sound in my head as I cross the desert by night. Imagine, now, an entire dome of stars turning quietly above your head, your caravan journeying by their light, but if stars could sound, they would do so low and sweet, like the bells on a tambourine. Because stars are music also. The camel's feet mete out a rhythm, and that rhythm too is music. You sway and sway in the saddle to that rhythm, and then you hear a voice... a woman's voice, either in your head or in very truth... that will resound forever, as age follows age, amid those cold, bare rocks. It is as if a woman, a beautiful woman who loves you, is singing softly through closed lips, for such is the sound of the magnificent Chinese violin from the land of Hu. No other instrument can touch the heart so. And that voice sounds, and in it you hear words – 'Do you remember me?' it says, and 'Find me.' "

I stopped at that and raised my eyes, to see Mansur watching me with endless patience and waiting for me to be done.

This man cares naught for music, I thought, and ended with a submissive sigh.

21

THE FLOWER

"Gyul, the Flower," the slave-trader said, and as he did, he pushed his lips forward with great relish, imparting to the word a distinctly Persian sound. "Gyol," is what he truly said.

A flower is, of course, a flower, whatever the language in which it is named. Even so, it seems to me that however much ancient Iran has given the world – all the poetry, music, domes and columns, all those admirable painted miniatures – the word that meant no more than "flower" will forever be its greatest gift of all. "Hua" is the sound of it the Celestial Empire, and I see the ephemeral white lacework of chrysanthemums and peonies. "Gyul" they say in this rugged land, and the nostrils fill with the spiced scent of roses.

"She's strong as a horse," the slave-trader went on, "but if you are battle-weary, then recline at your ease on cushions and she will become the rider, will saddle you and will gallop on, groaning aloud and squeezing you with her warm thighs, until you send her away. This is a rare piece of merchandise, and I have kept her for a rare buyer. Never have I permitted sun or dust to touch her face."

At which he slowly and solemnly threw back the grayish veil from the face of his rare piece of merchandise.

A wide, sensual mouth with snow-white teeth smiled indolently at me, while black eyes, curious as any bird's, examined me with a candid interest.

It was a dusky, a very dusky face, with a curved, elegantly arched nose. And it was a strange face, for all its features seemed overly large. I had the fleeting thought that had that mouth been but a trifle broader, the nose one whit the longer, and the eyes even more wide-set, it would quite simply have been a fright.

"She's twenty or twenty-five. From Medina, seemingly. Of the Arabiya. She speaks Iranian, at least, if not Sogdian?" I inquired.

The trader gave an honest shrug of the shoulders, as if to say that I had no need for merchandise such as this to speak much or often.

I looked at him closely.

"Fifty dirhams," he said, with ill-concealed pride.

I laughed quietly in his face. "Whence come such prices in this market of yours? I would have thought that ten dirhams would serve to a nicety. The price you name in this deserted place perplexes me."

"Yes," was his dignified reply. "Once our market was crowded, with hundreds of women to choose from, and a good number of men too. There were prisoners from Constantine's city. There were people from the north, from lands ruled by the tribes of the Sakalib, the Rus. But now there's little trade. War... In war, there's a lot of merchandise to be had, and at low prices, so much is true. But know this: I'm well aware of what happens when the war comes if not to its end then to a lull between the warring sides, because that's when the prices for my goods suddenly start to rise. Which signifies that people are beginning to buy, not just to sell. And at this time, that's where the prices are going. Upward, I mean. And this merchandise is truly a rarity. This is no ordinary woman. Forty-five."

I shook my head and turned away to adjust my saddle. And from the corner of my mouth said reluctantly, "Twenty is a price I would discuss."

But the slave-trader drew himself loftily up and became most serious.

"Esteemed sir," he said, "a sword in a worn scabbard hangs behind your shoulder. You have a bodyguard. And by your saddle, by the color of your face, I see that you come from a war in which you were no plain soldier. You could simply clap your hand to that sword, take the woman from me and pay me naught. Worse than that I have known. You could simply lay me low before you're done. But you're a Sogdian, which signifies that you're a good trader, and you will understand when I tell you this: If you want to kill me and rob me, do so now, but if you want to strike a bargain, then let us speak in earnest. Forty. What is this? You come from a war, you have come away alive – then can you not indulge yourself with a thing of rare beauty? What if there is war again and you're killed within the week?"

I could have thrown a hundred dirhams at him in place of the forty he was asking, but that would have verged on an insult. And the point in chief was that I was delighting in every instant of this colloquy. Trading had been my occupation, and with it I felt at home again, wherever that home was, and my colleague in this peaceable craft could see that well enough. And so I allowed the conversation to come to thirty dirhams on his side and twenty-five on mine.

Then the accursed fellow did something most unexpected.

"No, thirty it must be," he said. "But I will give you without charge an old woman who will bathe your beauty before she comes to lie on your carpet. And you shall watch that fine spectacle... Two women for the price of one – how does that suit? The old woman, now I think of it, is from Sogdia. She will understand you well."

From Sogdia? That changed all. And so two female figures garbed in not the cleanest rags followed me to the caravan, were seated on a camel, and arrived with us at the caravanserai by sunset.

We were already in Khorasan and approaching Merv, I and the forty-eight Sogdians and one Turk who were all I had gathered from the veterans of Zab. Of the Army of Cowards that I had once led westward with the promise of bringing them eastward again at last, to their homes, almost naught remained. Those who had come away alive had scattered into Kufa's merry chaos with its clatter of weaponry. The only chakirs with me still were Makhian, the once and future miller, and the taciturn Vanaspar. The rest were no longer among the living. As for the other Sogdians who had crossed the Zagros plateau with me, the matter was not that they did not want to go home but that none knew how to find them all. For two or three weeks I had hoped that the rumor of the Hawk's departure would reach all who could be reached. But few answered.

Some had been lured by Barmak, who at that time was mustering a small Turkic and Sogdian guard to protect the person of the young Caliph whose byname was as-Saffah, He Who Spills. Barmak had also given me money for my journey, saying: "How can you call it a debt? We are all in your debt, and deeply too."

We had made our unhurried crossing of the Zagros mountains in the early spring, following still the same route, past Rayy and on to Nishapur, but avoiding large towns or at least their centers, for the talk there was of naught but armies or detachments of Khorasanis, which was their name for any who bore arms in service of the new Caliph. But we handily found a way to avoid them all.

Yet as we approached Khorasan itself, Yukuk came alive and forced us to spend a whole week encamped between Nishapur and Merv, while he and a few hand-picked men spied out the road ahead and gathered a quantity of other useful information.

"Since, master, we must soon return to this place and begin our search for the one known to you," he said to me, "why not begin to make certain beforehand what is in store for us and in which guise we had best appear? And if you very much want to pass on this occasion along the outskirts of Merv, where the gardens lie, and to do so unnoticed, there is all the greater need to ascertain what transpires there."

And Yukuk was able to ascertain a great deal. My brother, with Ashkend and other of his comrades in arms, had made a scintillating job of it. Abu Muslim was now confined to Merv, and there he sat, trying to understand how it could be that the people of Merv, who had once venerated him, were now on the brink of rising in open rebellion, saying, "We who had supported the House of Ali did not attach ourselves to the family Abbas with a view to giving it our leave to shed blood and perform lawless deeds."

Driven thus into a corner, Abu Muslim, they do tell, started killing in numbers never to be tallied. And people began to say that he could not long endure so. In that, though, they erred. The general would live some years yet before his body, well hashed and rolled in a rug, was pushed into the river.

My brother had, furthermore, acquitted himself well in Bukhara too, where the fires of a revolt led by a certain Sharik had been burning for a year. Sharik had begun by contriving to make a stand against the unfortunate Marwan and against the House of Abbas both at the one time. And if that were not enough, someone – and who, if not the glorious House of Maniakh? – had pressed two others, the Emir of Bukhara and the Emir of Khorezm, who both feared the reach of the new regime and with whom we should long ago have settled our scores, into supporting Sharik. And so, to no one's surprise, the illustrious Abu Muslim, who still represented that new regime, had found himself compelled to send out against them ten thousand Khorasanis, with my old acquaintance, Ziyad ibn Saleh, at their head. He it was who at that very moment was hounding the mutinous Sharik, like an animal run to ground, somewhere in the vicinity of Bukhara.

I did not doubt that Ziyad's way to the post of emir in my Samarkand was already open to him.

The sole unpleasantness from all this was that, as long as that doomed revolt still smoldered in Bukhara, we would be well advised to make our way home through Balkh.

Yukuk had brought to light yet more, though, and in ways known only to him. The garden of paradise by Merv was now a charred and blackened ruin. The murderers no longer arose even in conversation. The preacher had vanished; he might as well never have been. Abu Muslim was seemingly making great efforts to sweep away the tracks, as though he would be the better off for that. At first, no one knew the whereabouts of the few denizens of that devastated garden who had escaped with their lives, including the woman who had previously been spoken of only in hushed tones. Then information came that some five had escaped with their lives and had been seen here and there, but there was great reason to doubt the reliability of such talk. And the woman seemed to have vanished from the face of the vernal earth.

"I've seen worse for a beginning," Yukuk acknowledged. "Apparently they weren't all killed. Well and good, then – if that be so, we shall return this way again, shall we not?"

THE PATROL LED BY YUKUK overtook me when I was already by the long, weed-choked wall of the caravanserai.

"Some curiosities are prowling hereabouts," he said. "Several horsemen. One is described as being adorned with a very large nose. True it is, though, that there's not a single woman among them."

"Then let them prowl. I, meanwhile, have procured not one but two women for the price of one," I replied wearily. "Once, long, long ago, I promised our physician a good helpmeet. And now I am bringing him one, it being time to make good my debts. We'd best not show ourselves at the hospital, but someone may easily be sent to deliver the woman. I asked the slave-trader – there's a slave market in the back streets there – for a woman with some strength, and he duly foisted a true beauty on me. And an old servant-woman with her. Oh, I should have made you a gift too. It never occurred to me. But soon we shall be in Samarkand, and there will be gifts aplenty."

"Slaves? A slave market?" Yukuk repeated, and his face grew thoughtful. And a few paces on, he said: "Sire, I must quit you again. I will give the guards their orders. And I will return before dawn."

I gave him leave to go with an absent-minded nod, thinking instead of warm water and clean sheets on a soft couch. And – why not? – of a good long canter on a rug with the dusky beauty who at that moment was leaping lightly from her camel, unmindful of the old woman who slid down from that same beast with a stifled groan.

As soon as I had secured a room with two chambers that gave out onto a quiet corner of the inner courtyard, I waved them in. This was a

very small caravanserai. Most of the guard had had to go to its nearby
rivals, which lay behind just such another long wall, on the other side
of a neglected wasteland bestrewn with trash.

"Water," I said to the women. "Do you understand: water?"

At that, the covering fell from the servant woman's head to rest on
her shoulders, and I saw before me the grayest eyes in all the world.

"Maniakh of the House of Maniakh, what do you here in this town
without a name?" The tremulous voice was so familiar I could have
wept.

Then we looked at each other and laughed, while my dusky young
acquisition watched us in wonderment from behind a corner.

The gray-eyed Khalima next sank – nay, fell – to the carpet and all
at once began to unburden herself. The words flew from her mouth,
crowding one upon another, while I sadly examined the bagging skin
beneath her eyes and chin, and her long-unwashed hair.

"Nanidat, how did we live, you and I, to see the day when the head
of the House of Maniakh would buy a woman from the House of
Ashkend? But tell me my price. Was it too great for me to repay? I
was captured in Bukhara – imagine, in Bukhara, nowhere but Bukhara.
It is true chaos there now. And I was taken far, far away... Ashkend
is probably beside himself with grief. How you have changed, but
then again, you are coming from a war – and oh! would that we, in
that paddock of ours, had had but the slightest notion of how that
war progressed. Are we carrying the day, Nanidat? Or are we at least
holding our own? And who today is that 'we'? Oh yes, we're carrying
the day, of course, else you would not have chosen that youthful beauty
for yourself. What would you want with such as her in a war? Thus
peace has come for you. But you don't yet know what you've bought.
Don't let her torment you to death. She thinks of naught but men, so
sick she is, the sorry slut. Every night we lie awake when she begins
to shudder quietly in the corner under her blanket, then at length she
arches her body with a hiss, and immediately begins again, and yet
again. A nightmare, it is. But what am I saying – we lie awake? We *lay*

awake, I should say. Because now you've bought me. My God, why are you silent?"

The flood of her words broke off then, and the tears flowed.

"Forgive me, Maniakh. I haven't spoken as a person does for many a long month. But now..." Here she stopped, to catch her breath. "No, let me say at once the thing that matters most. I shall say it and be done. I fear that I shall not be your slave for long, Nanidat. Even riding that camel was a horror. It itches, it aches, it gripes me so. We all know that we must die one day, but when I knew how and where I would die – that truly defied description... And our master knew it even earlier and so didn't drive a hard bargain over me, not so? He would sooner or later have discarded me altogether, to prevent his other women from taking sick as I have. And I would have died on the roadside like a dog. Once a month – only once, can you imagine? – he sent us to the bath-house. But the last time there, that slut" – this with a nod toward the swart-faced woman – "saw what was afoot with me and told all to him... Imagine, then, how I counted every day thereafter, wondering if I would be let alone in that pigsty of ours for one more day, only one more day..."

I sat down beside her and before I knew it had reached out to her temple, to feel her pulse. *What man am I who comes from the war*, I asked myself fleetingly, *warrior or physician?*

"Show me," I said, "what manner of disease this is. It seems I am bringing our physician not only a helpmeet but also another patient... The place is not far from here. You will not contrive to die so soon, judging by your pulse. Show me, then!"

"But it's everywhere," she said, bewildered. "On my stomach and my sides already. How can I show you that? At first it was a tiny sore. Then new ones appeared. And now my head reels from it. I want to sleep."

"If only you knew how I occupied myself for the most part in that war, you would not fear to alarm me with sores of any kind," I said, impatiently tugging at the hem of the shawl that covered her. "Disrobe completely and lie face down here. I know at least three kinds of sores, including the one that turns the skin white as bone, in large patches, and lasts a lifetime. But no one dies of sores such as those. Or of many others. Bring water."

That last I directed toward the other woman, who all the while had been standing with her head atilt, trying to understand what was transpiring here.

"Bring water," I snapped at her. "Ap... Op... Suk... Water. Two bowls."

And I showed two fingers and went to fetch the clay bottles from my traveling pouch.

And once again found myself thinking that all this afforded me the veriest pleasure.

Into the third bowl, which was the smallest, I poured three measures of white wine, double distilled, and seven measures of water. Then I took from my pouch a clean jacket of white cotton – I had naught else to hand – and mimed to the dusky-faced woman the tearing of it. She stood, stock still and thoroughly bemused, but when she turned and saw she whom she knew as an old woman lying on my couch, her back bared, she was altogether stupefied.

The sores came to view immediately, but not before I had thought that, even after several months of slavery, a woman of forty may still be youthful and handsome, save for the look of her careworn face.

I slowly passed a hand over that warm back, with a mind to muttering something like "there's naught here." But then I thought that there were at that time no women closer to me in all the world than those who had crossed with me the threshold of childhood and youth.

"The sores are shallow, only affecting the upper layer of skin, and they are well known. Soldiers call them the flower of Khorasan," I mumbled. "Gyul, you understand... They spread fanlike across the body if naught is done to stop them. Death is altogether possible. Fever and delirium set in... Our healer says that demons live in the air and the dust, each to its own country, which devour cuts and wounds, gathering strength, and thus these sores arise. But death is by no means certain. There can be healing too... Khalima, gratify the head of the House of Maniakh and show all the rest. When I was a boy and watched you with greedy eyes, I could not have dreamed of such happiness. Turn over."

"I am mortified," she whispered as was proper, for she evidently no longer feared that death was close at hand. "This is simply shameful, when all is said and done. Nanidat, have you truly turned physician too, or are you only recalling the fancies of your youth?"

We both laughed at that, and a strange expression came to the face of my younger slave, as she craned forward to see.

"Light," I said to her, pointing at the oil lamp. "And will you tear that shirt at last?"

I again took up my shirt, tugged clumsily at it – to which it yielded not in the least – and threw it back at her.

Knowing at last what was needed, in a single elusive motion she ripped it asunder with a quick, harsh sound, and then looked at me, waiting to see what I would do.

I raised my eyebrows in surprise – uncommon strength in a woman this was, but it would have visited no shame on a man either – and took a smaller piece from her. I dampened it in the water mixed with strong wine, and began carefully to dab that moist cloth against the sores.

After bringing the lamp closer, the dusky-skinned woman squatted down by me, interested now to see what I did. Then she nodded, understanding at length what was happening. She moved my bottles nearer. And she tore more pieces from the shirt.

"She'll make a good helpmeet for our physician. I bought the girl for that very purpose, of which she has as yet no inkling," I told Khalima, and again we laughed.

"So I shall see my home after all," Khalima said, taking pleasure in the touch of my careful, healing hands on her skin. "You know, I've been dreaming of late that I might be vouchsafed a glance, only a glance, at the flowering gardens around the city, albeit from afar. Just one. And then, let it all end. Even the sacred birds in the dakhma, last resting place of the dead, would have naught to do with me, I thought, would shrink from me, would fear contagion. Strange it is how little a person needs at such a moment. And now... now I begin to understand that joys lie ahead for me still... And, while I think of joys, you truly do have a physician's hands, Nanidat, and it pleases me most of all that they are so warm and careful... But that salve of yours has such a loathsome stench! Wherever did you find such a thing?"

After working long over every one of that multitude of pink sores, I waved a hand at the dusky-skinned woman, who slowly left the room with many a turn, still unable to believe that it was she and not the other who was being sent off into the second of my two rooms.

"There's one other ready means of proving to you that your illness is not so simply passed to others and that you will not be driven from my caravan," I said to my gray-eyed patient, who was now utterly calm. "Your breast is so heavy and there are no sores here, but perhaps if it is lifted, so, something will be revealed? Ah-hah, there's naught, but then I also need to run my fingers here..."

"Maniakh of the House of Maniakh, now I know why you bought me, and I shall never forgive you. Where were you before, when I melted with admiration of you and was not yet betrothed? Why did you depart then for your beloved Empire? Well, be all as it may, I have still to pay my redemption price and so must submit to you... Only be very careful with me. Very, very careful..."

I cast another glance through the doorway, to ensure that the other woman had followed my bidding and left, and at that very moment, she gave me one last look over her shoulder. I paid no attention to her eyes at that time, but now, many years later, that gaze comes to me sometimes in dreams, and I am gripped with horror.

WE PLAYED A LONG-DRAWN-OUT GAME, touching each other cautiously – "This way, Nanidat, no harder, don't hurt me" – after which the most refined of Samarkand's women was suddenly seized with embarrassment. She bit her lips, mumbled something about the shame of that which now afflicted her, that it would belike soon pass, and that a girl from a good family should afford pleasure to the man also, not only to herself, and, shutting her eyes tight, she hid her face in my shoulder, pressing herself into it closer and yet closer still.

I awoke amid a jumble of bowls, medicine bottles and scraps of what had once been my shirt, saw the dust motes in the sun's rays that slanted upward to the plaster ceiling, felt the warmth of my own back, against which was pressed a serenely sleeping woman. My war was over, and I was almost home.

And her drowsy voice came from behind me. "It was wrong, though. You're too much mine own. It's the same, you know, as loving your own brother, a passing strange feeling..."

"I shall take you home and give you again to your husband, never doubt it," I said, turning and looking into her half-closed eyes. "In good health. If need be, you may spend some time under the care of our physician, and it will be for him to decide. Then your husband will send for you. In a year or two, this will have left not a trace on your skin. And who knows, maybe this is the most good I have done in this accursed war. I went to war for one woman but will bring home another. I have not saved Zargisu, but Khalima I have saved. Then let that be so for now. But I will return... And soon."

"Zargisu? You spoke of Zargisu? What are you saying, Nanidat?" she murmured. "Zargisu died. Long ago."

It became very quiet. We looked at each other in silence, both full awake now.

"She was killed a whole year before you appeared in Samarkand," she of the gray eyes said, right perplexed now. And fell silent, looking into my face and then stroking my arm, still without another word.

At length she broke the silence. "Yes, Nanidat, she also ran mad over you, as we all once did. But that was long ago. And then... She asked Aspanak to give her a difficult job to do. She had no equal. What she did, none other could have done. Yes, yes, curb your surprise. We women too know something of our husbands' affairs, even such as are a deep, dark secret. It was my husband who went to meet with Zargisu that last time, in Merv. But she came to that meeting with an arrow in her bosom and could no longer speak. She fell into his arms... My husband did not even have the time to bury her. He barely made away himself, so much I know. It was a very easy death, Nanidat."

I went to the window and looked long at an empty courtyard covered in sand and reddish pebbles that cast the lengthy shadows of morning.

"You say you went to the war for Zargisu?" she asked quietly at my back. "Then no one told you?"

"Answer me this one thing. Who knew of her death, save you and your husband? No, I mean – did my brother know?" The question came through near-closed lips.

"Aspanak? How could he not know?" She was indignant now. "All went awry with him after she was killed. And then came you, as luck would have it... And, this I know, put all aright..."

A brief silence ensued, followed by a heavy sigh behind me.

"Don't judge your brother, Nanidat," the owner of the world's grayest eyes said at last. "There was such a burden on his shoulders. How could he manage without you? And the glory of war probably sits very well with you. What were you in that war? Ashkend didn't say, although he told me he had seen you. You were a physician? No, not that – you're a mass of scars. Perhaps you even commanded a small detachment of bowmen or the like? Zargisu would have been happy. She would have been proud of you. And they... they of whom you never speak... would have been proud too."

The quiet persisted, broken only by the distant, doleful creaking of the gates that led from the street into the still-deserted courtyard.

My poor little girl, I said soundlessly, staring out at that courtyard.

But it was no longer empty. An instant earlier through the creaking gates had ridden a horseman short of stature and swathed to the eyes in a traveling wrap that could not hide his very long nose. In his hands was a bow at full draw whose nocked arrow he swept warily from side to side. And behind him across the courtyard, his sword at the ready, came another, with a clip and a clop, also looking about him. And other shadows too fell over the ground by the gates and moved slowly forward, all in the yard overlooked by my window. Breath bated, I began to move to a corner of the window – slowly, so as not to draw the attention of the horseman with his bow.

But then the door of my second room crashed open, and my dark-skinned slave flew into the courtyard, her arms outspread, uttering as she ran a long, exultant wail mingled with words of an unknown language.

The howl broke off in a short, damp cough. The woman bent forward, her arms fumbling at the air before her and an arrow jutting from her bosom.

Bemused, the short-statured, big-nosed horseman looked at the empty bow in his hands, then turned his eyes to the woman as she sank slowly to her knees, holding with care the arrow that protruded from her chest.

"Gisu!" wailed the horseman at his side. Straining for breath, he raised his face to the pale, morning sky and again howled like an animal. And then, still howling, he slashed with his sword at the turban of the unfortunate bowman, who began to pull his head into his shoulders and silently leaned toward his horse's neck.

Three other horseman were moving fanwise from the gates across the courtyard, and I understood with great clarity that there might well be only one way out of this room, that being into a courtyard teeming with horsemen. Although I did seem to recall a dark corridor that led elsewhere...

At which time, from several doors that opened onto the gallery surrounding the courtyard, figures holding bows appeared. "Leave one for me!" I heard from somewhere to the left. Arrows hit the first horseman's saddle and fell away, but then three struck his shoulder together. Two more fell. "I told you to leave one for me!" That voice, a hoarse roar, I now recognized as Yukuk's.

The last horseman turned toward the gates, but his horse screamed in pain and began to fall forward. My bodyguard in full armor – not one of them could have lain down to rest this night – poured into the courtyard, black shadows amid the golden rays.

The entire yard seethed with movement. But I was looking only at a bare patch of ground strewn with little pebbles.

It was an empty, senseless world.

And very cold.

But Khalima came and threw a blanket over my shivering back.

EPILOGUE

"I had supposed long since that we were seeking not Zargisu but some other woman," Yukuk, swaying in the saddle, said in a husky and indifferent voice. "Yes, sire, do I have leave to speak her name from time to time? Because in that confusion of names lay the error. Gisu, Zargisu..."

Looking askance at him from my own saddle, I gave a distracted nod and turned away to scan the dun-colored, wrinkled backs of the mountains on the horizon, with hopes of seeing, if only on their sunny slopes, the pale pink specks of trees in bloom.

"I understand naught of brainsickness, but many such I have seen in my time," he went on. "They are diseased, and they need care and a watchful eye. It is ill with them. But this, by all accounts, was one who stood on her own, and it was noways ill with her. And that a woman from Iran's best family had not merely taken leave of her senses but had become a monster who dispatched dying warriors with a dagger – I'm no healer, but that is beyond belief. I tried, of course, to picture a woman, sent to a war by the House of Maniakh, falling into difficulties and being obliged to act the part of an emissary sent from paradise to the best warriors, in order to escape with her life. But that is an elaborate tale. Simple explanations must always be sought as a beginning. And the simplest was to ponder this: Who said that we were seeking one and the same woman? Why could there not be two?"

One, Zargisu, and the other, someone else, she who kills? But the very meat of the matter, sire, was that, to my understanding, you grew up with... that woman. Which means that she is well beyond thirty-five. But what she did, and before our eyes too... how she bounded into the saddle... Only someone young, very young, could do so."

And he tried to extinguish the look of wordless reproach that lurked in his eyes, whose cause was likely that Zargisu to me had remained forever young, slender and lithe, with hair of copper and gold streaming to either side of her.

I remained silent, not least because I had by then remembered – and was now remembering time and again – the exact words, to the very letter, that my wily brother had used when sending me on this fool's errand.

Belatedly I recalled that even as a child, Aspanak had hated lies. And for that reason, he had brought to perfection the art of speaking a truth so that it could be understood in a great – a very great – variety of ways.

"When lying, brother mine, best lie truthfully," he would say.

He had never averred, it came to me at last, that Zargisu was she who had become a murderous monster. No, he had expressed himself far more precisely.

She was gone, my brother had said – not vanished, gone. Only now could my heart admit the other meaning of that word, the saddest meaning of all. And then, he went on, "we heard" of a demon-woman, who... well, and all the rest of it. Not a word of this being one and the same woman. And he had ended with "Find her, Nanidat, and deal with her as you see fit. You alone are equal to this, and I simply cannot leave the city in these crucial times."

No, he had not sent me in search of Zargisu. That I had understood his words as I did was my error and mine alone. And it would have been laughable to reproach him for a mistake that I had made.

No less laughable than to ask him whose swords it was that rang beneath my window after he had determined to a certainty that I was about to tell him no and so broke off the conversation. *I bade you bring me musicians, my dear brother, not circus performers with swords... And who sent that suspect pair who chivied me all the way to Bukhara, as hunters chivy a deer?* They could, I now knew, have killed me often enough. And in Bukhara... But that was all most simple. They whom my brother had sent after me, who dogged my heels but were at the same time my bodyguard, were the ones killed in Bukhara. And the second pair of pursuers were the real murderers. At which point, Aspanak must surely have been fretted in good earnest, until my letter arrived.

There was also probably no reproaching him for what had befallen me in Merv. He had thought that we still had someone in place there.

Further, I doubted that the intent from the outset had been to use me as a fisherman uses live bait. My brother had, of course, assumed that the danger to me would be vanishingly small and that all would be over in no time. And later he also sent Ashkend with his bodyguard, the world's best. No, no, all was as it should be. All was well.

Meanwhile, we would hope that my brother had believed his own words – "Once you begin anything, Nanidat, for all your innate idleness, you end by doing it better than any."

So was my brother now to be reproached that, by his good graces, I had been made commander in a victorious army and the man to be thanked that our land, if all went well with it, now had an opportunity to change its destiny? Even if peace came belated by a year, or perchance five, still the opportunity had presented itself.

You have in truth made a Hawk of me, brother, I thought. *You and I have both had good fortune. And no matter that one of us is presently a little sad... That soon shall pass.*

And finally, how many brothers did I have in this world? Few enough.

Yukuk was still speaking. "I was long – very long – put out over that confusion with the names," he said. "That our demon was indeed named Gisu – there came a time when that was indisputable. But then I wondered if there could mayhap be two women named much alike, the name being none too rare. Especially as Gisu is not even a name in full. And I calmly went on ascertaining what was known of that woman warrior who was sometimes named so and not otherwise. Had I been seeking none but Zargisu, the Golden-Haired, I would have had a far more tangled time of it. Because, as you yourself verified, this playmate of ours had hair that was near to black. And an utterly savage woman she was, raving mad. And, of course, diseased in her own way. Her name remains unknown even now, but her byname was Gisuburida. Sadly, I learned this only today, from the last of the five, who lived yet a while after his morning call on you and the encounter we arranged for him. And whence that fearsome woman came, how it all began – no, that he had no time to tell. But what of it?"

"Gisuburida?" I said in surprise. "Meaning 'With unloosed hair'? In essence, then, a strumpet? Fitting indeed. And belike she made no objection to that byname... Or even took pride in it. But what transpired when her trail went cold?"

Yukuk stretched his sunken mouth into a gloomy smile.

"If such a woman wishes to hide herself, rest assured that you will never find her. She could engage herself as a servant in some house, she could be lost to sight in the marketplace... But she wanted to vanish in such a way that it would be flatly impossible to find her. Because, for better or worse, the... the city authorities know all the wives, the servant girls and the market women. Even in our troubled times, there are such authorities. But who would take an interest in a slave girl from a foreign land, until she is sold to one house or another? It was a stroke of genius and so simple – to sell herself into slavery and then, when the time was right, to flee. Or never mind that, she could simply have looked the slave-trader in the eye and gone her way at her leisure, while he stirred not a limb. She was only waiting for her friends to come for her. While they were waiting until they were no longer sought... And then they set out. There are not so many slave markets in these parts. And even if she had already been sold, all they had to do was ask the slave-trader who it was had bought her. Then they would go in search of the purchaser. As indeed it transpired..."

"Whatever of genius that was on her part, still you guessed it," I said, to cheer him.

"Such was my good fortune," he acknowledged. "As you remember, I had received reports that a detachment of unknown allegiance was prowling right close by, and one of that number, by his description, was very like to he who was known to you. That nose of his... I was about to increase the guard when a respected wine merchant happened to say, in passing as it were, that a detachment seeking a slave girl to serve them had asked the way to the nearest market. And imagine, master, that calmed me where it ought not to have. Even then I had never a thought worthy of the name in my head save that if those brigands were seeking a woman, they presented no great danger. They would have employment enough, and, besides, we would not tarry there long. But then you tell me that you have bought two women at the slave market. At long last my head began to work aright. I hied me back to find that market and put my questions to the slave-trader. That you might have bought the selfsame woman never entered my mind, but I hied me there with a vague presentiment that something was afoot and I must hurry... And indeed, the five of them had appeared there shortly after you, master. And the slave trader paled and fairly shook when I too began questioning him about that very woman... And I must have looked no better than he when I learned who it was had bought her."

"You did not throttle him, by chance?" I inquired, my voice hopeful and my mind on Khalima, who was at that moment in the care of our good healer in Merv.

"I came close," Yukuk replied regretfully, "but I was in great haste. Because the five, as I understood it, now knew all and had betaken themselves to... what would become their trysting place with us. They had wind of where we must all have passed the night, for here there is no other place. I also knew that I should have met with that band of ruffians on the road to the market, but they must have simply lain low behind a village wall on seeing my detachment approach. Which in itself says much. So we had to retrace our steps with all speed. We cut across the barren lands and came right timely to meet those good fellows with an ambush. They were not much pressed for time, since they had resolved to approach the caravanserai at daybreak, which was our good fortune. But I've been thinking back, through the entire course of our war, and have deduced that good fortune came to us often enough in it. Could it be you who bring such luck, master?"

I tried not to laugh.

HOW DOES A VICTOR ENTER his city? Under a rain of flowers, amid proffered goblets of wine, to the humming of strings and the pealing of bells? But my detachment and I were instead lost in evening streets thronged with carts, donkeys and camels. No one, furthermore, paid us any marked attention. *And this is excellent,* I thought. *I need no great ado, no gathering of friends. Two years back, if memory serves, I entered here with every hope of resting from my labors. There never was a better time than this to make up what was lost to me then.*

The underground baths, the renowned baths of Samarkand. Now I would have time for them, all the time I could wish. And time, too, to recline on cushions in my own home for a month on end, consorting with no one in particular, accomplishing naught in particular, and only waiting for the first apricots to ripen, followed by the peaches and, later, the melons. There was the opulence we had all so richly earned. What else could one wish, and why?

And then I saw that the cart closest to me, rumbling down the stone-paved street, was oddly heavy-laden and I heard iron clinking beneath the blanket that covered it.

At which I left off snuffing up the aromas of bread baked for supper that were sidling down the street – for the bread of Samarkand has an aroma like to none other in the world – to cast my eyes over all that surrounded me.

Here was another cart that also carried weaponry. And at the end of the street, a mounted detachment was moving toward the citadel. All of near the same age, the riders were – and a relatively young age at that – and wholly unarmed, and none too easy in the saddle. Their horses too were sorry jades. Belike these were artisans' apprentices who had just been told that they were now soldiers. There really was no other reason for this strange cavalcade even to exist.

On a signal from Yukuk, who had become all at once very stiff and serious, an orderly broke away from my own detachment and sped to the house whose flowering gardens could now be seen rising up a gentle slope.

My dear brother, have you fomented a war all to avoid a difficult conversation with me? was the thought that flickered through my mind. *Then 'twas all in vain. I would never have said a word to you. Never a word.*

I was already riding through the gates.

"Am I to understand that the ceremonial feast is postponed?" I chaffed my brother by way of a greeting, staring at his face, grown thin and solemn, and at the two lines that had come out of nowhere to furrow his forehead. "Who are we to vanquish this time?"

"The Imperial army has crossed the frontier," he said in an undertone. "Fergana and Chach came to fisticuffs, and the Empire determined that this would be the time to step in and support its own, the men of Fergana. And to stir up trouble, it seems. What its plans are, where the army is going and where it will halt, no one knows. Maybe here. Or maybe it will pass on, to Bukhara."

I surveyed the crowd that had gathered in the courtyard. All were looking at me, as on that first day when I had all of ten chakirs under my command. And here again, something was expected of me.

"The Imperial army, you say? This was a belated change of heart. Had they mounted their campaign a year ago, it would have gone right ill with us. Who is its general?"

"Gao Xianzhi," my brother replied, still in an undertone. And then I knew that this was serious indeed. The hero of the Tibetan war was the one man who could wreak much evil here.

The people in the courtyard had begun, all unbeknownst to themselves, to draw closer, and were following the movements of our lips. So Aspanak brought his forehead forward until it almost touched mine, whispering: "Ziyad ibn Saleh has just arrived and has appealed to us for aid, since he cannot muster more than six thousand soldiers. The rest are of no account – peasants, apprentices. Gao has thirty thousand, by our estimates."

I freed myself from my brother's embrace and placed my foot, as if inadvertently, onto the step that led into the house, thus gaining a slight advantage of height over him. Then I took him by the shoulder.

"It was with exactly the same balance of forces that we carried the day at the Zab," I said, loud enough to be heard, at least by those who stood nearest. "Gao Xianzhi? Then this is no Imperial army. This is an army led merely by the Protector of Anxi, the Pacified West. Gao is not the Emperor. And that changes much, dear brother. Because if Gao loses, the Emperor will cast the blame on him and say that he never issued the royal command to begin the campaign. That would not be the first time. So all we need do is assist the Emperor."

My brother was silent, and in his stolid face I could see that he had yet more bad news to tell.

"Karluks," he said at last, so low I could scarce hear him. "He brings a detachment of Karluk cavalry, some five thousand strong. And led by the Yabgu of the Karluks himself."

This was bad indeed. I forced myself to smile and, quietly this time, said: "And where is the Khatun, that young man's sister? Has it been long since she was last a guest in Samarkand? She's a very astute woman, Aspanak. She understands that her brother is in difficulties" – and with this, I smiled into his face – "and needs help. We shall invite her here. And shall prepare for her such a welcome as she has never before seen. Should she wish to sit in her beloved bath-houses for two weeks never setting foot away, let her sit. And, while we shall utter no such word as 'hostage,' someone must be sent to her field camp while the Yabgu's sister is taking her ease in our city. Now, my veterans will begin training the new recruits tomorrow morning, if only to teach their horses to hold in formation and the recruits themselves to look as if they know how to grasp a sword. The remainder they shall learn on the campaign."

"You'll lead the army, of course," my brother said, as if thinking naught of it.

"No," I replied, remembering Mansur's coal-black eyes. "Too many exalted generals are not what we need here. Has the House of Abbas appointed a governor for us? Then Ziyad shall have charge of the army. And we shall assist him, to a fare-you-well. But I... I need a hundred men, not of the choicest kind. Find them where you will, even in the prison if all else fails. All must be perfectly but lightly armed. My hundred must be such as could never be overtaken or outrun. And they must have no fear of moving through the enemy lines, in small groups or even alone. Because naught is as helpful to an army as precise intelligence as to what is transpiring in the enemy's ranks. And for a hundred men, a hundred horses – the best of horses, extraordinary mounts. And a hundred in reserve. And a field hospital. That will, I think, make a fine gift to the House of Abbas. I can't think of a better."

I stopped then and looked into my brother's face, a face on which only his closest intimates could read his feelings, and then not always right well. Was that joy? Satisfaction? Envy?

The courtyard was very quiet save for the jingling of a bridle.

My brother gazed up at me a while from below, then nodded. "Yes, Hawk," he said.

With my hand still on his shoulder, I raised my eyes aloft, to feathered clouds in a bright blue sky. If it is true that lines of verse live somewhere above the compass of the world, perhaps I would see them now? Perhaps it was they I spied, soaring aloft in the inaccessible heights?

O Samarkand the bright, o gardens soft and sweet,
O air to heal all wounds that lay man low there,
The hills, the leas, where silvered waters meet,
The caravans that drift to sunset's crimson glow there.

To we who own the gifts of native earth
The world shall bring tribute of joy and sorrow.
For yet we know, where others saw but dearth,
We see endurance, victory and a bright tomorrow.

O Samarkand, my own, so let my heart achieve
The wisdom of your hills, whose sweet citation
Papyrus page is waiting to receive,
Inscribing for all time this invocation:

"Our God and this wide world are all that live forever,
While man lives short, in squalor and downtrod.
Yet still a man has all he needs whenever
He loves the world and puts his faith in God."

FROM THE AUTHOR

THE KITES OF MERV AND THE VOICES OF THE HILLS
OR, MY THANKS TO THOSE WHO HELPED MAKE THIS BOOK

When a novel is written and consigned to the not-so-tender mercies of people who have had nothing to do with it until then, it's hard. It really is. And that's why in all my books, even after I've written the epilogue, I always have something more to say. I want to open up a corner of my workshop and show how I happened upon one scene or another. And to thank everyone who helped me. The upshot is that every novel of mine (seven of them published in Russia so far) ends with a couple of pages in what, for want of a better term, I call my synthetic genre.

Those postscripts include, of course, a catalog of acknowledgments, beginning with my eternal gratitude to my wife Irene, whose computer I borrowed to write this book. When it was done, though, she gave me a new one, because, as she said then, "Now you're a writer." And then they detour briefly into how the book was written, and they also contain a thumbnail bio and some bits that function as a post-epilogue. One time, good grief, I even blurted out the answer to a clue in the whodunit I had just written.

When preparing the American edition, though, I realized that my Russian postscript would have to be reworked, leaving some parts where they were, taking other parts out, and adding in some odds and ends.

Back in 2007, as I was finishing this novel, I asked myself how I had done it, where it had all come from. Beginning with the kites in the sky above eighth-century Merv. And I wrote, in a kind of self-justification:

"I passed through ancient Merv – now a not very large city called Mary in Turkmenistan – a long time ago and in something of a hurry, too fast to notice what birds were hovering in its stifling, crimson sky. And imagine how much harder it would have been to find out what birds were circling over the heads of the characters of *The Pet Hawk of the House of Abbas* thirteen centuries ago.

"So I borrowed the little black crosses of kites against a sky the color of burnished copper from present-day Delhi. You will see the inimitable Delhi sky full of kites if you stand in one of the ancient streets of the Chandni Chowk and look toward the Red Fort. Along that street to this very day, most likely, walks an old man with a grizzled beard framed with a border the color of fresh carrots, quite unaware that, without so much as asking his permission, I had transposed his shade, along with the kites, into eighth-century Merv.

"I owe them my thanks for having lit yet another spark of life in the crumbling stones of the old fortress that even today rises above the River Murgab."

Now I understand what it means to write a historical novel. (Back then I didn't understand at all, although I certainly did feel it.) It means nothing short of bringing bygones back to life.

Are those bygones really *gone*, though?

Whether of the eighth century or the eighteenth, the people of past times are still splendidly alive. All you have to do is listen to the voices that find their way to us. And it's not only Russians who know how to listen, no indeed. I took my portrait of the future – the great – Caliph Mansur from British scholar Hugh Kennedy's remarkable study *The Court of the Caliph: The Rise and Fall of Islam's Greatest Dynasty*. And, while I'm on that subject, my gratitude is due not only to many a learned historian but also to the bookstores of New York (and Delhi), which provided me with a wealth of fine books. *Muhammad's People* by Eric Schroeder, for instance, which is a collection of strange voices speaking to us and among themselves there in the unimaginable depths of time. Or *The Assassins*, a classic by the classical author Bernard Lewis, who tells us in no uncertain terms that the turbulent eighth century was indeed home to the predecessors of that famous sect.

Also back in 2007, I gave long and sincere thanks to Dmitry Mikulsky, once a fellow student at Moscow State University's Institute of Asian and African Studies. Now Professor Mikulsky, he is an Arabist who reads ancient Arabic manuscripts in the original, and he was floored by my version of the personal interactions that occurred during this particular civil war in the Caliphate. He was floored because he couldn't prove it wasn't so.

A historian is someone who honestly admits that we don't know why certain people were friends or enemies, because we no longer have the facts to hand. A writer is a hooligan who can do whatever he likes.

But I have never truly thought that I could actually do whatever I liked. Because there are always at least three or four people who know how it really was. There are even some who have more than a smattering of the vanished language of Sogdia, and I found them mostly at the University of Tashkent. Foremost among them are Academician Edvard Rtveladze and his colleagues, Rustam Suleimanov and Olga Kobzeva, without whom this book would never have been written. They are the ones who told me, "Yes, all the knowledge is here, in Tashkent, and it's yours for the taking, but there's also something more important than knowledge." They encouraged me to go from Tashkent to where Samarkand used to be. I say "used to be" because the city that was home to my characters was flattened by Genghis Khan.

That, then, was probably where it all happened. I sat on the warm ground among thousands of bare, sandy hillocks honeycombed with ground squirrel burrows. The proprietors of those burrows, standing stock-still and ramrod-straight by their homes, could not have been less welcoming. Swallows were swooping and gliding high in the pale sky, calling out to each other. But I was hearing entirely different voices, the voices of those who had lived there many centuries before. Because every one of those round and desolate hills had once been a house, part of a wall or a tower in one of the world's most astonishing cities. The city founded by Tamerlane the Conqueror that sprouted up by the ruins of its southern wall and exists to this day is a mere shadow in comparison.

What the voices of the hills said to me will remain between us, but I know now that I can return one day to the Samarkand that once was theirs and whisper my thanks to those who lived so long ago.

So, as I said before, I passed through ancient Merv – now a not very large city called Mary, in Turkmenistan – a long time ago and in something of a hurry.

Of course, the American reader could not be expected to know what I meant by that. There are even some Russians who would have missed the point. "A long time ago and in something of a hurry..." That was in the 1980s, when the city that had once been Merv was housing a military transit camp for Soviet translators and interpreters who were on their way to the USSR's Afghan War. They were fellow alumni, graduates of the Institute of Asian and African Studies, and some of them never made it home. And although I was there only a few hours, I never forgot that city. Something stuck in my head all those years, and it is the unseen shadow that lurks behind the pages of this book.

No two readers are alike. For some, this will be a book about Iran undone and reborn, and a beautiful Iranian girl gone missing on the paths of war. Incidentally, her name – Zargisu – and the name of her "evil twin" Gisuburida were provided to me by Colonel Petr Goncharov, an expert on Iran who also passed through that camp in what used to be Merv. But he still gears up for every trip to Afghanistan with the same shiver of happy anticipation that anyone else would feel when heading for the French Riviera. That's just the sort of hold the country has. For other readers, the book will be about something else. About our – and now your – Afghanistan. About those two wars. Or are they one and the same? One day historians will be able to answer that question, while writers will keep on hearing among the hills the voices of those whose wars have been fought on that ancient land.

Dmitry Chen
Moscow
Spring 2013

OUR PUBLISHING PARTNERS

This is an unusual book.

Not merely because it is a mystery thriller that takes place in eighth century Central Asia, was written by a Russian, translated on a mountain in Arizona, and published by a small company in Vermont.

No, what makes this book *truly* unique is that it flips the prevailing publishing model: avid readers – before seeing a single word, acting only on faith, trust and a healthy dose of whimsy – agreed to invest a rather large sum of money on the translation and crafting of this novel.

Through the magic of Kickstarter, over 100 partners joined us in taking a risk on this work of fiction. Our thanks and congratulations to all, and a special thank you to the following partners who were able to make larger donations.

Mary Ann Allin
Anonymous
Altaire Productions and Publications
B L Lindley Anderson
Kate Beswick
Stephen J. Bodio
Shelia Cassidy
Robert Krattli
Catherine Mannick
Jeff Nicoll
Harlan Ratmeyer
The School of Russian and Asian Studies
Kevin Walker
Ingrid & Graeme Waymark

ABOUT THE AUTHOR

Dmitry Chen is a pen name – in the honored tradition stretching from Orwell to Le Carre to Bachman – for a Russian author who has been observing and writing about Asia for more than 30 years. He has published seven novels (and some short stories), mostly spy thrillers, some of them positively medieval. His Silk Road Trilogy was immensely popular in Russia and earned him a reputation as the most "foreign" writer in contemporary Russian literature.

ABOUT THE TRANSLATOR

Liv Bliss began her translation career in Moscow, with Progress Publishers and Novosti Press Agency, in the late 1970s and has been a happy freelance translator, editor, and language consultant ever since. She has an American Translators Association certification in Russian to English translation, and is on the editorial board of *SlavFile*, the ATA's Slavic Languages Division newsletter. She lives in the White Mountains of Arizona with her husband, Jim, and an assortment of far wilder creatures. Her translation of *Godsdoom: The Book of Hagen*, by Nick Perumov, was published by Zumaya Publications in 2007.